Ward squinted at the form crouched beside the wall, thinking it was some reptilian desert creature. But the way it hid, the way it curled its claws around the wall and peered out, the way it moved within the shadow, said it wasn't a beast at all.

"Are you seeing this?"

Neither Rivka nor Zee answered.

The creature flinched but didn't run. It seemed to be watching them. Waiting.

Ward crept forward. The creature rotated to face him. It was a small person, Ward now saw, wearing some kind of leathery costume or armor.

"Target approaching," Rivka said. "Time to go, Zee."

"Almost ready," their driver announced.

"I think it's a kid," Ward said.

Then Rivka hit it with a light.

It wasn't human at all. The face, scaly and reptilian, was sunken. Where there should have been a nose, there were two lumps, like tumors. The eyes were bloated. The mouth was a disjointed crater.

It came closer, one slow ophidian stride at a time.

"What is that?" Ward asked.

I0608454

THE TYRANT GODS

RAFAEL WARD BOOK THREE

BY MICHAEL POGACH

For Lisa and Howard

ACKNOWLEDGMENTS

How much research did you do for this book?

I get asked this question a lot, so I'll going to start off with an answer: I did a fuck ton of research. And I couldn't have accomplished even half of it without the help of some great friends and colleagues.

I'd like to thank Dr. Holly Wendt for digging up some epic medieval poetry. Carrie Lisbon for her pictures of Jerusalem. Vicki Mizrachi for her help with Hebrew translations. Daniel Schall for finding the most obscure poets for those random quotes I throw into each of these novels. And my editor, Gwen Nix for always asking the right questions and providing the right answers.

In addition, I need to thank Michelle Tooker, Bright Kelly, and Daniel Schall again for all their input, suggestions, arguments, edits, revisions, and more. They make up the most effective writing and critique partners I could wish for, and each is a wonderful author in their own right.

I'd be remiss if I didn't thank all the people who participated in my dystopian curses contest, including Julia Brateen's *Uff Da!* Even though I didn't get to use all those entries in this novel, I've got them earmarked for future works.

This book is dedicated to my parents, Lisa and Howard Pogach, who always encouraged me to pursue whatever I wanted (except bringing home motorcycles or taking hockey warmups without a helmet on, but I survived all that anyway). Though my brother and I weren't allowed to get every toy we saw in every store we visited, we were always allowed to get a book. That's good parenting right there, friends.

Last, as always, I must thank my wife, Colleen, for putting up with me, for supporting me, and for being the best eyes on my work. And my daughter, Coraline, for reminding me what true imagination is.

PART 1: THE CONSTANT WAR

Through every generation of the human race, there has been a constant war, a war with fear. Those who have the courage to conquer it are made free and those who are conquered by it are made to suffer until they have the courage to defeat it, or death takes them.
—Alexander the Great, c. 320 BCE

And now you think to withstand the Kingdom of the Lord in the hand of the sons of David; for you are a great multitude, and with you are golden calves...
—Second Chronicles, 13:8

Sure they make a mess of things, but did you ever notice these Believers are never there when we have a parade with the military and tanks and jets? They're never there where there's construction workers or police. They're always there at a casino or an REC recruitment center when they outnumber true Citizens four to one. They're not a real threat. They're a false narrative. They'll go back to their basements and holes the minute we show them our true Republic might.
—Renata Lopes, Secretary of Defense, 30 October 2056

CHAPTER 1

Hannah MacKenzie paced the once grand lobby of the Hotel Congress in Tucson, Arizona. Nearly nine hundred miles southwest of Horeb, their headquarters in Denver, Colorado. Except, they were Horeb wherever they went now. The army had taken the name of the HQ. Horeb was the seed and the tree. The pebble and the mountain. The storm and the flood.

Before her stood the one hundred and eighty-seven soldiers of Bravo Company, at attention, three rows deep, waiting for her to speak. MacKenzie hated their waiting. She hated their anticipation. It weighed on her like battle fear, that moment of terror chilling up and down the body's nervous system a split-second before the first bullet flies. It made her want to delegate this process to a subordinate.

Not a chance, she thought.

Allowing fear to prompt her actions, to make her pass off her responsibility, would be a betrayal of herself, of her soldiers, and of God. It would be a betrayal of her guiding hand, the Seer. While there were few things she liked less than disciplining a soldier—and nothing she liked less than making discipline public—this was too crucial a violation to let go.

"Private Grierson," she announced, the lobby's acoustics making shouting unnecessary.

Grierson came forward. "Yes, General!"

General. An empty rank. A title, nothing more. MacKenzie had come back from Spain five months ago shaken and hesitant. The Seer had noted it immediately. He'd asked her the very question she'd been thinking. Did she want to give up her command? She'd said no, but he knew better, and he told her what she needed to hear: that she was of more use to God in the field. He insisted that was His plan all along.

Still, she doubted. She doubted herself. She doubted God. For the first time, she doubted the Seer, but when he insisted, she accepted. Colonel Thomas Aldrich, the Seer said, would be promoted to general and would take over operations in Colorado. She would return to the field to commission Horeb's first special forces unit: Bravo Company. It was a job for a major or a colonel, but she, still a general, reviewed each dossier in Horeb and chose her soldiers personally. Including Private Grierson.

Grierson was a good solider. Strong, dedicated, and likely for promotion. The kind of soldier you could clone a hundred and eighty-seven times and guarantee Bravo Company would never lose a battle. The last person MacKenzie thought would break rank and violate radio silence.

"Do you have anything to say in your defense?" MacKenzie asked.

Grierson looked momentarily uncertain. "No, sir."

"Major Chavez," MacKenzie said to her second-in-command.

Chavez came forward to stand beside Grierson. He was a good officer, if somewhat overly fanatical. More interested in clean weapons than clean footlockers. The chatter among Bravo Company was that they appreciated him but didn't much like him.

"Your recommendation?"

"Sir," Chavez said. "I don't believe we need to abort."

MacKenzie was caught off guard by the major's statement. She'd intended for him to make a disciplinary recommendation not a tactical one. Certainly not one that mentioned aborting.

"Aborting is not an option, Major," MacKenzie confirmed, irritated by the implication giving up would ever be an option for Bravo Company. Especially now. A delay at this stage would forfeit the advantage they'd gained in the last seventy-two hours. In a blitzkrieg advance, the entirety of Second Brigade had charged from Horeb to Tucson, with minimal fighting at the District Border. The revolution had begun, but it would not sustain itself. MacKenzie and the Seer had worked out a detailed plan for these first days and weeks, a plan Aldrich was implementing with audacity and precision, and Bravo Company was the key. They were the only ones who could pull off the rest of the operation to split the Republic's Southwest District forces in half. They were the only ones who could convince the Republic their precious Wall was in danger. The only ones who could be trusted to take the Wall at Nogales, sixty miles to the south. "Recommend sentence, Major."

"Private Grierson broke radio silence," Chavez said, "potentially compromising the operation. I believe the private's actions are grossly negligent at best. Treasonous at worst. I recommend stoning, as for an apostate in David's Kingdom of Israel."

Of course you do.

Grierson stared dead ahead, her face expressionless.

"Negative, Major," MacKenzie said.

"Sir?" Chavez said.

MacKenzie lined up Chavez with her best glare. She was angry now. She didn't like being questioned. She didn't like hiccups in her operations. She didn't like this damn hotel. It was old and cold, despite a late autumn heat wave. It was annoyingly historical, with placards everywhere about some bank robber named Dillinger who'd been arrested here more than a century earlier. An event Rafe would surely know about, and be willing to lecture on.

Thinking about Rafe made her even angrier. It made her want to forget discipline and dismiss the company. It made her want to order the assault immediately, intelligence and diligence be damned.

You've lost your peace, the Seer had told her before asking if she'd like to return to the field, surprising her that anyone could think she'd ever had a measure of peace. Now, however, she was sure she had lost something of herself. She'd forfeited her command of Horeb. Her soldiers were ignoring orders and questioning her command.

This last, she would not abide. Her command was all she had and all she was.

"Private Grierson," MacKenzie said. "You will be removed back to Horeb for punishment."

Grierson choked out two words: "My son."

"Your son what?" Mackenzie asked.

"My son, sir!" Grierson said, speaking quickly, her words tumbling over themselves. "I had to leave him when I joined. His father couldn't see God's plan. I had to leave him, and his father took him to his parents' place. I couldn't let him be caught in the middle."

MacKenzie had reviewed the private's service records as she had for each of Bravo Command's soldiers, but she'd only glanced at her personnel file. Had it mentioned a family? A son?

"Sir," Chavez said. "If I may, the private believes her ex-husband took her son to Nogales. She was trying to warn him to leave town in advance of our arrival."

For fuck's sake!

"And I'm only being informed of this now?"

"He's only twelve," Grierson cried. She broke rank and approached MacKenzie, her steps trembling, her right hand over her heart.

Chavez cut Grierson off, herding her back in place, shouting down her objections in a grotesque display of callousness that should have been the antithesis of what they were fighting for. Watching Chavez belittle Grierson forced MacKenzie to imagine what she might do to protect her own child in an impossible future in which she could be a mother. She imagined doing nothing. She imagined being a good soldier, disciplined enough to never consider saying *fuck it* to her duty and her revolution.

Then she imagined a baby girl cradled in her arms. She imagined her father, who'd spoken his final words to Rafe and not her, holding a red-headed granddaughter.

"Private Grierson!" she announced. "You will be placed on restricted duty at Horeb until I either return or send orders otherwise. Understood?"

Grierson stood once more at attention but couldn't stop the tears from rolling down her cheeks. "Yes, sir!"

"Major Chavez," MacKenzie said. "Your inability to maintain discipline and foresee this security risk is extremely disappointing. You will accompany Private Grierson to Horeb where you will receive a demotion in rank. You will both be redistributed according to Horeb's needs."

A murmur ran through the lobby. Relieving the major of command on the eve of such a crucial operation was not good for the op or for morale. She needed to replace Chavez immediately with a seasoned commander who already had the soldiers' respect.

"Captain Talbot," MacKenzie continued. "You are promoted to major and will take ops command. I want two teams of three each. First team, assess the extent of the comm leak and name all possible targets. You have two hours. Second team, extract the Grierson boy and plug all potential leaks."

Talbot stepped forward, clearly already staffing the two teams in his head. "Yes, sir!"

"We set out at zero-three hundred. I don't need to tell you how important this op is. Once the Wall comes down, our Mexican comrades can join us in restoring Faith to those who've been deprived of it for too long. Understood?"

The response came swift, one hundred and eighty-seven strong: "To Canaan!"

CHAPTER 2

"Does anyone know what this mountain is called?" Rafael Ward asked his students.

He'd missed this. Teaching.

Except that wasn't quite right. A teacher was a designation of rank and authority. A teacher gave tests and grades. A teacher attended meetings and assessed lesson plans and program outcomes.

Here, he was a teacher in name only. In truth, he was a storyteller, which was immensely more satisfying than teaching had ever been, even considering the circumstances.

He'd been here in this desert fortress for five months. Five months of sitting beside Sam while she slept, comatose, beside machines that beeped and clicked as if speaking a language only they could understand. Five months of being attended to by Bar-Ilan—the doctor who'd surgically installed the brace on Ward's leg—and struggling through the daily workouts he prescribed for physical therapy. Five months of morning chats with Sam's doctor, Rivka. Five months of not knowing whose army occupied this fortress or who they reported to or when Compano might return with answers.

"Masada," a ten-year-old girl named Esther said. She was eager and smart, though she had a heavy lisp Ward assumed would have been addressed long ago had she been in school in the Republic.

And she was right, which caught Ward off-guard. The geography and history of Masada was not on the relatively small list of approved subjects he'd been given when he began teaching three months ago. In fact, it was the one thing Ward had been explicitly told he should not cover in his classroom. But if his students, even the young ones, knew about Masada, why was it off limits?

"Correct," Ward said, "and does anyone know the history of Masada?"

A murmur of shifting bodies and awkward coughs echoed off the stone walls of the classroom. Like all "rooms" at Masada, or more specifically *within* Masada, it was a cave. The khaki walls had long ago been worn smooth, leaving few visible tool marks.

"No one?"

A subject both taboo and familiar? A subject his students would admit to knowing but wouldn't talk about? Maybe more than any other moment in the last three months, Ward felt alive. He'd found a mystery. A story to either tell or hear. A reason to think and be, rather than simply sit and talk and rehab and sleep.

"Last chance," he said. "If no one speaks up, I'm going to tell it whether you want to hear it or not."

Young to old, his twenty-nine students glanced around the room, the younger faces eager for someone to tell them what to do. The older ones daring the teacher to make them say things they didn't want to. This was the greatest challenge Ward faced teaching these kids: the wide range of ages. Twenty-nine kids too young, some by months and some by years, to serve in the army garrisoned here. The youngest ones were completely literal and devoid of irony. The oldest, meanwhile, veered toward boredom if Ward took too long explaining things to the little ones.

Twenty-nine of them for around a thousand adults. Another subject absent from the approved list: the fertility and other genetic issues he'd been told had contributed to the small ratio. Questions were not encouraged here by anyone other than Ward himself, as far as he could tell.

A boy in the front row raised his hand.

"You don't have to raise your hand, Jacob," Ward said.

The boy lowered his hand sheepishly. Two of the older students in the back—a boy with a healthy dose of teen attitude named Ben, and a girl named Mara sporting a buzz cut like many of the boys—laughed.

"Do you know the history, Ben?" Ward asked.

"Is this an open book test?" he shot back with an attitude recognizable as teenage rebellion anywhere in the world.

Ward waved a hand at the stack of half-century old textbooks on a table beside his desk and said, "Be my guest."

But Ben and the rest of the students knew better. Not once had Ward passed out those books or suffered the kids to read them. He was a storyteller, not a test giver, though he knew he risked his role by treading on censored subjects. Just as he'd risked his role when he was Professor Ward of Carroll University. Risk was part of education. You couldn't truly learn if you didn't risk. Whatever else his life was worth, he had decided when he took this job not to hide from the truth. Not to fear risks. He'd taken them back then, and he would take it now. He had to. Like coming up for air.

"What were you going to say, Jacob?" Ward asked, committing himself to this risk.

"My dad says there was a war here a long time ago," the boy answered.

"There sure was," Ward said. "Two thousand years ago, the name Masada was known throughout the region. It was no secret base like it is today, with all of us living below the surface. It was a landmark. Everyone for a thousand miles knew and feared Herod the Great's indestructible fortress Masada."

No eye rolls this time. Many of the students perked up. They knew Herod. Not much had survived the last two millennia, and even less had been offered to these kids as part of their education, but the name of the man who built the Second Temple in Jerusalem was still known here. As it should be. The greatest difference between Ward's experience as a teacher in the Republic and here was he was now teaching Believers. Jews. And even with their obviously limited knowledge of secular history, their familiarity with tradition was amazing. At times, Ward felt he learned more from them than they ever could from him.

"Does anyone know the story of the First Jewish-Roman War?"

Heads shook side to side. Esther eyed Ward like he was some kind of magician.

"It's a story of rebellion," Ward said. "Of conquest and of mass suicide. Who wants to hear it?"

Heads bobbed. Hands shot up. Even Ben seemed interested. Ward had them. It took breaking the rules, of course, but he had them. As it had always been for him, the experience was exhilarating.

He launched into his telling, setting up the impenetrable nature of the mountaintop fortress. The hundred meters of unclimbable mountain cliff on the west. The over four hundred meters of deadly cliff on the east, scalable only via the zigzagging Snake Path. Partway through, his eyes drifted to doorway. He wondered if they were listening now, or if they were recording him and would review it later like the administration had back home.

Not home, Rafe. You have no home anymore.

He shoved the thought aside lest it derail his story. He was in the moment. Whatever consequence that brought, he'd learned from MacKenzie and from Sam, to go with it.

And look how that worked out for them.

Unwilling to let those memories take hold, Ward went on with his telling.

"And when Rome sent its legions to put down the Jewish rebellion, a garrison took position atop Masada, housing themselves in the same buildings Herod had constructed a century earlier. The Jews of Jerusalem knew they would have to take the fortress, but they also knew it was impossible. In more than a hundred years, no one had even been able to make it halfway up the cliffs without being seen and killed. But the Sicarii knew a way."

"The scary were God's best soldiers," Lia, a girl barely six years old, said as if it were her lecture. Like the rest of the kids, she had an Israeli accent that made the word *scary* sound like the word *Sicarii*. Also like the rest of them, she was comfortable speaking in English. Such bilingual ability was almost unheard of back in the Atlantic District of the Republic.

"Not scary, Lia," Ward said. "See-car-ee. It means the wielder of a *sica*, a wicked curved dagger used by soldiers and assassins."

Lia, and some of the other younger kids, watched him with wide eyes. The older ones shifted as if uncomfortable or bored. Ward didn't worry about them. He was having a blast. He was almost, for the first time since he'd been brought here, not worrying about Sam.

She was stable, after all. Her unborn baby, now an obvious swell in her belly, was stable. Nothing in her condition had changed since she came out of the River Lethe in a coma. Virtually every morning, Rivka would tell Ward if Sam wasn't in a coma, she'd be up and about perfectly healthy, save for the hand Ker had cruelly amputated. There wasn't a test they'd done that could explain the coma.

Ward liked Rivka. She was strong but didn't hide her caring. She was honest. She was also one of the few people he'd met here without a modification. Like the exoskeletons many of the soldiers had on their hands for steady aiming and brute strength, the mods were practical but creepy. Even Bar-Ilan had one, a robotic eye he said helped him with his surgeries.

It was Rivka who'd convinced Ward to take up teaching again rather than sitting by Sam all day, holding her hand and waiting.

Slowly Ward became aware the class had gone silent again. Waiting.

"The Sicarii," he said, "were like special forces of the time. Stealth soldiers with the best training. Assassins."

"Who did they assassinate?" asked Ben.

"The Sicarii believed they killed at their god's command, like most fanatics, which meant their targets were Romans mostly." He left out the stories of Sicarii ravaging local villages, even massacring several hundred in one, including women and children, because the locals weren't revolutionary enough for their tastes. "Remember that the Sicarii were of this land. They had lived here for generations. Centuries, even. They were the only ones who knew how to penetrate the mountain. It was impervious to assault, but a few highly trained assassins were a different matter. They came at night, maybe climbing in the darkness, or maybe as some historians think, using secret tunnels to get inside the mountain. Whatever the case, a small number of them snuck into the fortress and killed the Romans while they slept."

"Even here?" a boy with bright blue eyes named Uri asked.

"In the palace, Herod's palace where we are now, you mean? Yes, probably. The Sicarii took the untakeable fortress then held Masada for six years during the war. The Romans couldn't figure out how to get inside. They couldn't climb up a mountain in heavy armor. They didn't have drones or helicopters, right? It was two thousand years ago. So, they built a giant ramp."

"Why did they let the Romans build a ramp?" Ben asked.

Smart kid, Ward thought. The answer was because they couldn't stop the Romans. There were legions at work, and only a thousand or so Sicarii, including families, on the mountain. Not all that different, or larger, than the small army here now.

"They sabotaged when they could," Ward said. "But they were under siege. You've seen the giant squares drawn in the desert, right? Those are the outlines of the Roman camps."

"No way," a red-headed boy named Yakov said. "From that long ago?"

"They weren't playing around. A Roman camp was a permanent military station. Walls. Guard towers. Imagine how many soldiers could live in those camps. Plus all the slaves the Romans brought. That was their trick. In addition to simple numbers, they used Jewish slaves to do a lot of the work, so any attack the Sicarii tried would kill their own. It was only a matter of time."

A matter of time.

How long would it be until he got in trouble for going off script like this? A day? A week? What if they threatened solitary confinement? Torture? What if they took Sam off her machines? All of a sudden, the plans Ward had been working on when they were first brought to Masada popped back into his head. Plans for escape.

But such plans were pointless. He would never leave without Sam. Whatever punishment was coming for breaking the rules, he would accept it. He would learn from it. Because eventually, Sam would wake. Then he could worry about escape.

"What happened next?" Ben asked.

"The Romans finished their ramp," Ward said. "They sent their legions in."

He paused for effect. His students' eyes were wide. A few kids' mouths hung open.

"Who won?" Yakov asked.

"We did," a fourteen-year-old named Shira said.

"Not so fast," Ward said. "Here's the thing. We have no records from Rome to tell us what happened next. The only recording of the assault was by a man named Josephus, and what he wrote has never been verified by another source."

"So it's all bullshit?" Ben said.

Mara elbowed Ben again.

"Look," Ward said. "The story is the story. We accept it because it's what we have, but that doesn't mean we can't be skeptical. Josephus says the Sicarii defenders took an oath to never be slaves nor to ever convert to Roman paganism, even under pain of torture or threat of death. They decided instead to deprive Rome of its victory. They drew their weapons and used them on each other."

"They killed themselves?"

"No," Ward said. "Suicide was prohibited in Judaism—still is, as far as I know—so they took turns killing each other until only one man remained, chosen by lots. Only he committed suicide."

The younger children sat blank-faced. Normally, Ward wouldn't tell a story like this to children, but here they were, at Masada. In a fortress whose history was taboo. What better reason to tell it?

"That's crazy," Uri said.

"No, it isn't," Mara said with a heavy voice and a strong glare.

"For them," Ward said, "it was the greatest middle finger to the Roman Empire they could offer."

"This finger?" Jacob asked, extending his middle finger.

Ward laughed. "Yes, that one, but it's not a nice thing to show people."

"Wait," Mara said. "If they all died, how do we know how they did it?"

"Good question. The story says one mother couldn't bring

herself to let her children be killed and hid them in a water cistern. The Romans found her, and she told them what had happened."

"Seems kind of convenient for the storyteller."

"Maybe," Ward said. "We know the Sicarii were here and the Romans laid siege and built their ramp. The tangible evidence tells us all that, but history is more than just evidence. It's stories. Just because there's no record of the story doesn't mean it isn't true. Just because the Romans made no record of it and no bodies were ever found doesn't mean it isn't true. Sometimes truth is simply waiting for historians to discover the corroborating evidence."

"What's corroborate?" Lia asked, her eyes shifting to the doorway before she finished her words.

Ward turned. A soldier stood at the entrance, rigid and unmoving.

That was fast, Ward thought, certain the soldier was here to order him to stop talking about prohibited subjects.

The soldier, however, didn't enter the room or interrupt. He stood, statue-still, as if waiting permission to enter. Ward sought recognition in the young man's face, but so many of the soldiers here looked alike. Medium height, medium build, strong jawed, variations of olive-toned skin.

"Yes?" Ward said.

"You're needed," the soldier said.

"I'm teaching." The declaration came out automatically, as if it was a trump card for whatever orders the soldier had been given.

"There's a problem."

"Are we under attack?" Ward meant it to be glib, but the sound of his students shifting nervously in their seats said it didn't come out as intended.

"No."

"Am I in trouble?"

The soldier cleared his throat. Suddenly, however, Ward knew what he was going to say. Panic rose from his gut. He was already moving before the soldier spoke.

"There's a problem with Samantha."

CHAPTER 3

Ward ran, the brace on his leg clicking and whining. His limp was virtually gone, but the bones in his knee still felt like they were grinding together. Not bad. Just there. The kind of irritation he was conscious of during normal activities, but which disappeared once adrenaline got pumping. Like during physical therapy when Bar-Ilan ratcheted up the resistance level on the treadmill each week. It was a wood-framed device, with exposed cogs and pulleys, devoid of modern displays or meters. The only assessment tool it offered was a single red cable Bar-Ilan plugged into the brace on the side of Ward's knee at the start of each session. The cable then connected the doctor's Port, the only Port Ward had seen at Masada, and apparently told the doctor everything he needed to know about his patient's progress and vitals.

As he navigated the tunnels of Masada, Ward pushed harder than he ever had during physical therapy. He bounced off walls as he rounded corners. He knocked people over as he shoved by them, barely hearing their complaints. He didn't care about their bumps or bruises. He didn't care about decorum or rules. Sam was in trouble.

It was his fault she was here. His fault she no longer had a home or a family. His fault her dog, Reina, was seven thousand miles away, maybe alive, maybe not.

Like Sam.

The first choking sobs hit him as he slammed into a wall at an intersection.

I did this to her.

The thought was both crushing and stirring. He tried to get

moving. His legs, even his braced leg, wouldn't comply.

Slowly, he became aware someone was shouting his name.

From up the corridor, the soldier came running, waving his arms. Bar-Ilan had told him that even with only one leg in a brace, he would be able to run faster and kick harder than any unmodded person. The soldier had no visible mods on his legs. Ward put the advantage to action and kicked back into a run. A few turns later, he reached the infirmary where Sam had slept— her status stable and unchanging—for five months. He didn't slow for the door. A single kick shattered it, splinters and hinges ricocheting off the walls all around.

The infirmary was an oblong cave of khaki dolomite, its walls and ceiling indistinguishable from the other rooms below the surface at Masada. Only its floor, a buffed and smooth poured concrete, set it apart. Ward hit this concrete and kept going, his boots sliding like skates on ice. He slammed into a gurney and knocked over a med kiosk and landed on his ass. He got up, trying to make sense of what he saw.

He'd come here every day, at least twice a day, for five months. First thing in the morning, then again in the afternoon. The same routine each time. Maneuver through the regimented rows of gurneys and patients, machines and kiosks. Sit beside Sam on her gurney, listening to the endlessly perfect beat of her heart on her monitor. Wheel her up to the surface once a day for fresh air, keeping her hidden beneath the canopies so no surveillance drones, or Eye-Ds, could see her. Talk with Rivka, the two of them sometimes sitting close enough their thighs pressed together.

The infirmary no longer resembled that room he'd sat in every day for months. Half the gurneys were gone. There were no patients. No doctors, nurses, or techs.

No Sam.

The solider arrived, his boots clomping on the concrete.

"Where is she?" Ward shouted.

"I tried to tell you," the soldier said, panting.

"What?"

"The baby," the soldier said.

Ward was running again before the soldier could finish,

before he was even aware of starting to run, as if his leg brace was wired directly into his brain and knew what he wanted before the signal could reach any other part of his body. He shoved the soldier aside. He knew where Sam was.

The infirmary was for minor injuries and stable patients. Sam was no longer stable. There was only one place they would move her. One place where Bar-Ilan did his work, installing mods in soldiers to keep them alive, and cutting them up to save them when their mods couldn't.

He ran for the operating room despite not knowing exactly where it was. He'd only seen it once, during the initial tour Compano had ordered for him the day they'd arrived. He knew it was in the southern portion of the subterranean complex, the opposite end to where he was now. It was enough direction to get started.

When he saw a tunnel he remembered he took it. When he reached an intersection he couldn't recall, he trusted his instincts, or maybe trusting the leg brace, to lead him the right way. Through brightly lit tunnels. Through dark corridors. Down hand-cut stairs. Across an ancient mosaic of exotic birds he'd examined sometime in his first weeks here. It was two thousand years old. Part of Herod's initial design, most likely. Now, however, he stomped across it as if it were no more than dirt and brick.

Sweating. Running. Slamming into walls. Running. Turning. Running.

Somewhere inside the mountain he became aware he was speaking, almost shouting, willing himself forward, faster and faster.

"Come on. For fuck's sake. Come on!"

He needed to get to her. He needed to be there. To save her.

Too late, Rafe. So long too late.

He rounded a corner, his toe catching his opposite heel, slinging him forward into a wall. He bounced off and landed on his knees and hands. The pain was surprising and inconsequential. He didn't have time for it.

Sam doesn't have time for it.

He got to his feet only to find himself facing a door he knew.

Control.

The room he'd only been allowed to enter once, to receive a comm—approved by Compano, presumably—from the Republic. From his brother Daniel.

The Seer, his brain corrected.

It was a connection he still had trouble making. How could Daniel, his big brother, be the Seer, the scourge of the Republic? Daniel, who'd died when they were children, only for Ward to discover three years ago he was still alive, a prisoner in a Labor Camp.

Daniel, who'd died again in an attempted escape from that Labor Camp.

Daniel, who'd appeared five months ago on a monitor on the other side of the door Ward faced, alive for the third time.

"Hi Raffi," he'd said in Control that day, as if they'd only been apart a few hours.

They'd stared at each other in silence a few moments before Daniel had asked him to do something dangerous. No smiles. No tears. Just a declaration that some part of his army had become corrupted and Ward had to help root that corruption out. He asked Ward to retrieve a device that an operative inside Masada had hidden in Control for this very moment. A device that would tap into Masada's comms. Ward found it behind a fuse box. He connected it inside the panel Daniel told him to open. And then he tried to ask his brother every question that had weighed on him for more than twenty years, but the comm link shut down before he could say a word. His brother was gone again.

But Daniel wasn't the issue now. Sam was. And she was in trouble.

He ran harder, aware his endurance was almost comical. Six months ago, he couldn't have jogged fifty meters without collapsing. Now, thanks to his physical therapy and the fact that alcohol wasn't allowed at Masada, he kept finding higher gears. Even as the brace on his leg began making sounds like a transmission chewing itself up, he knew he could go faster if the damn thing would let him. If Bar-Ilan would unlock the thing's potential rather than limiting it to prevent Ward from overexerting the damaged leg.

He reached the OR seconds later. This time, he hit the door with his shoulder. It offered the briefest moment of resistance then flung open, smacking the wall like a gunshot and spilling Ward inside.

The OR was huge. Carved out of brighter stone than most of Masada, it was so vast Ward couldn't see the far end. It could have been a hanger for small airplanes or large Eye-Ds. Rows of beds lined the poured concrete floor. Lights blinked incoherently atop machines next to every other bed. Like the infirmary, however, there were no patients in the beds.

"Hello," Ward called out as he moved deeper into the cavern.

Slowly, the darkness at the far end disgorged a series of drawn curtains hiding pockets of the OR from sight.

"Hello," Ward called again.

"You can't be here," a voice declared from behind the closest curtain.

Ward went for the curtain. Before he could grab it, however, the soldier was suddenly beside him. Telling him to back away. Grabbing at his arm. He fought for the curtain. Got a grip. Yanked. It came down with a series of pops, like shower curtain rings snapping, revealing a circular stall with a gurney in the center.

Sam's gurney.

She lay there, hair buzzed to her scalp, arms hanging wide, the cuff on her wrist heavy and absurd like a piece of drab robotic jewelry. Her face held the same serene look she'd had since she was pulled from the River Lethe five months ago, but below her neck was absolute carnage. Her abdomen was splayed open as if something had clawed its way out of her. Clamps and tubes and hoses ran from her gaping body like bones and intestines.

The room twisted around Ward. He was barely aware of Bar-Ilan standing over Sam, his scrubs splattered with her blood. Barely aware of the absence of the steady beeping from Sam's heart monitor. Of his legs, even the braced one, wobbling. Of the fact that he might fall. Might faint.

Then Rivka was beside him, holding him as his eyes locked on the expanding pool of blood beneath the gurney. She forced him back, keeping Sam's blood from touching his boots.

"You should have waited," she said.

He tried twice before he could force words from his throat. "What happened?"

"The umbilical cord," Bar-Ilan said, the surgical mask over his mouth bouncing with his words.

"What does that mean?"

"And then an aneurism, I think."

"The baby?" Ward asked.

Bar-Ilan's masked head shook.

I killed her baby, Ward thought. He wanted to cry. He needed a drink.

"But Sam's okay, right?"

Look at the body.

"Shay," Rivka said, using Bar-Ilan's first name.

The doctor shook his head again, refusing to look at Rivka. Refusing to look at Ward or at Sam. As if he was ashamed of what was on the table.

Ward tried to speak, but the room was spinning again. He leaned on Rivka who held him tighter.

Bar-Ilan's voice, coming from somewhere far away, said, "Samantha is dead."

CHAPTER 4

R afael Ward was going to escape.
It was a fact as sure as any he'd ever known. Daniel was alive. MacKenzie hated him. Sam was dead. Fact: he wasn't going to spend one more night as a prisoner in these tiny quarters, sleeping on this tiny bunk, and then he was getting out of Masada.

He'd been planning it from the start, knowing they might discover the comm tap he'd placed for his brother at any moment. He'd been memorizing the steps the way he used to memorize the lines of epics like *Beowulf* or the *Kush-Nama*. Step One: get out of his quarters. This was the key to everything. He was a "guest" at Masada, but no one made any secret about what that really meant. His single room, about the size of a small prison cell with no door handle on the inside, was locked each night. Though there were no handcuffs or escorts, he was as captive as anyone in a cell. More so even, and they all knew it.

Alive, pregnant, Sam had been better at keeping him here than the cliffs surrounding the mountain. Better than a GPS locator strapped to his ankle. Better than a gun to his head. The fact that she was in a coma didn't matter. The fact that she might never wake didn't matter. Compano, or whoever was in charge here, knew he would never leave Sam.

But Sam was dead. He'd refused to accept this at first. Refuse to be taken from her side. Someone must have guided him back to his quarters, though he didn't remember the journey. Bottom line, however, was she was dead. Their leverage over him was dead. It was time to leave.

Getting out of his quarters, however, was a problem. There

were no adjacent rooms or guards stationed outside he could call in under the guise of being ill so he could overpower them. There were no ducts to crawl through or ceiling tiles to climb up into. He would have to break out. Somehow.

Which would lead to Step Two: supplies. The storerooms were one level down and easy enough to get to. There were no guards. Everyone at Masada was, as far as Ward could tell, here by choice. They were soldiers and soldiers' families. They were all believers in whatever it was this army was fighting for. Or against. He hadn't bothered asking after the first few days of his inquiries were met with stone-faced silence.

Step Three: get topside. Again, this would initially be easy enough. Though there were a thousand people in Masada, the subterranean base, with at least four levels and miles of tunnels, could hold many more. Most days, Ward could stroll the corridors for hours and only run into a few soldiers if he kept away from key areas like the barracks, the mess, or the training caves. Assuming he could make it above ground, he would head to the western cliffs and climb the casemate wall near the fortress's beehives. This was the difficult part. Even where the wall was most eroded, it would still be a haul and scramble to get over. And it was exposed. Most of the plateau was under the camouflaged canopies, but there was a gap between the canopies and the wall, necessary to keep the shadows natural so the Eye-Ds would be fooled into thinking Masada was as barren as it had been for almost two thousand years.

Step Four was the hard part: the climb. Once over the casemate, he'd be visible to both to defenders and Eye-Ds all the way down. A hundred meters—he was sometimes surprised how quickly he'd taken to thinking in metric after only a few months away from the Republic—almost as vertical as a wall. An impossible climb, treacherous and hopeless, for an out of shape guy in his mid-thirties with a bad leg. However, thanks to Bar-Ilan, he wasn't out of shape anymore, and his leg brace gave him strength and stability he hadn't had in a decade at least. These facts took the climb from impossible to merely improbable, but if he made it, he'd be free.

Sort of.

The desert extended seemingly forever to the south and west. To the north, the impenetrable wall called the Jerusalem Line. To the east, across the Dead Sea, the Riyadh Quarantine Zone.

Which way was freedom?

I could stay, he thought.

Without Sam? Compano's pawn? A prisoner?

You can work in the status quo, Compano had once taught him. *You can learn its rules. Exploit its loopholes. But once it changes, all bets are off. All allies are potential enemies. All advantages are nullified. Everything needs to be re-evaluated.*

Except the status quo hadn't changed; it had been obliterated. Rivka was no longer his ally and confidant. Bar-Ilan was no longer his physical therapist and friend. They were military doctors. Soldiers. Enemies.

There was no time for grief. No time for questioning or guilt. Compano was returning at the end of the week, Rivka had told Ward yesterday. He had to be gone before she arrived. He had to shove his anger and anguish at Sam's death deep inside, deeper than where he kept his desire for the fuzzy clarity a shot of whiskey offered. He had to hide it until he could indulge it.

Maybe with a few explosions on his way out like he had at the Tower.

Stop it. These aren't the people to blame.

No, he couldn't help telling his brain. *I am.*

The anger, the need for a drink, lessened for a brief moment before swelling within him once more. He flipped the mattress off his bunk. Kicked over the wooden stool he used as a nightstand. Grabbed the metal bunk frame and threw it against the wall. The desire to claw through the sand-colored stone all around him was worse than the thirst tearing at his throat and hammering in his temples.

He was crying again. He let it run its course and then wiped his face and examined the mess he'd made of his quarters. The stool was on its side, one leg broken. The mattress was folded in the corner. The bunk frame was wedged at an angle in the other corner. His clothes, usually folded in a pile beneath the bunk, were scattered about the floor.

"Stupid," he muttered as he kicked the broken remains of the stool aside. With nowhere to sit, he set about righting the bunk and gathering his belongings from the mess.

It took longer than he expected, the small confines making it difficult to maneuver the bunk and mattress, but soon enough he sank heavily onto the squeaky bed, the only things he'd brought with him to Masada clutched on his lap. He looked at the jacket in his left hand as if it had worked its way there on its own. He squeezed its worn leather. It was reassuring of nothing, so he looked at his right hand. At the golden bee cradled in his palm.

The last of Childeric's Bees.

Once a symbol of wealth, of power, it was now a simple trinket weighing almost nothing. Its ruby inlaid wings reflected the room's single fluorescent bulb in a dull sheen. It looked lonely. The last of a swarm of three hundred. A sad reminder to Ward of forgotten history. Of faded empires. Childeric and his Merovingian descendants. Napoleon and his First French Empire. What remained of the conquerors who'd championed the Bees?

What did Ward himself have?

Nothing.

Tears were coming again. He clung to the bee, the stupid hunk of gold and ruby he'd stolen even before he met Sam, and let them come. He tried to force the bee into a reminder of her, but it wouldn't cooperate. The only images it conjured were of Commandant Gaustad and MacKenzie and Daniel.

"Stop," he whispered to the bee.

He was punishing himself. Evading one memory only to flog himself with another. He forced himself to think of Sam. To remember her determination. Her love for Reina. Her integrity, so much stronger than Ward's. But the only image he could summon was the last he had of her, lying on the gurney, body torn apart. Blood everywhere. Her closed-eyed stare locked on the hand-cut stone of the cave's ceiling.

He could still smell the operating room. Like a metallic pollen, the stench of Sam's blood, of her baby's blood, filled his head. He feared he might never escape it.

He got up, ready to go now. Ready for the infamous Rafael

Ward to disappear. Compano's war. MacKenzie's war. They didn't matter anymore. He needed to go wherever his past wouldn't matter. Wherever his name, and his legacy, would be unknown. Disappear into the desert if need be.

Never see Daniel again?

"Whatever it takes," he told the question, as if it were standing before him.

He slipped his jacket on over the fatigues they'd given him to wear. Stuffed the bee into his pocket. Grabbed the broken leg of the stool, figuring it was his best weapon to either pry or smash open the door. Before he could start, however, someone approached the door from the other side. He felt it more than heard it and went perfectly still. Waiting.

There was a knock.

A pause.

Then: "Rafael."

Ward almost let himself believe it was Sam's voice coming through the door, but he knew better. It was Rivka. But why? Was she here to console him? Or had they discovered the comm tap he'd placed at his brother's request? Was she here to coax him into opening the door so they could barge in? So they could shoot him in the head?

He considered staying silent, pretending to be absent, but that would only set an alarm. He needed them to think he was locked in nice and tight.

"What?" he said.

The door opened. Rivka looked tired. Her normally strong posture was slightly slumped. Her eyes were red as if she'd been crying.

"We need to talk," she said, pain obvious in her husky Israeli accent.

Part of Ward wanted to. Part of him wanted to open his arms and invite her in and hold each other to share their grief. Another part of him, the angrier part, wanted to go. To taste the desert air far away from here. To never see her again.

"I'd rather be alone tonight," he said.

"It can't wait." She pushed into his quarters, forcing him to back up almost to the wall, and closed the door. She looked at the stool leg in his hand. Stood her ground in the middle of the room like a dare.

Ward's pulse quickened. Not for a fight. A different rhythm. A beat he hadn't felt since Madrid. Since MacKenzie.

"Are you going to hit me with that?" she asked of the stool leg, her words like her. Short. Dark. Strong. She was close enough to kiss him. Or slip a knife between his ribs.

"Do I need to?"

She shook her head. "We have to go."

Ward didn't move. At first, he thought she wanted him to go with her to talk about Sam, or about what was changing now that Sam was dead, but he could see that wasn't it at all.

She was nervous.

"It's not safe," she said.

Ward understood. Maybe not all of it, for it was clear there was more motivating her than his safety, but enough to make him willing to go along.

"Where can we go?" he said.

"I know a way out."

"Of Masada?"

"*Ken.*"

It took Ward a moment to process the word. A simple one. Hebrew for *yes*. It was not one of the languages he could easily speak, though he could read it competently enough.

"Drop your pants," Rivka said, producing a device like the one Bar-Ilan used to calibrate Ward's leg brace.

"Why?"

"Do it."

He considered his options. Yes or no, both ended with him on the run, but only one offered a way out of Masada.

He took down his pants, his shirt and jacket partially covering his briefs, suddenly overcome with the desire to look away, as if Rivka were the one half naked and vulnerable. She knelt before him and attached the device to his leg brace with a small cable extending from its corner. A familiar shiver ran up his thigh and down his calf. She spent a moment navigating menus on the device's screen while Ward examined the ceiling, the walls, the floor. Everything but the woman kneeling before him.

"You're unlocked," she said. She disconnecting the device, causing that shiver once more. "No more physical therapy protocol."

"Thanks." He pulled up his pants. "Now what?"

"Now you follow me. There's no time left."

She exited the quarters. Ward, half-certain he was being led into a trap, clutched the stool leg tighter and followed.

CHAPTER 5

They started south, in the direction of the operating room. Where Sam died.

Ward wondered if Rivka wanted to give him the opportunity to say goodbye to Sam, but they soon entered a corridor that twisted a different direction. Before he knew it, he was lost, and they were descending a set of timeworn stairs far older than most of the tunnels and excavations he'd seen in Masada.

"Where are we going?" he asked.

"Down."

"I thought you said we had to leave. Leaving means out, doesn't it? Up?"

Rivka put a finger to her lips and hurried on, forcing Ward to follow and guess at her intent. Had her status quo changed with Sam's death too? If so, what did that have to do with him? And where were they going? They were already at least one level deeper than he'd ever been before. The LED clusters that had been embedded in the tunnel ceilings above were gone. Their only light was a small yet bright flashlight Rivka wielded one-handed like a pistol.

The tunnel they followed forked twice. At the first, they went left. At the second, Rivka shined her light down each new tunnel as if unsure which way to go.

"Where are we?" Ward asked.

Rivka returned her light to the right fork. "Almost there," she said.

This new tunnel twisted and turned more than the previous ones. They'd long ago left behind any indication of being in a military base. The tunnels were narrower and lower than what he'd gotten used to in the base. Their finish rougher, as if it hadn't been worth the time to smooth the walls.

They reached a dead end. Only it wasn't. Rivka slipped into a seam in the rock like a magic trick. One second she was standing there before Ward. The next she seemed to walk right through the wall.

"Come on," she said.

Using his hands to locate the seam, Ward followed. Inside they pushed through a crevice barely wide enough for him to fit sideways. Partway through, panic began to take hold. He imagined getting stuck. Being trapped for hours, or days, the mountain crushing the breath from his chest until...

"Rafael," Rivka called from ahead.

She shined the line into the crevice above Ward's head, giving him a direction, a lifeline, to follow.

Finally, he dragged himself from the seam to find Rivka at the head of a narrow, curving set of stairs. She began down, leaving Ward to navigate steps too shallow for anything but his heels. Down. Slowly, down. Hands on the walls as if there were anything there to hold on to should he slip. Three levels down.

At the bottom, they stood in a small chamber not much larger than Ward's quarters. Rivka shined the light around them revealing two short tunnels on either side of a third that was blocked by a massive boulder surrounded by a mess of smaller rubble.

"Tell me we weren't aiming for the middle one," he said.

Rivka ignored him, busying herself with picking up the occasional rock, appearing to carefully choose only ones about the size of coffee mug. She lifted each a few inches from the ground then dropped it unceremoniously.

"What are you doing?" Ward asked.

His mind had shifted back to Sam and his own escape plan. He wondered if he wouldn't be better off heading back up the stairs alone and out the way he'd planned. Over the casemate wall and down the cliff. Not that he'd be able to find his way back, especially not without a flashlight of his own.

He could take Rivka's flashlight. A solid blow to the back of her head with the stool leg would knock her out cold. But then what? It was a bad plan. An impulse born of stress. Fear masquerading as strategy. He didn't want to hurt Rivka. He liked her.

I liked MacKenzie too.

An invalid comparison, he would have told his students. He betrayed MacKenzie, not the other way around. Rivka had been on his side—on Sam's side—from the moment they arrived at Masada. More than that, there'd been something between them, hadn't there? A companionship? Maybe even a desire?

"Here," Rivka said.

She had knelt beside a textbook-sized rock and was hefting it with both hands. She managed to get it a few inches off the ground, but it didn't seem to want to go any higher.

"Let me," Ward said.

Rivka waved him off and braced for one more try. There was a click followed by a sound like an attic door breaking open for the first time in years.

"What was that?" Ward asked, backing away instinctively.

A section of the wall between Rivka and the small tunnel on the right moved. It was so slight, Ward wasn't sure he saw it. Then it sank into the wall around it like a giant invisible fist had punched into a wad of dough. Vertigo gripped Ward, prompting him to place his hand on the smooth stone to steady himself.

Rivka, meanwhile, was still raising the rock. When she got it waist high, Ward could see a cable attached to its underside. She pulled until the cable reached its maximum length, then gave one more tug. The cable recoiled like a tape measure, sucking the rock back to the ground with a thud and a plume of dust.

"What is going on?"

"I told you," Rivka said. "It's no longer safe here. We have to go."

She got up and motioned Ward back so she could put her hands on the portion of the wall that had moved. It swung open like a door. A burst of stale, acrid air hit Ward. Beyond was only darkness.

"These tunnels are very old," Rivka said. "Only a few know about them. It's safer than trying to climb down the Snake Path."

"And you're one of the few?" Ward said, an alarm sounding in his head.

"It's our only chance. We go now, or all is lost."

She entered the portal, went left, and vanished, leaving Ward alone and blind. The panic he'd felt in the crevice returned. He backed up, his heel catching his other foot and almost dropping him on his ass.

Then she was back. First her light. Then her. A green glow in her other hand. She handed Ward a chemlume glowstick that reminded him of his childhood. Games of hide and seek with his brother, with only that green glow to identify them in the night.

"Keep up," Rivka said. Then she was gone again, moving beyond the green glow of his glowstick, the brightness of her flashlight obscured by her body.

Ward followed, entering a new tunnel as if he'd come through a solid corridor wall. As soon as he was clear of the portal, it swung closed behind him with a creak and a thud. Stone façades were riveted somehow to both sides of a thick slab of wood on iron hinges. When it had settled noisily back into place, Ward passed his sickly green chemlume light over the wall but couldn't tell where the wall ended and the portal began. It was an ingenious system, virtually undetectable, with only a pile of rocks on the ground to note its location, one of which he guessed was the triggering mechanism for the door on this side.

Down the tunnel to the left, Rivka's light reappeared. Ward hurried to her across the uneven floor.

"Where are we going?" he asked when he reached her.

"I told you—"

"You told me we had to leave, but why? Where are we? How do you even know about this place?"

"We're in tunnels that were here before Herod built his palace above."

"Tunnels for what? Who built them?"

"I don't know."

"Did Herod build the secret door too?"

"No, the door is only a few hundred years old."

"How do you know?"

"You can trust me, Rafael," Rivka said.

Said everyone who's ever deceived me, Ward thought. But Rivka was different. She was a doctor. She cared for Sam. She tried to heal her. She treated Ward with respect and kindness. Even caring. She had no reason to trick him into these tunnels. If the soldiers of Masada, if Compano herself, wanted him locked away or dead, they could have left him in his quarters to rot. They could have kicked open the door and executed him before he even had a chance to object.

He had to trust Rivka. He couldn't *not* trust her. The situation demanded it. More than that, he wanted to trust her. The way Sam had finally trusted him on their escape from the REC in Arizona. Thinking of Sam brought back the guilt and the inherent unfairness—no matter how ridiculous it was for an adult of his experience to complain about *fair*—of her lying there on that blood-stained gurney while he was here skulking his way towards escape.

"This morning," Rivka said, "you didn't see what you thought you saw."

Blood. All he'd seen was blood and his friend torn apart like an insane vivisection.

She went on. "The baby—"

"The baby survived?" Ward blurted. If he could rescue the child, he could redeem his failure to protect Sam. "We have to go back!"

Rivka shook her head, but didn't respond right away, as if she were conflicted about what to say next.

"What?" Ward demanded.

Finally, she said, "It's too late for the baby."

Those six words hit Ward like a kick to the groin: a sudden sharp pain followed by a slow buildup of agony. He doubled over, unsure if he wanted to cry or scream.

"But it's not too late for Samantha," Rivka said.

"Not too late for what?"

"She's not dead, not yet."

Ward stood up straight. "What the fuck are you talking about?"

Rivka put a hand on his shoulder. "I can save her."

CHAPTER 6

Rivka was still talking, but Ward didn't hear her. He couldn't. His ears were ringing. Somewhere nearby there was a jackhammering threatening to bring the mountain down on top of them.

It's not out there. It's in here.

He shook his head, clearing out the jackhammer. The ringing, however, persisted, though it began to soften until it was barely more than his pulse, a steady beat, like a line of poetry. Four syllables. Stressed followed by unstressed. Trochaic dimeter.

I can save her.

No, there was no saving the mess he'd seen in the operating room. It was blood and death. It was impossible.

Then again, what did *impossible* even mean? What about his leg? Bar-Ilan's eye? The contraption keeping Compano alive? All might be seen as impossible to someone unfamiliar with technology and scientific advancement.

But what about Adrien Quinque, the four-hundred-year-old priest? What about the thing Ward had definitely not hallucinated coming out of the sea at Santorini? What about Ker's ritual?

A different kind of impossible. An impossible requiring belief.

What do I believe?

He didn't know, but he couldn't help imagining what MacKenzie would say: *Have faith.*

"She's not dead?" he asked, his voice weak in the darkness.

"Not yet."

"How?"

"Not here."

"Why not?"

"We have to move," Rivka said.

"You can save her?"

"*Ken.*"

She started ahead, but Ward was too stunned to follow. Soon, he was along inside a cone of green chemlume within an otherwise endless darkness. He called for her but heard no reply. He turned slowly, seeking her light, his balance abandoning him. Was he falling? Had he fallen? Was he still standing? Still spinning? Soon, his heart was thundering. Not adrenaline this time. Fear. Claustrophobia. He was having trouble breathing. The mountain was closing around him once more, squeezing him like carbon into a diamond. A punishment. A torturous death. Revenge for the machine Compano has become. For his betrayal of MacKenzie. For the loneliness and pain Sam must have felt at the end.

Compano's training teased him, the words floating around him like visible ghosts in the green glow.

Go up, not down, she'd taught him. *Go down and you're stuck. Down might as well be a coffin.*

Stop, he told himself. *Stop, stop, stop, stop.*

"Stop!"

Then Rivka was beside him, holding him up, giving him strength, like she had in the operating room. His heart slowed. His lungs inflated. He swallowed then spit out the dirt that had somehow made its way into his mouth the way it had made its way into his boots.

"We're almost there," Rivka said, leading him forward until he found his own pace once more.

"Where?"

"The first step to saving Sam."

"How do you know about this place, these tunnels?"

"Clan memory. Like the Dead Sea Scrolls."

"The Dead Sea Scrolls?" Ward repeated, familiar with the series of two-thousand-year-old documents and fragments, some pressed onto copper scrolls, which were found in caves above the Dead Sea a little over a century ago, not far to the north of Masada. How they connected, however, was lost to him.

"They were reintroduced to the world when they were needed."

"You're saying the Bedouins who found the scrolls knew they were there?"

"Such things are not easily forgotten. The scrolls were 'discovered' when it was time to establish provenance for my people in this land. It is the same for us and these tunnels as it was for the scrolls."

"Your people? Jews? Ah," Ward said, thinking he understood. "Establishing a right to this land immediately before the British withdraw and the first Arab-Israeli war."

"Not the first of such a war."

Ward didn't want to get into the political background of one of the most fought over slices of land in human history. "Do all Jews know about these tunnels, then?" he asked.

"Of course not, and you're missing the point."

"Is Compano one of you now? Is she Jewish?"

"She's been given a chance. And a choice."

"For what?" Ward asked. Then: "You know what, never mind. How can you help Sam?"

"This tunnel will lead us out, on the north end, a little above ground level. Someone is waiting for us."

"This someone will help Sam?"

"The science is complex, and the procedure is difficult. I don't have time to explain it now."

It sounded logical, if cryptic, but something didn't compute for Ward. If these tunnels really were secret, and if Bar-Ilan really could cover for them, then they had until dawn to get away from the mountain. It was before midnight when Rivka came to his quarters, and they couldn't have been underground much more than an hour or two, which meant they had five or six hours until dawn. Enough time to get more than twenty kilometers from here, even hiking through the desert.

"I say we do have time."

Rivka shook her head as if she'd known he would insist.

"We walk as I tell," she said, getting them moving. "Bar-Ilan kept trying after you left. He got a heartbeat. He got Samantha stable, as much as she was before, but he also discovered something in her blood. He thinks it's changing her DNA, like a cancer. She needs a transfusion. Blood and marrow and clean genetic bodies, like stem cells."

"You mean the way really rich people make designer babies?" Ward asked.

"*Ken*. Sort of."

Ward had read about it a little when he was a professor. Stem cell research had been banned in the old United States. It offended some people to think scientists could do what they believed was God's realm alone: decide life and death. When the Republic lifted the prohibition on stem cell work, it became the go-to for nearly every disease there was. It cured over a hundred types of cancer. Then it hit the open market. Medical research companies were bought by a new class of oligarchs who used the treatments to customize their unborn children's eye colors and artistic proclivities and other personality traits.

Soon, however, there were rumors of other enhancements. Exposes written by daring journalists, some of whom died tragically under mysterious circumstances, detailed changes to the human genome. Advanced intelligence potential. Super skillsets in toddlers. And side effects. Deformities. Mutations.

"You're not going to do something weird with the baby to save Sam are you?" Ward asked.

"It's experimental, not weird."

Ward didn't want to hear more. Harvesting Sam's baby to save her was horrific. Barbaric. He could see what had driven people to ban this type of research once. It was also necessary, he understood.

"It's the best we can do," Rivka said.

"Then do it. What do you need me for?"

"We don't have the proper equipment or the necessary sequencing."

"Buy it."

"No one is selling."

"Take it."

"It's not that easy," Rivka said. "We have soldiers, but so do they. Control won't authorize an op, and they won't allow anyone to leave Masada to get it. They don't see it as necessary to our mission yet."

Ward stopped, forcing Rivka to turn and face him. "You know who has it, right?" he asked.

"*Ken.* I can explain more once we're far away from here."

"Promise me you can save her."

"I swear it," Rivka said without hesitation.

"How long do we have?"

"Bar-Ilan thinks he can keep Samantha stable for now, and he can cover for our absence until Compano returns. Seventy-two hours from when I came to your quarters. She'll notice you're missing right away even if no one else does. She's obsessed."

Ward wasn't surprised by this assessment, though he still didn't understand it. Revenge maybe? Whatever the case, now wasn't the time to explore it.

"How many others know about these tunnels?" he asked. "Can we be tracked down here?"

"Unlikely."

When he didn't say anything else, she got them moving again, taking them through turns she seemed to know without needing to consider which to choose. Maybe five minutes. Maybe ten. Eventually, the tunnel opened up into a cavern perhaps as vast as the OR above, wide enough Ward could no longer see the walls around them. Here and there, his green glow reflected off smooth stones, like river rocks. And something else.

"Wait," Ward said, the need to examine these stones coming over him the way he'd needed to examine the confiscated art in Commandant Gaustad's office back in Philly. The way he'd needed to rescue the golden bee before destroying the Tower.

"No time," Rivka said. "I heard something."

But Ward had already knelt beside a small cluster of the stones. Except they weren't stones at all. They were bones. His green light fell on the knob of a femur. The socket of a shoulder. Fingers strewn about like pebbles. He peered deeper into the darkness then followed the glow. They were everywhere. Fragments. Skulls.

"Hundreds of them," he said.

Rivka came back to him. *"Ken.* Our contact is waiting outside. Not far. We have to go."

He couldn't see them all, but he could feel them. The skulls mostly. In groups, like gossiping children. In piles, like they'd died, or been dumped here, in cliques. Picked clean as if the flesh hadn't just decomposed but had been boiled away. Or eaten by insects. All of it cast in that sickly green pale.

"Golgotha," he whispered, the Aramaic word meaning *place of the skull* popping into his head. A dark and sentimental name given to the supposed location of Jesus's crucifixion outside Jerusalem. This was surely not that site, but the word struck him as appropriate.

Then the glint of metal caught his eye. He pushed aside an arm bone exposing a slightly curved length of iron, pitted and tarnished. Maybe the remains of a broach or a chunk of a circlet. Possibly the blade of a small dagger.

"We have to go," Rivka said again.

This time the alarm in her voice pulled Ward from the remains. Her knees were bent as if ready to run, her eyes locked over Ward's shoulder back the way they'd come.

Then he heard it: footsteps.

A flash strobed the cavern. The scene burned into Ward's eyes like a photograph. The walls. The ceiling. The bones. And there, behind the flash, almost obscured in its shadow, was a man with a gun. The report of the gunshot came a split-second later, so loud it felt like it might knock Ward off his feet. More gunshots detonated, at least two weapons. Rivka grabbed Ward's arm and pulled him into a tunnel he didn't see until they were in it, dragging him onward through turn after turn until there were no more turns. Until there were no more shots. Until the only sounds were their own footfalls and gasping breaths.

CHAPTER 7

"He's not here," Rivka said.

They stood in the mouth of a cave twenty meters above the desert floor, looking out at the night. Breathing the fresh air. Above, the stars flickered as if they didn't care one bit what happened below.

"Who?" Ward asked.

"Our man."

The silence of indecision settled over them. Ward wondered how long they could wait before their pursuers found them.

"Who was shooting at us?" he asked.

Rivka kept scanning the desert, then locked in on a boulder outcropping to the northeast. "Random patrol," she said. "They probably thought we were Bedouins who found their way into the tunnels by mistake and were shooting to scare us off. I doubt they'll raise an alarm."

"And if they do? Why are you risking your life for me like this? You are risking your life, right? They're not going to forgive you for helping a prisoner escape."

"I'm a doctor. Sam's my patient."

Ward wanted that to be it, but he was having trouble. It wasn't trust. It was motivation. The reason MacKenzie abandoned him at Santorini. The reason he tied her up and left her behind in Spain.

"You can't be risking all this for one patient," Ward said. "Sam's not even one of your people."

"No, she's not," Rivka admitted. "But helping her, proving that the procedure to help her is real and obtainable, will change everything for us. That's worth the risk. Putting us on even ground with our enemies is worth the sacrifice, if it comes to that."

"War," Ward said. "More killing."

"That's not all."

"What else then?"

"I—you, the way you cared for Samantha. You weren't the dangerous terrorist they said. I couldn't let them keep you like that."

"Compano was going to have me executed when she returned, wasn't she?" Ward asked, aware they were dancing around another subject altogether: their attraction to each other.

Rivka, eyes averted, apparently willing to keep dancing around it, said, "I'll explain everything, I promise, but we have to go."

She began down the slope at a half-scramble, half-slide, almost like she was snowboarding. Ward did his best to follow but was tentative having not tested his leg brace on anything this severe. That tentativeness cost him as he lost his balance more than once, hitting his knees, even doing a partial somersault, scraping his hands and winding up with fistfuls of earth in his boots and up his pant legs.

"Are you okay?" Rivka asked at the bottom. She appeared to be trying not to laugh.

Sitting on the cold desert soil, Ward looked up at the mountain looming over them. It was like looking up at a battleship in dry dock. He was lucky he hadn't killed himself.

"I'm fine." He began unlacing his boot to shake out the dirt.

"No time," Rivka said. She took off at a jog outcropping they'd seen from above.

Ward continued with his boot anyway, shaking out dirt and gravel before going after her. He caught up to her on the far side of the boulder where she was shining her flashlight around. Here, the desert wasn't tans and beiges and khakis like inside Masada. It was silted shades of grays. Like ash.

"Help me with this," Rivka said, apparently finding what she was looking for. She cleared a line of dirt and then another at a ninety-degree angle. "Lift," she told Ward.

He felt at the edge, surprised to discover it was a tarp.

Together they pulled it aside to reveal a shallow pit filled with two bicycles and two backpacks.

"Your man?" he said.

"Our man."

"This was the plan?"

"This was the backup," Rivka said. "Something must have happened."

"Can you contact him?"

"We're dark until he finds us."

Ward considered the predicament and then the bicycles.

"I haven't ridden a bike in twenty years," he said.

"They say it comes back to you." She set the two bicycles against the boulder and chose a backpack. She went through its contents, muttering in Hebrew before adding, "No guns."

"Was there supposed to be?"

Rivka swapped some items from her pockets into one of the packs and tossed the other to Ward who caught it awkwardly. It was heavy and tied with a drawstring. He tugged it open enough to see the contents. Some ration bars, a compass, a utility knife, a small first aid kit, matches, parachute cord, and a water bladder with a tube running through a hole in the pack like a straw. He took off his jacket and stuffed it inside then hoisted the pack onto his shoulders.

Rivka had chosen a bicycle and was waiting for him to get on the other one. They were the kind of bikes teenagers used to ride around the neighborhood when Ward was a kid. Low handlebars. Black seat. Black wheels. All exposed parts painted flat black. A memory of Daniel teaching him how to ride hit him like a sandstorm. Daniel jogging beside him as he pumped the pedals and gripped the handlebars so tight the front end wobbled. Daniel giggling uncontrollably each time he fell over in the grass. Daniel hugging him and encouraging him to try again.

"Rafael," Rivka said, her impatient tone familiar to Ward. A teacher's impatience. "We have to go. No light."

Choice seemed to have abandoned him. It was go or be captured. Escape or be killed. Succeed or let Sam die.

He buried his glowstick in his backpack and got on the bicycle.

"Stay at the edge of visibility," Rivka said. "Ten or twenty meters apart. I'll take the lead."

She pedaled off, leaving Ward to get used to riding again on his own.

It turned out to be true, what they said about riding bicycles. After the first few wobbly seconds, he got the thing rolling fairly smooth and straight considering they were riding on desert sand. He kept in the general direction Rivka had pointed out, able to see her only at intervals when the moonlight glinted off her bicycle, letting his mind wander back to the bones in the tunnel. Was it possible they were the remains of the Sicarii, the victims of the mass suicide he'd told his students about, lost for two thousand years? Could their internment deep within the mountain be why no evidence had ever been found to corroborate Josephus's story?

Up ahead, Rivka came to a stop. Ward pulled up alongside her, a bit short of breath and feeling the exertion in his leg but not in pain. He stretched and looked around to get his bearings. They'd left Masada behind them and were riding roughly north or north-west, he figured. To their left, the west, rose the shadows of looming mountains, rounded and flat-topped lumps of night at haphazard intervals. To their right, the horizon was flat. Above, stars punctuated the night like no other sky Ward had ever seen, bright and sharp and obligated to nothing and no one on this tiny planet.

"Doing okay?" Rivka asked.

"Fine." He pointed right, to the east. "Is that the Dead Sea?"

"*Ken*," Rivka said. She brushed some of the gray sand away with her foot revealing a stripe of white paint. "This was the highway 90, the Dead Sea Highway, once the longest road in Israel. Before."

There was no need to explain *before*.

Before the surprise nuclear attack the former United States launched on Saudi Arabia's capital half a century ago, wiping it and its six million inhabitants off the face of the Earth. The attack was the United States' declared retribution for the Saudi terrorists who flew planes into the financial towers in New York City. For the United States, it was a monumental victory. It was also the first major stage in the rise of the New Republic Party and eventually in the formation of the Republic itself.

For the rest of the world, however, that attack was the start of uncertainty and destabilization. For the Middle East, it was chaos. When the dust settled after a generation of war and hyper-radicalism, the land was divided. The north, its urban centers largely spared the damage of war, rebuilt. The south could only languish in ruin, its suffering growing worse each year. Syria, Lebanon, and much of Iraq were now caliphates of the Levantine Authority. Egypt had been torn apart by civil war, resulting in North and South Egypt approximating its ancient Upper and Lower Kingdoms. Nothing lived in the Riyadh Quarantine Zone.

"Shouldn't we be avoiding roads?" Ward asked.

"It's not a road anymore. Besides, only a fool would flee Masada to the Dead Sea. They won't look here."

They.

Which they? The army in Masada? The Republic, who surely had Eye-Ds hovering near cloud level all around the world? Others who might be interested in the Tower Terrorist, Rafael Ward?

As if reading his mind, Rivka added, "And our contact assured me the route would be clear of Eye-Ds until dawn."

She pedaled off at a steady pace, giving Ward time to catch up before she sped up. Around them, the shadowy shapes of the desert rolled by. He imagined a post-apocalyptic landscape reminiscent of a late twentieth century movie he'd once seen about a lone warrior hunting gasoline after the fall of civilization. Sickly puffs of bushes sprouting here and there. Closer to the sea, gnarled stumps, maybe palm trees, reaching up like fingers broken off at the top knuckle.

A short time later, the mountain shadows to the west disgorged the straight lines and right angles of human construction. A military installation, perhaps, or a hotel from the pre-war days, Ward guessed, but rather than exploring, Rivka kept them riding the highway until a barbed wire fence, or what was left of one, appeared on their left. She rode along it until they reached the remains of a steel gate hanging loosely on a post. Here, they angled inland.

Once lost among the hills and humps of the landscape, Ward half-expected to see palm trees and grass. Instead, they found a trapezoidal ruin far older than the installation they'd passed. It lay flat in the darkness, yet Ward could make out the remains of walls, columns, and the mosaic floor of an ancient structure.

He turned to ask Rivka where they were, but she was gone. He waited in the breeze and silence for her to return, totally alone in a way only a desert could offer.

Except, he wasn't alone. A darting shadow to his left, near the edge of the ruin, spun him low into a crouch. When he looked, however, there was nothing there. He watched the spot, feeling like he was being watched in return, but there was no other movement. He called Rivka's name, as loudly as he dared. Even the breeze didn't reply.

He waited another moment before starting down the slope, leaving his bicycle on its side. He made his way through piled rubble that had once been walls to the mosaic carpet. Even in the dark, it was beautiful. Birds, likely peacocks, were the main theme of the scene. The central square, the church equivalent of a nave, was gorgeous. A double border of pyramids surrounded thousands of interlocking ovals set to form circles in a symmetrical pattern that gave the impression of an M.C Escher painting. In the center, the four cardinal directions were noted by overlapping diamonds containing more birds.

He surmised he was standing in a late-Roman era church or synagogue. Using this hypothesis as his guide, he walked the layout as best he understood it, starting at the western point of the central compass, until he almost stumbled over a kneeling Rivka. Her positioning, on both knees with her back to him, brought the memory of his mother praying before Daniel's bed like a jolt.

"Quiet," she said. "Keep your eyes west."

"Why? What's west?"

She flicked on a small flashlight rather than answer and passed it over the desert floor, revealing a faded inscription.

"What is this?" Ward asked. "It looks like Aramaic."

Rivka switched off the flashlight. "It's nothing. An archaic spell."

"Spell?" Ward said, suddenly certain he knew where they were. "Wait, this is the Ein Gedi synagogue, isn't it? Where David rested while fleeing from King Saul."

"David rested at the oasis to the north, not here. This synagogue would not be built for many generations after David, though this land was holy long before David slew Goliath. The original temple, the precursor to this synagogue, is up on the ridge, a place to thank God for His abundance."

The story came together for Ward like stitching together the pages of a textbook whose binding had failed. "The Chalcolithic temple? I thought that was fourth millennia BCE, two thousand years before Abraham."

"Do you think God came into existence only when Abraham heard His voice? The temple on the ridge was destroyed in one of the wars that have plagued this land since humanity could walk. In the aftermath, the earth lay steeped in the blood of its faithful for an age. When the Romanized Jews came to build a temple, they couldn't cleanse the land, so they sought a sign. God shone a ray of light on this site, and here they built."

"And then carved a spell?"

"A warning."

"What does it say?"

He thought she would refuse again, but after a moment she touched her fingers to the inscription. "Whosoever rebels against the Word of God," she read, tracing the words, "or reveals the secrets of His garden, let his soul and the souls of his seed be forever denied Paradise."

"What secret?" Ward asked.

"It's an obsolete spell, like what is found among Egyptian pharaohs. It means nothing. Come."

"To the oasis?"

"To our man."

CHAPTER 8

The Ein Gedi Oasis was a lush wellspring known throughout the ancient world for its diverse vegetation, clear water, abundant wildlife, and gorgeous waterfall. It was a paradise in the middle of the Judean desert. It was proof of the Land of Milk and Honey promised in the story of the Exodus. It was where David—the boy who'd slain Goliath—hid from King Saul in the middle of the Judean desert in the years before the boy would become king. After the formation of the modern nation of Israel, it became an animal sanctuary so beautiful tourists used to hike two days through the desert from Jerusalem to visit its botanical garden and waterfall.

All of that, however, was before.

The war had changed more than the political landscape of the region. It had changed the climate. A brief nuclear winter was followed by a decade-long nuclear summer which scorched the diverse landscape of the Arabian Peninsula, extending to portions of Israel and Egypt. It killed the oasis, leaving behind a gray and scorched wasteland.

All of this Ward knew in a textbook manner, but to see it in person, in contrast to the photos he remembered of the falls and the lush groves of the oasis was disconcerting. It was downright scary.

They stood at the rim of a great depression, like an explosion crater, its walls seared black. Rivka seemed to be vibrating with anger, or maybe grief, at the scene before them.

"This was the wading pool," she said. She pointed to a cleft in the bluff overhanging the crater. "That is the waterfall. My *savta*—my grandmother—met my grandfather here when it was still beautiful. Before the wars. I didn't know her, but I know the stories. When I come here it's like I see ghosts."

Ward didn't know what to say. He became hyperaware of how close he was to her. Of a feeling between them, like static electricity rising from the desert itself. If he looked, he was sure he'd see her fingers twitching close to his, ready to entwine.

He didn't look. He couldn't take his eyes from the crater. He couldn't stop seeing a similar hollow, on a much larger scale, at the Labor Camp in Arizona. The Pit, where Daniel somehow survived the firebombing that incinerated every other prisoner.

That image then morphed into another. A void at the bottom of the sea within the Santorini caldera where he sent the Vase of Soissons. Where the priest Adrien Quinque proclaimed El cast Ba'el to Earth within his prison. From that abyss came a sound, like a voice, calling to him…

"This way," Rivka said, leading him higher into the hills. Soon, when the spoiled oasis had been left below, caves began to appear in the hills and cliffs like gaps between teeth. She chose a cave halfway up and said, "We're to wait here."

"What happens if your man doesn't show?"

"He'll be here at dawn."

They ducked into the cave, Rivka's flashlight leading the way. It was far larger inside than Ward expected. Not high. Deep and winding, like a surprisingly large closet in a small master bedroom. He wondered if this was one of the caves the Dead Sea Scrolls were found in, but he didn't ask. A few twists in, it opened up into an underground grotto with a pillar in the center, the way a great oak might grow in the middle of a meadow. Rivka rounded the pillar and sat cross-legged on the ground and began rummaging through her backpack.

Ward sat opposite her, leaning against the pillar while she produced two glowsticks and a couple ration bars. She set the glowsticks between them like a cold green campfire and offered Ward a ration bar. He took it hungrily, tearing off the wrapper and biting off half of it before she'd even opened hers.

In between chews, he said, "I think it's time you explain how we're going to save Sam."

"*Ken*," Rivka said. "First, understand I am not in intelligence.

I am told only what a doctor needs to be told, but I hear things. No one pays attention to the doctor when debriefing an injured soldier. No one remembers what they say when the meds kick in. I know far more than my security clearance allows. I know what kinds of forces and weapons our enemies have. I help keep prisoners alive when they are brought in."

"Keep them healthy so they can be tortured."

"It's always been so for doctors, I think."

Her tone changed. Ward read it as regret. A doctor who'd begun to question her direction as a healer. A soldier who'd begun to question orders. Another motive for helping him escape

"The revolution in your Republic is larger than you know," she said. "It is more than a war for a nation. It is a war for humanity itself, but we are not as united as philosophers would like us to be. There are many sides. Many allegiances."

"Which side are you on?" Ward asked, and immediately regretted it for the look of hurt on Rivka's face. She wanted him to respect her choices, her betrayal of her people. She wanted him to feel for her the way he suspected she felt for him. And he did, or he was beginning to, but he couldn't help his natural skepticism. Before he could apologize, however, she continued.

"We are all Israel has left," she said, "but I'm not so naïve to think we're the first soldiers to believe our cause is the righteous one. Humanity's mistake is believing Gods are more morale than we are. Then again, maybe we're nothing more than dead sinners walking a dead earth, killed by our immorality centuries ago."

"If that's the case, why bother helping anyone? Why be a doctor?"

"Because I'm not so jaded as I sometimes seem. Because I still believe in people and in love. Because a couple months ago, Bar-Ilan and I were brought into Control to discuss the type of protocols I told you about. Genetic customization. They wanted to know if it was useful for us."

"Compano wanted to know?"

"That one is a soldier, a useful tool, nothing more."

"She's not in charge?"

"She's not Israeli," Rivka said. "She's a traitor to her own people."

"So are you by helping me."

"I'm a doctor."

Silence filled the grotto. Ward imagined it filled with the crackling and popping of a campfire.

"The protocols," Rivka began again. "Bar-Ilan and I have been trying to make those breakthroughs for years, but it requires data and equipment we've been unable, or not allowed, to obtain. That is part of why we brought Compano in. We thought she might be able to provide access through the Republic."

"But she hasn't," Ward said.

"No, but she has led us to a faction who has what we need, at least partially. The intel is incomplete. I was able to get a copy of what we have, but it's a puzzle to me."

Of course it is, Ward thought, finally seeing why he was necessary to this operation. Which made him question if the attraction he'd felt had been a product of wishful thinking rather than true desire.

"Was all of this in motion before Sam and I arrived or after?" he asked.

Rivka took a moment to answer, never making direct eye contact. "It has been ongoing," she finally said.

"And Sam dying is just a convenient coincidence?"

"There is nothing convenient about a young girl's death," Rivka said, her eyes now locked on Ward's, fierce and daring. "Perhaps I wouldn't have had the courage to do this if you hadn't arrived, but you did. Such is God's will. Would you refuse to save Samantha because there were other motives before you arrived?"

"No," Ward said, feeling chided and small.

"Then help me."

Rivka shuffled around the glowsticks to sit beside Ward, a flimsy strip of paper in her hand. She offered it to him, but it slipped from his fingers, landing between their legs. They both bent to pick it up.

Their heads knocked together.

Simultaneous grunts. Smiles. Ward started to apologize as she leaned in for the paper again. Her mouth found his. The kiss was hard. Hungry. Frantic. Quick. Over.

"We shouldn't do that," she said, her fingers going to her lips.

"Yeah," Ward said, wanting more than anything to pull her to him once more. "I guess not."

Why not?

Because, he told himself, *look how it worked out with MacKenzie.*

She picked up the paper and handed it to him. Their fingers touched. She pulled away. Ward forced himself to look at the slip of paper. Forced his eyes to focus on the handwriting, not the woman beside him.

The first line was two words: *Honey Bee.*

The second was longer: *Lamented in death, Here lies Hannibal, the Barca.*

"Hannibal?" Ward asked. "As in the Carthaginian general with the elephants? Son of Hamilcar Barca?"

"*Ken.* It's an epitaph, which Control believes means the data is located where Hannibal is buried. Can you find it?"

"Hannibal's tomb?"

"We have found dozens of references to monuments and tourist attractions dedicated to Hannibal, but no information on a tomb."

Ward was struck by an awful thought. A claustrophobic thought worse than what he'd felt beneath Masada. Was this to be his lifelong formula, his *raison d'être*? Was he nothing more than a character trapped in a plot formula, like Philip Marlowe and Hercule Poirot and the other detectives he used to love reading about? Was he nothing more than the vehicle for others' mysteries, cursed to live a life of unending mystery, plot twist, and solution?

"Rafael? Can you find it?" she asked again.

"No," he said. "I have no idea how to find it."

CHAPTER 9

"What do you mean you don't know?" Rivka said.

"I mean, I don't know," Ward said. "It's like asking me where Alexander the Great's tomb is, or where Genghis Khan is buried. There are a thousand possibilities and none. Every town in the Greek world swore they had Alexander's tomb nearby, the same way almost every church in Europe used to swear they had a piece of the True Cross or Saint Peter's finger bone."

"But you solve these puzzles. Compano says so. Everyone has heard what you do. Everyone knows."

"Nobody knows. You don't know. I'm a prisoner. A nobody. Even out here, I'm still Compano's fucking prisoner. What do you think I can do, find the Ark of the Covenant? The Garden of Eden? Some things are just lost. Get a Port and look up how many Hannibal tombs or monuments there are. Probably five hundred. It's like trying to find a specific piece of hay in a haystack."

"What about the honey bee?"

"What about it? How many of those Hannibal monuments do you think are within a hundred kilometers of a beekeeper? Four hundred and fifty? Three hundred and ninety-five? You need more intel. I can't put together a puzzle with half the pieces missing."

"Please. For Sam."

"It's not about please," Ward snapped.

Rivka got up and crossed to the far side of the grotto, at the edge of the green glow. Barely visible. Like a ghost. Ward let her go. He was angry. At her. At Compano. At himself for being cast in this role again. For failing Sam.

For giving up so easily.

That was the alcoholic Rafe giving up, he knew. The man who'd tried to drink himself to death in Arizona. He wasn't that man anymore. He hadn't had a drink in five months. He had a purpose, a reason to live. There was a girl lying on a gurney counting on him. Anger didn't matter. Resentment at needing to solve another puzzle didn't matter. Only Sam mattered.

He got to his feet. "This is all the soldier gave you?"

Rivka came back into the green light. "*Ken.*"

"And we're looking for data and equipment?"

"Somewhere safe. Locked away. Underground probably, like a storage depot."

"Or a tomb," Ward said. "How big is the equipment?"

"Meaning how large does the tomb have to be?"

"Exactly."

Rivka thought on it a moment before answering. "Like a large desk," she said. "Big enough for you to lie upon."

Ward began pacing around the grotto. "That's not big, or small, enough to narrow it down. Give me some time to think it through. Maybe I can narrow down the options."

When he came around the pillar, Rivka was in a crouch, like a lioness about to pounce. He froze mid-step, but she wasn't looking at him. Her attention was on the tunnel.

"Someone's coming," she whispered.

Ward knelt beside her. "Your man?" he asked.

"He's not supposed to arrive until dawn."

Ward's hand went reflexively to his belt, but he had no weapon. He grabbed for his backpack as Rivka buried the glowsticks, casting the two of them in disorienting darkness.

Disorienting for Ward, at least. Rivka put her lips to his ear and said, "Stay here."

Then she was gone, leaving Ward to dig blindly through the backpack for the utility knife inside. Seconds later, the muffled crunch of bootsteps announced someone coming. At first, Ward thought it was Rivka returning, but she'd made no sound when she left, and the incoming strides were too long to be hers.

With the knife in one hand, Ward sought the pillar with his other hand. He found the edge of it and crept around to the far side where he would be hidden from an intruder with a flashlight. His heart was racing. His imagination conjured a trio of Masada soldiers with submachine guns. Then a squad of those militarized REC Agents that MacKenzie called Reapers. Then a single cyborg like Compano, only larger and deadlier.

Get a grip, he told himself, wiping sweat from his forehead. He hadn't been this pathetically nervous on his first operation in south Philly. The one where he'd met MacKenzie for the first time.

I'm going to get shot in the dark thinking about her again.

That was enough. He opened the utility knife and gripped it as Compano had taught him. A quick peek around the pillar revealed a flashlight beam bouncing with the intruder's gait. Up the tunnel. To the grotto entrance. Ward pulled back around the pillar as the light swept around the cave creating disturbing shadows on the back wall Ward was facing.

For a moment, he feared Rivka had left him, deciding his inability to decipher the intel made him a liability. But no, she'd risked too much to cut him loose that easily. And then there was their kiss. Dangerous. Exciting. Sincere.

The intruder came deeper into the grotto, rounding the pillar slowly, forcing Ward to move clockwise until he was, more or less, facing the entrance to the grotto. He tightened his grip on the knife and weighed attacking versus making a run for the exit. Neither felt right, not with Rivka's position and plan unknown. A true wildcard. One he would have to be prepared to improvise off of.

The flashlight and footsteps stopped, placing the intruder a quarter of the way around the column from Ward's position. The cave was silent, as if holding its own breath in anticipation of what was coming.

The flashlight beam turned to the opposite wall, giving Ward an opportunity to look over his shoulder around the pillar. Even with his eyes adjusting to the lack of light, the intruder appeared as little more than a shape holding the flashlight. Except the shape was moving unnaturally, as if part of it was leaning one way while another part was rising up at an impossible angle.

Impossible for a single person, Ward understood a split second later, but not for two separate people.

Rivka came up out from behind the intruder as if she'd opened a zipper in the darkness and slipped through with uncanny speed and silence. A curved dagger appeared in her hand and slipped around the intruder's shoulder.

The intruder gasped and dropped the flashlight, the beam briefly illuminating a dark-skinned man not much taller than Rivka, with her curved blade at his throat, before the light went out.

"It's me," the man said.

As Ward dropped to his hands and knees in search of the flashlight, Rivka said, "You're early."

"You paid me to be smart and flexible," the man said with the barest hint of a North African accent.

"What's changed?"

"Our route."

"Are we unable to enter Jerusalem?"

"We're going to Jerusalem?" Ward said, unable to hide his excitement as he continued to scramble for the flashlight. The center of the most populous, and destructive, vein of religions in history—Judaism, Christianity, and Islam—Jerusalem was a historian's dream. According to Republic news outlets, it was also a nightmare of instability and violence.

"As paid for," the man said, his voice oddly familiar.

Ward found the flashlight and switched it on. The light highlighted Rivka first as she was sheathing her dagger. Next, the intruder, from knees to face. Ward nearly dropped the flashlight.

"You!" he said, unable to believe who he was looking at.

CHAPTER 10

"Good to see you again, my friend," the man said with a toothy smile.

"What are you doing here?" Ward said, shining the flashlight directly at the man as if expecting him to disappear under the light.

"Zee's our man," Rivka answered.

"Indeed," Zee said, putting his hand up to keep the light from his eyes, the motion causing his sleeve to ride up, revealing a tattoo familiar to Ward: tree roots at the base of the wrist, with a vine-tangled trunk rising up the forearm.

Ward lowered the light. "I just wasn't expecting…"

"Who else is there for smuggling in the Mediterranean?" Zee said happily.

Rivka added, "He has arranged materials and service for us for a long time."

Ward looked Zee over again, but there was no doubt. The tattoo, the wide ears, the black and red kufi. It was Ziyad—known to his friends and clients as Zee—the man who helped Ward escape the island of Santorini after MacKenzie left him there. The same man who extended Ward his skills as a smuggler to arrange travel through Europe to Ireland to Iceland to Greenland, and eventually back into the Republic through the Canadian Districts. Who connected Ward with the first of the hackers who would eventually reprogram his REC ID card to get him into the Tower.

"You see," Zee said, throwing his arms wide. "I told you we would meet again in the future."

He came at Ward quickly, his lanky frame somehow

enveloping Ward in a bear hug. A confusion of thoughts and emotions still whirled in Ward, however. Zee had been a friend, but he was also a businessman. Was there an ulterior motive here? A debt Ward owed the smuggler? A client Zee had taken who had outbid Rivka's services?

"And I always keep my promises," Zee said, giving Ward a hearty pat on the back before letting him go. "Though I admit I thought this one would go unfulfilled. The world thinks you're dead, my friend."

"I've been close a few times." To Rivka, Ward said, "Did you know we know each other?"

"Not at first," she said.

"What am I, a reference?"

Zee said, "That's not exactly how it works."

Ward found the answer comforting if vague. If anyone could have led the REC to Ward during his years hiding out in Arizona, it would have been Zee. The fact the smuggler never did, Ward thought, spoke volumes about the man's ideas on friends versus clients.

"Are you here to find the tomb for us, or to take us to it?" Ward asked.

Zee said, "Tomb?"

"Zee is our transportation," Rivka said. "If we are still good to go."

"We are. There's a been a change to our primary route, but it's handled."

"I thought your people were reliable."

"The most reliable," Zee said, "as our good professor can surely attest. There are, however, other networks active in the region we should avoid."

"Masada?"

"Much more mundane than that, and unconnected to our movements. The new route I've prepared is the most direct I could arrange clear of Eye-D traffic through the Waste, but we must be at least twenty kilometers from here before the hour is up. We should go."

"What's the Waste?" Ward asked.

"Dangerous," Rivka said.

Zee shrugged. "For you, my friends, it is nothing. Come, the clock is ticking for us to reach Bayt al-Maqdis."

The use of the medieval Arabic title for the Jewish Temple in Jerusalem, and thus for the city itself, caught Ward off-guard. Hearing the name for the first time after a career of only ever having seen it written was like hearing a bird sing after a lifetime of being told they said *tweet*.

Rivka pushed Ward's backpack into his chest and said, "Let's go."

Outside, it was warm and still dark, the moon partially occluded by cloud cover. Below the cave, an off-road vehicle idled aggressively. Ward recognized it as an early-century Storm Mark III, an Israeli standard based on the American Jeep platform. Its four-door body, painted in foggy camouflage, looked a half-century old, but the engine sounded strong. They piled in, Rivka insisting on sitting in the back alone, and took off across the desert.

No one spoke as they drove west from the oasis, the Storm bouncing them around a good deal for the first few minutes. It quickly grew hot in the vehicle with no air conditioning and windows that wouldn't roll down, but Ward did his best to zone out and let his brain work as the sands rippled by his window like ashy waves.

Hannibal was as much a myth as a historical figure. There were three narratives of his death written in antiquity, plus a number of related anecdotes and references, none of them penned within a generation of the events they described. His death, most historians agreed, came at the hands of the Romans, his life-long adversaries, after his location in a kingdom called Bithynia, in modern Turkey, was betrayed by the king Prusias I.

These facts only prompted questions, however. Would the Bithynians have erected a tomb for Hannibal? Would they have given his body to the Romans? If so, would any of the purported tombs, including ones Ward vaguely recalled being attested in North Africa and across the Middle East, have housed his remains? Were his remains even the point? Rivka's intel seemed to indicate the tomb was a landmark for a storage depot or a meeting spot. What did that have to do with the honey bee in the first part of the message? Was it a coincidence he still held Childeric's golden bee in his pocket? He didn't much believe in coincidences, but he couldn't see a connection between the Carthaginian general and the Merovingian king who commissioned the golden bee six hundred and fifty years later, and half the Mediterranean world away.

"Honey bee," he whispered, sounding his way through it, seeking meaning in the words themselves rather than the relic in his jacket. "Bee honey. Worker. Queen. *Apis.*"

"Latin?" Zee asked.

Ward, who hadn't realized he was speaking loud enough to be heard, said, "The genus name for a bee. It's nothing."

"Don't get stung," Zee said.

"Hurts," Ward replied absently, still searching for a link between bees and Hannibal.

"Kills the bee," Zee said.

Ward barely heard. He was still playing on the similar sounds of the key words. "Honey, Hannibal, honey, hanni…"

"The general?" Zee asked.

"You know of him?"

Rivka made a sound communicating a clear message: *Don't share.*

"Of course I know of him," Zee said. "I'm from Tunisia."

"Carthage?" Ward said, naming Hannibal's ancient empire, the capital of which was now the capital of the North African nation of Tunisia. "I thought you were from Iraq."

"I was born in Sousse, south of Tunis, where I was orphaned during one of the revolutions of my childhood. There were too many to number or name."

He went on to describe a period of homelessness and fear and stark survival followed by a forced relocation for orphans at the advent of Tunisia's current government. Though Ward's own experiences in the foster system were far less physically perilous than near starvation and daily battles for water and shelter, he found himself developing a kinship with Zee he hadn't previously experienced. He also wondered why the smuggler hadn't shared his story in the couple months they'd spent together on Santorini and in southern Europe.

"They took us to Iraq," Zee continued. "I grew up there, near the border with Syria and Jordan, a few kilometers from the Quarantine Zone. I found my profession there, and now the entire Mediterranean is my playground, as your song says, from sea to shimmering sea."

"Shining," Ward corrected, biting back the impulse to also state it wasn't his song. "Sea to shining sea."

"Shining? It's nice, but I like shimmering."

"Have it your way," Ward said. "What do you know about Hannibal?"

"Rafael," Rivka prompted.

Ward understood her concern, but they needed information. "Do you know where his tomb is?"

"Which one?"

"See?" Ward said to Rivka.

She responded by looking out her window.

"He died in Turkey, you know," Zee said. "They built a monument there last century, on the exact spot where he died, they say."

"How long until we cross?" Rivka asked.

"We'll make it to the next safe zone in time. From there it depends how long it takes to cross the Waste."

"Safe zone?" Ward asked. "From Eye-Ds?"

"They cycle over the Waste day and night, but I've arranged some hiccups in their pattern. Relax. Enjoy the sights."

Ward turned to the window, seeking some definition in the partial moonlight but finding only hints of the bushes and stunted trees he'd imagined near Ein Gedi.

"Are the transport options I asked for arranged?" Rivka asked.

"Jerusalem is prepared. Haifa and Tel Aviv are on standby as required," Zee said.

"No problems with getting us across?"

"All is arranged."

"Wait," Ward said, only now putting together the obvious. "We're crossing the Jerusalem Line?"

Zee chuckled. "Did you want to tunnel underneath?"

Ward suddenly found himself beset by anxiety. The

Jerusalem line had been erected in the aftermath of the Arabian War, a wall partitioning north and south Israel like Hadrian's Wall in Britain, as impenetrable as Masada had been at the height of its rebellious power. It was said the Line had served as the inspiration for the Republic's Wall along its southern border. Only the Line was more effective. More impenetrable. More imposing than the Great Wall of China. Deadlier than the Berlin Wall. No account Ward had ever read of people who'd stolen across it. In fact, were it not for the slender dimensions of the nation itself, the Line might have cut Africa off entirely from Asia and Europe. Though no pictures of it existed in Republic textbooks or media outlets, it was said to be a true wonder of the modern world.

"We're going to go over it?" Ward asked.

Zee said, "You've never seen it, have you?"

"No."

"Sit back. The Line is nothing. It's what we encounter first that brings danger."

"What do we encounter first?"

Neither Zee nor Rivka responded, leaving Ward to sit silent and uncomfortable as they sped toward the deadliest border humanity had ever built.

CHAPTER 11

"Almost there," Zee said.

Ward startled awake, trying to hide his surprise with a yawn and a stretch. The moon had finally broken through the clouds, bathing the desert in a pale light that cast everything silvery like iron. Like the earth here might never hold reds and greens and browns again.

They were no longer bouncing over rough sands and through narrow wheel ruts. Beneath them the sands were packed and tight, almost like a road. Beside them, whipping by as Zee revved the Storm to near one hundred kilometers an hour, were husks of buildings Ward first mistook for outcroppings of stone and bramble and shrub. A closer look revealed them to be the remains of buildings, homes even, Ward thought, though there was little left to judge aside from broken walls and piles of debris.

"Is this Jerusalem?" he asked.

"No, my friend," Zee said. "We must pass through this first."

He pointed Ward's attention to a dusky cityscape ahead which, for the first time, gave the desert perspective and depth. They were on a rise descending a slight angle toward the urban landscape. Of course it wasn't Jerusalem, Ward understood, feeling foolish. That fabled city waited on the other side of a great wall.

"Are you sure this route is wise?" Rivka asked.

"No, but it is what could be arranged."

"Do you have the weapons I requested?"

Zee patted the steering wheel. "We're armored. Speed is our best weapon."

"Against what?" Ward asked, wondering what society, or threat, could exist in this wasteland.

Rivka leaned up between the seats and pointed ahead. "Speed's no good if you can't see the bomb in the road."

Zee jerked the wheel hard left. Ward's shoulder slammed the door as the Storm slalomed around whatever they had seen. Ward turned to look through the vehicle's back window. Growing small in the distance was a patch of road slightly darker than the rest of the gray surrounding them. Like a clue in a video game, highlighting that spot as a secret door. Or a trap.

"Good eye," Zee said, as casual as ever.

"What was that?" Ward asked.

Rivka, with an attitude that said if Ward didn't know maybe he shouldn't be here in the first place, said, "A bomb."

The city ahead disappeared as the road began angling now uphill, leaving them in the company of the broken homes and small buildings on the side of the road like decrepit, nervous sentinels trying to warm them off.

"Who planted it?" Ward asked after a moment.

His question hung in the Storm unanswered. A moment later, Zee swerved again. This time Ward spied a rusted, industrial-sized soup can in line with the right wheel of any relaxed drive through the ruins.

Zee kept up speed as they crested the rise along a harsh curve, the Storm's tires squealing ominously. The view spread beneath them might have once been brilliant. Ward imagined it looking like Cadiz in Spain, the whitewashed buildings climbing the next rise like the sun itself had laid them down. A gift, an urban oasis, in the desert.

As beautiful as it might have once been, however, the ruins ahead were a thousand times more awful, as if the sun had grown angry and come down from the sky, as in Ovid's *Metamorphoses*, and charred the city with its rage. The buildings that stood were blackened. The ones that no longer stood were fused mounds of tumorous destruction.

"What is this?" he asked as they raced toward the cadaverous city.

Zee said, "This is Bethlehem."

"Bethlehem."

Bethlehem. Of course. Once a city of more than twenty-five thousand people, it was most famous as the birthplace of Jesus Christ. Before that, it was where Rachel, matriarch of Judaism, died and was buried. Centuries earlier, perhaps even before Jerusalem was settled, it was a Canaanite city named for Lahmu, the god of fertility. What Ward saw, however, could not have been that city. Even here, south of the Jerusalem Line, such devastation could not be real.

"What happened?" he asked. There was no color but char and ash. A stillness hung over the remains, penetrating the Storm and cutting Ward's heart cold "Was there a war?"

"There still is," Rivka said. "The oldest war in history. People have been fighting it as long as humanity can remember."

"You mean for the Holy Land? Jews and Muslims?"

"I mean long before Muhammad or Abraham."

"Religion is an excuse," Zee said. "War with each other is the only thing they know. Like leaving room for dessert. You're going to indulge it anyway, even if you're full. It predates cities. It even predates tribalism. They've been killing each other since they could walk upright."

"They?" Ward asked.

"We," Rivka said.

Ward thought he understood. "The Arabian War."

"That was fifty years ago. The war we speak of is more than fifty centuries old. It is eternal. Tribes, governments, Gods, good, evil. Excuses. Your war, your bombs, were only one part of it."

"But Riyad is almost two thousand kilometers..." He stopped. He didn't want to argue ownership of America's bombing of Riyadh anymore.

"What, Rafael?" Rivka said, creeping up between the seats again. "Did you think your bombs fell only in Arabia? Did you think they were the beginning and the end of the war?"

"They're not my bombs. It wasn't my fucking war!"

"Please, friends," Zee said. "It's difficult to keep us from getting blown up when you yell about bombs."

Rivka returned to her seat, her desire to get the last word tangible in the Storm, but she remained silent. Ward set his sights on the carcass of the city they were now cutting through, swerving hard around objects and discolored patches of road. Maybe debris. Maybe bombs. Of those who'd left the traps, he saw no sign.

Until he did.

They slowed to take a sharp branch left at a fork, giving Ward the first sightline around the turn. Something separated itself from one of the broken structures. A flicker of motion too small and too quick to be a person.

"Did you see that?" he asked.

Zee was locked in on the road and shook his head. Rivka didn't respond. Whatever Ward had seen was gone. A jackal, maybe. Or a monitor lizard.

Or my imagination, he added, noting his lack of sleep and intense stress levels of the past twenty-four hours.

He settled back in to his seat and watched out the window for other signs of life, but the city was a corpse. They continued another kilometer or so, slowing and slaloming at intervals, before the landscape began to change. In time, something appeared on the horizon, taller than what they'd seen so far. Less blackened. As they got closer, its height, maybe three meters, became apparent.

"Is that the Jerusalem Line?" Ward asked, excitement bubbling in his belly. It wasn't a venerable ruin, but any edifice of such legendary proportions was enough to spark his inner historian.

Zee said, "That is what's left of the Palestinian Wall, the West Bank Barrier, from long before the bombs."

Ward examined the barrier as they got closer. It looked like the steel scales of a xylophone staked upright in the earth. He wondered how this, of all the structures in Bethlehem, was still standing. Could the tribes Rivka mentioned be using it, even upkeeping it, as part of their war?

The road took them to the barrier then turned west, parallel to it. A few minutes later, the scales of the barrier began to shrink. Then, some went missing, giving the thing the appearance of a gap-toothed grin. Not long after, the barrier appeared to simply dissolve away.

"The Tomb of Rachel," Zee said as they neared the barrier's last stubborn scales.

"Here?" Ward asked, trying to contain his excitement. Rachel's Tomb would be a wonderful site to visit. He leaned into the window as they passed two large masonry pillars. Other than the barrier, they were the largest structures they'd seen in Bethlehem. Between the two pillars hung, barely, a gate. Its mate had long since disappeared into the desert.

"Alas, the entrance is all that remains," Zee said. "The tomb itself was wiped away many years ago. Apologies, my friend."

Ward was about to express his disappointment when an explosion went off outside beside the Storm. The vehicle lurched left, Zee fighting the steering wheel to keep them from crashing into the ruins alongside the road.

"Down," Rivka shouted.

The Storm careened to a stop, mostly still on the road, a few meters from the entrance to Rachel's Tomb.

"No contact," Rivka said.

"Was it a bomb?" Ward, pressed against his door, asked.

"No," Zee said. "The tire."

"A trap," Rivka said.

Ward's awareness of the situation returned slower than it should have, embarrassingly so, compared to his companions who were already assessing possible solutions. The Storm, he realized, was sitting cockeyed, leaning forward and left, thanks to the driver-front tire being blown out.

Zee said, "We can run on a flat if we need to, but it would be difficult in the sand ahead."

"We need weapons," Rivka said.

Zee didn't respond.

"Zee," Rivka said.

"Beneath your seat."

Ward watched Rivka feel around under the vehicle's back seat. There was a click. She slid over and let the cushion rise. From beneath, she withdrew a black bag.

Zee elbowed Ward in the arm. "Come, stand watch. I'll make the swap. It's a quick change."

Rivka got out first and called, "Clear."

Ward exited. It had gone from warm to hot outside, but it was still cooler than inside the Storm.

"I've got Zee's back," Rivka said, handing Ward a bullpup assault rifle. "Watch this side."

"For what?"

"You'll know."

Ward took position, holding the bullpup, which was the same color as the desert itself, tighter than he'd been taught to hold a weapon. It was a sleek weapon, maybe three times the weight of an RT40. Probably slightly less heavy than a full-sized assault rifle. He'd seen plenty of similar bullpups before; they were favorites of undercover REC Agents who preferred the compact size and short exposed muzzle due to its action and magazine being set behind the trigger. REC models were also rumored to work off a GPS guidance system linked to each Agent's Port. He'd never used one, however, and found its lack of extension disconcerting, especially out here in the open.

More than its design, however, Ward found the weapon itself troublesome. He'd done all he could to avoid killing since the Tower. The guilt of those deaths still weighed on him. He didn't think he could bear more. Trying, however, wasn't enough. Once at Masada, he'd sworn to himself he would never take another person's life again. Even if it cost his own. Only it wasn't his own life on the line. It was Zee's and Rivka's. It was Sam's.

The sudden desire for a burning gulp of whiskey surprised him to the point he barely recognized the flash of movement to his left. He turned slowly, as if on a delay, but there was nothing there. He watched and waited, holding his breath until he no longer could. Exhaled. Inhaled. Held it again, still watching. Nothing. He stood and looked over the vehicle's hood. Rivka was still scanning the far side. Zee popped up beside her, said something Ward couldn't hear over the Storm's idling engine, then ducked back down.

"All clear?" she asked Ward, shouting to be heard.

He saw nothing at the barrier and was about to announce *clear* when he saw it again. This time he wasn't the only one.

"Contact," Rivka shouted.

"Don't shoot," Zee said.

Ward tightened himself to the vehicle but remained standing, the bullpup ready but not aimed. He squinted at the form crouched beside the wall, thinking he was right before. It was a jackal. But the way it hid, the way it curled its paws around the wall and peered out, the way it moved within the shadow, said it wasn't a beast at all.

"Are you seeing this?"

Neither Rivka nor Zee answered. The vehicle dropped off its jack.

The creature flinched but didn't run. It seemed to be watching them. Waiting. Then it turned, like it was listening for something back in the city. A deliberate motion. A human motion.

Ward crept forward. The creature rotated to face him. It was a small person, Ward now saw, wearing some kind of leathery costume or armor.

"Target approaching," Rivka said. "Time to go, Zee."

"Almost ready," their driver announced.

"I think it's a kid," Ward said.

Then Rivka hit it with a light.

It wasn't human at all. The face, scaly and reptilian, was sunken. Where there should have been a nose, there were two lumps, like tumors. The eyes were bloated. The mouth was a disjointed crater.

It came closer, one slow ophidian stride at a time.

"What is that?" Ward asked.

No answer from his companions.

"Rivka," he said, louder, terrified by what he saw. "What the fuck is that?"

Zee said, "Don't shoot."

"They're called Nephilim," Rivka said, coming to his side of the vehicle.

"Fallen angels?" Ward asked, familiar with the Biblical name for a generation of angels who chose life on earth with humans rather than in Heaven.

"It's just a name," Zee said, coming around to return the jack to the equipment box on the back of the Storm. "They're mutations."

"Mutated from what?"

"Did you think the Quarantine Zone was for fallout?" Rivka said. "Did you think the Jerusalem Line was for keeping out radiation?"

"You're saying nukes did this?"

"You didn't drop nukes. You dropped something far worse."

Ward was speechless. The thing crouched by the barrier, he now thought, didn't even move like a human. It slithered and jerked like a special effects monster. He couldn't take his eyes off it.

In return, it watched them, the way a cat watches a bird outside the window.

"We shouldn't stay," Zee said. "They don't like outsiders."

"Why not?"

"They're tribal. Two tribes, we think. They live in the Waste and fight each other over what's left of this city. The traps are theirs, one side's or the other's. Keeping us from getting through their city is a nice distraction for them from killing each other. A trophy they can gloat about. A one-up on the other side."

"You seem to know a lot about them."

"It pays to know the obstacles of a place if you're going to do business there."

Suddenly, the Nephilim's head popped up as if it heard a new sound coming from the city.

"Let's go," Zee said. "Now."

As Ward reached the door, he heard whatever the Nephilim had heard. The grinding of metals, like an iron dragon chewing a mouthful of cars.

"Now what?" he asked, the sound growing louder.

Zee and Rivka flung themselves into the Storm.

"Rafael!" Rivka ordered.

Ward went for the door, unable to help a look back toward the sound. What came out of the ruins was a nightmare, slow and angry and hungry.

A tank.

CHAPTER 12

"Go, go, go," Ward shouted as he dove into the already moving Storm.

He twisted in his seat as the vehicle's momentum slammed the door shut, half to make sure he'd seen what he thought, and half to see the amazing beast again. It was the color of night, seeming to suck moonlight rather than reflect it, as it crawled through the ruins of Bethlehem the way Ward and Daniel used to roll trucks over Lego towers a lifetime ago. It could have been a century old. It could have been Israeli or American or Russian. Ward didn't know enough about tanks to make a guess, but he was certain he'd never heard anything louder. Not jet turbines. Not the destruction of the Tower. Even from inside the Storm, the distance between them and the tank growing, the grinding of its steel tracks was deafening.

"Is it Masada?" Ward asked.

"It's the Nephilim," Zee said. "I don't know which side."

Rivka asked, "I don't think it matters which side."

"How the fuck can the Nephilim drive a tank?"

"They've been forced into a new evolutionary path, my friend. They're different, not broken."

Ward wasn't interesting in further explanation. "Can we outrun it?"

Rivka said, "It's not trying to catch us."

Ward watched it come, slow and deliberate, wondering how one tribe of Nephilim could have a tank and not already be victorious. Unless both tribes had them. Which begged more questions, such as where they got gasoline in a desert and if they had ammunition for the massive gun sticking out of the tank's face like a phallic joke.

"We're almost there," Zee sang, as if having the time of his life.

"This is fun for you?"

"Why not be happy our tire blew on the way out rather than the way in?"

At first, Ward thought Zee had lost his mind, but he quickly understood that if they'd been forced to pull over on their way into Bethlehem, the delay might have led them straight into the tank's path on the narrow road through the city. They'd have been sitting ducks.

"It's slowing," Rivka said.

Before Ward could ask if the Nephilim were giving up the chase, the tank belched fire.

"Hold on!" Zee cried.

Ward gripped the sides of his seat. There was a sharp whistle. Then the desert in front of them exploded. The Storm jerked left, blown off track by the force of the blast. Ward hit his door then was flung the other way, his head striking something hard. Zee's shoulder, or maybe his skull.

"—out of here," someone was shouting.

It took Ward a second to recognize Rivka's voice through the ringing in his head. Another second to comprehend their situation. The Storm had stalled. The passenger side and back windows were blown out. Zee was jabbing the starter, trying to get them moving. Behind them, the tank was still coming, a cloud of gray dust behind it like a cape.

"Almost," Zee said.

"We don't have time for almost," Rivka said.

The engine cranked over. The Storm roared to life, lurching into motion, throwing Ward back in his seat. He took the opportunity to buckle himself into the chair's five-point harness.

"Serpentine," Rivka said.

"Understood," Zee said, his enjoyment of the chase noticeably diminished.

"Got anything we can use?"

"Grenades. Behind the seat. Tan bag."

"Got it."

Ward, facing forward like a terrified child in the front seat of a roller coaster, listened as Rivka heaved grenades out the back window. Their detonations were barely more than bubble gum pops compared the roars of the tank and the Storm. He imagined tossing grenades at a tank was like tossing water balloons at a charging bull. He counted the seconds, wondering how long it would take the tank to reload. How many seconds he had left to live.

I'm sorry, Sam.

"Miss," Rivka said for the second or third time. Ward wasn't counting.

I'm sorry, Daniel.

Rivka called more misses. Then: "Hit!"

Despite himself, despite not wanting to see the muzzle flash that would announce their deaths, Ward looked. The tank was still coming, smoke puffing from its left tread.

"No effect," Rivka said. "We need something bigger."

"I think it won't matter," Zee said.

Ward faced forward. Zee was pointing ahead, but there was nothing there to save them but the nighttime horizon, like a line across his vision separating the dark sky from the slightly darker land.

Or was there?

Ward squinted until the line appeared to shimmer on its own, running forever east and west as far as…No, there was something else. A shape, like night on night. A building, maybe, or a small tower.

"It's slowing," Rivka said.

"It should have stopped by now," Zee said. "It shouldn't come this close."

"This close to what?" Ward asked.

"The Line."

Ward saw it now, sticking up like a middle finger to the desert's emptiness. Only it wasn't so far distant now at all, and the shining line wasn't floating. It was set atop posts every few meters, about chest high, like a thick, single-filament spider web.

"The Jerusalem Line is a fence?"

Zee didn't answer.

"You're telling me the Jerusalem Line—the most impenetrable barrier ever built—is a fucking fence?" Ward asked again of the cable fence that wouldn't stop a beach ball from blowing across.

"The fence is only a marker for the true blockade, my friend."

"What blockade? All I see is a fence."

"It's—wait, here we go."

The tower, perhaps two hundred meters ahead, seemed to turn, as if the top third of it was a head deciding to look their direction. This strange analogy bore out for Ward when the turning head offered a nose coming around. Only it wasn't a nose at all. It was a turret, fronted by a massive cannon that made the tank's gun seem like a straw stuck in a rotten potato.

It continued turning until it pointed directly at the approaching Storm.

Ward forgot how to breathe. His heart forgot how to beat. His body clenched, getting as small as possible, as he waited to be blown to dust.

CHAPTER 13

"Brace," Zee said.

The tower cannon fired with a resounding *whump* that made Ward's ears pop. The sand around the tower burst as if someone had lowered a straw from the sky and blown a shot of air at it. Ward closed his eyes and grasped his harness, silently prompting Zee to drive faster. Or slower. Or turn. Anything to keep them from being annihilated, as if they could outmaneuver the incoming supersonic shell.

They didn't swerve, however. Nor did the Storm speed up or slow down.

Most disconcerting of all, they didn't explode.

But there was an explosion.

Ward opened first one eye then the other. They were definitely still alive. Definitely still speeding toward the tower. Half a kilometer behind them, where the pursuing tank had been, was a geyser of sand rocketing into the sky. A second later, the shockwave hit, kicking the Storm across the sand like a kid's wagon being dragged sideways. Somehow Zee kept the Storm moving forward, fishtailing out of a potential rollover and racing straight at the tower as chunks of the tank landed around them like shrapnel.

"Injuries?" Rivka called.

"Good," Zee said.

"I'm okay," Ward said. "I think."

"I thought they'd have learned not to get too close by now."

"Maybe they were hungry," Rivka said.

Ward couldn't tell if she was joking or referring to some cannibalistic tendency of the Nephilim. He wasn't sure he wanted to know.

"Are we not worried about that thing?" he said, pointing at the tower.

"We're no threat to the Line," Zee said, "so it is no threat to us."

The Line. Ward had almost forgotten. He'd expected an impassable barrier, not a cable on posts. "Is someone going to tell me how that fence is the Jerusalem Line?"

"Do they still teach the old propaganda in the Republic?"

"I—"

"One photo of El-Mabka gets miscaptioned, and it spreads across your social media until everyone believes the Line is brick and stone," the smuggler said.

"It's not my social…wait, El-Mabka?" Ward was stunned. El-Mabka was the Arabic name for the Western Wall, the last standing retaining wall of the Second Temple complex in Jerusalem. The Second Temple, or Herod's Temple—built Herod, the same Roman King of Judea who built the Masada complex—was destroyed by the Romans in 70 CE, three years before the mass suicide at Masada Ward had told his students about yesterday.

"A convenient mistake. What do they call it, the Mandela Effect?"

Ward still wasn't willing to believe it. "What about eyewitnesses or Eye-Ds?"

"No one comes south to the Line. Why should they? You've seen what lives in the desert. To the southeast, Arabia is dead. Anyone who wants to go to Egypt goes by plane or boat."

"The Eye-Ds see the Line," Rivka added, "but walls and cables are difficult to differentiate three kilometers up. Besides, who's watching the drones?"

Who indeed? Certainly no one who would leak classified information. It was both unbelievable, and yet somehow perfectly right.

"So, even the impenetrable stuff is bullshit?" Ward asked.

"Not at all."

"It is as uncrossable as you've heard," Zee said. "Thirty meters deep in the sand to the fifty meters high in the sky, it's impossible. It's an energy network. It fries organic material like lightning."

Ward still wasn't sure. "What about planes, then? Couldn't

someone fly a bunch of troops over the Line for an invasion? Or load up an Eye-D with a few bombs?"

"You want to drop a bomb on Jerusalem?" Rivka asked.

"No, I'm just saying how impenetrable can the Line be?"

"If some army wants to invade Jerusalem, they'll come across land from the north or across the sea from the west."

Zee added, "The Line isn't meant to stop invasion."

At first, Ward didn't understand. Then he got it. "The Nephilim."

"For the first few years they came to Jerusalem like magnets drawn to iron," Rivka said. "It cost thousands of soldiers to clear the desert between Bethlehem and Jerusalem. They've stopped coming north now, and they rarely venture south. The southern desert is theirs, though they tend to stay inland, away from the sea. Mostly they wait in Bethlehem and fight each other."

"Wait for what?"

"The return of their savior to lead them in conquest of the Land of Milk and Honey promised to their ancestors," Zee said. "The opening of Paradise so they may be cleansed and suffer no more."

"Both tribes believe in the same savior?"

"Who says there's only two tribes?" Rivka said.

They were close enough to the tower now for Ward to see it was a steel structure shaped like an A with the top gap filled in. The bottom gap was two lanes wide and blocked by a metal gate. As they got closer, a trio of soldiers covered head to toe in desert camo exited a door in the left leg of the A, assault rifles aimed at the Storm.

The lead soldier waved them forward. Zee pulled up then shut off the vehicle. The soldiers circled them, never getting too close, each examining the same portion of the vehicle the previous had in their rotation. Then they did it again, this time each with a Port outstretched, scanning the vehicle and its inhabitants.

Ward asked, "So we just drive through?"

Zee said, "Did you doubt me?"

"Have you been through the Line?" Ward asked Rivka while the soldiers finished their inspection.

"No."

"You've never been to Jerusalem?"

"I said I've never been through the Line. There's plenty of other ways to the north."

Rivka and Zee appeared calm and confident, but Ward was unsettled. He didn't like the look of the tower. He didn't like the look of the soldiers. He felt like things were going wrong somehow. Not like with MacKenzie. Even when she'd forced him to go to Paris, an unknown country supposedly engulfed in chaos, there'd been his academic familiarity and her absolute confidence to keep him on target. This quest to save Sam had neither. From the start, Rivka's plan had been full of setbacks. Zee not meeting them at Masada. The vague intel about Hannibal. The Nephilim. The tank. The Jerusalem Line being little more than a tollbooth.

On the other side waited a city he knew precious little about. A city rumored to be chaotic and lawless in the world, according to Republic reports, not that he trusted such sources anymore, but there was no doubting the history or Jerusalem as the most fought over real estate in written history.

Nothing was adding up. Nothing was falling into place as it had with MacKenzie. He felt lost and vulnerable.

The lead soldier approached Zee's window and motioned for him get out. He did, leaving the door open, and exchanged a few words in Hebrew with the soldier. Ward didn't understand any of it, but Rivka didn't object to anything.

A second soldier then motioned for Rivka to exit the Storm. She did as ordered, again conversing in Hebrew. Ward expected the third soldier to order him out of the Storm as well, but the command never came. A moment later, Zee and Rivka were back in the vehicle.

"You seem worried," Zee said. "This is not like the man I remember, the one who told me he would walk across the ocean itself in order to get back to the Republic with bombs in hand."

Ward didn't have a response. He was a different man then. He no longer had revenge in his heart. He was focused on life, not death. Sam's life. He couldn't fail again.

"What did they want?" he asked.

"To verify my arrangements," Zee said. "But you?" he added to Rivka.

"She recognized me," the doctor said. "She knew my brother."

"You have a brother? At Masada?" Ward said.

"Not anymore."

"Are they going to let us through?"

"Yes," Zee said. "And our safe house is prepared and waiting."

"Safe house?" Ward said, hesitant to waste any more of Sam's time, though the truth was he had no idea where they would go once they made it into Jerusalem. He still didn't know where to start looking for Hannibal's tomb.

"For how long?" Rivka asked.

"That depends on where you want to go next," Zee said.

Rivka raised an eyebrow, telling Ward the decision was his.

"We're not sure yet," he said.

"Then use the safe house until midmorning," Zee said. "Our encounter with the tank has raised the tension level in Jerusalem, so some extra time to solidify our options is not unwelcome."

Rivka added, "We should sleep."

"It is settled."

They sat in silence a long time. Eventually, the east horizon began to lighten. A short time later, the gate opened like a garage door rattling on its tracks, almost as loud as the tank had been.

"The door is actually unnecessary," Zee said. "A formality. The energy network is the real barrier. They can pause it beneath the tower. Or, if need be, they can reactivate while we are passing through and fry us. Or they can collapse the tower on top of us, closing off the portal altogether."

"Pleasant," Ward said.

They came out the other side to a wonder. Even in minimal light, Ward could see the desert here was no longer gray, as if the Line itself kept the decay at bay. The sudden abundance of earth tones was like coming out of the darkness into bright sunlight. Browns and tans and khakis and golds. And greens. Small shrubs. Thin, wispy trees. Had they driven through to Oz in that old movie about witches and munchkins, Ward would not have been more surprised.

"It's beautiful," he said, feeling immediately stupid for doing so. It was still a desert. Still practically a wasteland. But it offered promise, something Bethlehem had lacked entirely.

"Wait until we get on a little further," Zee said.

For the first time in months, Ward found his fear, that sense of malice hanging on him since Sam went into her coma, lifted. He was excited. He was alive, like he'd been so briefly in the classroom at Masada, and eager to reach the fabled city of Jerusalem.

CHAPTER 14

There was one road into Jerusalem, and they were the only ones on it. Surrounding them as they drove north was an ever-increasing menagerie of colors until they were no longer in a desert at all. As if the desert had been replaced, almost imperceptibly in stages and then all at once, with a rich landscape that reminded Ward of Southern California's Encino Valley.

Soon, buildings appeared. There were no suburbs. No spattering of municipal sheds for water or electricity. No military barracks. It was desert, then fertile landscape, then cityscape. Jerusalem. It rose out of the horizon like someone had pressed a button. From their southern approach, as dawn neared, the right side of the city was afire. The left was shrouded in shadow.

"Excuse me a moment," Zee said, "while I set our approach."

He tapped a few buttons on the Storm's console. A voice popped through the vehicle's speakers in Hebrew. Zee said hello in an Arabic dialect Ward barely recognized then slid a comm bud into his ear, cutting off the speakers.

"What do you think?" Ward asked Rivka.

She seemed the doctor once more, the young woman, maybe a couple years younger than MacKenzie, who had sat with Ward and Sam beneath the canopies on Masada and watched the sunrise each morning. The caring woman who'd urged Ward to do something with his time. To teach. Get a leg brace and do physical therapy. Get involved in the cause, though what exactly they were fighting for at Masada, she never said.

"He doesn't want us to hear."

"No, I mean about the tomb. Where we need to go. Any ideas?"

"You will figure it out."

Ward didn't know if he was comforted or terrified by her faith.

Zee ended his conversation, and they began to pick up speed. One moment, Ward was wondering about trust and plans and what he would feel when they entered the city, and the next they were in it. What had, at first blush, appeared a city built of sandstone and brick became something far more alive once they were within its embrace. Ward thought of the ruins of Ancient Greece, such as the Parthenon in Athens. Stark white marble that blanched the modern world's view of the Athenians. The truth, however, revealed through spectral and chemical testing, was the Hellenic Greeks lived lives of vivid colors, their buildings shining with reds and blues and greens.

Jerusalem wasn't a city of paint. It was a city of glowing signs, bright marquees, lush trees, and small roadside and rooftop gardens. All it lacked was more people, which Ward assumed would change as the morning turned to day. The few people he saw were a mix of orthodox and secular. Traditional black hats and ball caps. Head scarfs and hair flowing free. Light and dark skin. Bright clothes. Big smiles. A diverse population that could have been at home in any European city.

"What do you think, Rafael?" Zee said. "A beautiful city, no?"

"A little surprising so close to what we drove through."

"You were expecting fallout? Or a militant religious hub, perhaps?"

"I don't know what I was expecting."

"The Old City is now the religious center of Judaism. It is almost its own country within the old walls. Orthodox attitudes. Orthodox laws."

"And the rest of the city?" Ward asked.

"Jews, Muslims, Christians," Rivka said. "The contented, all living together, unwilling to fight."

"Fight what?" Ward asked.

Rivka didn't answer, so he asked, "Are we going into Old City?"

"Only the Orthodox are allowed to enter the Old City,"

Rivka said. "All others are forbidden."

Zee said, "Our safe house is not far from the Old City walls, as requested, and there are plenty of other sites to see." He pointed to a row of buildings fronting a tall bank of earth. "On the other side is King David's Tomb, and beyond that the Zion Gate and the Old City. Once, long ago, you could see the Dome of the Rock from here."

Ward strained to see between the buildings, hoping for a glimpse of the tomb or the gate. The Dome of the Rock, he knew, had been leveled in the aftermath of the Riyadh bombing fifty years ago, the first strike in the Jewish-Arab War that resulted in the destruction of nearly every non-Jewish building in Jerusalem's Old City.

Zee laughed as if he'd goaded Ward into a game of made-you-look.

"Where are we staying?" Rivka asked.

"The Republic Consulate."

"That," Ward said, "does not sound inconspicuous at all."

"You misunderstand. It was one time the consulate building for the old America, but no longer. Now it is one of the most exclusive residences in Jerusalem."

"And *that's* inconspicuous?"

"Nothing buys discretion better than the appearance of money."

Rivka grunted an approval, and Ward gave up the argument. Anything had to be more inconspicuous than the rumbling Storm with its busted-out windows.

Soon, they exited the main road for narrower streets. The buildings around them grew even taller, precluding any hope of a glimpse of Old City, but also closing in the neighborhood they'd entered. Discretion, Zee had said. Maybe. But when the streets became one-way fares, with concrete pylons preventing sidewalk access, Ward grew anxious.

"Have you used this safe house before?" he asked.

"Only for the most important clients."

"Who is your man inside?" Rivka asked.

"Baghel. He does a lot of errands for me. He earns every shekel."

Ward flinched, thinking Zee had said Ba'el. *I need sleep*, he thought, knowing Baghel was a common enough name meaning *ox* in Arabic. *My mind is playing tricks on me.*

"He's good?" Rivka asked.

"The best. We're almost there."

Zee took them down a winding road that was barely more than an alley. Then out of it, toward a large park, as green as a golf course or a cemetery. They turned right and pulled over in front of a sprawling building that would have seemed more at home in a resort on the Mediterranean. Six stories tall, its main entrance looked like a modern, marble-clad interpretation of a medieval synagogue, complete with a massive portcullis aperture. Only, rather than a heavy latticed grillwork, the opening was covered in glass giving an almost unobstructed view into the lobby.

It was beautiful, but it did not appear very secure.

"Wait here a moment, please," Zee said.

He got out of the Storm and hurried up the street to a boy in a dirty white thawb crouched beside one of the many palm trees lining the sidewalk. A homeless boy, if Ward had to guess. Zee spoke to the boy then waved Ward and Rivka over.

"This is what you arranged?" Ward asked the doctor.

She shrugged and got out. Ward followed, surprised at how much cooler it was here than in the desert. Sunny and breezy, it was like a nice autumn day in Philly; the perfect weather for a comfortable stroll in a t-shirt or maybe a light jacket, as if the Jerusalem Line kept even the sun's wrath at bay. As he caught up to Rivka a thought—a problem—occurred to him, one he felt stupid for not having recognized sooner.

He touched her arm but didn't grab her.

"You contacted Zee because he dealt with the soldiers at Masada, right?"

"*Ken.*"

"So they could have used this safe house before?"

Rivka started to say yes, then set her jaw. She seemed to be going over exactly the problem Ward was getting at. If they were discovered missing from Masada, how long would it take for someone to track down Zee or his safe houses?

"No one who will tell," she said after a moment. "No one knows I contacted Zee."

"Not even Bar-Ilan?"

Another pause. "He'll cover for me."

"Until Compano shows up."

"We will be back by then."

She crossed the street, giving Ward little choice but to follow.

"Baghel says all is ready," Zee said proudly as they met him.

"This is Baghel?" Ward asked.

The boy was maybe fourteen. Nearly emaciated. Dirty. Grinning like Zee, though unlike the smuggler's perfect teeth, the boy's were crooked and gap-filled. At least three were missing altogether.

"He's a beautiful boy," Zee said.

Baghel stood and put out his hand. Rivka didn't move, so Ward shook the hand. Or rather, the boy shook Ward's hand, yanking on his arm and squeezing his fingers. Ward tried to pull away, but Baghel wouldn't allow it. He grinned even bigger, almost innocently, at first making Ward think of Lennie Small, the mentally disabled migrant worker whose strength surprised nearly everyone, including himself, in *Of Mice and Men*. But Ward quickly saw Baghel was no homeless stray unaware of his own strength. He was smart and calculating. And the moment Ward understood this, the boy let go of his hand, leaving Ward to wince and flex his fingers.

"Security?" Rivka asked.

"Baghel has made sure one of my men is working security tonight," Zee said. "You are in good hands, my friends. The best hands on the best street in the safest neighborhood of Jerusalem's outer city. Now, it is time we go inside."

Baghel waved as Zee took them through the automatic sliding doors of the glass portcullis beneath a sign in Arabic, Hebrew, and English declaring the name of the building: The Consulate. The lobby was ostentatious to say the least. The floor, ceiling, and walls were all either clad in gold or bordered in gold leaf. A huge chandelier shaped like a tornado, glittering with at least a thousand bulbs, hung low in the center of the lobby, it too glistening in gold trims.

Without thinking about what he was doing, like he'd innocently entered a roadside motel, Ward started across the reception hall to the check-in desk. He made it to the middle of the lobby, below the chandelier like an arrow above his head, before Zee grabbed his elbow.

"Wait, wait," the smuggler said. "Cams cover the lobby and main areas. Our room is ready this way. Come."

He led them to the elevator bank, skirting the lobby, then down a short hallway to the stairs. As they went, Ward noted there were no guards. None he could see, at least.

"We are secure in this stairwell," Zee said, pointing to the ceiling. "No cams, see. The elevators are no good."

Zee took them to the fourth floor, Ward's leg brace handling the stairs without any issues. They exited the stairwell into a hallway styled with Persian carpets and the wallpaper striped with reds and golds.

"Here," Zee said, stopping before room 414. He handed Rivka a device about half the size of a Port. "The doors are keyed to residents' palm prints."

Rivka activated the device and rotated it so Ward could see. The screen lit up, showing a red palm. Zee nodded to a gold plate beneath the door handle. She tapped the red palm against the plate. The door opened.

"Whose palm print is it?" Ward asked.

"None of ours," Zee said. "I'll return in four hours. I suggest you get some sleep."

"You're not staying?" Ward asked.

"Have no fear, my friend. You are safe here. I promise. I will see you soon."

Rivka, apparently disinterested in whether or not Zee stayed, entered the apartment, leaving Ward and the smuggler in the hallway.

"There's everything you need inside," the smuggler said. "Stay in the room. You're safe here. It's a nice place. I would tell you to try the swimming pool and sauna, but maybe don't do that."

"Got it."

"It is so very good to see you again, my friend."

Zee hugged Ward unexpectedly. Tight. Earnest. Then, almost in embarrassment, he pulled away. Ward watched him leave then pushed open the door Rivka had left slightly ajar. He closed the door and set both its bolt and chain locks.

She caught him from the side before he'd taken three steps into the apartment. If not for the wall, he'd have lost his balance and hit the floor. Her hands grasped at the side of his neck. He tried to get his arm free for a counterstrike, but she was all over him. Her hands found his face. Pulled it close.

The kiss was harder and hungrier than the one in the cave. She began pulling at his clothes. He forgot about safety and deadlines and tombs. He forgot everything but her hands, her mouth, her body.

CHAPTER 15

Ward woke confused, in the softest bed he'd ever slept in. After the initial kiss, he and Rivka tore off each other's clothes, discarding articles like shredded birthday present wrappings, on their way to the bedroom where the details of the night got lost in their appetites.

He didn't remember falling asleep afterward, but obviously he had. He remembered rolling over and stretching and the two of them agreeing without saying so to take a break. Rivka had lain her head on his shoulder, where it still was, and they'd talked briefly about being hungry and how Rivka's grandmother used to like a clandestine cigarette on the balcony after sex according to her family's stories. From there, they must have both drifted off.

It was morning, according to the lines of light around the gold trimmed curtains opposite the bed. He vaguely recalled there were tall, glass French doors through those curtains leading to a small balcony. Filtering through those doors and those curtains were the sounds of a lazy city start to the day.

He had to pee, but he saw no en suite. He didn't remember passing a bathroom on their way to the bedroom either, but then again, his attention had been on other things.

MacKenzie would have cleared every corner of the apartment first.

MacKenzie. He hated how she popped into his head like that. Hated how she could take over his mind even now, with Rivka sleeping beside him. Hated how he didn't know who he hated most for it: her or himself or Rivka.

Needing a distraction from his self-loathing, he sent his mind back to the intel and the tomb. The honey bee. Hannibal. He made a list of every tomb the Carthaginian general had, or was claimed to have. He came up with twenty-nine, most in either North Africa or the eastern Mediterranean. It was too many. Rivka's intel was too fragmented. They were missing the key word or phrase. Or maybe knowledge of who the transmission was sent to or from. The frustration built again, as did the need to pee. He tried to wriggle out from under Rivka.

"I was comfortable," she said, rolling onto her back, a sliver of light through the curtains drawing a line from her navel across her right breast to her shoulder.

"Sorry," Ward said.

She stretched and sat up, letting the sheets pool around her waist without a hint of modesty. Ward looked. She let him. He almost lost his train of thought, caught up in the sudden desire to kiss her and draw her to him for another round.

"Were you thinking about the tomb?" she asked.

"Yes."

"And?"

Ward sought a conclusion, but the best he could come up with was, "It turns out Hannibal Barca, the scourge of Rome, the man who marched an army of war elephants over the Pyrenees into Italy to wage war on Rome itself, is dead somewhere."

"That's not helping."

Her stomach growled.

"We'll think better once we've eaten," Ward said.

Rivka rubbed her belly, then slid her hands to her breasts, slowly, her eyes locked on Wards. "Okay," she said. "Feed me."

"You're enjoying this," he said.

"Didn't you?"

"I meant teasing me."

She shrugged. Ward stood but, struck by a momentary anxiety, kept his back to the bed while searching for his jeans. He'd never been comfortable with his own body. Even when training with Compano, when he'd been in pretty decent shape, he'd lacked the kind of two-percent-body-fat physique he believed women drooled over. Until now, anyway. He looked at himself. Bar-Ilan's intensive physical therapy, had given him the body he'd always lacked. The slight flab he'd gotten used to around his middle was gone. His core was tight and strong. He could feel Rivka examining him from behind. He turned slowly, battling the anxiety, letting her eyes linger over him the way he was lingering on her. If he'd become flab free, she was downright solid. Ripped wasn't the right word. MacKenzie was ripped, all tense, coiled muscles screaming for action. A taut steel cable. Rivka, on the other hand, her body shaved clean from the neck down, was more like a Greek sculpture of a goddess. Soft and feminine, yet athletic and powerful. Maybe stronger than MacKenzie.

She's going to be the death of me and she's not even here.

"If you're done with your exam," Rivka said, "I'm hungry,"

Still naked, Ward entered the hallway to the living area of the apartment. Two doors set opposite each other halfway up the hall offered a second bedroom and a bathroom. Ward poked his head in the bedroom first. It was furnished similar to the bedroom he'd exited, with gold accents everywhere and the same limestone floor tiles that ran throughout the apartment.

The bathroom featured an oddly outdated quartz countertop over a vanity accented in gold. He peed and washed and splashed warm water on his face and then followed the hallway to the rest of the apartment. The living room, dining room, and kitchen made up a large open square with the apartment's front door off the kitchen. High end gilded furniture occupied the rooms as if staged by a real estate agent for a gaudy royal family. Over the dining room table, which was set for eight, hung a smaller replica of the huge tornado chandelier in the building's atrium, this one decked in more gold trim than the one downstairs.

Flung over the couch, he found his jeans and Rivka's bra. Her pants were under one of the dining room chairs. One of his boots lay on its side near the kitchen island. He didn't see the other. Their backpacks were tossed on the couch. He considered collecting their clothes but decided he'd rather watch Rivka wander the apartment naked.

The kitchen island and countertops were a dark green stone, maybe granite, flecked with gold. The whole apartment felt like a model unit. The kind of display that would sell the space but that no one would actually choose for their own style. Only the paintings on the walls, all in gold frames, seemed personally chosen. They featured bright colors and impressionistic landscapes. Ward leaned in to one to read the artist's signature: Shmuel Katz. He knew the name. A holocaust survivor and one of Israel most prominent artists in the twentieth century. He had no doubt it was original.

Even with the paintings, however, the apartment couldn't escape its simulated feel. It both comforted and worried him.

While trying to erase the worry, he did a quick sweep of the apartment. All the curtains were closed over the windows, forcing him to switch on a few lights. There were no obvious security risks. He backtracked to the kitchen. A clock on the stovetop said it was a little after eight. Enough time to eat and shower and maybe get dirty again before Zee returned. He opened the refrigerator. It was stocked with fruits, vegetables, meats, greens, and a dozen different types of bottled drinks. There were three kinds of steaks in the freezer, plus two whole frozen chickens. He closed the door and rummaged the cabinets. He found breads, scores of canned foods, boxes of ration bars, chips, pretzels, and more. There was enough here to host a massive house party. Or to withstand a siege for a few weeks.

In the final pantry next to the dining room, he found the liquor. Four kinds of vodka. A few rums. Close to twenty bottles of wine, mostly red. Gin. Tequila. Brandy. Whiskey.

Close the door. Close it now.

But he didn't. He counted the whiskies. Canadian. Irish. American. Greek. Israeli. He catalogued each in his mind, noting the color of each. The proof of each. He imagined their smells. Their burns.

In the back, he found a bottle of Bowmore single malt Scotch. His tongue rubbed the roof of his mouth as if it could get at the bottle from here. He lifted it from the pantry. It was heavy and cool. Unopened. Perfectly amber. He could almost taste it through the glass. Through his hands.

"Don't make me come out there," Rivka called.

Ward almost dropped the bottle. He put it back quickly,

clanking it against the other whiskies. His father had caught him and Daniel once as they'd hunted through his nightstand looking for loose change. How old were they then? Nine and seven? The sound of his father in the doorway, clucking his tongue at them, had sent Ward's heart into his throat so fast, it had pushed tears from his eyes before he even comprehended they'd been caught.

The way his pulse had rocketed at Rivka's voice wasn't quite to that level, but it was close.

"Be right there," he said.

He closed the pantry and grabbed a fruit tray and two bottles of water from the fridge and hurried back to the bedroom. Rivka had propped herself up on the pillows to a half-sitting position, still boldly naked as if basking in the intruding light from the hallway. That self-conscious anxiety gripped Ward again when she looked at him, still naked.

"Looks good," she said.

The desire in her voice banished his angst. "I was going to say the same thing."

She straightened up a little more as Ward placed the tray and bottles on the night table on her side of the bed. She chose a bottle of water and took a long drink.

"Feed me," she said.

He sat on the edge of the bed and chose a slice of mango. Placed it to her lips. She pulled it from his hand with her teeth. She grinned.

"There's a ton of stuff in the kitchen," he said. "Do you cook?"

"Because I'm a woman?"

"Because I can barely make pasta."

It was true. When it came to cooking, he was as clichéd a bachelor as there was. His best meals were frozen pizza in the toaster and melting cheese over tortilla chips in the microwave and calling it nachos.

"Are there eggs?"

"Yes, and steaks."

"Steak," she said, like she hadn't considered it. "I can make steak and eggs."

"You're hired."

They took turns feeding each other slices of apple, mango, papaya, and some green, fleshy fruit unfamiliar to Ward, his attention slipping back and forth between her naked body and the list of places where Hannibal's tomb could be.

"Something more interesting on your mind?" Rivka asked.

"What?" Ward said, at first unsure what he'd been accused of. "No, I was thinking about the tomb again. Zee said they built the one in Turkey a hundred years ago, in the place where it's said Hannibal committed suicide."

"Suicide?"

"The Romans were closing in on him. He was an old man by then, unable to fight as well as he once could, and he didn't want to give them the satisfaction of claiming they'd killed him. Legend says he waited until they surrounded his house and then drank a dose of poison he kept in a ring on his finger. A final *fuck you* to all of Rome."

"A soldier's death, then," Rivka said.

Her comment struck Ward as odd coming from a doctor. Then again, she was a soldier too. At Masada, no less. Why wouldn't the nobility of suicide be lionized among an army that made its home there?

"In any case," he said, "we're talking almost twenty-two hundred years ago. Who knows when the first monument was built on that spot. That week? A hundred years later? A thousand? There's no way to know."

"But it's the right spot, yes?"

"As near as history tells us," Ward said. "Libyssa, on the shore of the Sea of Marmara, in Gebze, Turkey. I think..." He trailed off, his mind wandering over possibilities and stories until his eyes found Rivka's confident nakedness once more.

"Should I get dressed?"

Ward felt his cheeks flush like an embarrassed teenager. "Maybe."

She got up and wrapped a blanket around herself. "There. Now tell me what you think."

"I think Zee was right. The tomb in Turkey is the place to go. It's the only one that makes sense."

"Convince me."

"Think about it. You're sending a comm to someone, but you don't want to tell everyone who might be listening where to go. Codes can be broken even without code keys, so you preset a number of locations that only need to be identified by a simple yet vague title. 'The lighthouse' could mean the harbor in Alexandria. 'The river' could be a preset location on the Euphrates or the Jordan or whatever river they'd already agreed on. Hannibal's tomb would be a monument that's still standing. The one in Turkey, right there where he died."

"And the honey bee?"

"I can't swear to it, but I think I remember reading once that Turkey was in the top five in honey producing nations in the world."

"Good enough, then," Rivka said. "I'm going to get some more fruit."

She left the bedroom still wrapped in her blanket. Ward didn't watch her go. He was going over again in his head—Hannibal, Turkey, honey—making sure it was the right decision. Making sure he wasn't forgetting something. Convincing himself he was right.

Until the alarm sounded.

It was so loud, he sprang from the bed as if it had thrown him out. Rivka charged into the bedroom, the blanket she'd wrapped herself in falling away as she met him beside the bed.

"What is it?" he screamed, certain she would have to read his lips to understand.

In response, an electronic voice sounded from the living room, repeating two short phrases in Hebrew.

"Fire alarm," Rivka mouthed, translating the message. She put her lips to his ear and said, "It says we should leave down the stairs and congregate in the park across the street."

"Legit or are we in trouble?"

She went to the curtains and slid them back a little to look outside. Ward joined her. People were already beginning to spill out into the street, many in pajamas and robes. They moved purposefully but not panicked. This was Israel after all, a nation that had been at almost nonstop war since its modern inception a century earlier. Or, according to Zee, since humanity learned to walk upright.

"We should go," Rivka said. "If it's about us, I'd rather fight outside than in here."

"Right." Ward said. "Let's get dressed."

CHAPTER 16

Ward started for the living room to grab their clothes, but Rivka called him back. She had flung the closet's louvered doors open wide and was standing there completely naked and grinning.

"As good as the refrigerator," she said.

The closet was, in fact, stocked better than the fridge. Piles of neatly folded clothes lined the shelves on one side. The other side was packed with dozens of hanging shirts and trousers and jackets. On the floor, pairs of shoes, from dress to casual to combat, sat in rows around a blue trunk with gold trim.

Rivka went for the trunk first. Matching pistols waited inside, each atop a stack of neatly folded tactical fatigues, one stack black, one khaki. Rivka lifted the pistol from the black stack and examined it, still naked, like a pinup girl posing for a photoshoot.

"Jericho," she said, naming the Israeli-made pistol. "Zee did good."

Ward squeezed in beside Rivka and took the other pistol. It was similar in size and weight to the Republic's RT40. It fit his hand perfectly, its slightly contoured grip the only noticeable difference from the RT40 he'd trained with and come to rely on over the past few years.

They placed their pistols on adjacent shelves and dressed quickly, Rivka handing Ward khaki fatigues while choosing black for herself.

"Good fit," he said of the multi-pocketed trousers and lightweight, ventilated shirt.

"Here," Rivka replied, pulling a taupe sport jacket from a

hanger. "And this over your head," she added, handing him a white and blue tallit, a Jewish prayer shawl with knotted fringes at its corners.

He put on the sport jacket then draped the tallit over his head.

"I'll do it," she said, repositioning the shawl more like an extremely high collar than a hood. "Good enough."

She finished dressing, choosing a white thawb to wear over her fatigues. She added a multi-colored headscarf to her head, matching the style Ward had seen as they drove through the city, a common custom for married Orthodox Jewish women.

"Should we contact Zee?" Ward said as they moved to the living room.

"I can't."

"You don't have a way to contact him?"

"He sets the protocols. We're blind."

Ward hunted for his boots, preferring their broken in comfort to the new ones in the closet, while Rivka filled her tactical pack with provisions from the kitchen.

"Do you smell smoke?" he asked. He'd learned from MacKenzie not to trust coincidences.

"No."

He finally found his second boot lodged between the couch and the wall and put it on. Rivka waited for him by the front door, her backpack from the desert over her shoulders, her pistol in one hand, Ward's pack in the other. She tossed him the backpack and cracked open the door. Ward grabbed his leather jacket from the floor and shoved it and his pistol into the pack.

"We should stick with the crowds," Rivka said.

"Through the lobby? Isn't that a bit exposed?"

"If this is about us, they'll know to watch the back exits and stairs."

It made sense, but Ward didn't like it. If the alarm was about them, trying to sneak out in the crowd was not only foolish, it would put innocents in danger. Then again, if the alarm was a way to flush them out, the crowd might be the only chance they had of getting away. If they were cornered in a stairwell, people would die.

Rivka said the hallway outside the apartment was clear led them out. The first thing Ward noticed was the alarm wasn't as loud out here, as if the speakers were only present inside the apartment. The second was they were the only ones in the hall, leaving him to wonder if they'd had the floor to themselves. Rivka checked the stairwell they'd come up with Zee but closed the door without entering.

"Clear," she said. "This way."

She tucked her pistol under her thawb and took them down the hall to the main stairwell. It was obvious before she opened the door that these stairs were not empty. The echoes of voices and footfalls rattled around like pebbles in a can even over the sound of the alarm. They slipped into the press of evacuating residents as if they'd lived here for years. It was slow and loud, but they eventually made it to the lobby, which was even slower and louder. It was organized chaos. There was no single direction of flow. Voices shouted to be heard above the alarm, a raucous mix of Hebrew and Arabic, with Ward catching occasional words in English, French, and Spanish. Some residents hurried to get outside. Others mingled about, as if ready for coffee and a conversation with their neighbors. A significant number of them were older and relied on canes or walkers to try to push through the crowd.

Rivka grabbed Ward's hand, her fingers interlacing his in an aggressive parody of a couple's affection. "Stay with me," she said.

Ward tried, but he was on sensory overload, his eyes darting this way and that seeking enemies. Strike teams. Snipers. Until they nearly steamrolled a stooped couple, probably in their eighties, the man hobbled with a cane and the woman barely squeezing through the crowd using a four-pronged walker. When the woman tottered, nearly losing her balance, Ward pulled free of Rivka and went to them, catching the old woman before she went down. She looked up at him as if expecting to know him, a dutiful grandson perhaps, but seeing it was a stranger, she tried to right herself. The old man said something Ward couldn't hear. He didn't need to. He pointed at the crowd to indicate he wasn't going to abandon the couple and then set himself to shoving a path wide enough for the walker.

Rivka caught up as the trio neared the entrance and pushed aside, almost violently, the last few people keeping the couple from getting outside.

The old man bowed his head and thanked Ward in Hebrew. His wife put out her hand like a princess expecting it to be kissed. Ward placed his hands around hers and squeezed gently. Her hand was feathery, barely even there, but the woman smiled. It felt like the first good thing Ward had done in years.

"We have to go," Rivka said in his ear. "Now."

The old man said something else in Hebrew which Rivka answered. Then she pulled Ward away toward the growing mob across the street, holding his hand tight, as if determined not to let him get away again.

"Into the crowd," she said.

But the crowd was an amorphous thing, moving and shifting as residents filed in while others wandered off, presumably in search of breakfast or simply a break from the cacophonous mix of resident chatter and the alarm. They aimed for the center of the throng but soon found themselves closer to the north edge, the rest of the park sprawled before them, shining in the early morning sun like a green carpet. Further to the north the greens faded and the landscaping faltered. Here, the land was unkempt and browned, with only pops of haggard trees here and there. And tombstones?

Ward tried to create a map of the city as best as he knew it—which meant a historical map a few centuries old—and guessed he might be looking at Mamilla Cemetery. Suddenly, the evacuation didn't seem so awful. He wasn't going to get to see any of the sights in Old City, but here he was, a few meters from one of the oldest cemeteries in Jerusalem. The site of a horrific massacre of thousands in the seventh century. They could easily slip away from the crowd and take a look.

At that moment, Rivka pulled him back through the crowd to the west. He tried asking what she was doing, but she kept moving without looking back to answer. Behind them, two police cars screeched to a halt in front of the Consulate, blocking the road. Rivka slowed to a quick walk, matching the pace of those around them.

"We should look for the kid, Baghel," Ward said.

"The safe house is blown. We can't trust him."

Ward asked, "What about Zee?"

The broke free of the crowd to stand alone in the park, too distant from cover for Wards' liking.

"I don't see a fire," Rivka said.

She moved off at a quick walk, crossing the flagstone walkways snaking through the park, out across the open grass. Ward's leg brace keeping him moving, matching her speed. Away from the Consulate. Away from their best position to contact Zee, leaving Ward to wonder if she knew something he didn't.

Had the alarm simply spooked her?

Did she no longer trust Zee? It was his building after all. His setup. His security.

Ward had trouble accepting the smuggler had betrayed them. He was a mercenary, yes, but he couldn't see that kind of treachery from the man. Not with their history. It had to be Baghel.

As they moved through the park, Rivka sped up once more to a jog. Whatever she believed, Ward knew he had to trust her instincts. It was her op. Her country.

Near the far end of the park, the ground rumbled as if the earth were gathering itself for a monumental belch. Rivka slowed. There was an immense *crack*, as if the world itself had fractured. Then a sound like the *whump* the tower cannon had made at the Jerusalem Line. The ground beneath Ward's feet seemed to liquify. He put out his arms for balance, but there was nothing to grab on to.

Earthquake!

Only it wasn't. It was more focused. More…predatory.

The air around him seemed to quiver then gathered to form an impossible pressure, like being sucked through a black hole. Something was coming. It was all Ward could do to put his hands over his head and get as tight as possible before the earth stopped spinning.

Before everything went black.

PART 2: HOME

If there is a witness to my little life,
To my tiny throes and struggles,
He sees a fool;
And it is not fine for gods to menace fools.
—from The Black Riders and Other Lines,
  by Stephen Crane, 1895

In response to the growing rumors of attacks along the Wall at
the Republic's southern border, President Barclay declared today,
"We will find the perpetrators of these false narratives and shut
their lies down. You can bet on that, Citizens. Our Wall, the truest
symbol of our homeland, will stand. It will be standing next year
and in fifty years and in a hundred."
—Paul Welles, Republic One News, 15 November 2056

CHAPTER 17

The world shook and the girl opened her eyes and stared into the sun.

No, that wasn't right. She didn't *open* her eyes at all. They were already open. They'd been open a long time. One moment she wasn't seeing. The next, she woke and was blinded by the relentless eye of the sun.

Except that wasn't quite right either. She hadn't woken. One moment, she *wasn't*. The next she *was*.

She wondered if this was birth but quickly dismissed the idea. She wasn't a baby. She wasn't new, though she felt blank. Vacant. Even austere, though she wasn't sure she knew what that meant. She was an adult, though barely. A girl. No, a woman, though *girl* was more comfortable. She examined these facts. Accepted them as truths. Trusted them, even if she didn't know how she knew them.

She blinked at the sun, wishing it would dim or go away. She tried to bring her hands to her face to shield her eyes, but she couldn't move them. She was, in fact, unable to move at all. Panic shivered through her body. Good. At least she had a body.

She tried to move again. This time, she felt her arms move a little. A few twitches. Better than nothing. She tried harder, recognizing that they were tired. Weak. But her strength was growing by the moment.

She turned her head so the sun would stop glaring directly in her eyes. To her surprise, her head responded, lolling to the left. Revealing the sun wasn't a sun after all. It was a bright light mounted to a metal arm, like in a dentist's office. It occurred to her she didn't quite know exactly what a dentist was, but that she once had known. As if she were two minds in one body: one trying to make sense out of where she was—*who* she was—and the other, with answers at the ready, unable to communicate. Yet.

She let herself believe that the two separate minds would converge in time, the way her strength was slowing returning.

She glanced around, using what limited mobility she had to turn her head left and right and up and down. She was lying on her back. Indoors. Not a building, however. Something more natural, with a rough stone ceiling and walls the color of sand.

A cave.

She'd been in a cave before, but when? Where?

A series of images flashed through her mind like a flip book: a cave, bats, a river, dark water, blood, cold, sinking, blackness.

The images hurt her head, in part because she didn't know what a flip book was and was trying too hard to understand. She shut her eyes. Squeezed. Opened them again.

She was still in the cave beneath the dentist light. Still on her back. On a table, cold and hard, not a bed. She took two deep breaths like gulping water. She thought she might have the strength to sit up, so she tried.

Too quick.

Her head spun. The cave spun. She tried to brace herself, but her arms were still weak. Still tingling with the rush of blood. She fell back. Hard. The pain started at her shoulders and extended up her spine into her head.

"Hello?" she tried to say, but her voice caught in her throat. She coughed. Tried again. "Hello?"

No one answered. The cave was silent. Except for a steady beeping she hadn't previously noted, though she was certain it had been toning regularly since long before she'd become aware.

"Anyone?" she said, her voice stronger. "Please, help me!"

Me. The word was familiar, but empty. Like a box that should be full of photos and memories yet holds only dust and cobwebs.

A shiver, like a tickle, began in her fingers. Then her feet. Arms. Legs. Until tremors wracked her body.

"Help," she shouted. "Anybody. Where am I? Who am I?"

Who am I?

She sat bolt upright at the sound of the voice, her elbows locking to keep her up. The tremors died down to intermittent quivers in her arms and legs. There were more beds around, and more dentist lights, but all the beds were empty, and all the lights were dark. She was still alone.

Had she imagined the voice?

Where am I?

It was no hallucination. The voice was there. She could hear it as plain as she could see the light and the machines and hear the beeping.

"Where are you?" she said.

Where am I? the voice asked again.

Fear bled away. She was no longer alone. The fact that she couldn't see her companion, or hear him with her ears, didn't matter. She wasn't alone!

Wait, was the voice a *him*?

When I need to be.

There was no doubt it wasn't her voice. It was another voice deep in her mind, so deep it almost didn't exist. And it was lonely. As she recognized this, she too became lonely.

She decided to get up. To go find someone who could explain who she was and why she was here. She tried to slide off the table, but something tugged at her arm. With her left hand—an awkward motion that told her she was right-handed—she reached for the underside of her right bicep. There was a length of tubing inserted into her arm. Now that she knew it was there, it felt like a snake nestling in her muscle. The other end of the tube was connecting to the beeping machine. Two more lines from the machine ran to the sides of her forehead. These were thinner and felt like they were applied with adhesive rather than implanted.

Hospital.

"Yeah," she said. "Hospital. Do you know why I'm in a hospital?"

We.

"Sorry. Why *we* are in a hospital."

The voice didn't respond. She waited a moment. When it didn't return, she shifted her attention to the wires and tube connected to her. Like a trio of leashes.

A rage suddenly erupted in her like…like…

An image. A soda bottle. Shaken up. Its cap yanked off.

She had no idea what a soda bottle was or what was supposed to happen once the cap came off. Only that, like the cave with the river and bats and blood, it was her image. A product of her mind. A memory, perhaps. Whatever the image's source, it seemed to quench the rage that had almost overwhelmed her. Slowly, she swung her legs over the side of the table. Her feet dangled a few inches above the ground. It wasn't a floor so much as it was a counterpart to the ceiling. Carved stone. Mostly smooth.

She edged off the bed, putting weight on her feet inch by inch. The tingling that came with each inch of pressure threatened to drive her mad, but she kept at it until she was standing. Her legs trembled. Almost buckled. When they didn't, when they held, she stood tall. It felt good, like accomplishing something. Like finishing her leg of a relay race. Whatever that meant.

She tried to walk, but the machine came with her, the wires and tube dragging it along the length of the bed. The rage began to rise again. She grabbed the wires in her fist and yanked. They popped off with a series of soft *plops*. The tube in her arm, however, didn't come off. Her first tug felt like a hard pinch. She got a better grip on the tube and tried again.

It resisted. Because it wasn't *on*. It was *in*.

She inhaled deeply and held her breath. Pulled. The tube resisted. She pulled harder. It started to come, like drawing a vein from her arm.

She screamed.

The voice in her head screamed, maybe not so far away as it had been.

The room spun. Her vision funneled to a point. She was going to pass out. Dimly, she was aware the steady beeping from the machine had become louder and faster, but she refused to let go of the tube. Refused to stop pulling. A spurt of blood arced through the air before splattering on the floor near her feet.

It was almost out. She called on the voice in her head, willing it to keep her conscious long enough to draw it the rest of the way out.

Something grabbed her wrist, stopping her from pulling the tube out any further. A hand. Another person's hand! Then a face, all blur and shadow, floated before her.

"Don't let her pull out the central line," a voice said. A real voice, not her own, not in her head.

Another said, "Stabilize it. I've got her."

She could understand them even as she was aware she didn't know the language they were speaking. Even as her vision was blurring into a swirl of deepening shadows.

"Where's the sedative?"

"Is that enough for transport?"

"No, this one stays."

"Her?"

"We need twenty-five of us for this kid?"

"She's dangerous."

"I'm losing her."

Then she was falling back into darkness.

CHAPTER 18

MacKenzie stood atop what was left of the Wall, looking across at the Mexican army encampments. She couldn't see much in the dark, but she knew what was out there. One hundred and forty years ago, the Battle of Ambos Nogales—or the Battle of Both Nogaleses—between American forces in Nogales, Arizona, and Mexican forces in Nogales, Sonora, was fought in a single day, establishing the permanent border between the two nations. The Republic's Wall was built on that exact border. It was a battle of ancient history, yet MacKenzie had read about the night before Bravo Company's invasion of Republican Nogales, unable to resist the pull of the story, as if Rafe had infected her with a whimsy of the past and the long dead.

Behind her, at the bottom of the Wall, sat the remains of Righteous Road, the razor wire beach that once served as an intimidating obstacle to those who might want to hazard climbing the Wall. Beyond that, Republican Nogales was a bustling small city of about thirty thousand. It was one of the Republic's most important trading posts, the place where they took in goods that had been extorted from Old Mexico the way a schoolyard bully collected milk money. It was a city that welcomed Bravo Company with open arms and very little violence. A city that shut off its televisions and silenced the propaganda when MacKenzie and her troops marched its streets.

On the other side, in the direction MacKenzie was looking, lay Mexican Nogales. Once, it had been a civic and industrial hub of nearly a quarter million people. It had been a city center and suburbs and schools and museums and monuments to the Battle of Ambos Nogales. After the rise of the Republic, however, it devolved into little more than an urban warehouse. Until two weeks ago. With Bravo Company on the move, the Mexican army marched on its Nogales, expelling the police and Republic's self-declared International Peacekeepers.

Out there now, in the dark, were the Mexican encampments that would reinforce Horeb. Out there now were the soldiers who would fight side-by-side with Bravo Company to liberate the Republic from its tyrants. And then Old Mexico from its politics of submission. And then the American continents. And then the world.

All of which was too much for MacKenzie.

She wanted freedom and vengeance. She wanted war and victory. And more and more, she wanted a quiet place to sit in the sun when it was all over and let God's glory warm her the way her father and the traitor Torres and the Seer had all promised.

But that was getting too far ahead. She couldn't afford to lose focus because of the future. Or Rafe's goddamned history. She was a bullet, already fired from its gun. Already on its trajectory. The Battle of the Nogales Wall was won. The two-front assault had accomplished in less than twenty-four hours what had been projected for up to twenty days. The revolution was rising. The Republic army was already on its heels. Horeb had tripled the size of its forces with the addition of the Mexicans.

The victory the Seer predicted for next summer might find itself within reach by the start of the new year.

The sound of approaching soldiers turned MacKenzie away from Old Mexico. Graciela, the commander of the Mexican forces, approached with two soldiers, all dressed in charcoal fatigues.

"It is good to see you again, General," Graciela said, her accent thick but her confidence in speaking English clear.

"You too," MacKenzie said, surprised at the intensity of her emotions at seeing the stocky commander again. It had only been about five months since she'd aided MacKenzie in Teotihuacan, Old Mexico, but it felt like years. She was a good commander, loyal and reliable. She helped save Oren's life and facilitate MacKenzie and Rafe's pursuit of Ker, who'd kidnapped Sam and taken her to Spain as part of some kind of vendetta against Rafe.

Then again, Sam had only been in trouble because MacKenzie unwittingly led Ker, her tech officer, to Sam and Rafe. Which meant she'd also been the one who led Ker to that moment when he shot Oren in the stomach.

She felt herself spiraling down the rabbit hole of memory and emotion. Oren had been her lover for a brief time. He was a good man, the conductor of soldiers and spies and supplies between the Republic and Old Mexico and Europe. He was the kind of man who would never betray her or Horeb the way Rafe had.

As if reading her mind, Graciela said, "The conductor sends a message."

"He is not with you?" MacKenzie said, hating the obvious disappointment in her voice.

One of Graciela's attending soldiers came forward with a Port and offered it to MacKenzie.

"It is off grid," Graciela said.

MacKenzie swiped open the Port. On screen were three words:

Protect the Grossmutter.

"What is this?" MacKenzie said.

"There was an infection," Graciela said. "We thought he was healing, but a fever took. He asked I give you this."

MacKenzie read the message again, refusing to understand what she was being told. The Port grew uncomfortable in her hand. She pushed it back at the soldier, not wanting to know. Her hands shook. Her eyes watered. She sought a weapon, something large and powerful. Something to blow another hole in the Wall and make her feel more like herself.

Graciela said, "He died four months ago."

"And you're just telling me now!"

"Crucial comms only was our agreed protocol."

MacKenzie sought any hint of compassion in her voice but found none. She hated the Mexican commander. She wanted to grab her by her thick neck and shake her until the truth came out that Oren was fine.

Except she didn't hate her. Oren wouldn't let her. He'd always demanded she be honest with herself. He'd always expected her to be better than her rage and hunger for violence.

You're right, she told Oren. *It's not her I hate. It's me.*

After her return to the Republic, she'd sent two soldiers to the abbey in Spain where Rafe had left her, but there were no bodies. No hints that Sam or Rafe or Ker had ever been there. No evidence she herself had ever been there. Still, she'd ordered those two soldiers to keep searching. She'd kept them there for three weeks, until the Seer asked her to bring them home. She'd done all that, but she'd never sent a single comm asking about Oren's condition.

"I'm needed on our side," she said.

Graciela placed a strong hand on her arm. "The conductor was my friend as well."

MacKenzie faced her counterpart. Graciela was older, probably in her late forties, and her pain was clear on her face, regardless of her composed voice. MacKenzie wondered if she'd loved Oren. It was a thought devoid of jealousy. She never could return Oren's love. If Graciela could, then she was glad. He deserved to be loved.

"We should send troops east," Graciela said.

MacKenzie understood she meant to Eagle Pass. To the Grossmutter, Oren's grandmother. She wanted to say yes. She wanted to dispatch a squad right now and lead them herself, but the Seer's orders were her guide. He spoke for God, and God wanted Bravo Company in El Paso, Texas, no later than the day after tomorrow. If she was meant to see the Grossmutter again, she would.

Providence, as her father used to say.

"I'll take care of it," she said.

One of the soldier's flanking Graciela touched his ear and then said in Spanish, "A soldier is coming."

A moment later, the sound of a soldier running up the steps to the battlement. They waited. It was one of MacKenzie's. A corporal named Foules.

"Report," MacKenzie said.

"Jerusalem, sir," Foules said. "A bomb."

At first, MacKenzie thought she'd misheard. There were no places called Jerusalem in the Republic. There were no cities named after religiously significant places or people, like San Francisco or St. Louis, anymore, and she couldn't recall any strategically significant cities called Jerusalem in old Mexico.

"In the Holy Land?" Graciela said.

Of course. Jerusalem, in Israel. MacKenzie felt like an idiot. She blamed her stupidity on the shock of Oren's death, but knew it was a lie. Her focus had been lacking since she'd returned from Spain.

Since Rafe...

"Affirmative," Foules said. "Confirmation came through Horeb."

MacKenzie compartmentalized her distractions. "Was it REC action?"

"Unknown, sir."

"I will leave you to discuss this development," Graciela said.

MacKenzie watched her and her soldiers depart, demanding a full report from Foules when they were alone.

"That's all we have, sir. Republic news feeds are not reporting the incident yet, but Horeb believes it was a considerable attack. Possibly nuclear."

"Understood. Thank you, corporal. Dismissed."

Foules retreated, leaving MacKenzie alone on the Wall. A nuclear strike in Jerusalem was a game changer. Any significant shift in Jerusalem's careful balance between Judaism, Christianity, and Islam could have critical repercussions. Should a vision of God's Word that contradicted the Seer's claims come to dominate the Middle East, it could change the international support the revolution had been amassing.

She wondered how the Seer was taking this news. He'd never explicitly stated Jerusalem was in his plans, but he was God's prophet. A pilgrimage to the Holy Land was surely part of his destiny. Would this bombing change that fate? Would it alter the plans they'd put in place for the revolution?

Not my concern anymore.

She was in charge of Bravo Company now, not Horeb. Not the entirety of their military plans. Aldrich would make those determinations. If he wanted her input, he would ask. For now, she would do her job. She would follow orders, and she would win battles. Such was her role.

Providence.

As she started for the stairs, shouting on the Republic side broke out. To the west. She sought the source but couldn't see any movement. The shouting got louder. Then it ended abruptly. There was a tense moment of silence. Then: small arms fire erupted. A pocket of Republic loyalists, no doubt. Which ignited a dangerous hunger in MacKenzie. It was the kind of hunger that got people killed. The kind of hunger that could only be ignored so long before it made her feral.

She told herself to trust her soldiers. She was Bravo Company's commander, not part of a strike team. There were no reports of Agents or Reapers in the area. No need for her to get her hands dirty. They'd taken Tucson and Nogales without her firing a shot. They could handle minor resistance like this.

But that hunger was burning.

She located the muzzle flashes about three blocks away. Drew her pistols. Charged down the stairs, eager for battle.

CHAPTER 19

Ward didn't know where he was. His head felt like it was filled with cotton. Like he'd left the shower head pointing right into his ear for a good hour before toweling off. It took him some time to realize he couldn't hear.

The initial panic of being deaf was interspersed with moments of wonder, like when he realized he could feel the pounding drone of the helicopter rotors above. Like when he realized those helicopters weren't flying against a blue sky but rather a gray one, almost the color of the desert south of the Jerusalem Line. Like when that tinny ringing began far away within his skull and slowly grew closer and louder until he knew he wasn't deaf anymore, and then the sounds of sirens leaking in behind the ringing.

All of that was before. He didn't know how long. The clock in his head only began ticking again a few minutes ago. What happened prior was lost to him, bobbing away from him like a ball in a swimming pool. He knew only the present, and in the present, he was on his ass, his mouth full of blood and pain.

Where was here? Why was the sky gray?

Every movement, every thought, was slow, but he was regaining himself. He was seeing and understanding. First, the sky wasn't gray. It was filled with smoke. Second, he was bleeding in more places than his mouth. That wound was because he'd bitten his tongue. His cheek, below his eye, hurt like it had been sliced open by a hot knife. His back and neck and legs—well, his unbraced leg, at least—felt as if someone had worked them over with a sledgehammer.

Third, he'd lost Rivka.

Fourth, he still hadn't figured out where he was or what had happened.

Four was enough things to know. He tried to stand but his head spun and his unbraced leg got wobbly and he flopped back onto his ass. He wiped the back of his hand across his face. It came away smeared with blood. He'd almost forgotten about his cheek. With memory came more pain, followed by more memory. They'd been escaping the Consulate. Then the ground had gone all spongy. There was a massive *crack*. Then nothing.

A heavy dread settled over him. He got to his knees and turned around.

The Consulate was gone. Where it had stood was now a circle of ash. Nothing else. No ruins. No rubble. Just a circle of black earth.

He'd never seen such devastation. Had there been broken walls or smoldering remains, he would have compared it to Bethlehem, but there was nothing. It was as if someone had placed a cosmic tube over the spot and cremated everything inside it. All that remained within the circle was ash and smoke, rising to a slowly dissipating mushroom cloud.

Ward shouted for Rivka. No one responded. No one looked at him. No one. Which meant there were other people around, a fact he registered for the first time since the clock started again in his head. Some were screaming. Some were running, away or toward or just in circles. All as the sirens continued to wail, getting closer, and the helicopters continued to hover overhead.

Aftermath, he understood now. Because he'd seen it before.

He'd caused it before.

The chaos wasn't all that different here from what he'd seen outside the Tower. Dazed and bloody survivors. Onlookers, distant and afraid. The dead strewn about as if tossed from a tornado. Bent and twisted at unnatural angles. Flattened into the earth. A woman, rocking and weeping, cradled a mess of flesh that might have once been a child. A man whose arm had been torn off held the severed limb under his other arm like a briefcase.

Look for the helpers.

Who had said that to him when he was a boy? Mom? Daniel?

Some television show host? He couldn't remember. It didn't matter. There weren't enough helpers.

"Rafael!"

Rivka came through the smoke, limping and bleeding from her forehead.

"You're hurt," he said.

She pulled him to his feet and began dabbing at his face with the tallit that was still, somehow, around his shoulders. Then she turned him to examine the back of his head, which faced him right at the blackened circle. It was maybe half a kilometer in diameter, terminating close to thirty meters from where they stood. Outside it, the grass remained green. The trees remained standing. People darted this way and that, around others lying still on the ground.

Inside the circle, there was nothing. No cars. No trees. No sidewalk. No street. No bodies. Nothing but the ash and the smoke and the almost glassy earth near the center of the circle.

"You're okay," Rivka said, turning Ward around again. "Nothing broken. Hold still."

She produced a small tube and bandage from her pocket. The gel inside the tube was cold. The bandage was tight on Ward's cheek. He didn't care. He was trying to make sense of what he was seeing in the circle.

"What happened?" he said.

"A bomb."

"What kind of bomb can do that? Or this?" He pointed at the boundary between grass and char.

"Later. We have to go."

"We can't," he said. He'd left after the Tower came down, while survivors struggled to stop their bleeding or find their limbs. He'd walked away without helping a single person. He wouldn't do that again.

He couldn't.

"Rafael," Rivka prompted.

"You're a doctor."

"Do you think this was a coincidence? Someone tried to kill us."

Look for the helpers.

It was his mother's voice now, commanding him.

"We're the helpers," he said.

He pulled away from her and found a woman motionless in the grass. Went to her. Touched her face. Too late. Her chest had been pulverized flat, like someone had deflated it. The wailing of victims mixed with the rising song of sirens. He sought someone else, someone he could save, but Rivka was there again, grabbing at his arm.

"Help is here," she said, pointing at the far end of the park where a series of police cars were pulling onto the grass, spewing forth officers who looked more military than civil. Following the police cars, four ambulances drove in a line over the curb and onto the grass. "We have to go. They have to think we're dead."

Ward relented, dragged back to reality by Rivka's words. *They*. The ones who'd set off the bomb. The ones who'd tried to kill them. His brain swirled with possibilities, names and faces whipping by like confetti in a hurricane. Who could have done this? Who would have killed so many just to get at him?

Compano.

Why? For what? Revenge? She could have had that any time in the past five months. She could have had that by sending more than two helicopters and a few Reapers to take him at the Pit near the Grand Canyon. It made no sense why she would do this.

Unless it wasn't her. Unless it was someone else's revenge.

For the Tower.

"They're going to lock down the city," Rivka said.

She shoved Ward away from the crowd, toward the ambulances where a police barricade had already been set up at the curb. The paramedics were triaging survivors. The dead. The walking and crawling and moaning wounded. Those who could move on their own, they shuttled toward the barrier.

Rivka kept them in line long enough to blend in, and then she turned east and took them through the cemetery. No one stopped them. At the far end of the cemetery, they clambered over a small stone wall onto a sidewalk. The streets were emptying. People were disappearing indoors. Half a block away, a police car had parked crossing both lanes, its lights flashing. In the distance, a military transport was speeding their direction.

"My backpack," Ward said, suddenly aware he'd lost it.

"No time."

He didn't tell her his pistol had been in the pack. Rivka took them across the street and into a market. The bearded man behind the counter paid them no attention, nor did the other customers. Their faces were all buried in their Ports, presumably watching coverage of the bombing.

Rivka left Ward near the door and found a man who appeared willing to share his Port. She leaned over his shoulder and watched the feed for almost a minute before returning to Ward.

"We have six minutes," she said.

"Until what?"

"Until Jerusalem locks down. When there's a terrorist attack, they set up a perimeter, probably a kilometer out for this, maybe two, and squeeze everyone against the walls like a grindstone."

"Can we get through?"

"I doubt it. This isn't the Republic. Terrorism isn't an anomaly here. They know what they're doing."

"So we're going into Old City?" he asked, the prospect of setting foot in the legendary city was exhilarating despite the morning's events.

"Most of the gates will be closed already. They leave one open at each of the four directions for the religious to get inside. Only the religious. I don't know if they will accept any ID I have, but we should try. The Damascus Gate is closest."

"What if we can't get in?"

"Follow me," Rivka said. "And pull up your tallit like a hood."

Ward did as instructed and then followed Rivka out the back. Here, the sidewalks were empty, but the streets weren't. Cars packed the lanes, traveling slower than Ward expected in an emergency, as if they were happy to either make it to their destination or not. Rivka didn't wait for a break in the traffic. She crossed with confidence, Ward following, in the direction, he hoped, of the Damascus Gate—one of the oldest continually used gates into Old City, built in the sixteenth century over the remains of an older gate dating to Roman Emperor Hadrian in the second century.

As they reached the far curb, a silver sedan pulled over. The driver honked and rolled down his window. Rivka kept on, but Ward stopped and leaned down to see who it was. A stupid move. He could have been leaning into an assassin's bullet. Instead, he was peering at the couple with the cane and walker he'd helped get out of the Consulate.

"We don't have time," Rivka called.

"We might."

She approached the car, much more cautiously than Ward had, and was visibly surprised to see the folks inside. The driver spoke in Hebrew. Rivka responded. They went back and forth for a few seconds.

"They're trying to get into Old City and saw you," she explained. "He wants to give us a ride to thank you for saving them earlier."

The click of the car's doors unlocking made Ward's decision. He got in the backseat and slid over so Rivka could join him, and the man pulled back into traffic.

"Does he understand English?" Ward asked. He watched the man's eyes find him in the rearview.

"Not much."

"Then we need to talk."

"The fire alarm."

"Lucky for us," Ward said, though he didn't believe it at all.

"The building must have had some kind of alarm that detected the bomb when it was armed."

"You think it was internal, not a missile or something?"

"No, it was small. The kind of thing a smuggler would use."

"But what kind of..." Ward stopped. "You think Zee did this?"

He hadn't considered Zee. He'd locked in on Compano right away without examining the options. A stupid mistake. Almost as bone-headed as leaning down to the car to see who had honked.

No one else is going to have to try to kill me, he thought. *I'm going to get myself murdered all on my own.*

"Who else knew we were here?" Rivka said.

Ward looked out the window as the car turned. They were now driving parallel to the Old City Wall, a pale limestone edifice that could have stood in a textbook as the epitome of a medieval city wall. The excitement he'd felt earlier at the thought of the archaeological treasures of Jerusalem was now absent.

"Why would he blow up a whole building just to kill us?" Ward said.

"He does what he's paid for."

"He's my friend."

Rivka said something in Hebrew Ward was sure meant *idiot*, or the equivalent. She was probably right. He hadn't wizened up in the past thirty seconds.

"Why would he try to kill us?" Ward asked, thinking it sounded like a smart question until it came out of his mouth.

"Us," Rivka said, "or you?"

"Someone must have talked. The kid, Baghel, maybe."

"He works for whoever pays the most. Someone must have outbid me."

"Who?" Ward demanded, seeking another option. Someone to blame other than Zee. But why? What did he owe the smuggler?

Nothing. Other than whatever getting me off of Santorini and giving me everything I asked for to return to the Republic is worth.

Rivka and the driver began conversing in Hebrew, leaving Ward to look out the window again, seeking answers to make sense of such an excessive assignation attempt. What he found was a medieval castle staring at him. The Damascus Gate. A familiar sight from textbook photos, but this was much larger. Much more real. Breathtaking. He took it in with a historian's eye, a moment of pure academic immersement. The battlements. The arrow slits. The machicolations, those bracketed open-floor balcony structures defenders could use to drop stones or boiling oil on attackers. The crenellated turret over the gate. The towers flanking the gate itself, each topped with a large Jerusalem flag—two broad horizontal stripes of blue on a white background like the Israeli flag, but with a lion rampant on a crest rather than a Star of David at its center—whipping in the wind.

They turned off the road onto the large flagstone sidewalk, which was packed with cars the way South Philly residents parked on medians because there was no room anywhere else. The driver stopped behind a parked car.

"There's too much traffic," Rivka said. "We won't get close enough for them to make it on foot. He says we have younger legs and should go. We might make it."

The old woman turned in her seat and offered Ward her hand as she had earlier. He took it again. Squeezed it again. The driver touched his hand to his heart and then to his head. Rivka got out. Ward followed.

They made it barely a hundred meters before Rivka stopped. The two Jerusalem flags that had been flying were gone. In their place, two red flags were slowly being hoisted. Rivka watched them silently, without moving, until they were fully raised.

"We're too late," she said. "They've locked it down."

CHAPTER 20

They followed the crowd toward the Damascus Gate. The red flags, Rivka explained in a low voice in case anyone around them understood English, were flown only when Old City went on lockdown. At that point, the Jerusalem Guard—who, on a normal day, were simple gatekeepers turning away all but the Orthodox, and those they invited in for business purposes—became an armed military force on the walls and at the gates. When the red flags flew, no one got in or out.

"Then why are we going to the gate?" Ward asked.

"We're invisible in here, in the crowd, for now," Rivka said.

"Unless they have cams, or someone is recording this on their Port. All it'll take is one ID scan of me and we're done."

Rivka slowed a moment as if considering this point, and then pushed ahead, deeper into the crowd. Down a series of amphitheater-style stairs to a patio which narrowed to a stone bridge spanning above the original Roman era gate ten meters below. At least a hundred people, mostly men and mostly draped in tallit like Ward, pushed toward the closed Damascus Gate. Too many people. Not enough bridge. They weren't getting anywhere.

Fighting a wave of claustrophobia, Ward broke free of the throng and sought the bridge's railing. He hung his head over the side, gulping whatever fresh air he could, and found himself staring at the ancient Roman gate below.

Rivka appeared at his side, eyeing him with a confusing mix of anger and a doctor's concern.

"What about that?" he said, pointing at the older gate.

"That was walled off five hundred years ago," she said. "Wait here."

Doing his best to hold his ground, Ward waited. It was all he could do. She might have been gone five minutes. It felt like an hour.

"Deployment is unpredictable," she said when she returned.

"Meaning?"

"I have a contact, but she must have been assigned to a different gate. We don't have time to check them all."

"So what do we do?" Ward asked.

Rivka led them back across the bridge, shouldering her way through the crowd which was growing more combative with each passing minute. Shoves were becoming violent. Shouts were becoming threats, recognizable even in Hebrew. The hum of violence grew in the air like static electricity.

Halfway up the stairs, they got stuck in a bottle neck. A large man in a black hat grabbed Ward's arm. The man spoke Hebrew and pointed at his Port then at Ward. It took Ward a second to understand the man wasn't talking to him but to another man in a similar hat beside him.

"Sorry, don't speak Hebrew," Ward said pulling free.

Rivka shouldered the large man aside, making a path. They cut through and up the stairs.

"They're setting the perimeter," Rivka said at the top. She pointed to the sky. A few helicopters remained hovering over the blast site, but the rest, at least ten, were spreading out to set the edge of the lockdown.

Beside them, a man in a tan business suit was also looking up at the helicopters, his Port angled so Ward could see the screen. The scene was dissolving from a studio shot to the blast zone, from the vantage point of a helo-mounted cam. The picture scanned over the smoking wreckage, the mushroom cloud had dispersed, pulling up to show the entirety of the scorch circle Ward had noted earlier. A perfect ring. Black and dead inside. Green and bustling with survivors, police, medics, and more outside.

The scene zoomed in even more on a girl trying to stand on a leg that hung from her like a bag of bones. A girl who looked like Sam. Dark hair. Dark skin. An innocent victim. She collapsed, staring up at the helicopter, not even bothering to cry for help.

"Rafael!"

"What?"

"I said, I have an idea."

Ward tried to wipe the injured girl's face from his mind, but he couldn't. It stuck the way his last view of Sam stuck—torn open from the inside like...

"Now," Rivka shouted, pulling him back up to the street.

Ward expected her to take them across the street, maybe to a cellar beneath one of the shops. It wasn't uncommon in ancient cities to unearth tombs or other archaeological finds in basements or during renovations. An entire subway had to be rerouted once, in Rome, when a two-thousand-year-old military complex was discovered on the proposed trackway. And nearly a century ago, a homeowner looking to expand his basement in Turkey discovered the subterranean city of Derinkuyu, which had previously been thought of as a myth. Instead of crossing the street, however, Rivka kept them tight to the Old City wall where it sloped back down from street level and away from the Damascus Gate, serpentining from paved walkways to grass paths. A hundred meters later, it brought them to a small grotto and another sunken gateway in the city wall, this one was covered with iron grillwork that had been painted green a long time ago. A sign, in Hebrew, was posted beside the gate.

"What's this?" Ward asked. "I thought the closer we get to the walls, the closer we are to the grindstone."

"Unless we go through the grindstone."

"You want to go under Jerusalem?"

"Not exactly." Rivka pointed to the sign. "This is Solomon's Quarry."

Ward knew of the quarry, which legend said had provided the stone for King Solomon to build the First Temple, the one featured in the Old Testament, but he didn't see how a quarry was going to help them.

"You want to hide inside?" he asked, letting his tone indicate he doubted a semi-famous tourist site with a sign out front was going to fool Jerusalem's counter-terrorism forces.

Rivka said again, "Not exactly."

She knocked on the gate, which clanged and rattled. There

was no response. Ward watched the path they'd come down, but it remained empty. Rivka knocked again. After a moment, a stooped man in a yarmulke came to the gate. He examined Rivka up and down, and then did the same for Ward, having to rotate his upper body at the hips because his neck, seemingly, couldn't lift his head back. He muttered something, maybe in Hebrew, maybe not.

Rivka got close to him and answered in Hebrew. He responded in kind and then unlocked the gate and waved them inside. Once they were in, he locked the gate behind them.

"Now what?" Ward said.

"How well do you know Jerusalem?" Rivka asked.

"I don't."

"Not this city. The historical Jerusalem. The stories. You know of the siege, right?"

"Which one?"

"The Babylonian siege, under king Nebuchadnezzar."

"Of course," Ward said. He knew it well enough. Sixth century BCE. The start of what was called the Babylonian exile, or the Jewish diaspora. "What does it have to do with us?"

"Lead the way."

"To what?" Ward said. "What the fuck are we doing in here?"

The old man hissed and shook his head, either due to Ward's tone or the fact that he understood and didn't appreciate the language. Rivka spoke to him in Hebrew. He waved her off, and she motioned Ward deeper into the cave. To their left, immediately upon entering, was a small booth, possibly for selling tickets to tour the quarry, set in the wall. Beyond the booth, a series of stairs led them to a landing with a portable toilet to the side. The ceiling was low and roughly hewn. Lights glowed at intervals, highlighting the golden color of the limestone surrounding them.

Underground again, Ward thought, the claustrophobia he knew he should be used to by now returning. *Might as well start digging with my hands. Or my mouth like a fucking—*

"There's stories about the quarry," Rivka said. "Secret paths and entrances used to smuggle things out of Jerusalem in times of trouble."

"What are you...you mean the Ark of the Covenant? It disappeared after Nebuchadnezzar's siege, but how does that help? Jerusalem is locked down and you want to escape through a myth?"

"*Ken.*"

"This is crazy," Ward said.

Blank faced, almost clinically, Rivka said, "What if it isn't?" She watched him. Waiting. Giving him little choice but to blunder off into the quarry, or to think about it. The quarry. He didn't know what she wanted, so he began talking it through. Reasoning it out. Thinking as he spoke. Some people did their best thinking while pacing or while writing. He did his while talking.

"Solomon's Quarry is at least five acres of caves of tunnels. Herod the Great used its stone to renovate the Second Temple. The Ottoman's used its stone as well when building the current walls around the city. Josephus mentioned it. I don't see how any of this helps."

"Go on," Rivka said, her confidence apparent, though in what Ward had no idea.

"Legend says Solomon quarried the stone for the First Temple from here, which is why Herod chose this as his quarry. By Herod's time, it was better known as Zedekiah's Cave, which..."

He stopped. Zedekiah was the last Biblical King of Jerusalem, the one wearing the crown when Nebuchadnezzar laid siege to the city, eventually sacking it and destroying the temple. Zedekiah's legacy was mixed. He was installed as a puppet king by the Babylonians, but he achieved fame by smuggling the Ark of the Covenant out of the city before it could be taken or destroyed.

"Tell me," Rivka said.

Ward was certain she already knew, but he went on anyway. "Archaeologists and treasure hunters have examined the quarry for centuries. No evidence has ever been found the Ark of the Covenant came through here. No exit has ever been found but the one we came through, which was well known and not suitable to a secret escape. In fact, Zedekiah himself tried to hide from the Babylonians down here, but he was caught. They put his sons to death before his eyes then blinded him. That's an ominous choice for an escape route."

"But," Rivka said, "there have been engravings found, and if the caves are as large as stories say, extending both beneath Old City and out in what was once the wilderness, perhaps there's way out behind the perimeter."

She was saying *if*, but there was no mistaking that continued confidence. Ward had seen it below Masada.

"What do you know?" he asked. "I've never heard of any excavations that even hinted at an exit."

Rivka gave a MacKenzie-like grin. "I have," she said. "But I need your help to find it."

CHAPTER 21

The girl woke.

Again.

Memory came like drips from a broken faucet. She was still on a table she remembered. In a cave she remembered. Beside her, a machine she remembered was still beeping. Of herself, she remembered nothing.

Who am I? a voice that wasn't hers asked in her head.

Panic coursed through her at the sound of a voice not her own in her head, sitting her up. Making her dizzy. Making her angry.

"Who are you?" she asked the voice.

No answer.

More drips of memory. Last time, she tried to get up, but she was attached to the machine. It stopped her. People arrived. They stopped her.

She couldn't stay here, but she was wary enough not to go running off without a plan. She had to take her time. She had to collect more information. The cave around her was quiet. There were rows and rows of beds and machines. All the beds were empty. All the machines, save hers, were silent. She remembered one of the people in the room saying something about transport. Something about her not going.

She shifted her attention to herself, starting at the top. The wires she'd torn from her head were reattached. She was wearing a blue-gray gown of light fabric, barely enough to keep anyone warm, but she wasn't cold. Surprisingly, the tube that had been inserted into her right bicep was no longer there. A thick gauze bandage covered her arm where it had been. Upon seeing the bandage, her arm began to throb, the pain thumping up and down her arm. Up to her shoulder. Down through her elbow, her forearm, to her...

There was no hand at the end of her wrist.

A sudden pain flared where her hand should have been. She wailed and doubled over, fighting the need to vomit, afraid she might pass out as the excruciating misery of having her hand cut off with shears replayed in full.

Someone cut off my hand with fucking garden shears!

The memory was so thick and painful in her skull she thought she her head might explode.

Eventually, the pain subsided, and the memory let go, leaving only a throbbing in her forearm. She'd fallen back on the table and had to fight to sit up once more. The thought of looking at her arm, at the hand that wasn't there, nauseated her, but she knew she had to. She forced her eyes down her arm. To her elbow. To her slender forearm. To her wrist, covered in a black cuff that appeared both metallic and not. The cuff was hard and smooth and rounded over the stump of her arm. Thick fibers, or maybe wires, ran through it like veins, and it was pocked with small tabs and ports. The tubing that had been inserted in her arm was now attached to a tab where her thumb should have been.

On reflex, she clenched her fist. She felt it close. Felt the fingers bite into her palm. Only there were no fingers. No palm. Only a tingling pain in the shape of a hand. Like a ghost.

She cried and cradled the cuff to her chest. It was cool, like steel. Or death.

Yes.

The voice made the girl jump.

"Where have you been?" she asked it.

Death, it said, closer than she remembered.

"Who are you?"

Death. Closer still.

"What do you want?"

We, it said like it was whispering in her ear. *We want death.*

It was no longer in the deep. No longer separate. It was beside her now, conjoined. A partner. A twin.

Yet still an other.

The sound of a door opening startled the girl. Fear pulsed through her as if it'd been injected. People were coming. People who didn't want her getting up. Or getting out.

No more sleep, her other voice said.

The girl was in complete agreement. She—*we!*—would not let them put her back to sleep, but she also didn't want to antagonize them. Not yet. She had to play it cool, the phrase *play it cool* occurring to her like it was something she might have said in her previous life. If she had a previous life.

A man in beige clothes entered the cave. He was young, probably not much older than she was, though she had no idea how old that might be. When he saw her sitting up, he stopped mid-stride and his eyes grew wide like bottle caps. He shouted over his shoulder in that language she didn't know but somehow understood, calling for more people to enter the cave.

The girl swung her legs over the edge of the table, prompting the man to remove a device from a pocket below his waist. It was dark and metal and sinister. It reminded the girl of the cuff on her arm.

Gun.

Yes, a gun, she agreed. A tool for killing.

She was suddenly thirsty. And hungry. A tremor began in her core, extending to her arms and legs. Her fingers tickled and twitched. She pulled the wires from her head, first the left side then the right. She pulled the tubing from the cuff, ignoring the dragging pain flaring within her phantom hand. She slid off the table.

The man in beige backed away, his gun aimed at the floor near the girl's feet. Two forms appeared in the doorway behind him, a man in white and woman, also with a gun, in beige. The trio exchanged looks then approached together, cautious but determined.

"Where are you going?" the man in white asked.

The man with the gun first.

The girl accepted the other voice's assessment. The man with the gun, the one who'd first entered the room, was directly ahead. The girl angled his direction, but she was weak, her steps labored.

"Please," the man in white said, "I'm here to help. You've been through an ordeal."

The girl believed him. But the two in beige weren't here to help. They were here to contain. To subdue.

The man in white came around the man with the gun. The woman in beige maneuvered wide, taking a better angle but a longer aim. New formation. Same goal. The man in beige with the gun first.

The girl took a step and felt a strength rising within her. Another step and she felt even stronger, as if a battery deep inside her had been switched on. The man in beige was only a leap away now.

"What are you doing?" the man in white asked.

Death.

The girl said, "Death."

CHAPTER 22

Every so often, the low, wide caverns of Solomon's Quarry opened in an auditorium-like expanse before closing in once more. Water drops occasionally let go of the ceiling, splashing on the limestone with almost no sound. The fluorescent lights meant to keep tourists from getting lost had long ago been left behind. This deep underground, their only light was Rivka's bright but narrowly focused flashlight.

Early on, she refused to slow for Ward to examine the quarry. As they continued on, however, she indulged him more and more often, allowing him to run his fingers along the chisel marks lining the walls, or to inspect the unfinished blocks, half-carved from the earth and abandoned for some imperfection a stonemason had discovered a couple thousand years ago. Relics of such age were beyond rare in the Americas even before the rise of the Republic. There'd been the Norse dig Ward had gone on in graduate school in Newfoundland, and analytical work he'd done on finds from pre-Columbian sites in Old Mexico and South America, but nothing of this scope. The only thing of this age and size he'd studied was the Lynch Quarry site in North Dakota, but that was a series of small pits spread over almost seven hundred acres, and dating back thirteen thousand years. None of the sites he'd studied had offered this kind of pre-construction grandeur or inspired the kind of romantic imaginations of these unfinished blocks and potential secret escapes.

It was the idea of escape that forced Ward to examine their progress pragmatically. They'd started out traveling directly under Jerusalem's Old City wall. A few twists and turns followed, but then the tunnels straightened out quite a bit. In the past few minutes, they hadn't varied trajectory much at all. He did his best to calculate distance and direction and came up with a concerning conclusion.

"I thought we weren't going into Old City," he said, certain they were a good half-kilometer south of the quarry entrance. Or right under the center of Old City, maybe close to the Western Wall, the last standing foundation wall of Herod's Second Temple.

"We're not," Rivka said, moving through the tunnels with a confidence Ward found unnerving.

"Where are we going?"

"This way."

The tunnel chose that moment to split. Or rather, the tunnel they were in met with another coming in on their right to form the top branches of a Y converging with the stem. Rivka didn't spend any time choosing. She took them back up the other branch of the Y, to the northwest, Ward guessed. He didn't ask why, following along dutifully, trusting in her confidence because he didn't know what else to do.

The tunnel here was less refined than the branch they'd come down, like an unfinished decision. Which bore out a few minutes later when they came to an abrupt stop. A massive limestone slab marred by a snaking fissure near one edge filled the tunnel. One of the aborted blocks found throughout the quarry like a two-hundred-ton roadblock positioned here at least a millennium before tractors and cranes were invented.

As he opened his mouth to ask Rivka her plan, the light went out. One blink, it was there, illuminating the limestone block, the next Ward was blind. He felt like he was both falling and rising, flying and being thrown down. Weightless, dizzy, terrified, and timeless, as if each second was both a fraction of itself and an eternity. Compano was right. This was how he died. Alone in the dark. Buried alive.

He called for Rivka, certain she'd abandoned him. Betrayed him as Zee had. Expecting no response but the echo of his own voice. But she did respond.

"*Ken,*" she said. "I'm here."

Relief flooded Ward like a glorious Scotch. The light returned. Not like a switch the way it had gone out, but like it was emerging from a tunnel, offering a hint of light followed by an approaching form, as if coming out of the roadblock itself. Then she was there, posing like a gameshow hostess.

"Don't look so close," she said, motioning to the fissure in the stone. "Don't look straight on."

Ward started to ask what she meant, but then he saw it. The fissure wasn't an imperfection. It was an overlapping flange hiding a tunnel. A mirage. Like beneath Masada.

"You knew," he said.

"*Ken.*"

"Was this made by the same people as in Masada?"

"This is older."

"Solomon," Ward mused.

Rivka said nothing.

"If you knew, what do you need my help for?" he asked.

"You'll see."

She pushed into the fissure, forcing him to follow or be left behind in the dark again. It was tight, leaving little light to filter back from Rivka in the lead, but Ward's claustrophobia had fled. He was no longer afraid. He was fascinated, fully engrossed in the moment and the scene. Thrilled to be among the first to walk these tunnels in two thousand years or more. As the earlier tunnels had, this one narrowed and then opened into another auditorium. Rivka took them a few meters into the cavern and then stopped, shining her light around as if seeking something. Ward took the opportunity to move to the edge of her light, following it around and exploring. The cavern was huge, its ceiling and far end lost in darkness, but there was little else to discern it from previous caves. Slowly, Rivka moved through the cavern until she'd lighted upon three exits in addition to the tunnel they'd come through, one in each of four directions, though Ward had no idea which direction each went anymore.

Finally, she found what she was looking for, stopping near the center of the auditorium and shining her light on the floor. Ward knelt to examine what he thought at first was a series of chisel marks. With the light at the right angle, however, he saw it was an angle, its long wings spread like scissor blades about to slash closed.

Except it wasn't an angel. Its face was too child-like. And familiar. Like a pre-adolescent version of a man he knew. Someone he'd spoken with. Someone he'd seen a photo of. The Grossmutter's house popped into his head. Her fireplace mantel, with all those picture frames...

"You see it?" Rivka said.

"It's a cherub," Ward said, whatever else he'd been thinking of glitching away. "The Old Testament, the Torah, is full of them. God places one, or sometimes the angel Uriel depending on which version of the story, at the east of the Garden of Eden to protect the Tree of Life once Adam and Eve are driven out."

"With a flaming sword," Rivka said.

"Right. The Holy of Holies in Solomon's Temple was also adorned with cherubim, and they were said to be part of the prescribed construction of the Ark."

"*Ken*," Rivka said, as if waiting for him to draw a conclusion.

"That's it, isn't it?" Ward said. "You want to follow the path of the Ark, the way it was smuggled out of Jerusalem."

"This is the way."

"And it will take us," he had to pause, knowing how stupid it would sound the moment he spoke it, "to the Ark?"

Rivka didn't mock him the way he expected. "No one knows where the Ark went when it left these tunnels. That secret was lost long before I entered this conflict."

She offered him the flashlight, like a prompt. Or a challenge. He took it and began investigating the floor, Rivka always beside him. It was a slow process. The marker they were looking for would be, he assumed, as difficult to see as the cherub had been. In the end, he found nothing on the floor and started on the walls. Here, he discovered a marker quickly. Next to the first of the three exits from the cavern. A cherub, holding a shining sword.

"Here," he said.

Rivka placed her hand on the faint image. "The sword. The guardian of Eden. Let's go."

She put her hand out for the flashlight, but Ward didn't hand it over.

"Wait," he said. "Did you expect it to be this easy?"

"How is this easy? I can barely see the little cherub."

"But a few thousand years ago it might have been more visible. The one on the floor might have been more obvious. If it's a secret path, they wouldn't advertise it."

He took the flashlight to the next exit where they found not one but two faded cherubim facing each other, as if praying toward an object between, or below, them, their wings flowing forward so their tips almost touched.

"Come on," Ward said, taking them to the final exit. Beside it was another faded image. A cherub with four wings and four faces: the boyish angel, a lion, an ox, and an eagle.

"Which one is it?" Rivka asked.

"The more important question might be, what happens if we choose the wrong one."

"You expect danger?"

"If this is a puzzle to keep the way of the Ark secret, yeah I expect danger."

Rivka said, "This is why I needed you."

He expected as much, but hearing her say it got under his skin. Worse, doubt got under his skin. Had she known all along they would have to come down here? Had the sex been nothing more than a way to guarantee his cooperation?

"Is it the sword?" Rivka said.

"Why would you choose that one?" Ward couldn't help the rhetorical response. It was a teacher's comeback. Let the student defend their position, and then proceed once that thesis had either been confirmed or refuted.

"Eden," she said. "The first destination, and the last."

"I thought heaven was the final destination."

Rivka shrugged.

Ward said, "Look, the one over here with the four faces is from the Book of Ezekiel where the cherubim carry god on his throne, and this one, with the two facing each other, this is how the Mercy Seat, or the cover for the Ark of the Covenant, is described as being adorned."

"We go this way, then," Rivka said without hesitation. She motioned for him to go ahead.

The tunnel was long and straight. Not to narrow. Not too low. Ward found himself worrying about booby traps like in an adventure movie, but the way was easy and unobstructed. Until they found it blocked by another slab with a familiar fissure near the edge.

"This is where we're either proven right or crushed by a landslide or something," Ward said.

"We're right," Rivka said, but she let Ward continue in the lead.

Once through the fissure, the way continued long and straight once more, giving them time to talk.

"Do you know what kind of bomb that was?" Ward asked.

"They call it subnuclear. Focused blast with an implosion wave."

"I've never heard of it."

"You really don't know what your country did here during the war, do you?"

"I wasn't even born," Ward said. "The Republic wasn't even born."

"But you're a teacher," she said, her tone making it clear she didn't accept his age as an excuse. "A historian."

"And history says it was a nuclear strike on Riyadh, followed by a brief assault and occupation. American forces were completely withdrawn in less than a year."

"American soldiers never set foot in Arabia. By the time the clouds cleared from the bombs, there was nothing left but ash. The peninsula wasn't quarantined to protect people from radiation. It was quarantined to protect people from what survived."

"Like the Jerusalem Line," Ward said.

"What we saw in Bethlehem was the outskirts of the fallout. Nothing in the quarantine zone survived longer than a month."

"Will Jerusalem face that kind of fallout from this morning? Will we?"

"No, the bomb this morning was something new. We've only recently received intel about it. This was the first I've heard of it being used on civilians. It's more dangerous than conventional nuclear weapons because its implosion wave keeps the blast zone focused."

"Isn't that better than nukes?"

"What keeps governments from using nuclear weapons?" Ward said, "Fear of them being used in retaliation."

"*Ken.* Because mutual destruction serves no one, but a weapon which destroys so completely yet leaves the rest of the city intact could be deployed without that fear of mutual destruction."

The idea was chilling.

"What Zee did this morning was targeted," Rivka added. "It was not for mass destruction. It was for being thorough."

"You really think it was Zee? You really think he did all that just to kill me."

"He didn't do it to kill me."

"Coincidence?" Ward asked. "Random terrorist attack?"

Rivka didn't answer.

"Fine. It was about me."

"Which means it was either Zee or someone who paid Zee. Unless there are others who know you didn't die in the Tower."

There were, but none Ward could think of who would try to kill him like that. Sam, MacKenzie, Da—*the Seer*—and Compano and presumably some of her Agents or support staff at the REC.

"The only people I can think of would prefer to keep the illusion going," he said, "not blow it up all to shit. Too risky. Too big. If they wanted me dead, they would hire a sniper not a bomber. They'd poison me and hide the body, not demolish half a city. Are you sure it's not about you?"

"My people would never betray me."

"They shot at us in Masada."

"It was dark. You have no idea. We are bound by more than promises and blood."

"We have to consider all options."

"That's not one," Rivka said.

Ward considered pressing her on it, but up ahead the tunnel widened, revealing three lines of dull light. The outline of a door.

The need to get out of the dark, and out from underground, nearly prompted Ward to rush ahead, but suspicion caused him to hesitate. Where was the booby-trapped ceiling or the bottomless pit to threaten those who dared trespass? Were the secret tunnels through the fissures really all that had kept this way secret for millennia?

I'm being paranoid. True, but not without cause. Not without precedent.

Rivka shared none of his hesitancy, however. She charged on, leaving Ward to either follow and fall into the hypothetical bottomless pit with her, or to stand there alone in the dark. He followed, arriving at the wood plank door as she began banging on it. The jangling of locks being opened preceded the door swinging wide to frame the same stooped man in the yarmulke who'd let them into the quarry back at the Old City wall.

"Is that the same," Ward started, but Rivka shook her head to cut him off.

She and the man exchanged a few words in Hebrew. The man then led them through another cave to another door. Ward noted his stoop and limp were not as pronounced as he recalled, leading him to suspect it was not the same man after all. A twin, maybe. Rivka motioned for Ward to wait in the grotto while she and the old man spoke in the open doorway. He found a bench and sat. The sun shone bright but not too hot overhead. It was late morning, he guessed, and he tried to get his bearings on where they were, but the best he could come up with was they'd either crossed all the way under Old City and come out the other side, or they'd doubled back and were now further north than where they started. He wondered if either option was far enough to get them beyond the lockdown perimeter.

With Rivka still talking to the man, Ward got up and wandered the grotto, trying to figure out where they were. At first, he found nothing distinctive, until a small doorway set into the wall like an opening in a cave caught his eye. Or rather, the green-gated door in the cave opening caught his eye. Because he knew it. He'd seen it before in photos.

"Son of a bitch," he said.

Rivka and the man stopped talking. They glared at him as if he'd broken a favorite dish. Or spoken sacrilege. Which he sort of had, considering his companions.

"This is the Garden Tomb, isn't it?" he said, naming the

supposed site of Jesus Christ's burial and resurrection. It was noted in REC records as one of the first declarations of fraud enacted by the Republic upon its formation. It had been visited and tested, according to REC history, more than three decades ago, those tests concluding the tomb was no more than nine hundred years old.

"There's a car waiting," Rivka said.

"Did we get behind the perimeter?"

"*Ken.*"

Though he would be disappointed to leave Jerusalem, getting past the lockdown was crucial to saving Sam. "Can you get us out of the city?"

"I can, but there's another problem."

CHAPTER 23

MacKenzie washed her hands in the fried chicken restaurant's restroom. Blood and grime came off easily enough from the backs of her hands and her palms. With some scrubbing, even her fingernails gave up their filth. Fingerprints were another matter. Those little whorls held onto dirt the way some people held onto their past.

One of the men her mother lived with for a time—*what was his name?*—had been a mechanic. She remembered standing by the bathroom sink watching him wash his hands with a thick orange soap. She couldn't have been more than eight or nine.

"How come your soap is a different color than mine?" she'd asked.

"Don't you have dolls to play with?" he'd said, not looking at her, not even in the mirror, as he turned his hands over and over in the water.

"How come I can't fix things like you?"

"You don't know how."

"How come you can't teach me?"

"For fuck's sake, kid," he'd said. "Do you ever say anything other than 'how come' all the time?"

She always braced for more when he said those three words: *for fuck's sake.* Too often they preceded a verbal lashing. Not physical though. That only came when he was drunk, without warning, when Mom was already asleep.

When he didn't keep going, she asked, "How come you don't wear gloves at work?"

He stopped scrubbing and looked at her, his glare backing her up against the toilet.

"You can't feel it with gloves," he said. "You've got to feel it to know how to fix it."

Newton! she remembered. *The prick's name was Newton.*

Newton hadn't known much about raising a kid, or being a good boyfriend to MacKenzie's mother, and he'd been a half-competent mechanic at best, but she'd learned over the years that he was right about the gloves. They were a barrier. A separation. Not worth the risk. What if the fabric caught on the trigger guard? What if it caused a millisecond delay between intending to pull a trigger and actually doing it? No matter the advantages, gloves weren't worth it. So she scrubbed away what she'd done, slowly becoming aware her hands were shaking like a raw private's hands after her first kill.

"Out of practice," she told her reflection.

The skirmish had been brief, almost over by the time she arrived in the parking lot outside. Four loyalists inside, dressed in Republic National Guard uniforms, had two Bravo Company teams pinned down behind the cars in the lot. A quick assessment said the best strategy was cover fire to keep their attention on the parking lot while a small number of soldiers slipped in through the back. She should have ordered it. She should have maintained a safe vantage point and watched it be executed with perfection.

Instead, her adrenaline up, she charged.

It was her first action, her first kills, since returning from Europe. There was no slow motion. There was no calm resolve. It was fast and chaotic. Almost like her first time. She chose a break in the suppressing fire from inside and charged. Four shots took down three of the loyalists before she even reached the entrance. The fourth tackled her as she crashed through the door. He was big. He had leverage and a stun dagger in his hand. His advantage lasted maybe a half-second. Then the dagger was in MacKenzie's hand, and she was plunging it into his chest, that soft spot below the throat. As he hit the floor, his eyes wide in pain and surprise, she noted he was wearing gloves.

MacKenzie's Charge they were calling it already. Not to her face, of course, but she'd heard as she made her way to the restroom. The Seer would hear about it.

So what, she thought. *I'm not Horeb's general anymore. There's no regs preventing me from engaging in combat.*

But she knew it wasn't about regulations. It was about the Seer insisting she remain cautious even as a member of Bravo Company. It was about his insistence there was a more important role for her in the revolution than killing loyalists in a shithole fast food joint. No matter how good at it she was.

How many had she killed in her life? Dozens? Hundreds? Would it be thousands before she was done? Why not? She killed Newton when she was nine.

That was a lie. Newton had been killed in an accident at work. A car had fallen off a lift, crushing his chest and pinning him underneath for almost ten minutes before they got it off him. At that point, little Hannah MacKenzie had heard while eavesdropping at the hospital, the car itself had been keeping his organs in place. When it was removed, everything had gushed out. He'd died within a minute.

But she knew, even then, it was her first kill. She'd goaded him all that morning, practically begging him to hit her. To prove to her mother what an asshole he was. Instead of taking the bait, however, he'd gone to work, the tires of his car screeching away from the apartment building in a rage she'd wanted directed at herself, but which made him careless instead.

She hadn't dropped the car on him—or shot, stabbed, strangled, or any of the other countless other ways she'd killed people since—but she knew it was her. And Someone else. Maybe even that Someone her mother whispered about sometimes. God. Had God heard little Hannah's voice begging for Newton to be taken away?

It was the first time in her life she'd considered such a thing as God. Soon, she would be having conversations with her mother about God. Soon, they would be reading the Bible and praying together. For the time being, however, at nine years old, all she had was the guilt of it. The guilt and the power. The knowledge that Someone had chosen her. That she was meant for better. That she could fix anything if she prayed hard enough and kept her faith that God would see her through.

Still, the guilt never really went away. Newton's was the

first face that appeared shadowy and horrific in her dreams, gaping like a fish trying to breathe on land. They all gaped like that, the faces of the people she'd killed, when they haunted her nightmares. They'd come often in the night when she was younger, frightening her awake so her hands shook until morning. Like they were shaking now.

That was a long time ago, though. She barely remembered how that fear felt. What she remembered more when those faces came to her at night, what clung to her like the slickness of sweat, was the rage that accompanied each kill. She imagined it was similar to the way some people could remember what clothes they were wearing on a particular day. Like the rage itself was a shirt she wore. An emblem. A mask.

Like the one she wore in Old Mexico. The one that had cut down more than ten Mexican police. The one that had saved their lives.

The one that had so disturbed Rafe.

"Damn it!"

He was in her head again. He'd poisoned her somehow. Snaked a piece of his hypocritical righteousness into her soul when he'd jabbed that stun baton into her neck. Made the simple act of killing into a moral anchor threatening to drown her.

"General," a soldier said from outside the restroom.

MacKenzie shut off the water. "Come."

It was Foules again. "We have confirmation, sir."

"The bomb?"

"Subnuclear."

The paper towel dispenser was empty. "Shit. Do we know who's responsible?"

"Negative, sir, but Target Abel was confirmed in the vicinity."

Target Abel. Horeb's number one most wanted individual on the orders of the Seer himself.

Rafe.

Why him? Why call him Abel? MacKenzie didn't know and didn't care. Or wouldn't let herself care. Or refused to believe she cared.

For fucks sake!

As it had been for the last five months, the slightest thought of him was enough to send her into a rage. She fought it. She refused to give him that power. She concentrated on Oren, dead somewhere in Old Mexico, on the anger and grief she'd felt the moment Graciela told her about him, until she was numb to the news Foules had delivered. The bomb might as well have detonated on the moon. Foules might as well be telling her a pile of rocks was sighted in the vicinity.

"We have this," Foules said, offering a Port.

Mackenzie shook her hands dry and took the Port, relieved her grasp was steady. Two photos, side-by-side, filled the screen.

"A few minutes after the second image, the bomb went off," Foules said, clearly eager to discuss this development.

Of course he was. Every soldier in Horeb had standing orders from the Seer himself to apprehend Target Abel on sight, regardless of collateral risk. The target's safety, however, was to be guaranteed. No matter what.

"Communication from Horeb?" she asked.

"Orders are for Bravo Company to continue its operation and take El Paso."

"Not to pursue Target Abel?" MacKenzie said, unable to hide her surprise. The way her voice echoed in the small restroom, it sounded more like a child's petulant disappointment.

"Sir, he didn't—"

"Dismissed."

"Yes, sir," Foules said.

He exited the restroom, leaving MacKenzie alone with her reflection and once-again trembling hands. The long-held suspicion—anchored in the back of her mind since she'd returned from Spain—burst like a migraine, a jackhammer pounding away behind her eyes: *The Seer doesn't trust me.*

Of course he didn't. How could he trust her with this when she'd let her past and her feelings get in the way in Spain? He wouldn't trust her until she proved herself.

"Foules!" she announced.

"Yes, sir," Foules said, re-entering the restroom.

"I want Nogales locked down by dawn. Then get me a transport east. I want to be in Maverick County, Texas, by nightfall tomorrow."

"But sir..."

"Now!"

"Yes, sir," Foules said, hurrying from the restroom.

MacKenzie examined her reflection in the stained and cloudy mirror. Blood had splattered the collar of her shirt. A few spots stood out like large freckles on her cheek and ear lobe. She looked closer. Lines had grown around her mouth and dark circles hung under eyes like the shadows of doubt.

She made up her mind.

Then second-guessed.

She clenched a fist but stopped herself from punching the mirror. Instead, she turned on the water again and splashed some on her face, not bothering to wipe off the blood.

"I'm still following orders," she told her reflection, swapping back to her initial instinct.

Bravo Company would sweep the border to El Paso as planned. They would continue to raze the Wall's defenses, attacking from both sides with Graciela's assistance, all the way to the Gulf of Mexico. All MacKenzie was doing was scouting ahead. Things were handled here. She'd be back with Bravo Company at Las Cruces in twenty-four hours as they prepared for the assault on El Paso. Done and done.

Satisfied, she wiped her face dry on her sleeve and pushed out of the restroom. Right into Graciela. It was like walking into a wall. Neither woman gave an inch.

"He says you should remain here," Graciela said.

"Who?"

"The Seer."

"Does everyone have a fucking line to him now?" she said, stomping away from Graciela.

She didn't want to talk anymore. She needed to get away. From Nogales. From Bravo Company. She needed solitude to think and plan and figure out how to earn the Seer's trust back. She needed the kind of wisdom she suspected the Grossmutter could provide.

When she sighted Foules, she said, "I want that transport ready to go in five."

She left him saluting and marched to the temporary command center tent that also served as her personal quarters and ordered everyone out. Five minutes. Plenty of time to pack and prep and get her head back in the game. Five minutes, then she'd be gone, on her way to Eagle Pass.

CHAPTER 24

"Unidentifiables?" Ward asked. They were driving slowly north, caught in evacuation traffic with everyone else who'd either been cleared to exit the lockdown zone or who'd already been outside the lockdown and wanted to get even farther away from trouble.

Rivka, in the driver seat, said, "Asmauth Airport is under constant surveillance. Drones. Cams. Sensors like the one in the Consulate. Every airport in Israel is a potential combat zone."

This was the first part of the other problem she had mentioned at the Garden Tomb. They got beyond the lockdown but finding transportation to Gebze was going to be difficult. Hearing about the amount of security at the airport made Ward think it might be far worse than difficult.

"If the airport is such a danger, why are we going? What about another..." The answer came to him obvious enough. "You're tapped into the surveillance, aren't you?"

"*Ken.*"

"And the old man at the tomb who could have been the twin of the old man at the quarry told you there's some people at the airport we'd be better off avoiding?"

"Facial recognition is registering no match for a handful of people on site."

"Let's skip it then," Ward said. "There's got to be other airports."

"Our arrangements are for Asmauth Airport."

"So we improvise. Do we have any money? Can we buy tickets to Turkey somewhere else?"

"Tel Aviv, but we need travel passes to enter the north corridor. Zee had those arrangements."

Ward sat back. The car was small but comfortable enough. Its air conditioning worked. Still, he was anxious and began fidgeting as they continued on at ten or fifteen kilometers per hour, with stops every few minutes that Ward assumed were due to checkpoints somewhere ahead.

"But you've got eyes on them, the unidentifiables, right?" he said. "We can avoid them."

"My intel is static, not live. I know what I was told when we got the car. I can't track them in real time."

Ward thought this over, trying to picture it the way MacKenzie might. They had a goal. Enemies were in the way. They needed to strategize. Except the more he tried to design a MacKenzie-like plan, the more people died. He changed tactics. Concealment rather than assault. Costumes.

"They're probably tapped in too," he said, seeing the flaw in that plan. A hat and sunglasses wouldn't fool cams or recognition software, and if Rivka's people could hack into the airport's system, so could Zee's. His disappointment became confusion. "Wait. We're dead, right? Why does Zee have people at the airport in the first place?"

Rivka looked at him like he'd asked why the sun rises in the east and sets in the west.

"Could this not be about us at all?"

"Do you want to take that chance?" Rivka asked.

He didn't have to think about it long. *Always prepare for the whole thing to go to shit,* Compano had taught him.

"No."

"Zee is thorough," Rivka said. "We both agree on this, correct? Until he verifies body parts, he'll assume we're alive. Therefore, we should assume these are his people at the airport."

"But you have a plan," Ward prompted. "Your little old man at the quarry arranged something, right?"

"I have a contact at the airport."

"Who? Another mercenary?"

"You don't trust me?"

"I trust you," Ward said, without hesitation. Because he did.

It was everyone else he couldn't trust. "I'm just concerned. Your first contact didn't work out so well for us."

"He was your contact," she said.

My man. Your contact. A distinct shift from *our man* earlier.

"This is different," she went on before Ward could reply, her tone defensive yet soliciting approval. "It's someone I know personally."

"A boyfriend?"

"Are you jealous?"

"I'll hug him if he can get us out of here."

"He's a former patient. A man I helped start over after Masada."

"After?" Ward said. "I figured you were all in for life."

Rivka hit the accelerator, launching the car forward to slip in ahead of a yellow truck in the next lane over.

"I'm a doctor, not a soldier," she said. "I have a job, like anyone else. So does Noam now. I trust him."

It was enough. It had to be. Still, Ward couldn't help but focus on what she'd just said: *I'm a doctor, not a soldier.*

Those six words struck him as both an accusation and an excuse. They also made him think. The way she moved, the way she thought and spoke and reacted, was more than just a doctor. Plus her belief in whatever it was they believed at Masada. It was palpable on her at times. She was as much a soldier as everyone else there. Even the children, the ones in his classroom. Would they all grow up to be as devoted as Rivka? Would his life have turned out differently if he'd been as devoted to the Republic?

Traffic slowed to a stop-and-go rush hour pace, giving Ward a headache. He pushed the button to roll down his window for some fresh air, but Rivka stopped the window with a button on her side.

"Not safe," she said. They lapsed into silence again for a few minutes until she asked, "Who else knows you're alive?"

The implication of the question was clear: who hired Zee?

"If it's not Zee himself for whatever personal reason," Ward said, "it has to be the Republic that hired him. I still don't think this is the way they would do it, with a bomb like that, but I can't think of anyone else."

Except he could, now that he was thinking about it in terms of personal reasons. After all, personal vengeance was the basis of everything Ker had done. He'd blamed Ward for the death of his brother in the Tower, going so far as to infiltrate MacKenzie's army and kidnap Sam, eventually cutting off her hand, for the simple consuming sake of vengeance.

"Whoever it is, if they find out we're alive, they'll try to finish the job. Either Zee or whoever hired him, or even an open contract at this point." Ward was sure he'd seen movies like that, with assassins all over the world picking up contracts on a mark. It seemed legit enough to be concerned. "There could be five others out there looking for us. Or fifteen."

"I think we should worry about the one we know about," Rivka said.

She was right. They couldn't be looking over their shoulders at everyone. They would end up walking right into a wall. Or a trap.

"What's your plan?"

"Get to Noam at the airport," she said as if it had been stupid to ask.

Ward let it go. They were both stressed. Being on the run was difficult. He'd lived like this before. Rivka hadn't. She was a doctor and a soldier. She knew orders and routine. She could fight and kill and heal. Living on the run was different. He had to be the one to keep them on point. Like he had with Sam.

Sam, who was dead, but who was maybe now alive. Like Daniel had been dead and was now alive. Like Ward himself. Dead to the world. Until this morning when Zee, or whoever had paid him, killed dozens, maybe hundreds, to make Ward's supposed death real and permanent. It was all enough to twist his mind into something that no longer resembled sanity.

Traffic began to spread out. Ahead, the horizon flattened out as the city finally gave way to the desert, with only a few pops of construction visible at a distance. A line of military transport trucks and armored vehicles rolled by them in the opposite lane, toward Old City. A few minutes later, a domed building atop concrete posts like an art deco spider of cement and glass rose above the trees. Two more turns and, like an oasis in the desert, the airport appeared.

"It looks like a shopping mall," Ward said.

"It was Israel's first airport, operated by the Jordanians until we took Jerusalem by God's will. It was closed for a time, but after the Jewish-Arab war, it was rebuilt and renamed Asmauth. Independence Airport. What do you think?"

"It's kind of ugly."

"*Ken*. Very."

The road brought them around the main terminal to a squat parking garage. They parked on the third level and took an elevator to a walkway.

"You've lost your tallit," Rivka said. "Keep your head down, but be vigilant."

Ward didn't bother asking how he could do both. The walkway, with a dark blue carpet that reminded Ward of a casino, led them to the airport terminal, the body of the concrete spider, which turned out to be very much a mall after all. Storefronts and fast food restaurants beckoned from beneath neon signs. Huge televisions covered the walls above the signs, many with flight numbers and times on them. Customer service kiosks, each staffed by an armed soldier and a teenager in an employee uniform, dotted the two wide avenues of people shuffling this way and that, quickly but politely.

If this was an airport post-lockdown, Ward wondered what it would take to change this population into a terrified mob. That thought led to another: how many bombings would it take before Philly—or any city in the Republic—became so used to them it went about its business in this matter-of-fact manner? Hundreds? Thousands? He'd watched the news feeds in the aftermath of the Tower bombing. The city had gone on lockdown for a week, followed by a month-long curfew extension blocking out sixteen hours each day. He'd heard rumors, as well, of door-to-door searches, major increases in black bag disappearances, and more.

Yes, hundreds probably.

"Noam will be over there," Rivka said. "Stay out of trouble."

"Are you sure he's expecting you?" Ward asked, but she

was already gone, blending into the crowd like a raindrop in a storm. He slid the other direction, letting his eyes adjust from the chaos of the full scene to the individuals surrounding him. To his right, two crowds of teens, maybe college students, clustered near a café, chatting boisterously. Occasionally, they shouted at passersby who ignored them. Until one didn't. A man in a brimless cap shouted back. Ward only understood a few of the words, but he caught on quick enough. The teens were Israeli. The man in the cap was an atheist. They blamed him for the bombing this morning.

Shouting turned to pushing. A soldier tried to get to them. Someone threw a punch at the man in the cap. The airport hummed like it might explode.

Ward pushed against the crowd, trying to get away from the epicenter, heading up the concourse until he found an empty table where he sat with his forehead in his hands like a man with a migraine. His heart was racing. It wouldn't take someone recognizing him to make this place the combat zone Rivka had warned about. It might explode on its own. They needed to get out of here fast. He sought Rivka in the crowd, but she was long gone, so he sought Zee's people. Anyone not seeking company. Anyone watching the crowd not the monitors for their flight's status. Anyone out of place in the flow.

Like me.

More shouting erupted from the opposite end of the terminal as the teens. He tried to ignore it, now clinging to the edges of his table as if it were a flotation device after a water landing. He searched the crowd, but the more he looked, the more he lost focus on faces. The more his eyes kept returning to the giant screens above. The ones not displaying flight statuses were showing scenes of the bombing aftermath. Some replayed the forming of the mushroom cloud from different videos taken at multiple angles from residents' Ports. A few screens showed survivors and rescue workers interacting. The largest screen, mounted to the back wall of the bus station, lit up with two columns. The first was Hebrew text. The second was numbers. Different than the flight status screens. Next flights boarding maybe. The more he looked, however, the more that didn't make sense. The numbers were dates not times. Including today. Then he understood. The screen was showing a list of bombing locations in Jerusalem in the past five years. There were more than thirty of them. The dates were worse than the scenes of death and destruction on the other screens.

He looked away, he had to, and found a man in a green shirt staring right at him from across the terminal. The man could have been a car salesman or a CEO, if it weren't for the way he was locked in on Ward, ignoring the increasing number of scuffles breaking out. The man said something. Ward watched his lips go, but there was no one near him listening. He was talking to himself. Or to a comm. Reporting Ward's location.

Ward started in the direction Rivka had gone. He risked a look over his shoulder. The man was following. Ward found a restroom and ducked inside. Its entrance was one of those turn-right-turn-left layouts which opened to a bank of urinals on the right, broken up by two sinks in the middle, and row of stalls on the left. Two men were at the urinals, one on each side of the sinks. Ward caught a look at himself in the mirror. His face was streaked with dirt and a little blood. His jacket was dirty. His shirt was stained, and his trouser pocket was torn. He looked homeless again.

One of the men at the urinals finished and approached the sink. Ward started to back away but stopped himself. He needed to blend in not draw attention to himself. He approached the open sink and splashed some on his face. When he looked at the mirror again, the man he'd seen in the terminal entered the restroom.

What would MacKenzie do?

The answer: *Call me an asshole for not having figured it out already.*

No, she would use the assets the setting gave her. A sparsely populated restroom in an airport on the morning of a terrorist attack. An airport on the verge of breaking out in chaos.

The man beside Ward headed for the exit. The man in the green shirt came up behind Ward, framing himself in the mirror. His hand came up, his sleeve pulling up his wrist. Revealing a mark. A tattoo. A tree, its roots extending beyond the sleeve's reach, its trunk, what little could be seen, entwined with thick vines. Like Zee.

"Bomb!" Ward shouted, hoping the word *bomb* was one Israelis knew in every language.

They did.

The man at the urinal screamed. The man who'd been leaving the bathroom ran. Someone cried out from one of the stalls. The man in the green shirt with the tattoo flinched. It was enough.

Ward flung himself backward, throwing his head back into the tattooed man's face. He felt the crunch of a nose breaking on the back of his skull. The man went down. Ward went with him, leading with an elbow to his chest. Then Ward was up and running.

Outside the restroom, an impromptu perimeter had already been established by a few men and one woman who were keeping the crowds back with outstretched arms, delineating the supposed safe zone rather than forcefully keeping anyone back. Shouts and sirens and the rumble of people running filled the terminal like shockwaves.

Someone pulled at Ward's arm. He spun, ready to fight.

"Did you do this?" Rivka said. She was wearing a headscarf and sunglasses.

"They're here," Ward said.

"You fucked this up."

"He was on me."

"Who?"

"Zee's man. Green shirt. Tattoo on his forearm. He had me cornered in the bathroom. What was I supposed to do?"

"Not shut down the airport."

"I—"

"Didn't think about that, did you?"

He had no answer. He felt like a foster kid again, unable to explain why he thought he should be allowed the final slice of pizza when his foster parents' real son was still at the dinner table, never mind the kid had already eaten three and he'd had only had one.

"Put these one," Rivka said, handing him a gray hat and chrome-rimmed sunglasses.

He did and they crossed the terminal, away from the crowd. She asked where Zee's man was. He scanned the terminal. The crowd. The stores and restaurants. Like before, however, his eyes kept roaming to the televisions.

"Oh no."

"What?" Rivka asked.

He pointed up at the largest television. It no longer displayed dates and locations. Instead, it showed a recording of a large hotel lobby with marble floors and gold trim and a massive chandelier and customers meandering this way and that. A familiar lobby.

"The Consulate," Rivka said.

The video, a security cam feed taken from up high behind the back wall to show the door and everyone entering and leaving, zoomed in and froze on a man in the middle of the lobby. A clear shot of the man beneath the chandelier. Eyes wide. Mouth slightly open.

The image of himself on the screen, ten feet tall, taking in the opulence of the hotel moments after they entered, seconds before Zee pulled him away from the cam's eye, hit Ward like a mule kick.

"We have to leave," Rivka said.

But Ward was frozen like a deer hoping that standing still would keep the bright lights from seeing him. And like a deer, it wasn't working. Already, people in the crowd were turning their direction. First one, then another. Examining him. Up and down. Looking to the television and back, recognition on their faces, but not belief. Not yet. If he moved, however, if he showed life, he was certain confusion and disbelief would become fear. The Tower Terrorist, the boogeyman bomber, was alive in Jerusalem. All it would take was a single step, a small turn of the head, a blink for the crowd to accept it. To split into two factions: one would run; the other would come for him.

Then Rivka was in his face, her mouth pressed to his. Trying to shield him. Trying to embarrass others into looking away. A hard kiss, her hands on his cheeks, like last night. Like a death-row prisoner's last kiss. So out of place in the commotion, Ward thought it might work.

It almost did.

Part of the crowd split off, attention returning to the commotion. The soldiers were coming out of the restroom, one of them waving his arms. All clear. False alarm. No bomb.

We might make it.

Then the Ports came up, held high, angling at the kissing couple. Pressing in for the best photo. The one that would prove the boogeyman was alive.

"Rafael Ward," an accented voice called above the sirens and the shouting. An accusation. Followed by strobe-bursts of other words Ward recognized.

Terrorist.

Bomb.

Kill.

Die.

Rivka broke off the kiss. They were out of options. It was too late to run. Too late to do anything but fight.

The crowd crashed in on them.

CHAPTER 25

"Be ready," Rivka said.

Instinct brought Ward's hand to his belt, but there was no weapon there. The pistol he'd taken at the Consulate was in the backpack he'd lost in the aftermath of the bombing. Not that it mattered. A gun in his hand was a deterrent at best. A club at worst. He wouldn't shoot these people. He wouldn't spill anymore innocent blood.

Rivka shouted in Hebrew, loud enough to carry over the crowd. Heads turned. She shoved Ward. Shouted again, this time pointing at him. The approaching mob hesitated. In it, a face among many, was the tattooed man. Zee's man. Rivka shouted again, putting up her hands as if expecting him to hit her.

Or explode.

He understood. He'd become expendable. His purpose in this operation had been to decipher the Hannibal intel and get them through the quarry. Mission accomplished. He was useless now. A loose end threatening to drag her down. A sacrifice to be made in order for her to escape.

She played me.

Like Compano.

He should have known. He should have seen. They were both military. Both dedicated to their causes. He was a tool, one they'd each used carefully then discarded.

Zee's man was now at the front of the crowd. Ward wondered, with a sense of hilarity, if the man would get him or the crowd. If he would be taken away and executed, or murdered right here in the terminal, torn apart like Caesar or Pizarro.

Only they didn't grab him. Because Rivka wasn't pointing at him. Still shouting in Hebrew, she was pointing past him. At the crowd. At Zee's man. As one, the crowd turned. All but Zee's man. He remained locked on Ward, until Rivka shouted again. Ward understood. She wasn't betraying him. She was aiming the crowd at their enemy. Relief flooded through him. As did guilt for doubting her.

Zee's man understood as well. His eyes widened as those closest to him backed away, leaving him exposed, like a stretch of beach when the sea withdraws before a tidal wave. His hand went to his pocket. Too slow. Too late. The mob hit him, all at once, the tidal wave crashing down. Ward wondered if the people of the Republic would do it like that, if they would turn as one on a threat to protect themselves and their neighbors.

He doubted it. Then the soldiers arrived, seemingly from all directions, and Ward no longer cared about the tattooed man or hypothetical Republic reactions. He and Rivka fled, breaking through the crowd to where it thinned. Here she slipped her arm through his like she wanted him to escort her to the dance floor.

"Quickly," she said.

She led him to the far side of the terminal so they could double back around the crowd to an escalator where they got in a patient line for the ride down. Those in line tottered nervously, but no one pushed or tried to leapfrog ahead. Once they were on the escalator, everyone rode down patiently, staying on their stair. No panic. A city that had known more than thirty bombings in the last five years.

"He'll tell Zee," Ward said.

"We'll be gone."

"We have to come back."

They reached the bottom of the escalator. Rivka checked the signs then started down a concourse to the right.

"They'll open the flights soon," she said. "They don't keep them grounded for fake bomb threats."

"I think he had a gun."

"This is Israel. Everyone has a gun."

Except me, Ward noted. "He'll tell Zee. Once we find the

data, we have to come back here. For Sam," he added, as if she didn't know.

"We'll think of something."

Halfway down the concourse, a service door popped open. A head peered out. Ward slowed.

"This way," Rivka said before he could ask. She dragged him to the door.

A hand appeared below the head as they approached and waved them into a wide corridor. Were it not for the unpolished floor and exposed cabling along the ceiling, it could have been another part of the concourse.

"This is Noam," Rivka said.

Noam was a head taller than Ward. He wore a military style flight jacket and gloves and had the kind of face that seemed not to know how to smile.

"We are to be good for flight," Noam said, almost comically confident in his broken English. He ushered them to the end of the corridor where a door opened to the jetway which took them not to a plane, but to a flight of stairs.

"To run," Noam said.

They did. Down the stairs with Noam in the lead and Rivka bringing up the rear, across the tarmac, between two blue and white airliners, to a hanger barely large enough to be considered a maintenance shed. Inside waited the kind of jet Ward assumed only billionaires and royalty got to enjoy. They boarded quickly into an opulent cabin that made Ward think of the high roller rooms he'd occasionally glimpsed at various casinos.

"Be sit," Noam said before entering the cockpit. "We will takeoff number one when cleared is made for airport."

The cabin presented two rows of seats, doubles on the right and singles on the left. Each seat looked like it might fully recline. In the back third of the cabin, the seats were replaced by a long couch on one side and a full wet bar and two hotel-sized refrigerators on the other. The only thing missing was windows.

"What's with the blackout option?" Ward asked of the oblong slots that had been filled in like the windows of an old South Philly factory.

"The plane belongs to people who value privacy," Rivka said.

"What people?" Ward asked.

"Does it matter?"

Ward wasn't sure, but he wanted to know. He also wanted a drink from the bar and some food from the refrigerators. As if reading his mind, Rivka pulled two sealed trays from the closest fridge.

"Sit," she said.

Ward chose the closest seat to her on the right. The feel of her eyes on him as he got settled made him anxious. Part of him wanted a drink. Part wanted her. He looked up expectantly, ready for her to sit beside him. She maneuvered to the aisle and tossed a tray on the seat next to him and chose a seat on the left three rows up.

Ward watched her get comfortable without ever looking back at him. Disappointed, he went the other direction. To the wet bar. The upper cabinets had glass-inlaid doors making the glasses inside visible. The lower cabinets had solid wood doors, but he knew what was in there. Rum. Vodka. Gin. Whiskey. Maybe even Scotch. His mouth watered and his tongue felt dry. He hadn't wanted a drink this bad since he'd left Spain. He got up. Went to the bar. Put his hand on a lower cabinet knob. Took a heavy breath. Opened an upper cabinet and took out a glass and filled it with water and brought it back to his seat. He opened his tray and ate the surprisingly good turkey sandwich and fruit cup in silence.

Soon the jet's engines began to whine. A moment later the jet lurched forward as they taxied to the runway, a disconcerting motion without windows to see the runway whipping by. Then they were taking off. Almost immediately pressure began building behind Ward's eyes from the pressurized cabin. Soon, he would have a raging headache.

"Is this thing stocked with medicine or anything?" he said.

"Full tactical support," Rivka said after a beat. "Weapons and gear."

"Not what I meant."

"Motion sickness?"

"Migraine."

"Will you take medicine if I give it?"

This time, Ward had to pause before answering. "Why wouldn't I?"

"I saw how you looked at me in the airport. You thought I betrayed you."

"No, I—"

"The small cabinet above the refrigerator," Rivka interrupted.

"Rivka," Ward said, but he couldn't deny what he'd thought. He couldn't explain it away. And she wasn't turning around to hear him out anyway, so he got up, fighting a moment of vertigo, and went to the cabinet. It was full of bottles, dozens of them, all with bilingual labels.

"It's a two-hour flight," Rivka said. "Take the pills and go to sleep."

Ward found a bottle of migraine pills and brought it back to his seat. He took three pills, washing them down with water, and waited to fall asleep, as the doctor had ordered.

CHAPTER 26

The girl stood in the sun, the real sun, arms wide like a lizard trying to warm its blood. Around her, the heat rose off the desert plateau in shimmering waves. In time, however, the warmth became tiresome. Uncomfortable. Like a good idea that didn't live up to expectations. There were canopies nearby, casting shade that might offer relief from the heat, but she didn't want temporary relief. She wanted the coolness she'd left when she'd followed the stairs out into the sun. She wanted the darkness of the caves she'd left below.

She lowered her arms and embraced herself, as if to prove she was real. The cuff on her wrist was warm and coated in a sticky film like drying maple syrup.

Mom used to make pancakes with maple syrup.

Not that she remembered who Mom was or what pancakes looked like or what maple syrup tasted like. If nothing else, though, it was her own voice offering the thought. Not her Other, as she'd begun to think of that deeper-down voice. She could tell the difference, though she couldn't describe it. Other didn't have a different tone or sound. It was just Other.

Why did we do this? she asked Other.

We enjoyed it, Other replied.

She couldn't deny that. Other was usually right, she'd learned in their short time together, which both disturbed and comforted her. Usually, but not always. Other called them *we*, but she knew better. She knew they were separate. Other was a part of her, yes, but Other wasn't her any more than the cuff was her.

A breeze ruffled the papery gown she was still wearing.

Barely. It hung on her, torn and stained dark and stiff the way clothes get when they dry in the sun. Its purpose had been modesty, she understood, but she didn't care so much about that, especially now that there was no one left to see her. She tore it off, the fabric disintegrating into flakes that fluttered away as if they'd never existed. Naked, she embraced herself once more. In time, her hand slid to her belly. To the stitches traversing her abdomen where her pubic hairline should have been. To the stubble covering her flesh there like sandpaper.

What is sandpaper?

Who cut us? Other said.

Once, she thought—in a vague way that was less than words but more than emotions; a way she'd learned her Other couldn't hear—she'd truly been two. Once, she'd had another life in her. A separate life. A potential that was not her and not Other.

We can kill them all, Other said. *Everyone who did this to us.*

"We already did," the girl said aloud because she sometimes liked hearing a voice outside her head.

She looked at her hand, dark with blood. Her arms, too, and her chest and her legs. All covered in blood. If she wiped her palm across her face, it would come away syrupy like the cuff on her wrist.

There are more, Other said. *More who are responsible, but who are not here now.*

The need for more death burst inside the girl like a fountain of strength and adrenaline. She could have sprinted from one end of the plateau to the other and jumped to the desert floor a thousand meters below like a...

What's the word for that thing we're not allowed to say?

The answer came like a wind through dry leaves: *God.*

The word made her cold. It extinguished the fountain. Something inside her uncoiled and rose from her intestines to her heart. The feeling of the blood crusting across her flesh made her want to run, not like a god, but like a child afraid of the shape in her closet. She wanted to no longer be naked. She wanted to no longer be alone.

She wanted to cry.

"What have I done?" she said, her voice so small it evaporated almost as soon as it entered the world. "What did you make me do?"

A bird cawed somewhere, lonely and hoarse.

The need to get the blood off her, confusing and irrational, took over. Frantic, she sought something to wipe herself clean, but there was only sun and sand and stone as far as she could see. There was only one hand. She used it to rub at the blood, but it wouldn't come off. She clawed at it with her fingernails, but the gore remained stubborn. She grabbed a handful of sand and began rubbing.

Sandpaper! She understood it now, as she rubbed handfuls of desert over her flesh until her own fresh blood began to mingle with the dried remains of all the people she'd killed.

Home, Other said, startling her.

Sometimes she thought Other carried on conversations without her, only letting her in on the conclusion.

"What home?" she said. "I don't remember a home."

...home go home go home go home...

"I'm not going anywhere with you. Look what you made me do."

Home!

The force behind that single word was like a sledgehammer inside her skull. It knocked her off her feet, sprawling her out hard on the hot ground. Lying there on the sand, spread out beneath the sun, she began to shiver as if the temperature had dropped to below freezing in a split-second. As if a god had set its finger on her heart to mark her for its coming.

I've done something horrible, she thought. *Something the person I used to be never would have done. Something that deserves to be punished.*

But she didn't know what she'd done. She didn't understand virtue or vice. Discarding her gown and bludgeoning a man to death with her cuff were as indiscernible as drinking water and eating fruit. She only knew she didn't like the blood on her. And that her friend would be disappointed in her.

Friend. She knew that word. She understood it, as if thinking it had made it real.

"I have a friend," she said, liking the way the word felt on her tongue and in her ears.

But who was this friend? And where?

We are our friends, Other said. *We are new. We are free. We need no one else.*

The girl stopped shivering.

"Free?" she asked, that word igniting pleasure in her even more than *friend.*

Free.

There was a change in Other with that word. It felt less... other now. More a part of her. As if she'd accepted it and it had accepted her. She felt as close to whole as she had since she'd opened her eyes to that false sun in the cave below.

Home, Other said, reassuringly.

"Where is home?"

I'll show you.

"Yes," she said, standing. "Show me."

CHAPTER 27

The Chihuahuan Desert, pocked with yuccas, agaves, and tarbush, occupied most of the territory between Fort Stockton and Eagle Pass. To MacKenzie, at a thousand feet and two hundred miles per hour, it could have been the Sahara whipping by below. Aside from blurred and muted greens throughout the otherwise drab landscape, the only features were the Wall to the west and the distant line of retreating Republic forces on their way north from southern Texas, probably to Dallas.

The old Black Hawk helicopter, retrofitted by Horeb's mechanics with salvaged twin e-mag turbines, was tight with a pilot, copilot, MacKenzie, and the kid Lieutenant Porteus had insisted join her when she'd boarded the helo at Fort Stockton.

"The Eye-D you ordered lost contact before reaching Eagle Pass," Porteus had said, standing at the most rigid attention in the command tent outside the town's courthouse. "We can't confirm the Republic's presence in the town, or that of hostile loyalists. Regulations state officers may not enter occupied territory alone."

MacKenzie wasn't familiar with the regulation he was citing. She'd been responsible for establishing Horeb's regs and procedures, but the truth was she'd delegated most of that task to others. The responsibility she'd focused on was her soldiers. She drilled them. She taught them about pain and killing. She drove them to be committed to the revolution and to the Seer. As for regs, she assumed her staff borrowed liberally from the Republic's military standards. It wouldn't surprise her to discover Porteus had been involved in that process. He was a military man through and through. A good soldier. A decent mid-level officer. A total shit-filled waste as a thinker. He followed orders and passed orders on. Armies needed men like him, but MacKenzie preferred they kept their distance from her.

"You're a bit short on personnel here, lieutenant," MacKenzie had said. "Besides, are you suggesting I squeeze a squad into that helo?"

Porteus had looked at the Black Hawk being refueled on the grass in front of the courthouse as if he'd never seen one before. Which he may not have prior to its arrival. The lack of air support was the one deficiency Horeb suffered. They had a few dozen jets and planes and maybe two hundred helicopters, most of them older retrofits like the Black Hawk, stolen from decommissioned yards and civilian service. Less than three percent of the Republic's active equipment. Not enough to spare, but being Horeb's general, even if only in title now, had its advantages. When she asked for a helo—if she asked the right person—she got one.

"No, sir," Porteus had said. "But regulations are clear."

MacKenzie had needed to squeeze her fists until her knuckles cracked to keep from punching Porteus in the jaw for his obstinate allegiance to the regs. Two other soldiers in the tent stood at attention, barely daring to breathe, while a cadet stood dead still practically in mid-stride, a stack of folders in his hand. The cadet, who would be promoted to combat forces on his seventeenth birthday as per Horeb policy, looked unsure if he should stay or run off and never speak of this again.

"I'll take him," MacKenzie said.

"Cadet Bryce?"

"Regulations fulfilled," she said and left the tent.

Cadet Bryce, a baby-faced kid with bright copper eyes matching his skin tone, now sat opposite her in the helo, his back to the cockpit, gripping his harness with one hand and tapping his finger and thumb together the way kids who'd been weaned off Lito did. He looked like he might vomit.

"It gets better," she told him through the headset. Talking in the helo without a headset was impossible, but MacKenzie liked the noise, the way it silenced everything else, allowing her to think without distraction.

"If you say so, sir," Bryce replied.

MacKenzie left him to his terror and watched the Wall pass below like a line drawn across the earth by a drunk god. *Damn you Rafe*, she thought. *Now I'm blaspheming because of you.*

A lie. A comforting one. Like the deafening roar of the helo. Like the Wall.

It was a lie from the start. Sold as a way to protect the Republic, it was never anything more than a delicate bird cage, unable to keep the cat out or the bird in. Now the impenetrable Wall had cracked. Porteus had delivered the news first thing on her arrival in Fort Stockton. After Bravo Company's victories, the Republic had abandoned the entire southern border from the Pacific to El Paso. All central and east Texas forces had been ordered north. The only question was the status of the Wall south of El Paso through Eagle Pass and beyond. She simply couldn't tell from this height at this speed.

The intel Porteus had shared indicated the Republic was setting an east-west line along Route 40, almost three hundred miles north of El Paso. They were expected to try to cut off the Horeb and the south from coast to coast, but MacKenzie thought that was a bit ambitious considering their losses and the disarray that surely had to follow Horeb's lighting strikes throughout the region. Still, that intel had prompted MacKenzie to want to finish her task quicker than she'd initially planned and get back to her soldiers for the assault on El Paso.

Not that she was concerned with losing. Victory was God's will. The Seer had declared it. Providence. Such knowledge should have alleviated the pressure on MacKenzie, but the longer she spent away from her soldiers, the more she doubted her decision to divert resources for this personal task. Was it worth a helo? Was it worth the danger they could be in?

She searched the landscape for hostiles, but there were no signs of Republic stragglers or loyalists. Not that it would be difficult to hide from a single passing helo.

As if he'd been reading her mind, Bryce said, "Should we be flying this low?"

"Intel says the region is clear," she said. A lie. Intel was inconclusive, but there was no need to worry the kid. "In any case, we would see most antiaircraft defenses, they're usually vehicle mounted, and RPGs have a max range of about a thousand feet, so we're good."

He bobbed his head but didn't respond. The pilot added they were flying at eleven hundred feet and they would be approaching Eagle Pass in ten minutes. MacKenzie looked ahead to the vertical lines and pink haze of small city on the horizon before letting her mind drift back to the loyalist problem.

They'd planned for it, but seeing them in action, like in the fried chicken restaurant, was different. They fought for the Republic, the very government that oppressed them, with an almost religious fervor that the Republic regulars didn't express. Regulars surrendered—there were over four thousand Republic prisoners at Nogales alone—but all reports said loyalists did not. Ever.

Would they stop fighting when the revolution was over? Were they capable of understanding the irony of being willing to die for their belief in the Republic while claiming Faith was an unforgiveable vice?

Where would Rafe fall on a spectrum between Believer and loyalist?

She hated that he'd hijacked her thoughts again, but she let her mind run all the way back to the last time she was in Texas. He'd been in the front seat while MacKenzie and Sam had sat in the back, Sam whispering her concerns about Rafe. Was he insane? Could he really help her? Was he trustworthy?

MacKenzie knew Rafe could hear them, at least a little. She didn't lie. He was a good man. His word was worth something. He wasn't perfect, but his intentions, she'd told Sam, tended to be in the right place.

That was all before, however. Something had changed in him. Because of the Tower. Because of Sam.

Because of me?

No. It was on him. He never had real Faith. He was a good man, but he was a Godless man. Which meant he was vulnerable. That was why the Seer had wanted him to be the symbol of the revolution once upon a time, she guessed. His vulnerability represented the population of the Republic. In Rafe, they might see one of their own, even as they hated and feared him for what he'd done in Philadelphia, destroying the Tower and killing those hundreds of Citizens.

Compared to how many I've killed?

All the more reason to see the Grossmutter. The need to tell her about Oren's death was there, as was the excuse that she should hear it from someone who knew him, but more than that MacKenzie wanted a kind voice to tell her she was still doing God's work. Doubt had found her because of Rafe, and she feared only the Grossmutter could cure it. Like a priest taking confession.

Once, it would have been the Seer she went to, but that was before Spain. That was before he'd offered to put her back in the field.

I'm a fucking mess.

This doubt would get her killed. She was still the Seer's chosen. She was still doing God's work, simply on a smaller scale. She was a soldier now, not the General. She didn't have to singlehandedly bring Faith back to the Republic. She would fight like a soldier. She would kill like a soldier. And when it was all over, she would retire like a soldier. Find somewhere quiet and warm and devote herself to God's word.

This was a recent development in her plans for the post-war world. She'd long refused to think about life after the war. Somewhere in the last few weeks, however, she'd begun wondering about the possibility someone like her could have a peaceful life, maybe even a family, in the aftermath. She knew it was at least a half-foolish fantasy. Soldiers like her needed to serve as much as they were needed. But maybe, she'd begun telling herself, her service could be to God. Not the Seer. Not the army. To God and God alone.

Like the kid, who didn't have to worry about the war strategy or governance. As a cadet, he only had to worry about the small tasks afforded him, yet he did so with a certain gravity she didn't find in many other cadets or even soldiers. He seemed to understand that even apparently inconsequential actions were bricks in the foundation of God's returning glory. He was a good kid. She liked him and his stoic way of dealing with his discomfort in the helo. He would make an excellent soldier. In time, he would make a far better officer than Porteus.

"Five minutes," the pilot said.

The plan was to land on the Mexican side of the Wall and cross the border in a vehicle Graciela had arranged. As the pilot steered them to the Wall, MacKenzie and Bryce were turned momentarily perpendicular to Eagle Pass. What struck MacKenzie was the haze. It was like looking at a sunset glare through dark sunglasses.

"Sir?" Bryce said.

MacKenzie ignored him. "Pilot, are you seeing this?"

"Yes, sir," the pilot's voice crackled in her headset.

The pilot brought them around perpendicular again. There was no doubt. Eagle Pass was burning.

CHAPTER 28

Someone was coming.

The girl didn't need eyes or ears to know. She was aware of it the way birds were aware of a coming storm. The way magnets were aware of nearby iron.

She had the impression—not a memory exactly; more a perception or vague knowledge—she would have once been scared by her awareness of the coming stranger. She had the impression she was once scared of the dark. Neither of these impressions were true now. She awaited the stranger with curiosity. She sat cross-legged in the dark in complete comfort. She had confidence Other would protect her.

Other had brought her here through tunnels devoid of light. Other had guided her, step by step, until she began to see in a pale grayscale. Then Other simply told her which tunnel to take when there was a choice. Other was better than a flashlight or hand holding hers. Other was more reliable than a person. Other couldn't get lost. Other couldn't abandon her or be killed. Other was inside her, safe and powerful and empowering. Like a baby.

Other had led her deep into the mountain, finding their way like a dog tracking a scent. The girl had the impression she liked dogs.

Dogs are loyal, she'd thought.

We are loyal! Other had insisted with such force the girl had lost her footing.

She'd sent her thoughts then to that abstract place Other didn't seem able to hear. It was a place of impressions and bits of memory like the flakes of her gown floating away. One of those memories was warmth, like two bodies cradled together. It was a warmth similar to what she felt when Other spoke to her. Protective and needing and prodding and...furry?

Other had interrupted to instruct her to squeeze through a narrow crevice she would have otherwise never seen. She'd done so, pushing into more tunnels. It seemed they were endless. Not like above. Not like the corridors where the bodies lay. Those were smooth and worn. These were rough and not well-traveled. These were older, but someone had been here recently. She knew it because Other knew it. Other smelled it.

Eventually, she'd entered a cavern much larger than any of the rooms and caves and cisterns above. She couldn't see the far end. She couldn't see the ceiling. She couldn't see the walls to the sides. They could have been on the dark side of a planet for how vast the cavern was, the only planet in a solar system whose sun had died, leaving nothing behind but the memory of light.

Yet, despite the expansiveness, the girl had felt embraced by this cavern. A part of it like a drop of water in an ocean. *This* darkness was made for her. *This* cavern had been waiting for her. *This* was home.

Home, Other had said.

It sure felt like it, not that she remembered a specific home. Only an impression of what home was. She found a wall and walked the perimeter of the cavern before discovering a place to sit next to a small mound of old things. Debris. Strips of cloth. Pieces of steel. Bones. Death. Ancient forgotten death.

Home, Other had said again.

Golgotha, she'd thought despite not knowing the word or what it meant. Only that it fit this place and her and Other.

"What do we do now?" she'd asked.

Other hadn't answered.

"Why did you bring us here?"

Other had retreated the way the girl sometimes did. She wasn't fully alone, but neither was Other close. So, she waited, comfortable among the debris of ancient death.

Until now. Someone was coming. For the first time she became aware of her nakedness as a vulnerability. Not shame for her body, but the lack of protection her flesh offered against attack. She got to her feet and surprised herself by raising her nose and sniffing at the air, as if that might tell her who was coming. It didn't. She smelled only dust and disuse and the cuff on her wrist. The strength of its carbonous metallic scent surprised her. She hadn't smelled it before. Now she almost couldn't ignore it.

Flee, Other said, breaking their silence and startling the girl.

"You said home was safe."

Flee!

A route filled the girl's mind, as if it had been uploaded to her consciousness.

What is upload?

A darkness entered the cavern from the same direction the girl had come, like a shadow wrapped in more shadow.

Too late, Other said. *We must kill.*

Above, when she'd been threatened, the girl had listened to Other and killed. Now, however, she waited. Someone was coming for her. Was being drawn to her. She wanted to know who. And why. She held her ground.

"Who are you?" she asked.

The newcomer, with a voice as artificial as the cuff on the girl's wrist, said, "You don't remember?"

It was too dark to see who'd spoken, but the girl got the impression the stranger was larger than the people she'd killed in the caves above.

"I am...new," she said. "Who are you?"

The newcomer said, "A friend."

CHAPTER 29

The vehicle Graciela had arranged was a crew cab pickup truck with steel planks welded to the sides and front with cutouts for navigation. The rear was covered in smaller planks which gave access to a belt-fed machine gun mounted to the truck bed. It was stocked with assorted small arms and ordnance in the back seat.

At first glance, it struck MacKenzie as an insult that this ridiculous jumble of parts was the best Graciela would offer. Then she noted the machine gun was a Republic model decommissioned more than ten years ago. Closer examination revealed the truck was also obsolete—a Republic Motors vehicle at least forty years old that ran on gasoline.

She understood. It wasn't an insult. It likely was the best the troops here could offer. Old Mexico had been an oppressed vassal nation so long, it didn't have its own military equipment any more than Horeb did. They made do. They scavenged. They stole. They bought obsolete weapons and supplies from the very government which erected the Wall and prompted the economic tailspin that had destroyed their own infrastructure.

The revolution was theirs as much as it was Horeb's. If Horeb was the Republic's pet, a dog to be put down because it snapped at its owner's hand, Old Mexico was the feral cat begging for scraps at the back door. Ever unfed. Ever ignored. That would be the Republic's downfall. The feral cat had found a way inside and was working with the angry dog.

Thinking of dogs made MacKenzie want to get moving. The sergeant who'd given her the keys to the truck offered three soldiers to accompany them over the Wall, but MacKenzie declined.

"It is not safe," the sergeant said, his English deliberate but confident.

Nothing ever is, MacKenzie thought.

"But the fires are to the north, correct?" she asked.

"*Sí.*"

Which meant the Grossmutter's house had likely been spared. "Are there Republic troops?"

"No."

"Loyalists?"

"*República patriotas?* No."

"Then we're good."

She gave Bryce the keys. He looked at them uncertainly in his hand as if they might bite.

"Can you drive?"

"Yes, sir."

"Then drive."

He did, quickly and adeptly, taking them across the Rio Grande on a makeshift bridge erected over the remains of a portion of the Wall, not far from where Oren had shown them the structure on MacKenzie's first visit. On the other side, they entered a city on fire like a nightmare parody of the Eagle Pass she remembered.

How is it possible it's not even been half a year?

She directed Bryce to drive a few blocks up the street parallel to the Wall before turning into town. The buildings on either side of each street were either actively on fire or smoldering ruins. No more than one or two per block remained relatively intact, but even these had broken windows and were spotted with bullet holes. They saw no movement. No signs of survivors. No indications of active loyalists.

"We can't see who might be hiding out there," MacKenzie said. "We're a rolling target in this thing. Pull over." She didn't add it was hot as fuck in the truck and she wanted to get out.

Bryce rolled two wheels up on the curb in front of a blackened shell of a house that might have once been brick. Charred ceramic tiles spoke of a Spanish style roof. MacKenzie got out and peered into the ruins as the smell of Eagle Pass hit her hard, as if the entire city had gotten together for a bonfire and decided to burn all of the town's plastics and used tires in addition to wood and a few hundred rodents. She coughed and wiped at her eyes. Seeing no threats in the ruins or up and down the block, she moved to the driver's side as Bryce was opening the door.

"Stay in the car," she told him.

"My orders are to stay with you, sir," Bryce said.

"You're going to keep me safe?"

His cheeks flushed. His feet dangled above the ground.

"Who gave your orders?" MacKenzie asked.

"Lieutenant Porteus, sir."

"Is Lieutenant Porteus a general?"

"What?"

"Is Lieutenant Porteus a general?"

"No," Bryce said, clearly confused by the question. Then, getting it, he said more firmly, "No, sir."

"Stay in the fucking car."

He pulled his legs back in the truck and MacKenzie closed the door. From the back seat she chose an RT 5.56mm assault rifle, preferring the balance of the full weapon to the urban assault bullpup rifle next to it. She added a second RT40 pistol to her current sidearm, holstering it to the opposite hip, plus a radio and a bag full of ammo, grenades, and gear.

"Turn the truck so it's facing the river," she told Bryce, "Keep it running and keep the radio on. If shit goes down, speed your ass back to the bridge. Got it?"

"Yes, sir."

She hiked up the street, covering two blocks before stopping to analyze the damage. One house burned to the ground beside one with only a broken bay window behind another whose southern wall had been blown apart. East of her position, nearly a full block of storefronts sat undamaged and unoccupied, their doors swinging open. She headed that way, only to find a pile of smoking rubble a block long.

This was no airstrike or organized assault, she understood. It was a battle. Street to street and house to house. The silence of the town made it feel like an extermination. There were no engines humming. No voices calling for help. No birds chirping or dogs barking. There was only destruction and fire and heat and smoke.

She kept going another block deeper into town, able to envision what had happened here as clearly as if she'd been watching it on an Eye-D feed. When news of the Nogales victory overwhelmed the censors and made its way to the public, Believers took to the streets, armed with hunting rifles and baseball bats. Thinking they could intimidate the soldiers who'd been occupying the town since the Wall was built. Thinking they could join the revolution for freedom and bring Horeb to Eagle Pass to back them up. Thinking they were ready for a fight.

The Eagle Pass police department came out first. There was a tense showdown, probably near where Bryce sat in the pickup, sweating and waiting like a good soldier. Someone got pushy. Maybe a Believer threw a rock. Maybe a police officer jabbed too hard with a stun baton. The clash grew larger and louder. It began to boil. The Wall commander sent down a squad of troops with orders to end the discord. Another rock was thrown. Or another stun baton was jabbed, this one catching a Believer—an Eagle Pass resident; a neighbor and a friend—in the throat or the eye. Someone struck back. It was only a matter of time now. Some residents understood and fled. Some cops hesitated. Then someone swung a shovel or fired a shot.

And the soldiers did what soldiers do.

They cut down the first line of residents in a matter of second. The rest fled. The soldiers gave chase. There was no rational voice from the Wall trying to end it before it got worse. There was no instinct in the troopers to contain the traitors. They went house to house, punishing the innocents who cowered behind their walls of stucco and OSB with salvo after salvo, slaughtering them as they hugged each other and wept and prayed. But it was taking too long. The Republic commander determined a full assault would be more prudent. A better deterrent. Maybe the orders had already come through for them to abandon the Wall and they thought they had nothing to lose. Maybe they simply wanted to use their heavy arms and artillery before packing everything up. Either way, they stopped worrying about individuals and began targeting the homes and stores where people hid.

They were ruthless. They were efficient.

They did what I would have done.

Without realizing she was doing it, MacKenzie began stalking up the street, her weapon to her shoulder, looking for someone to shoot. Someone to blame. Someone to kill. No survivors. No bodies. The only remains were strewn about the streets and lawns and parking lots. A shovel lying against the curb. A pistol shell on the crown of the street. A pile of rifle shells in a pothole. A finger in the grass. Blood in drops and splatters and pools.

Sound spun MacKenzie to the left. She faced a mostly intact laundromat. She sighted each machine with her rifle. Heard the sound again. The soft padding of a careful step, maybe. She approached the door from an angle and kicked it open. No one came at her. Nothing scurried off. Inside was a mess of broken machines, shell casings, and a small fire dying away in a trash bin. She waited until she was sure it was either a weasel or an armadillo or some other small and frightened animal before backing out of the laundromat and continuing up the street.

The eerie silence, and lack of human remains, made her think, somewhat inexplicably, of the Alamo a hundred and fifty miles to the northeast. *Remember the Alamo,* the tourist placard had said, a battle cry echoed by Reclamationists during their war to kill God and Believers alike. It wouldn't be long until Horeb was shouting *Remember Eagle Pass.*

What the Republic did here would only strengthen Horeb. It would make recruiting easier, but this fact didn't assuage her anguish at marching through this destruction. Nor did it explain what happened next, after the full assault. The Believers would have seen what was happening. They would have known they couldn't hide or flee into the desert. They would have gone on the offensive. They must have. They were fighting for their lives. For their souls. They may not have been trained soldiers, but they were the Seer's people. They were God's people. Surely, they would have fought back. Surely the Mexicans would have joined the battle. Surely, once the Republic ordered their troops north, the survivors of Eagle Pass would have begun to rebuild. So, where they?

There were no faces peering out from the rubble. No curtains being frantically drawn. It was as if once the battle had ended, both sides had decided there was no reason to stay. So, where did they go? The caravan moving north she'd seen from the helo had been troops. It was too big and too orderly to have been refugees. Plus, a quick count of smoldering vehicles on the streets she'd seen so far indicated there'd been no mass exodus.

"Something's wrong," she muttered, the sound of her voice swallowed by the crackling and hissing fires around her.

Only one of the hisses wasn't the fire. It was more intentional. Alive. MacKenzie hurried across the street to a smoking husk of a home, its remaining façade grinning like a charred skull. She crouched at what had once been the front porch. She touched her fingers to the soot and brought them to her nose. A flamethrower, no doubt.

She sought motion in the ruins, but there was only stillness. She listened for the sound she'd heard, but there was nothing...

There! She spun, rifle up, to the wreck of a house next door. Had it been a footstep? A rat in the rubble? A bird fluttering?

She crept closer, hearing it now the way a slight breeze becomes audible if you listen carefully enough. Breathing. Small and labored. Cautious. Withdrawing.

MacKenzie followed the sound, to the right and up the street. It stayed always within the ruins, from building to building. She tracked it carefully, a few feet then stopping to find it again. Blocking out everything else and focusing on the sound alone as it led her into town.

She reached an intersection. Whatever was breathing in the ruins would have to come into the open if it was going to continue this direction. MacKenzie noted where they were. Two blocks from the Grossmutter's house. She wanted to go—she *needed* to go—to the old woman, but she couldn't turn her back on the sound. She was a soldier. She wouldn't expose herself. Discipline led to survival. Impulse led to surprises and ambushes and death. But she couldn't just stand here all day waiting. She approached the damaged house on the corner where she'd last heard the sound.

A coyote, dirty and thin, burst from the rubble. MacKenzie crouched, all instinct, her rifle to her cheek as she sighted the thing. She almost pulled the trigger. She wanted so badly to shoot something, anything, that she almost tore the animal in half with a three-round burst at over three-thousand feet per second. Her trigger finger twitched but didn't squeeze. She lowered her weapon and watched the thing go. Near the next intersection, it stopped and turned. As if waiting for MacKenzie. Beckoning her to follow.

She did, slowly at first, for no other reason other than the mangy animal was heading in the direction of the Grossmutter's house. She expected it to take off, or to charge her, but it never did, keeping a slow enough pace for her to follow. At a quarter block distance, it whined. At a dozen paces, it sneezed. If she didn't know any better, MacKenzie would have thought it was smiling at her. Like it had been waiting for her. Like it knew her.

MacKenzie looked at the beast again. At its soot-covered legs. Its matted and dirty coat. Its ribs showing. Its yellowed fangs. Its collar.

"Reina?"

The dog—Sam's dog—barked and trotted to MacKenzie's and nuzzled her thigh. MacKenzie dropped her hand to its head. It—*she*—whined happily. MacKenzie marveled at the dog, almost unwilling to believe both that it survived and that it remembered her.

"What happened here, Reina?"

The dog nuzzled harder.

"You miss Sam, eh?"

Reina barked then howled. She looked like she'd been sleeping in the ashes and ruins for a month. MacKenzie imagined her lapping at soiled water and eating charred rat corpses.

"Come one, girl. Let's go find the Grossmutter."

Reina yipped then took off down the street at a loping pace MacKenzie could follow, taking her straight to the Grossmutter's house. MacKenzie recognized it immediately. Most of the homes on its block had been damaged or even demolished, but the Grossmutter's was standing defiantly, despite a number of bullet holes in the walls and most of the windows broken and the grass out front charred.

"Grossmutter," MacKenzie shouted, forgetting the need for stealth.

She started to the house, but Reina blocked her way. The dog rubbed her head against MacKenzie's thigh until she received the ear scratch she was looking for. MacKenzie had never had a pet, and she'd found Reina mostly a distraction when she'd first met her. She was a child's companion, nothing more, but the simple act of rubbing the dog's head seemed to lower her heart rate. It was almost like the gentle petting created an outlet for the tension that had been building in MacKenzie since she'd heard about the bombing in Jerusalem. Since Spain. Hell, since as long as she could remember.

Maybe I'll get a dog after the war when I retire.

"Stay here," MacKenzie said.

Reina plopped down. Halfway to the door, MacKenzie looked back. Reina was still sitting on her haunches, watching her the way Bryce had watched her she left him in the truck.

MacKenzie looked through the glassless front window. The house appeared empty. She tried the door. It was unlocked. She slipped inside to a dark foyer which led to a dark parlor.

"Grossmutter," she called. "Hello?"

The echo of her voice confirmed what she'd already intuited: no one was here. At least, no one alive. There was, however, a hint of home cooking in the air, though it was faded and stale. She cycled room to room, her stomach fluttering with each door she opened, afraid she would discover the old woman's corpse, but there was no one here. She entered the kitchen last and took a moment to stock her pack with some dog food and treats, a couple water bottles, and a leash she found by the back door.

Outside, Reina waited patiently. MacKenzie gave her one of the bone-shaped treats. Reina yipped cheerfully as she munched on it.

"Where'd she go, Reina?"

The dog was too busy chewing to answer, bobbing her head up and down with each crunch of the treat. Then she stopped and cocked her head toward the end of the street.

"Hear something?" MacKenzie said. Then she heard it too. A car approaching from the north. She took cover by the porch, Reina following without missing a chew, and lined up her sights on the street.

A moment later the vehicle she'd heard came into view. There was no mistaking the armored truck. MacKenzie strode into the middle of the street and waited for Bryce to pull up beside her and open his door.

"I told you to stay put, soldier," she said.

"Yes, sir," Bryce replied without hesitation. Or fear.

"And?"

"I saw that," he pointed at a flock of large black birds circling to the northwest, a mile or two away perhaps, "and thought with all the fires and signs of battle it was weird they were only over that part of town."

How did I miss that?

Despite her disappointment in herself, and in Bryce's inability to follow directions, MacKenzie had to admit the kid's initiative and instincts were impressive.

"I drove through that side of town before coming to find you," Bryce continued. "I think you should see what's out there."

"You should have asked permission to leave your post," MacKenzie said, knowing learning the lesson was as important as the kid's intuition. "If you ever disobey me again, I'll have you whipped then placed on lifetime latrine duty."

Bryce flinched but didn't back down. "Understood, sir, but you need to see this."

"You need to learn discipline or you're no use to Horeb."

"Sir!"

She almost put him on his ass and taught him about insubordination right there in the middle of the street, but the look on his face told her discipline could wait.

"Enemies?" she asked.

"Please, sir."

Now MacKenzie's intuition was screaming at her. They

piled into the truck, with Reina fighting for the front seat. MacKenzie finally shoved her into the back as Bryce drove up on the Grossmutter's lawn to make a U-turn and drove them north then west. In a few minutes, they neared a school. A few dozen pickups and a handful of cars filled the school's parking lot, along with three school busses. Two of the buses had been so badly charred no hint of yellow remained.

The parking lot wrapped around the school building to an immense field. Dozens of birds circled above like the mouth of a whirlpool seen from below, plus close to the same number hopping about in the field. Vultures. MacKenzie opened the door. She braced for Reina to go bounding into the field, scattering the birds, but the dog stayed by the truck and only offered a little whimper.

"Did you go see?" she asked.

"Yes, sir," Bryce said, his voice shaky.

"Stay here."

He did. She crossed a small line of bushes denoting the edge of the parking lot, Reina a few paces behind, and took in the sight.

"God help us," she whispered.

They'd fallen in rows where they'd been shot. Where they'd been lined up, like targets, their backs to their executioners. Thousands of them. Maybe tens of thousands. The entire town, as far as MacKenzie could tell, Believers and loyalists alike. Everyone who wasn't approved to evac north with the troops. They were probably brought here with the promise of a refugee shelter in the school. They were probably lined up in the field for a role call or a soup line.

MacKenzie knew death. She knew combat and retribution and rage. This was different. This was slaughter. This was evil.

She expected to feel thunderous fury, a driving need to set upon those responsible the purging hand of fire and vengeance, but she didn't. She was empty. As if someone had scooped out her guts and left her a hollow shell.

She became aware Reina was whining some rows over. She picked her way through the corpses, trying not to step on them, the smell of decay and blood pluming each time she did. They were two days dead, she guessed. Maybe three. The vultures had done their work on many of them, plucking away the clothes and flesh to get at backs and buttocks and thighs, but so many remained untouched.

Reina was pawing a corpse the birds had not yet gotten to. MacKenzie had never wanted to do anything less than what she was about to do. With shaking hands, she rolled the body over. The Grossmutter looked up at her, eyes open, face arranged in an expression that might have been contentment. Reina whined. MacKenzie placed a hand on the dog's neck, needing to feel her warmth.

Together, she and Reina cried.

PART 3: THE FIRE AND THE SWORD

…there sprang a new band of outlaws, called Sicarii, who slew the enemies of the Zealots in the day as well as in the night.
—The History of the Jewish War Against the Romans,
  by Flavius Josephus, c. 75

Vowed Hannibal: I shall pursue Rome with the fire and the sword which felled Troy, and neither gods nor treaties shall still my blade. This I swear by the war god and the shade of Dido, my queen.
—Punica, by Silius Italicus, c. 90

Are not half our lives spent in reproaches for foregone actions, of the true nature and consequences of which we were wholly ignorant at the time?
—Mardi: And a Voyage Thither, by Herman Melville, 1849

CHAPTER 30

The flight to Turkey was quick and smooth. Rivka napped most of the way. Ward tried to, his leather jacket rolled up behind his head for a pillow, but each time he closed his eyes, he saw the aftermath of the bomb in Jerusalem. He saw his face on the monitors. He saw his guilt in the minds of every person in the world. It didn't matter that he didn't do it. The media said he did it; therefore, despite not hurting anyone, he did it. Perception was truth. Add a couple hundred more to his body count.

He finally began to drift not long before the sound of the landing gear lowering woke announced their approach. He thought maybe he'd dreamed of MacKenzie in that flat in Spain. The way she'd attacked him. Driven him to the bedroom. All while the museum usher was tied up and scared for his life in the other room.

Looks like I have a type, he thought.

But Rivka was a doctor not a killer. Yes, she was assertive, even rough, in bed, like MacKenzie, but so what? She wasn't the type to assassinate non-Believers or robotically slaughter police who were trying to flee. Her intensity and drive were assets not flaws. She would stop at nothing to find that data and save Sam.

She'll leave me, in the end, he thought as they touched down, a self-delusion he found more comfortable than the truth: the people he loved didn't leave him. He betrayed them. His mother, his brother, MacKenzie, Sam, even Compano and Ken Hickey. He'd betrayed them all. Let them all down. It was the only constant thread in his life, aside from running down these ridiculous puzzles and mysteries whose only purpose seemed to torture him.

How many times could Sherlock Holmes find himself in a locked-room mystery before he began to suspect there was something about him that invited the circumstance? How many times could Hercule Poirot gather a lineup of suspects before he wondered why the universe kept placing him near such convoluted crimes? They were characters, puppets whose strings were manipulated by authors who never let them, for all their insights, understand they were locked into a pattern.

Ward didn't have that problem. He understood his pattern. Crisis. Puzzle. Betrayal. He reported his mother to the REC. He let Oren get shot. He broke his promise to Sam, letting Ker take her, and cut her hand off, and all but kill her. He stunned MacKenzie and tied her up. Ken was just doing his job, and Ward stabbed him in the chest with a two-thousand-year-old spear tip. He shot Compano in the face.

Rafael Ward. Tower Terrorist. Betrayer of friends and lovers.

The only question was how long until he found himself in a situation that required him to turn on Rivka too.

They taxied a while before Noam appeared in the cabin to open the door. They'd parked in a small, otherwise empty, hanger. As when they boarded, there was a mobile stairway waiting. Rivka and Noam exchanged a few words—directions to the tomb, Ward assumed—before Rivka gathered two bags from the back of the plane and descended the stairs to a nondescript black sedan waiting for them, its engine humming quietly, inside the small hanger. She put both bags in the trunk, which also contained a large case, and got in the driver side as if their roles were defined and beyond questioning.

Gebze could have been any European city of modest socioeconomics. The area around the airport looked much like Philly near its airport. The closer they got to the university, the nicer the buildings became and the less they saw of graffiti and trash along the curb. It was a relatively short drive, the roads clearly marked. There were no secret codes to follow. The street signs tended to be bi- or even trilingual, each offering directions in Turkish plus one or more of Arabic, English, and Kurdish dialect Ward didn't recognize.

"What will we find there?" Rivka asked as they passed a

sign which said: *Hannibal's Tomb 25 kilometers.*

"A monument of some sort," Ward offered, though he wasn't certain at all. "Maybe a mausoleum. If it's the latter, I assume we'll need to find a way inside, or into the crypt beneath."

It was the first they'd spoken since they were in the air. In fact, they hadn't spoken much at all since they had sex. Logistics. Directions. History. Orders. But not talk. Not a discussion.

"If it's not a mausoleum?"

"I don't know."

Silence for a time. Then a sign directing them south: *Hannibal's Tomb 10 kilometers.*

Ward asked, "Are we looking for a storage locker of some sort? A cache of data bars? Or are we talking a military base with armed guards?"

"A cache or depot," she said.

"You're sure?"

"If you doubt me, why ask?"

Ward wanted to say it was himself he doubted, but the way she snapped at him, he wondered if she wasn't suffering from the same uncertainty.

"I don't doubt you," he said. "I just don't want to make another mistake. We can't afford to waste the time. Sam can't afford it."

"We'll hope for a depot but plan for armed resistance."

"Okay."

Neither spoke until the next sign: *Hannibal's Tomb Entrance.* They turned in.

"It wasn't always a university," Rivka said, craning her neck to read the rest of the sign as they drove beneath it. "It used to be the Turkish Aerospace Research Institute."

"Odd place for a memorial," Ward said. "Maybe not for a secret military base or intel cache, though."

Rivka grunted her agreement as they drove down the narrow lane bisecting a sprawling green of manicured grass. Beyond the grass stood tall trees, like pillars, in the kinds of rows nature didn't bother with. Here and there, pockets of people lounged or strolled or played catch on the grass. It was a scene Ward knew well. A college quad. Which only increased his apprehension.

Was the data they were after part of an aerospace project?
Was the Turkish government somehow a part of all this?
Was the college a cover?
Would they find beekeepers on campus?
Or was the presence of the tomb here a coincidence?

Ahead, the narrow road terminated in a square parking lot which offered four walking paths back out in the four cardinal directions. A sign posted at the lot's entrance indicated the east path would lead to the tomb.

"Full gear," Rivka said.

"It's a college," Ward said, blanching at the idea of himself stalking onto a university campus in full tactical gear. "We should blend in, not look like an assault team trying to scare the kids off."

Rivka thought on it then agreed. They went with their packs and pistols, which they each concealed under their shirts. It was a quick hike to where the path broke through the trees and the scenery opened up to a familiar college tableau: students congregating, lazing about, flirting, playing catch, and studying in the shade. Intermingled were obvious tourists snapping photos of the monument in the middle of the field, which was not what Ward expected.

The monument was a massive boulder set in the middle of perfectly manicured circle of grass like the hub of a giant sun dial.

"I don't think this is it," Rivka said.

"Maybe that's the point."

The memorial, they discovered as they approached, consisted of a carving of Hannibal's face on the side of the boulder, and an epitaph carved in five different languages—Turkish, Arabic, French, German, and English—onto a large stone block nearby.

"I'll go this way," Ward said, indicating the stone block.

He walked around the block, pausing occasionally to make sure he didn't end up accidently in the background of someone's family photo. There were no access panels at the base or in the grass nearby, so he settled for reading the epitaph. He examined the English and French, noting they told the exact same story of Hannibal's military prowess and victories. Using them as a primer, he began looking over the Turkish in an attempt to pick up some vocabulary.

Rivka appeared at his side when he was halfway through. "I see nothing about the monument that looks like a tomb," she said. "Maybe we translated incorrectly."

"No, I think we're just missing something."

"*Ken.* A better idea."

Ward broke off his examination of the inscription and headed for the boulder, walking a clockwise circle around it while thinking over the two lines of intel that had brought them here. No matter how he tried to twist them, however, he could decipher no new meanings in those ten words. When he came back to Rivka, a trio of tourists, two women, one in a purple hat, and a man in a tan vest, were taking turns photographing each other kissing Hannibal's face.

A better idea occurred to him.

"Do you speak Turkish?" he asked Rivka.

"A little."

"Good enough. Find me a Port."

"To steal?"

"Borrow. Tell someone ours is broken and we need to look up how to get to our hotel."

Rivka scanned the crowds and homed in on the woman in the purple hat. A minute later, she had the woman's Port in hand, with the woman following close behind.

"Now what?"

"Does she speak English?" Ward asked.

"I don't think so."

"Okay. There has to be a reason they chose this spot for the monument, right? And there had to be a reason the intel brought us here. Pull up a map of the area."

Rivka did so, showing Ward a road map of the campus in grays and whites.

"No, we need a satellite image," he said. "Or a shot from a plane. Anything overhead."

Rivka kept working on the Port while the woman in the purple hat hovered nearby.

"Here," Rivka said.

The screen was centered on the clearing where they stood. Around them spread a halo of green, the trees, and beyond them the campus itself. He zoomed in as much as he could, sliding the screen a centimeter at a time.

"What are you looking for?" Rivka asked.

He didn't know, but he kept at it, examining every square meter of the campus for some indication of another structure or tunnel or stairs or depression or sink hole. There was nothing.

"Forget it," he said. "Give this back."

She returned the Port to its owner, her body language shouting about disappointment and frustration. He couldn't blame her even as he wanted to defend his choice to come here. It was the best starting point. The only definitive location. But without the ability to see underground, the best they could do is get shovels and start digging.

"We don't happen to have ground-penetrating radar in the case in the car, do we?" he asked.

"*Ken*, but in a field this large it would days to properly grid search."

"What about night optics?"

"We don't have time to wait for night."

"No, the kind of optics I've seen work on infrared and other spectrums. On the right setting they should be able to see a structure or a void in the ground."

"Like a tomb," Rivka finished.

She took off for the parking lot while Ward was still working through the possibilities his idea could work. He caught up to her at the car as she was opening the case in the trunk. It was stocked with guns, ammo, explosives, helmets, and more, including a couple shovels and some other gear Ward didn't recognize. Rivka rummaged around in the case, coming up with a set of optics that looked like expensive, albeit bulky and uncomfortable, sunglasses. They returned to the monument where Rivka put on the optics and rotated a full circle.

"I don't see anything," she said. "You try."

Ward put them on and examined the boulder in the circle in fields of greens, blues, and reds. He was no expert on interpreting the optics, but he saw nothing to indicate a space below them to house a secret tomb.

"Maybe I was wrong," he said, still examining their surroundings. "Maybe it's one of the other hundred or so tombs of Hannibal."

"Or the intel is wrong," Rivka said. "Or the translation."

"Translation?" Ward pulled off the optics. She'd said translation a moment ago as well, but it hadn't registered.

"*Ken.* The honey bee part was Greek," she said, as if he should have known all along. "The part about Hannibal was—what was the name—Phili...no, Phoenician."

"Phoenician! Are you sure?"

"*Ken*, he said Phoenician. What is it?"

Ward backed away, needing to shut her out. To separate his mind from the distractions of the crowd and the monument and the doctor.

"Rafael," she prompted.

He shushed her and paged through his mind, looking for those pieces of obscure research he'd so loved finding in graduate school.

"Lamented in death," he recited. "Here lies Hannibal, the Barca."

"You know it?"

"I never would have thought of it except for knowing it's a translation. It's totally obscure. A one-off theory by a Scottish historian who wrote an essay in the early nineteenth century about a Phoenician inscription he claimed was the epitaph of Hannibal Barca. No one believed him, though. I only found the article by accident in a grad school archive. The epitaph was uncovered during construction near an old fort on Malta."

"Malta," Rivka said, sounding both impressed and unsure. "Why so far?"

"It wasn't far, not really. According to one version of Hannibal's life, he was born on Malta. Plus, it was a Carthaginian territory, on and off, in the third and fourth centuries BCE. That historian, Sir Walter Drummond, argued someone discovered Hannibal's remains sometime in the first millennium, probably right near here where he supposedly committed suicide, and that person then brought the remains to Malta to lay Hannibal to rest in his own soil. Plus, and here's the best part, you said the honey bee piece of the intel was translated from Greek, right? Well, the Greeks called the island of Malta *Melitē*, meaning honey or honey-sweet."

"Malta," Rivka said, slowly, like she was tasting it. *"Ken,* we'll go to Malta."

Again, she took the lead to the car. This time Ward kept pace so they came through the trees at the same moment. And stopped at the same moment. Because they saw the two men at the same moment.

They lounged against adjacent cars like salespeople, barely trying to look casually disinterested in who was coming up the path. They were so obvious, Ward doubted his first impression even as the taller of the two, wearing a skullcap the color of the gray sands of southern Israel, locked eyes on him. The other, wearing a tan fedora, tensed but didn't move.

"Zee's men," Rivka said.

"How do you know?" Ward asked, but she was already on the charge.

CHAPTER 31

Rivka went left, toward the man in the skullcap, forcing Ward to go right or leave her flank exposed to the man in the fedora. The two men stood firm. Waiting. Watching.

Baiting.

Ward understood too late. The third man, also in a skullcap, appeared as Rivka drew her pistol. She didn't see him coming out from behind a van on the far side of the lot, a rifle raising to his shoulder, locking on Ward like a wildcat ready to pounce. The tactic was either extremely foolish, with Rivka clearly being the more dangerous target, or brilliant, forcing Rivka into a two-on-one. Either way, Ward had a split second to act.

"Shooter," he shouted as he drew his pistol.

He couldn't see if Rivka reacted to his warning because his gun caught on his belt. He looked down. Lost the gun. Lost his balance. Something whizzed by his head, about where his chest had been before he began falling. Palms first, then cheek, then shoulder hit the asphalt, the impact nearly knocking his organs loose of their moorings. He rolled, scrambling for his pistol. Shots rang out. Screams from every direction followed.

He came up with his gun. The man with the rifle was gone, probably seeking a new position from which to fire. Ward turned on his knee like a pivot, keeping his head low, until he saw a plume of red in the distance behind him, like a bright rose in the grass. A dart, the kind that might put a tiger to sleep at a zoo.

More shots rang out, bullets not darts, leaving Ward little time to contemplate why these men would try to stun him mere hours after Zee had blown up an entire building in an attempt to kill him. He found the man in the fedora but lost his target as a wave of screaming civilians fled to their cars. The man with the rifle and the tall man in the skullcap were also gone. He lowered his weapon and looked for Rivka as sirens sounded, their distance impossible to calculate. He found her not far from their car.

"We should go," she said.

"They were shooting darts."

"Not the first two."

"Why would the one with the rifle use darts but the others use bullets?"

Rivka got in the car without answering. They were among the last to exit the lot, speeding to get in behind the line of fleeing cars as if they were one of them.

"Put your hands over your face like you're crying," Rivka said as they neared the exit where three police cruisers had already setting up left-right switchback to slow the cars down so a full roadblock could be constructed.

"We're not going to make it," Ward said.

"Cry," Rivka ordered.

He put his hands over his face, leaving room to see through his fingers like when he was a boy watching a scary movie. The police monitoring the switchback were glaring hard at each passing vehicle but not stopping any of them. Ward thought they might make it until a police truck arrived to complete the roadblock. Brake lights lit up. Police lined the sides of the switchback and the access road, pistols and shotguns aimed low at each car. To take out tires not kill innocents. A good sign. A precaution, not a positive identification.

Rivka wasn't waiting, however. She turned the wheel slowly at first and then said, "Hold on."

There was no point in protesting. The tires were already screeching as the car lurched forward, smashing the rear bumper of the sedan ahead of them. The driver of the sedan must have panicked because that car then jumped into the back of the one in front of it. Horns blared. Police shouted to halt. Rivka stayed on the accelerator, pinning Ward to his seat as they cleared the line. For some reasons—shock or an unwillingness to fire without orders—the police didn't shoot. They hit the switchback at full acceleration. One car to break through rather than three or four plus the truck at the roadblock.

Finally, the police opened fire. Ward ducked low in his seat as glass shattered and bullets sheered through the car's body panels.

"Get up," Rivka said. "Shoot!"

They were through the switchback, which meant they had an angle that might get them around the roadblock. It also meant any return fire would risk the lives of all the people who'd been trying to flee the shutout at the parking lot.

"For the love of God, now," Rivka ordered.

Ward aimed out the window, following the lead of the police's initial strategy. He shot at tires as they sped away. Ten rounds, enough to force the cops down for cover as Rivka plowed through the police cruiser on the edge of the roadblock. The sound was like two trucks colliding at top speed. A police officer, a kid in his mid-twenties maybe, was in the passenger seat of the cruiser, eyes wide, mouth agape, watching them go without ever making a move for his weapon.

And then they were through. Rivka took the first turn at full speed. Seconds later they were out of range and right of the police, and the road ahead was clear.

"I think they were Zee's people," Rivka said.

Ward looked behind them. They were not being followed. "You said that. Why?" he asked.

"You talked to him about Hannibal and the tomb. By now everyone knows you're alive. Of course he sent his people here."

"What about the darts? First he wants to kill me, then he wants to capture me?"

Rivka shrugged as if to say: *So what? Plans change.*

Ward hated it. He'd had so few friends in his life. His bartender Carrie, who he ruined any chance at a relationship with. His officemate Ken, who he had to kill. MacKenzie, and calling her a friend was more than a stretch, especially now. Sam, who would probably never want to talk to him again even if he could save her, or restore her, or bring her back to life, or whatever it was they were doing. Now Rivka. It wasn't a big list, and he'd wanted so badly to include Zee on it back in the desert and in Jerusalem. After all, he'd gone out of his way to befriend Ward even when there was no profit in it.

Ward had hiked down the beach from where MacKenzie had left him on Santorini, concussed and confused and limping horribly. He'd been close to giving up and collapsing and waiting for the tide to come in and drown him when the blurry shape of a man appeared in the distance. A mirage, probably, but that promise, and the shade of the cliffs above, kept him going until he was close enough to see the man was real. Lanky and wearing a black and red kufi hat, the man stood in a boat just offshore, fishing.

Ward had called to him and remembered nothing else until he woke in the hospital. The man, Zee, had brought him to the hospital and stayed with him for two days, telling the doctors he was a family friend—a lie which Ward was certain no one believed, but which no one seemed interested in questioning—and even paid for his recovery.

When Ward was released from the hospital, Zee insisted he stay with him at his home, a small flat overlooking the caldera. Ward let himself be convinced, and the two soon found they shared a love of history, including Santorini's, as well as an intense dislike for the Republic's oppression. The next thing Ward knew, Zee had arranged meetings and contacts and routes to get him back to Philadelphia and the Tower.

Zee had taught him how to make a bomb.

"It doesn't matter now if it was him or not," Rivka said. "No one knows about Malta but us. Here we go."

She turned them down an alley beside a brick apartment building. They still weren't being tailed, though Ward could hear sirens in the distance getting closer. He was surprised not to hear helicopters above searching for them. The alley brought them to an underground parking garage. Rivka didn't switch on their headlights when they pulled in, though Ward suspected they were too damage to light up anyway. They parked in an unnumbered space near the back of the single level garage.

"We could have made it back to the airport," Ward said.

"Too risky. We need a new vehicle."

"How do you propose we find a Port for one of these?"

"I don't," Rivka said.

She got out and strolled up the row, leaving Ward to watch and wonder, before returning. Ward got out as she opened the car's trunk, which was pocked with four bullet holes. From the case, which showed no damage, she dug out a device about the size of a Port.

"The blue coupe over there," she said, pointing. "Bring the case."

"What is that?" Ward asked.

"A key."

She left Ward to maneuver the case out of the car's trunk by two straps along its length. It was heavier than he expected, and it dropped hard, echoing throughout the parking garage. He managed to get the straps over his shoulders like a duffel bag and bring the case to the blue coupe. It was a Mercedes, probably expensive once, though it was at least ten years old. It started up as he arrived.

"It should fit in the back seat," Rivka said of the case. She didn't help Ward get it inside.

"How did you get it started?" Ward asked, panting form the effort, once he was in the car.

Rivka showed him the device she'd used. It looked like an old CP1 Port, only its screen showed a single red button on a black field and nothing else. From its bottom edge dangled a cord with a pronged box on the end.

"It plugs in and overrides the system, if the car is old enough," she said. "Now tell me, is it Malta? Are you sure?"

Ward went over it all again. The Greek for honey bee. The Phoenician inscription. The record of the epitaph and the promise of the tomb.

"Yes," he said.

"You don't sound positive."

"I'm not, but it's the best we have."

"I agree," she said. "Let's go to Malta."

CHAPTER 32

When she was little, MacKenzie remembered the drive home—from the store, from the mall, from the shore— was always faster than the ride there. She liked to imagine they'd cut a path on the way there and, therefore, were able to drive so much faster on the way back.

The flight north from Eagle Pass was excruciatingly different. It was slower. Longer. Like the smoldering husk of the city was trying to keep her from leaving. Like it was trying to bring her back to complete the work left undone. To bury the bodies left unburied.

Reina nudged her foot. MacKenzie pushed back on the dog, who hadn't strayed more than a couple feet from her since they left the Grossmutter. Reina whined, a silent pantomime in the concussive storm of the helo's rotors. MacKenzie, who hadn't put on her headset, was thankful for the helo's deafening silence. She didn't want to talk.

Bryce did. He was sitting across from MacKenzie, headset on and facing forward, an allowance she'd made based on how uncomfortable he'd been facing backward on the way down. He'd tried to get her attention two or three times already, his stare attempting to will her to make eye contact. He had questions. He had suggestions. He had moralizing judgements. She wasn't interested in any of it, diverting her gaze to the desert below whenever she felt him staring at her. Like now.

The cold, wet push of Reina's nose on her hand surprised her. The intimacy the dog sought, the pure neediness of it, both comforted and annoyed her. She shoved Reina with her shin. Hard. The dog moped to Bryce and sat on his boots.

He continued to stare at MacKenzie. Fed up, she grabbed her headset, determined to order him to keep his eyes and questions to himself.

"What would you do about Eagle Pass?" she said, surprising herself as much as Bryce based on the face he made.

He didn't answer at first. It was a bit of a loaded question. She'd wanted to bury the dead, but he'd argued against it, stating succinctly and correctly the two of them could never bury so many alone. Even if they solicited the help of the Mexican soldiers at the Wall, they would waste hours and still only manage to inter a fraction of the town. All the while, they would be exposed, and Lieutenant Porteus would be getting anxious back at Fort Stockton.

He'd made all those arguments while she'd stood mute, listening. Really listening. Not like when she let Porteus speak, who was probably freaking out about their whereabouts and doing stupid shit like ordering his troops to do calisthenics or clean latrines. That's what shitty officers did. They ignored thought and initiative for rote physical activity. Bryce was half as old and twice as thoughtful as Porteus. If she'd been willing to admit it, MacKenzie might have commended him for being wiser than virtually every soldier in Horeb. Instead, she'd simply agreed with him and gotten back in the truck.

When he'd gotten in the truck, he'd been slumped, as if in defeat rather than victory. There'd been no pride or smugness in him. Rather, he'd seemed sad that she'd agreed with him, as if he'd hoped she would overrule him and settle a battle raging inside between pragmatics and virtue. He'd offered to bury the Grossmutter at least, despite not knowing who she was.

MacKenzie wasn't interested in peace offerings or conditional surrenders. She'd told him it no longer mattered. The Grossmutter was one of them. She'd died with them. She would be buried with them. They'd driven back to the Wall and boarded the helo in silence.

"It's not my place to say, sir," Bryce said, finally answering the question.

"Maybe not, but I'm asking."

Bryce opened and closed his mouth twice before answering.

"There should be trials, sir," he said. "We won't find them all, but we'll identify many of them, the ones who did...what we saw. Even if the ones we find say they were only following orders, there should be trials. We're doing this to be better when it's over, when we're in charge, right?"

Trials, MacKenzie thought. *But who will stand as judge?*

The answer was obvious. The Seer was God's chosen. He would be God's mouthpiece, His arm of judgment. He would be Moses leading the freed Israelites to Canaan, while MacKenzie served as his...not his Joshua. She was no longer the general of the Seer's army. She was Caleb, maybe, who kept faith in God when spying in Canaan. Or perhaps Judah, who led the Israelites after Joshua. She sought comfort in her role as God's warrior, but she found herself inexplicably empty and afraid.

Only it wasn't inexplicable. She knew exactly why.

Because Bryce is right. We'll never catch them all. We'll never know if we got the one who murdered the Grossmutter.

"Will that make us better?" MacKenzie asked. "Will failing to bring all the guilty to trial make us a better people? Will holding executions as the first act of our new government be a better start?"

"We have to try. Otherwise, what's the point?"

MacKenzie knew there was an answer, that it wasn't simply blasphemy masquerading as rhetoric, but she couldn't see it. She didn't have time. Bryce's eyes went wide.

"What's that?" he said, pointing behind MacKenzie, who was buckled to the cockpit facing backward.

"Hold on," the pilot's voice shouted in her headset.

The helo bounced like a balloon caught in an updraft. A cone of smoke charged by the portside fuselage, turning a wide arc back toward them.

"What's happening?" Bryce asked.

There was no time to explain. The rocket had missed on its first pass because the pilot had deployed a belly-loaded countermeasure to confuse the rocket's guidance and executed a nifty jump maneuver over it. But it was coming around. Their only hope was that it was a rocket powered grenade or a short range portable surface-to-air missile. If they ascended quickly enough they could outrange it.

The pilot understood. The helo pitched back, the angle giving MacKenzie a view of nothing but sky. She couldn't see if there were troops on the ground or vehicles large enough to launch a more substantial antiaircraft missile. She had no idea what they were up against.

The helo skipped again, hard to the port side. Reina slid across the cargo floor, her paws scrabbling for purchase, before slamming into MacKenzie's seat between her legs. She closed her knees around the dog to keep her from sliding out the open door.

"Keep climbing," MacKenzie shouted. It was an unnecessary order. The pilot clearly knew what he was doing, but she was strapped in, helpless, unable to do anything but shout useless orders.

An explosion split the sound of the rotors like God dividing the Red Sea. The helo dropped like a stone. MacKenzie's stomach threatening to burst from her throat. She couldn't open her eyes. Voices shouted in her head, like songs. Or prayers. From each of the souls she'd murdered in her service to God.

Why are they praying for me?

An odd calm washed over her as they continued to dive, twisting into a flat spin, faster and faster, centrifuging her consciousness until there was nothing left but oblivion.

CHAPTER 33

Before they crashed, the town might have looked from above like a couple parallel lines drawn in the desert, their outer edges blurring off into nothingness. That was how MacKenzie imagined it: two thick rows of buildings butted up against each other on either side of a wide street, with smaller homes radiating out east and west a couple blocks. An Old West town, now barely a relic. No more than five hundred residents. No more than a few dozen vehicles driving through each day.

Now, it would look like an H, with a crossbar of fire.

The chopper had crashed right in the middle of the street, right in the middle of the two rows of buildings. The pilot must have been trying to avoid collateral damage by aiming for anything other than the buildings. He succeeded. Cockpit first. Neither pilot nor copilot survived.

And all for nothing. However many residents there once were, they'd all evacuated some time ago. Bryce's recon had confirmed it was an evac not a massacre. They'd crashed in the middle of what was now a three-pickup truck, one-laundromat, two-barbershop, one-general store town.

Reina yipped and yapped ahead of them, not too far, as if trying to prod them faster north, away from the burning wreckage of the helo. They'd salvaged MacKenzie's sidearm, and a first aid kit, which Bryce had used to bandage the numerous lacerations she'd suffered. Nothing more. At first, after waking to Reina's rough tongue licking her face, MacKenzie had been angry at the lack of supplies and weapons Bryce had gathered, but when she saw the wreckage she relented. He'd done well to get them out alive, especially her, strapped in to the wall between the cockpit and the cargo area.

"It was Reina," he'd told her. "She woke me up and helped me drag you out."

"How'd she survive the crash?" MacKenzie had asked.

"I have no idea."

There was no need to press. They were alive. Whoever had shot them down would be coming to collect their prize. As soon as MacKenzie was able to get up, her head swimming and her balance off, they got moving. It had been at least ten minutes. They were moving faster by small degrees. What worried her was her eyes. She was having trouble focusing, and her vision kept bursting like she'd looked too long into the sun. Definitely a concussion, in addition to a messed-up knee, some damaged ribs, burns on her shoulders and her ass, and general soreness everywhere as if she'd been shoved into a barrel and rolled down a gravel hill. Thinking was like trying to run underwater. She knew enough not to force it. One slow thought at a time.

The shooters.

"Why aren't they here yet?" she asked.

"They're on foot," Bryce said.

"Not military then but definitely military equipped. That was some range on the rocket that took us down."

"Maybe they bartered with passing soldiers for something better than an RPG."

MacKenzie didn't have a counterargument. However they got the rocket, if they were in a vehicle, they'd be here by now. They couldn't have been more than a couple miles south when they were hit. Which meant their attackers were on foot, or maybe bicycles. Which meant there wasn't much time. With her limp, they would never make it out of town before they were overtaken, and even if they did, where could they go? Out in the desert, they were as good as dead. They had to find a place to hide. Or take a stand.

"Hold up," she said. She rotated slowly clockwise, giving her brain time to catch up and catalog their surroundings and potential assets, starting with the storefront to her three o'clock. A post office. This stopped her before she'd even really started. She hadn't seen a post office since she was a little girl. She guessed it had been a hundred years since any moderately sized town had needed one. Which only seemed right because this town appeared to be happily stuck at least a hundred years in the past, like being in the middle of a virtual rendering of an Old West town in a museum. All it would take was some tumbleweeds and piles of horseshit rather than macadam to make the tableau complete, especially with nearly all the storefronts sporting swinging saloon doors in front of their steel and glass entrances. It was a perfect place to meet at high noon for a duel.

"Tell me again," MacKenzie said to Bryce.

He recounted his reconnaissance as he had when she first woke, only this time she was able to better focus on the details.

"I didn't find Ports for any of the three remaining pickup trucks," he said. "It's possible they're in the houses they're parked in front of. Most of the stores are touristy, and the first few houses checked had been pretty well cleaned out. The general store up ahead looks like our best shot at getting resupplied before leaving town."

"Suggestions for leaving town?"

"Other than the trucks?" He shook his head. "Maybe the pilot sent a distress call before we went down."

MacKenzie wasn't willing to bet on maybe. She drew her sidearm and checked its magazine. Fifteen rounds plus one in the chamber. No spare magazine. If there were two or three loyalists on their way into town, they might be able to hole up and fight them off. Or even ambush them. Maybe they could take on five if they had enough time to prepare and she could get her brain clear. Any more and they were fucked.

She started north again, but it felt suddenly like the earth was pulling away from her boots.

"General," Bryce said, though she sounded far away.

She fell slowly, like she was thinking slowly, until Bryce grabbed her arm, below the shoulder. He tried to prop her up, his hand fumbling up her stomach to her breast. He made a sound like he'd been bitten and pulled away. She hit her knees.

Pain exploded in both, then spiderwebbed up her thighs. Bryce knelt beside her, not touching her.

"Sorry," he said, muttering it a few more times.

Reina yipped and bounded back and forth before them.

"You're fine," MacKenzie said. "It's fine."

She propped herself on a knee. Bryce backed away, eyes averted. She almost laughed. The soldiers of Horeb bunked together, men and women. They used the same latrines. They got dressed at the same time. Tits slipped out. Cocks popped erect. People fucked. There was no place for embarrassment or modesty in war. The kid would learn eventually.

"What should I do?" he asked.

"Give me a minute."

MacKenzie willed her head to clear. It did, somewhat, allowing her to stand, a little unsteady at first but getting better with each breath.

"Let's get to the general store and see what's what," she said.

He kept by her side, but did not touch her, as they moved through the town. It was a slow go, giving her time to examine the town in more depth. She'd heard the phrase *one horse town* before, but she'd never expected to be in one. It wasn't difficult to imagine a billiard hall and a brothel beside a stable and a saloon, with their hitching posts out front occupied by pawing horses while stagecoaches rolled through on their way somewhere more exciting.

The Lonestar General Store, with its ridiculous saloon doors in front of its contemporary steel and glass façade, was the last stop on the west side of town. Beyond it, the road continued until it shimmered into nothingness at the flat horizon. They had to be at least fifty miles from the next town.

"We need a vehicle," MacKenzie said, her thoughts coming a little quicker now. "I'll resupply here. You find us transportation. Check the houses with the trucks out front. If not, check garages. Look for something old that runs on gasoline and doesn't need a Port."

"Won't that need a key?" asked Bryce.

"They might be in the car if it's in a garage. On the seat or up in the visor. If not, try kitchen drawers or garage cabinets. Worst case, I can jumpstart it. Take Reina and meet back here in fifteen or when you hear shots fired."

"Yes, sir," Bryce said. He started back toward the nearest side street, but Reina wouldn't follow. "Come on, girl," he coaxed.

"Forget it. She can stay. Get going." When he was gone, she asked Reina, "What do you say, girl? Find some pain meds and water?"

Reina barked happily and slipped under the saloon doors. MacKenzie followed, swinging the doors aside to stand in a small trapezoid formed by the store's inset entrance. The locked glass door was covered in warning posters.

Report all strangers in town to the sheriff, and *Are your neighbors acting strange? Witness-Report,* and *Have your children become withdrawn? Witness-Report,* and *Do you know where your children are? Witness-Report.*

And, of course: *Official Witness-Report Station,* and *Unity for Peace.*

MacKenzie drew her pistol and aimed at the Witness-Report bill, but she didn't pull the trigger.

I'm smarter than this, she thought. Even with a concussion, she should know better than to waste a bullet and announce their location to the loyalists who'd shot them down. If her brain was going to be this slow countering impulse, she would have to be more careful.

Her alternate plan was to heft a nearby trash bin nearby and throw it through the door. The lifting and twisting motion of the throw sent a spike of pain through her back and knee. As if in the same pain, an alarm wailed.

Fucking brilliant!

She'd saved a bullet but announced their location all the same.

Reina barked happily, however, and charged into the store, paying no mind to the broken glass all over the floor. MacKenzie followed slowly, still limping. A glance around the store made her feel instantly better. There were aisles of nonperishable food, racks of clothing, and a huge sign hanging from the ceiling pointing the way to a camping supplies section in the back. She started down one of the food aisles, grabbing three bottles of water, intending to take a backpack from the camping section and return for more provisions. What she saw in the camping section, however, stopped her cold.

"Jackpot," she told Reina.

The back wall of the store, next to a door labeled for employees, was the sporting goods section. Or, as translated from the Texan vernacular, the gun wall.

Most of it had been cleared out, probably by residents when news of the revolution arrived, but a glass display case still held a few pistols and a number of hunting and multipurpose knives. The wall behind the case was set up to display about fifteen rifles. Four remained. Three shotguns and a hunting rifle. Below them, wire racks held close to a hundred boxes of various rounds, no more than ten percent of the display's full capacity. MacKenzie fought the urge to grab a gun first. She needed to be smarter. Plan better. She put the three bottles of water on the glass case and limped back to the camping section and found two backpacks. She filled each with five bottles of water and a handful of protein bars. Next, she got a bottle of pain medicine and swallowed handful of pills with half a bottle of water. Finally, she returned to the weapons, the alarm still howling.

She chose a 9mm pistol for Bryce and two folding knives, one for each of them, before examining the rifles on the wall. She chose a pump-action shotgun and a scoped, bolt-action .300 hunting rifle and set them on the case and topped off the backpacks with ammo. Then Bryce was beside her. She nearly jumped at his sudden appearance. It was the alarm, she told herself, but she knew it was more than that. She was hurt. Her head wasn't clear. She was making mistakes.

If I don't get it together, I'm going to get us killed.

"They're here," he said, over annunciating so she could read his lips, the alarm wailing so loud it was almost impossible to hear.

"Vehicle?"

He shook his head. "Not enough time."

There never was. MacKenzie was calm, however. This was

her arena, not giving orders or organizing armies. Battle. Killing. Adrenaline was focusing her vision and her thoughts. The pain and the fear and the doubt was peeling away. There would be no more mistakes. She handed Bryce a backpack. When he'd strapped it on, they loaded their weapons, side-by-side. He was good, even with his hands shaking a bit.

"Find the back door and make sure no one comes through it," she told him. "And shut off that fucking alarm."

"How?"

"I don't care."

"Yes, sir."

Holding the shotgun uncertainly, he set off through the employee door.

He's still a kid, MacKenzie reminded herself, but he was all she had. They were all each other had. He would do his job. She would do hers. She slung the backpack over her shoulders and picked up her rifle. Her hands were steady. She was ready to kill.

CHAPTER 34

The Lonestar General Store was not set up for defense. Its front windows were wide and open to the interior of the store, set with mannequins on the left in a fishing scene. The right window was decked with a canoe and more mannequins styling cowboy hats and boots of various colorful styles. Inside, the store offered a wide-open center lane, with clothing racks to the left and the food aisles to the right.

The smart move would be for the half of the loyalists to keep her pinned down with fire from across the street while the other half breached the rear of the store. Which meant MacKenzie's smart move was to make them abandon strategy and come in for what appeared to be an easy frontal assault. She had to work quickly, dragging one mannequin from its fishing boat to the clothing racks and setting it up behind a tall display of hunting vests. She was crossing back to her position in the food aisle when the alarm hit an awkward tone, like a cat whose tail has been stomped on. Then it shut off. Reina offered a thankful yip. MacKenzie didn't waste time being impressed with Bryce's resourcefulness, or the remaining ringing in her ears. She felt rather than saw the loyalists in the street. She got low so she could see up the aisle and under a couple racks of dusty cowboy boots.

They didn't move. They stood perfectly still in the middle of the street, stances wide, as if daring her to come out. There were only two reasons to be that reckless. Either they were idiots, inexperienced and out of their depth, or they knew something she didn't. Judging by her own recent errors, MacKenzie calculated it at fifty-fifty.

"Hey," one of them shouted with a solid Texas accent. "You in there?"

"Shh," she told Reina.

The one on the right shifted his stance, maybe taking aim with a rifle. They weren't coming in. That was okay. MacKenzie scurried deeper into the store so she could cross the main aisle without being seen. She got down on her belly, ignoring the pain lumbering from her leg to her back as she got into position. She took aim on the right guy's knee, just below the bottom of the saloon doors. Her heart slowed. Her vision tightened. For the first time since the crash, she felt completely in control.

She squeezed the trigger.

She was on the move before the echo of the shot came back to her. Before the guy hit the ground screaming. Before his partner returned fire. She slid into the food aisle and shimmied back away from the center lane as the partner lit up the store. Three seconds and it was over. Thirty rounds on a single pull, emptying the magazine of what sounded like an old AK-47 style assault rifle.

Amateurs.

MacKenzie crept forward into the aisle, Reina still beside her as if she'd been trained to keep calm under fire. The first guy was on the ground, wailing and writhing, a cowboy hat beside him and the top of his head exposed. The second, was standing wide-legged, probably reloading his weapon. Still right in front of the door. MacKenzie worked the bolt on her rifle and scoped in on the man's knee. She squeezed. He dropped beside his partner. She worked the bolt and put a round through the top of the first guy's head. It exploded like a water balloon. The second guy was doing his best impersonation of the first. MacKenzie racked the bolt and put a round through his chest.

Three seconds. Three shots. Two dead. She pulled back out of the aisle and reloaded.

"How we doing back there?" she called to Bryce.

"All clear," he returned.

They were making the same mistake she had in Nogales, when she stormed the fried chicken restaurant. Only they weren't her.

She got up to peer over the chip and pretzel half-wall, her knee popping and grinding horrendously. A haze hung above the racks. Plastic shrapnel from exploded mannequins and tattered threads from the shredded clothing racks filled the aisles. Somehow, the mannequin she'd set up by the vests remained standing. None of the others did.

Other than the corpses in the street, there was no sign of the enemy. She refused to give in to overconfidence, though. She had to be smarter than she'd been so far. She had to compensate for a concussion. There was no way those two idiots took down a Black Hawk on their own. Five, maybe six, idiots together could do it. Or two idiots and one real soldier.

She inched into the center aisle, seeking motion outside. Expecting a breach or a flanking maneuver through the rear of the store.

"Still good?" she called.

"Affirmative."

She caught the muzzle flash out of the corner of her eye. It lit up a second floor window across the street and detonated a can of mushroom soup the next rack over. She dropped to her face and scrambled away from the center lane as more return fire came in. She kept shimmying back until she was pressed against the wall beneath a display of running shoes that were leaping off their racks as if excited to begin dancing.

Four shooters, she guessed, from the angles of the return fire. Two in the second floor windows at wide angles. Two on the first floor, close to dead center. Not the best strategy, but not the worst. On knees and elbows she worked her way around the store's perimeter until she found a sight line to the first floor shooters across the street. She was marginally exposed, but their spray said they were firing blind. The contrasts of their interior lighting to the sunshine in the street to the interior of the general store reinforced that they had no idea what they were aiming at.

Which meant they didn't have scopes.

But she did.

The salvos from outside ceased. Footsteps, boots on linoleum tiles, thumped through the store. One set. Light and quick. Reina barked softly. No alarm.

"Get down, damn you," MacKenzie said as Bryce approached in a crouched run, following the same path MacKenzie had taken to get to her current position. "I told you to cover the back door."

"There's no one out there," he said, his confidence both reassuring and maddening.

Amateurs. But trusting amateurs to never get anything right was how veterans got killed.

"What about since you abandoned your position?"

He looked at his boots, briefly, before looking her right in the eyes. "The door's locked with two bolts, and I shoved a big desk in front of it. There's no way anyone is getting in without alerting us."

Good enough for this situation, MacKenzie accepted, but only good enough to get them killed against more effective enemies. Still, his instincts were strong. He understood the immediate danger versus the longshot. He was an impressive cadet, but she wasn't going to tell him that while he was disobeying orders.

"There's four of them out there," she said. "I'm going to take one out. The rest will light this place up. Stay low and tight and ride it out. Got it?"

"Yes, sir."

"Get me that," she ordered, pointing to a narrow blue cooler full of bullet holes.

Bryce slid it to her, and she set up with her rifle propped on top. The scope was good for hunting in a daylight desert but not so much for urban combat. The lighting contrast prevented her from seeing fine details. She saw motion well enough, though. It would do.

"When they stop shooting," MacKenzie said, "I want you to get to the corner of the front window and tell me what you see."

"Shout it?"

"What? No. With your fucking hands."

His brow wrinkled. MacKenzie reminded herself he was just a cadet, a kid, as much as he often thought and acted like a seasoned soldier.

"Like this," she said, miming the directions.

He nodded as she spoke. Took a moment to process. Said, "Like this?" He mimed out *two shooters, one front and center, the other second floor.*

"Exactly. Now stay low till they cease fire."

She took aim, seeking movement on the first floor across the street. There wasn't much. A blur. A shape. She chose her spot. Measured her breathing. Squeezed the trigger.

The return fire was immediate and wild. MacKenzie rolled to her right to get out of the center lane and covered her head. Shrapnel flew. Cans and shoes and bags detonated. Something burned her arm. She kept tight, not brushing it off. Three seconds, she counted. Three shooters. Ninety rounds. Amateurs.

"Go now," she told Bryce.

She rolled back into the center lane as he scurried out of sight. The cooler had taken more hits but felt strong enough to serve her purpose. She set up the same as before. Found the remaining first floor shooter. Marked the spot. Scooted left and stood to look over the racks. Bryce was at the corner. He mimed *one second floor, one first floor, one unknown.*

Good enough. She told him to get back to her and then set up again on the cooler. Her target hadn't moved. Bryce arrived. She fired.

There was no return fire this time, as she expected.

"Two left," she said. "They know they're facing a sniper. If they've got any brains, they're considering three choices. Retreat, flank us to the rear, or breach the front. They're not smart enough or equipped to come in through the rough."

"I'll get to the back door."

"No. If they were going to flank us, they would have already. They're coming through the front."

"What do we do?"

She could see he was scared, but he wasn't backing down. He had complete confidence in her. For a moment, his faith buoyed her, then she faltered. How many soldiers had she gotten killed because of her bravado? How many times had she put her own troops in harm's way when another tactic might have served better?

"Sir?"

There was no time to second guess. She'd set this plan in motion when she first entered the store.

"Set up over there on the right. Keep low. When they come in, they're going to lay suppressing fire waist high. Then they'll turn their back on you. When they do, shoot."

"Which one?"

"Whichever one is closest to you."

"How do you know they'll turn?"

"Are you studying for a test?"

He didn't reply.

"At least one of them will turn," she said. "Get in position."

He started up the wall. Reina whined from deep in her throat.

"You want to go with him?" MacKenzie asked. "Go ahead."

The dog scurried after Bryce. MacKenzie shoved the cooler aside and backed into the aisle, needing to stay out of sight until the shooters had been drawn fully into the store.

Only they didn't come in.

"Hey," one of them shouted. They were in the street, but not in the middle. Not where MacKenzie could see them. "You're not soldiers, right?"

Bryce's head popped up. He mimed *don't answer*, but MacKenzie knew they weren't going to present themselves in the middle of the street like the first two had. She needed them in the store.

"I know you're not," she called.

"We're true Texans," the shooter said. "If you're on our side tell us so no one else has to get hurt."

"Probably should have said that before I killed all your friends, you fucking redneck atheists."

Bryce was desperately waving his hands. *Don't shoot. Don't kill.*

"Are you Believers?" the shooter asked, his voice shaky, as if asking whether or not they were boogeymen.

"We are Horeb," MacKenzie shouted.

They stormed through the front door, shoulder to shoulder, and emptied their magazines the same way they had from across the street. The same way the two in the street had. It was over in three seconds.

"There," one of them said.

MacKenzie imagined him pointing to the silhouette of a head peeking over the vest rack. The mannequin she'd dragged there at the start. Somehow, despite all the gunfire, it remained standing.

Providence.

The sounds of magazines dropping and being fit into assault rifles filled the otherwise silent store.

Shoot, MacKenzie thought, willing Bryce to act. Only he didn't. *Shoot, damn you!*

The thunk of a magazine being pounded home declared time was up. MacKenzie rolled into the center lane. Both shooters had turned to the mannequin and were raising their rifles. Bryce was nowhere to be seen. MacKenzie sighted the loyalists. Two shots. Less than two seconds. Silence filled the store.

"What the fuck, soldier," MacKenzie roared, getting to her feet. She charged to Bryce's position where he crouched, shotgun white knuckled against his chest, with Reina panting happily beside him. "I gave you an order!"

"Yes, sir," he said, standing.

"You could have gotten us killed. Following orders isn't optional, damn it!"

"Yes, sir."

She waited for him to say more. He didn't.

"What in the holiest fuck of shit were you thinking?"

He came around the aisle, not avoiding her, not trying to escape discipline. When he neared the center lane, he said, "I saw them."

MacKenzie joined him in the middle of the store. The shooters lay still in a spreading pool of their own blood, one on his shoulder, the other on his face. Their cowboy hats were flung up the aisle. Bryce stepped gingerly into the blood and nudged the closest one from his shoulder to his back.

It was a kid. No older than Bryce. A boy with half his face blown off and the kind of scruff on what remained of the other half that said he couldn't grow a full beard if he wanted to. Bryce looked like he was going to say something. Instead, he went outside with Reina at his heel.

MacKenzie wanted to call after him that enemies were enemies. That it was kill or be killed. What did he want her to do, threaten to send them to bed without dessert if they didn't abandon their attack?

She wanted to make him understand, but she barely understood herself. She'd never killed children before. Not like this, anyway. Not directly. Maybe as collateral. Maybe...

She didn't want to go down that road, but neither could she abandon it entirely. She knelt beside the remaining loyalist and pushed the body over. It was a girl. Pretty, maybe. No chest. No way to know she was a girl the way she was dressed. Probably thirteen or fourteen years old. MacKenzie's .300 round had taken off the entire top of her skull.

She looked like Sam.

MacKenzie's hands began to shake. Her rifle clattered to the linoleum, splashing blood on her boots. She managed to look outside, to make sure Bryce wasn't watching, before she threw up.

CHAPTER 35

The Malta Freeport's airport was small, with a single runway that also served as the road in and out. They parked in a hanger that was eerily similar to the one in Turkey. Also similar was the sedan waiting for them in the hanger, the same make, model, and color as the one they'd abandoned in the parking garage in Gebze. There was no conversation with Noam this time. They took their gear, and the heavy case, and loaded up the car and drove south from the Freeport, chasing Ward's best guess for their destination.

His first impression of Malta was it felt like a time capsule whose seal had rotted away allowing sprays of modernity to seep in. On the east side of the road, the Freeport was a symbol of progress. Its rows of colossal oil tanks had been converted to water storage more than twenty years ago for the largest purification plant in the Mediterranean. Beside the tanks, like fields of shimmering wheat, ranged arrays of solar panels to power the charging stations for one of the busiest seaports in Europe.

To the west, Malta was untamed history. Tall Mediterranean palms and umber topography that would have been at home in a Homeric myth combined with spreads and bursts of stunningly colored flora. Crumbling stone walls ran along the road and meandered into the hills while the remains of the Benghisa Tower, one of many Order of Saint John era watchtowers built around the island's coast, whispered of life here four centuries ago.

What really struck Ward when they got out of the car, however, was the air. It smelled familiar. Like his life. His past.

A brief moment caught between the timelines of the two sides of the road.

"Like Santorini," he said.

"The island?" Rivka asked.

"Sorry, thinking out loud."

Rivka opened the car's trunk and began unpacking. They'd already discussed strategy in light of the incident in Turkey and decided to gear up with everything they could carry from the start. They each took a Jericho pistol, a backpack full of ammo and other supplies, and a folding spade similar to the entrenching tools Ward remembered from basic training. In addition, a telescoping radar device was strapped to Rivka's backpack.

"These too?" Ward asked about the compact assault rifles Rivka dug out of the case in the sedan's trunk.

"We can't be caught unprepared again."

She started across the street from where they parked on the shoulder. She paused at the old wall, her hand on its stone like a historian trying to identify its age, and looked up the rise at the ruined tower. The evening sun lit her like a painting, causing Ward to stare. Moments like this left him confused, or maybe just conflicted, about his companion. When she sat with him and Sam beneath the canopies of Masada, she was compassionate and open. Other times, like in Bethlehem or much of their time together since the Consulate, she was fiery and determined and severe. Like MacKenzie. One extreme to the other, consistent only in her vacillation between them.

It was no wonder he was drawn to her. He'd always fallen hardest for the women he knew he couldn't, or shouldn't, love. The ones who couldn't return his feelings. But Rivka was different. Wasn't she?

It was a stupid question. Of course she wasn't. She was another MacKenzie. A Believer who would always put her faith before him. Then again, she was a doctor, not a killer. She was a healer.

He watched her standing there, by the wall, and wondered if she would even consider a life exiled somewhere with a teacher and a teenager fresh out of a coma.

Am I really thinking about this?

He slung his rifle over his shoulder and joined Rivka at the knee-high remains of the wall. He placed his palm on the wall, as Rivka had, and was struck by the warmth in the stone. Again, he was reminded of Santorini. The cliff. The beach. The Beast— even now he couldn't convince himself one way or the other if he'd truly seen it—rising from the sea. MacKenzie. Always back to MacKenzie.

"Where is the tomb?" Rivka asked.

Ward turned to her only to find himself staring into MacKenzie's eyes. A flash. Then it was gone. Rivka stood before him, doubt clouding her face. Doubt filling his mind. He had to get a grip. MacKenzie and Zee and Compano and whoever else wanted him dead could wait. Sam needed him, and he needed her. She was his only chance—likely his last chance—to do something good with his life.

"There's no map," he said, surveying their surroundings, trying to place them in the historical framework he knew of Malta and the story of Hannibal's tomb. Trying to fit the puzzle pieces together. "In the seventeenth century, thirteen watchtowers were built around Malta's coast to protect from pirates and invaders. The island was perpetually changing hands. Phoenicians, Persians, Carthaginians, Romans. In more recent history, it was the French, the Ottomans, the British. By the late eighteenth century, the watchtowers needed major upkeep. That one, the Benghisa Tower, got a full restoration, including new fortifications and a wide perimeter wall."

"This wall?"

"The age appears about right. There are two reports of a discovery during the restoration and construction that might point the way. One said a sepulcher was discovered in or near a tenement owned by the Falzon family, one of the wealthier Maltese families. Their patriarch, Antonio, was a pioneering Renaissance architect, and there is some evidence to indicate he owned some of the land in this area. Though the construction of the wall would likely have destroyed all evidence of such a building, the report gave a crude description of the tomb, indicating access was through a vertical chute."

"A hole in the ground no one has been able to find for almost three hundred years?" Rivka said.

"Correct."

"And that's what we're looking for?"

"If the tomb is on Malta, that's what we're looking for."

"If?" She got close to Ward, almost threateningly.

One extreme to the other.

"You gave me two lines of text. This is the best I've got. The second report is the one I told you about by Sir Walter Drummond, where he details the tomb and the inscription he insisted identified Hannibal. What works in our favor is his essay on the inscription indicates the sepulcher was undisturbed."

"The tomb remains unopened?" Rivka asked, now intrigued, maybe even excited.

"He was writing about fifty years after the tomb was discovered and made no mention of himself or others opening it. My concern is there was a new fort built over there," he pointed west, "in the early twentieth century. They tore down the tower and razed its fortifications to give a clear line of fire from the fort to the port. I don't even know where to start looking, let alone what landmarks we might be looking for."

"We should use the radar."

"Where? Like you said in Turkey, it would take forever to do a proper grid search on this terrain."

"We use our eyes then. We look for anything and everything. It's getting late. We should split up. We'll find something," Rivka insisted, as if ordering Ward to believe. "We have to."

She started up the north slope, leaving Ward to go south. He crossed the wall a few meters down the road where it had crumbled, leaving a path. The landscape was jagged and covered in rocks and boulders and bushes and grass. After ten minutes, he became concerned the entrance might be overgrown. They needed a team of trained archaeologists not a doctor and a former teacher. Still, he kept on. As Rivka had said, he had to. He kicked at rocks and occasionally pulled up bushes and got on his hands and knees to examine outcroppings or hollows. As he neared the sea, doubt began to take over again. He wasn't smart enough, or lucky enough, to locate the tomb. He was a bookish fraud. A failure. A letdown.

Let me count the ways.

But he didn't count. He remembered the night optics they'd used in Turkey. He got them from his backpack and put them on. The landscape lit up in shades of blue and black and green, the colors cooler than what he'd seen in Turkey. Nothing to indicate a tomb. Rivka came over the rise as he swept back to the north, the blues and blacks morphing into a funnel shaped cone descending into the hillside.

"I've got nothing," Rivka said. "Should we switch sides?"

"Hang on," Ward said. He hiked up the hill further to the west than where Rivka stood, needing to climb over two more low rock walls to reach its summit.

"What do you see?" Rivka called.

Not much, Ward thought. He lost the cone of blues and blacks and took off the optics. The sun was dipping toward the horizon. The road was empty, as it had been since they arrived. There was no activity at the port. It was as if they were the only people on the island. He swept clockwise from the runway to the mouth of the inlet to the water tanks—a single maintenance truck scooted between the tanks, the first sign of life he'd seen—to the gated entrance with its barbed wire fence and conspicuous cams. To Rivka. To the sea. To the remains of the fort in the distance. To the rise. To more lines of rock walls in the northwest.

He tried tracing the wall they'd been walking, imagining it as part of a defensive fortification. Where would they have carved the line to protect the watchtower? Where would a large tenement have been? Even from this minor height, the lines reminded him of the remains of the Roman camps outside Masada. They traced history like ghosts condemned to follow the same path, trudging ruts through time until even memory was washed away. He imagined a small line to the west as the outer wall of a farmhouse. Two lines pointing an arrow north might have been part of a goat pen. There, to the northeast, a half-moon shape that could have been a well. Nothing large enough to be a tenement.

Then again, how large would a tenement building have been?
If it was late Roman era, it would have been an *insula*, basically
an apartment building of six to eight flats. If it was built during
Muslim rule, it might be marginally larger. Later eras would lead
to even larger buildings. Too large for the ruins he was seeing
below, with their straight lines and ninety-degree angles. Except
for the well, the only curved line in sight.

"What do you see?" Rivka asked, having approached while
Ward was lost in thought, effectively sneaking up on him again.

"You're going to give me a heart attack," he said.

"You've found something. I can tell in your face."

"Maybe. See there, on the other side of that drooping tree,
there's a section of wall that curves?

"A well?"

"Maybe."

He put the optics back on and sighted the curved lines. He
couldn't locate the funnel shape he'd seen before and was about
to give up when he realized he'd changed the angle by climbing
the hill. He wouldn't be seeing a cone, only the mouth of it. A
circle distorted by angle. An oval. He swept left to right again,
this time finding exactly what he was looking for. He removed
the optics and was staring right at the well.

He took off at a jog and was soon running. Rivka didn't
question, sprinting beside him. What they found wasn't a well at
all. It looked like half a stone fire pit. Or an arch that had fallen
over, its stones somehow still linked.

"Radar," Ward said.

Rivka shrugged out of her backpack and unhooked the
telescoping radar device. Extended to its full length, it looked like
a generic metal detector. It even offered a steady, dull beep every
few seconds. Where it differed from a metal detector, however,
was its display screen. Ward pressed close to Rivka to see the
readout, a confusing mesh of white, green, and yellow lines on
a cloud-colored background. It made less sense to him than the
optics, but the more Rivka swept the device around the arch, the
more clearly the lines at the bottom of the screen flattened out.

"This is the bedrock, no?" Rivka said, pointing at the bottom
lines.

"No idea. Can we check the instructions?"

"No. We can dig."

They unfolded their spades and started with the overgrowth, hacking their way through until the arch and surrounding area was clear. Then it was time to dig. When the sun finally set, they made do with glowsticks and flashlights. More than an hour later, possibly as many as two or three, they hit solid stone. Or, more accurately, layers of stone. Perhaps the remains of the wall the arch had once lorded over. After a brief, and silent, break to drink a couple bottles of water, they went at the stone, using their spades as pry bars, removing layers of brickwork until they hit a slab of limestone too large to be part of the wall they'd been uncovering.

"Is this the entrance?" Rivka asked.

Ward, still on his knees, brushed off the slab. It was hewn smooth, its edge at the open end of the arch true, its angles clearly once ninety degrees.

"Maybe," Ward said. "If the tomb was closed off rather than filled in when they built the fortification wall, they might have placed a stone like this on top."

"We don't have time for maybe."

You don't have to tell me, Ward thought. How much time did Sam have left? Forty-eight hours? Thirty-six? He barely had any idea what day it was, let alone how much time had passed since Rivka arrived at his quarters in Masada and told him Sam was still alive.

"We can't second guess ourselves now," he said. "It looks like the top edge is under the arch. Let's pry from the bottom."

They set to with their spades, but it was nearly impossible to get a grip on the slab. It must have weighed three or four hundred pounds.

"We have dynamite,' Rivka suggested.

"Too risky. It could collapse the whole thing. Make it impossible to excavate without a backhoe and six months to waste. We have to pry it up."

They got back to work, pushing and grunting and swearing. The tip of Rivka's spade broke off. Ward lost his grip more than once and could feel blisters already forming on his palms.

Finally, his spade bit through. He pushed.

"*Ken,*" Rivka said, moving to his side, ready to slide her spade in if he could open a gap. "More."

He pushed with all his weight and all the strength in his braced leg to leverage his power, all the time wondering what kind of data was down there and who locked it away in such an improbable location.

"Almost," Rivka said.

Ward's spade began to bend. His arms, shoulders, and back hurt. He found he was screaming and didn't care. Then, just as he was sure either he or the shovel would break, the earth gave way. With a sound like a pressurized bottle opening to release a thousand moans of anguish, the slab popped clear.

"I've got it," Rivka cried.

Together they pushed the stone up and over and got on their knees to slide it aside, revealing the tomb below.

CHAPTER 36

The drop was too tight for gear. Ward took off his backpack and rifle and set them beside the entrance. He dropped a glowstick into the hole. The green glow at the bottom was barely visible.

"Drop your shovel," Rivka said.

He did, counting off barely more than one second until it hit bottom, right on top of the glowstick, almost entirely smothering its light. "Six meters?" he said.

"*Ken.* We can climb it."

"There's no rope in my pack."

"I have it. Here," she said, setting her pack next to Ward's and taking out a bundled rope. "Tie it off there."

He wound the lightweight nylon rope around part of the arch, tying it off with his best knot. Rivka dropped her end into the hole. It dangled above the floor, maybe a few centimeters, maybe a meter or two. There wasn't enough light for proper perspective.

"Are we expecting a tomb or a welcoming committee?" Ward asked.

"Looks like a tomb. Would you prefer I go first?"

Tactically, he did prefer she go first. She'd already proven herself an adept soldier, but if this was Hannibal Barca's tomb, it was his arena, not hers. More important, this was about Sam. Being her doctor didn't outrank Ward's own responsibility, and culpability, in this mess.

"I'll go," he said.

He lowered his feet into the hole and began wiggling his way in, thinking if he ever got the chance to teach at an actual university again, he would require his graduate students experience a drop like this into the unknown.

"Stop," Rivka said, crouching beside him.

He looked where she was pointing and found his pistol caught on the rim like a wedge.

"Can you?" he asked.

With a little maneuvering and some uncomfortable twisting, he was able to shift enough for her to unclip the holster from his belt. She placed the pistol on top of his pack, and he continued down. At chest deep, with his feet dangling in the unseen darkness below, a childish fancy crept up on him, a nightmare snarling in the green pale of the glowstick, waiting for him to drop lower so it could pounce.

Grow up, he told himself.

He shimmied deeper until he was hanging by the edge of the entrance, shifting his weight from the rim to the rope. It held strong, and he climbed down, his feet touching bottom right when he ran out of rope. He gathered his spade and glowstick, its light too soft to penetrate much into the darkness, and listened for an approaching adversary. There was nothing, not even the scurrying of insects or bats.

"Clear," he called up to Rivka. "Come on down."

"Catch."

Her backpack came tumbling toward him. He caught it awkwardly, almost taking the attached radar on the side of the head. A moment later she was in the tomb with him, digging a couple flashlights from her backpack before sliding it over her shoulders. They shined their lights around. It was no doubt a tomb, not some natural void or cave. A low tunnel was cut into the far end, and the walls were still plastered in spots. The floor was littered with the broken remains of ceramic vessels, matching what Ward remembered from Drummond's description.

"I don't think anyone has been down here in our lifetime," Ward said. "Are you sure the intel you got was about the data for Sam?"

Rivka kept shining her light around, not responding.

"Rivka, are you sure?"

"Maybe there's another way in."

Ward didn't think it likely, but they were out of options and getting closer to being out of time. "In there," he said, directing her to the tunnel. "It's the only way to go."

Rivka drew her pistol and locked her flashlight to its barrel. She got on one knee and examined the tunnel.

"I'll go first," she said.

"My gun?" Ward asked, reaching for it instinctively.

"I put it in your pack."

She was crawling into the tunnel before Ward could argue. Seeing little chance of running into anyone who needed to be shot, he followed. The tunnel was tight, with a downward pitch, allowing Rivka, who was smaller and faster, to quickly outpaced him. When he came out the other side on his hands and knees, she was already up and examining the walls of the next chamber. It was wider but not much higher than Ward was tall.

"I don't see a grave," Rika said, sweeping the chamber with her flashlight.

Neither did Ward. The walls here were well-plastered, and there were no ceramic remains on the floor. There were no other exits. No nooks or crevices. No secret fissures to squeeze through.

"This isn't right," he said.

"Where are his remains?"

"Who would store data bars or equipment here? How would they even have gotten it inside?"

Rivka began moving wall to wall, banging her fist on the plaster every meter or so.

"Yeah, okay," Ward said, shining his light on the wall to his right.

He followed her lead, though he didn't believe there was anything behind the walls. The plaster was at least medieval, if not older, and showed no signs of being patched. This wasn't a depot. It was a tomb. What could an empty tomb offer Sam? Still, he kept knocking on walls, if only to have something to do. Something to make him feel like he wasn't giving up. Like he wasn't failing Sam.

Halfway around the chamber, his light found a stele inserted in the plaster. He almost moved right past it, so certain was he of finding nothing. It was barely visible on the stone, forcing him to trace it with his finger to work out the letters. Not exactly Phoenician. More like a Phoenician foundation blended beautifully with medieval Hebrew and Chaldaic. Ward's heart raced. He was looking at the epitaph Drummond had written about. Hannibal's epitaph.

Softly, he recited the translation from memory as he ran his fingers over the letters:

Within this inner Chamber of the sanctuary
Of the Sepulcher of the Outlaw,
Beloved in calamitous exile,
Lamented in death:
Here lies Hannibal, the Barca.

"What is it?" Rivka asked.

"The epitaph." Ward felt giddy. He knew he shouldn't. Sam was counting on him, but to make a discovery of this significance could offer a new paradigm in the understanding of Carthaginian history. "This is it. Hannibal's tomb."

She shined her light around again. "Where is he?"

"I don't know, but this is really it."

This time, she aimed her light at his face, forcing him to put up his hand and look away.

"You don't know?"

"It's more than two hundred years," he said. "Ceramic doesn't last forever. Any one of the urns in the other room could have been Hannibal. His ashes could have been scattered anytime over the centuries due to an earthquake or any number of military engagements and bombardments on the island."

"Ashes?"

"In Hannibal's time around the Mediterranean, the Jews were really the only people who buried bodies. The Greeks, Romans, and Carthaginians all bought into the same basic idea of preparation for the afterlife. Cremation, libations, and prayers to the gods for a safe journey. They honored ashes, what the gods left behind once the soul had been freed by fire, not bodies."

"Ashes?" Rivka said again, more forcefully, an exclamation as much as a question. "There's no body here? No possessions?"

She was coming closer, her light growing brighter. Ward kept backing away until he hit the wall, only now realizing that if her light was pointing at his face, so was her gun.

"Put the light down," he told her, fearing a slip of her finger. A pull of the trigger.

"I didn't come here for ashes."

"Your gun, Rivka."

"Where is Hannibal?"

"Rivka!"

She stopped, her gun a meter from Ward's face. Slowly, she lowered it. Flashes strobed his vision. He rubbed his eyes.

"He has to be here," she said.

"Why? How are his remains going to help Sam? What about the data?"

"You have to figure it out," she said, her coming halfway back up his chest. "You have to do your job."

"What are you talking about? I did my job. I brought us here. This is it. There's nowhere else to go. No other rooms. No..." He stopped, an idea—a hope—forming.

"What?"

"Hang on." He went back to the stele, feeling his fingers across the letters. "...inner Chamber of the sanctuary Of the Sepulcher," he read, then repeated the word *sepulcher* a few times.

"What is it?"

"The word. The lines." Ward paced. He thought better sometimes when he paced. "A sepulcher is a tomb, but not every tomb is a sepulcher. It depends on region and language and religion. For Sephardic Jews, for example, a sepulcher would mean specifically a rock cut tomb."

"We're in a rock cut tomb. What do Sephardic Jews have to do with it?"

"It's the language and the history. Sephardic means Spanish. There were Jews in Spain two thousand years ago, and their descendants began settling on Malta in the first century. Drummond theorized this tomb was cut for Hannibal sometime between then and when the Jews were expelled from the island at the end of the fifteenth century. I know fifteen hundred years is a big window, but in Spanish dialects of Hebrew, the word *sepulcher* doesn't only mean tomb."

"But this is Phoenician, not Hebrew."

"They're both Semitic languages that evolved side-by-side. Their alphabets are incredibly similar, with both Paleo-Hebrew and Aramaic evolving from Phoenician. Modern Hebrew is often used to help translate Phoenician texts. The point is, the Sephardic idea of the sepulcher means the whole of the tomb. Its complete construction, as in the mausoleum or the building or the cave."

"So the sepulcher isn't just this room."

"Exactly. It's both rooms. Following that logic, the next room you reach in the tomb, usually down a descent, is the sacred or private room. The sanctuary."

"The inner chamber of the sanctuary," Rivka said.

Ward nodded. "There's another room."

"You couldn't have said that? You had to give the full lecture?"

"Sorry," Ward mumbled. "I was still working it out."

"Where is it, this inner chamber?"

Ward pointed at the stele and said, "I would start right there with the radar."

Rivka operated the device jealously, keeping Ward from seeing the screen. It didn't take long. She found a void about three meters wide to the left of the stele.

"Is he in there?" she asked.

"Only one way to find out."

Rivka grabbed her spade and measured an overhead swing. The roof was too low. She took a sidearm aim and began hacking at the wall.

CHAPTER 37

Ward lost track of the time and the soreness in his back and shoulders. Had they been digging through soft earth, they might have excavated a hundred yards. Instead, he began to wonder if they would ever break through the wall. He began to doubt they would discover anything in the void beyond other than dust and emptiness. No data. No equipment. No twenty-two-hundred-year-old remains. Only vacancy and lies.

But whose lies?

Was the intel misinformation? Had the soldier who'd provided it to Rivka deceived her?

As much as he wanted the answer to be yes to either of those questions, he was becoming more certain with each swing of his spade that it was Rivka who was hiding something.

He took a step back and began to watch her, trying to find a truth in the way she was attacking the wall. She was here to save Sam, he accepted with the kind of faith MacKenzie would be proud of. Maybe the truth was wrapped up in how she planned to save Sam.

What if it wasn't modern technology they were after? What if it was the rediscovery of an ancient procedure they were seeking, and Rivka hadn't shared that fact because she was afraid Ward wouldn't believe her? History was full of such findings. The third century ceramic pot constructed around a copper tube and iron rod which resembled a wet cell battery and was quickly coined the Baghdad Battery. Viking compasses nearly as accurate as GPS. Greek robots powered by weights and pulleys. The incredibly strong and complex carbon nanotubes of Dark Age Damascus steel. The countless plants used in ancient

China and Mesopotamia for medicinal purposes that modern pharmaceuticals were only now recognizing.

It was a plausible enough theory. A comfortable one that set his suspicions at ease. Still, it was time they discussed it. Cleared the air. Trusted each other.

"What do you—" he started to ask.

A powerful swing by Rivka cut him off. The wall cracked. A large chunk of stone crumbled inward as dust billowed out.

"Help me," she said, coughing and waving away the cloud.

Ward didn't hesitate. They used their spades to open the hole, dragging out larger and larger chunks until a channel was revealed, giving the complete tomb an L shape when measured from where they'd entered. Rivka shined her light, still attached to her pistol, inside.

"It's deep," she said.

Ward examined the surrounding wall and ceiling. "Looks sturdy enough."

Rivka took point, leading the way with her light. Ward started right behind her, leaving his spade at the channel entrance because of how tight it was. For much of the way, he was forced to shuffle sideways. At one point, she got far enough ahead that he was left in near darkness, his own flashlight pointing at his boots as his arms were virtually pinned to his sides. He fought through, battling the familiar claustrophobia, along with an apprehension that came from not having a gun. Slowly, however, he convinced himself there would be no one waiting for them on the other side. The way was as ancient as the tunnels beneath the Pyramid of the Sun. A forgotten tomb. The only danger was a cave in burying them alive.

He caught up with Rivka where the channel opened to a cavern not unlike the previous two, only this one was punctuated by four alcoves, like shallow caves. Or chapels. Ward thought again of the Pyramid of the Sun and the clover leaf grotto beneath it. Unlike beneath the Pyramid, however, there were no murals or decorations and the chapels were partially filled with debris.

"This is really it," Ward said, shining his light about anxiously, dust dancing in the beam like a soft mist.

He hurried to the first chapel on the right, Rivka at his heel. She shouldered him aside at its entrance, shining her light in like she was stabbing with it, illuminating a large flat boulder surrounded by loose stone and gravel.

"Not here," she said, moving counterclockwise to the next chapel.

This time Ward hurried to keep up, wanting to spend more time examining the first chapel and the boulder which struck him as a type of bier or altar. He soon forgot the first when he saw the second. Its condition was much the same as the first, only upon its flat boulder rested a stone box about the size of a deep desk drawer.

"Looks like an ossuary," Ward said.

"For bones?"

"Or ashes. Sometimes possessions."

Rivka entered the chapel and examined the ossuary as if measuring it with her hands before leaning over it to look in.

"I'll check the next one," she said, leaving Ward alone in the chapel.

He leaned over the ossuary the same way Rivka had. A piece of fabric rested inside, possibly a shroud or a cape. It might have been blue once. And something else. He reached in carefully with his flashlight and slid the fabric aside. Part of it crumbled to dust as he did so, but it revealed a brass, or maybe gold, ring.

"Here," Rivka called.

Ward rolled the ring over. The insignia was too faded to identify, but he was certain it was a signet ring, the kind used to emboss wax seals. A wonderful find, but not one that could help Sam.

"Rafael!"

Ward abandoned the ossuary. He glanced into the third chapel—it was empty like the first—on his way to the fourth where Rivka stood as if afraid to enter. Inside, the boulder at the center was lower and flatter than the previous three. Upon this bier lay a corpse. A man, judging by the tufts of beard clinging to his otherwise fleshless skull. A soldier dressed in armor so decayed it appeared ready to disintegrate at the slightest touch, with a sword clutched upon his chest.

"It's him," Rivka said.

Could it be? Ward knew better than to make an identification based on anything less than strict scientific study. It would take months, if not years, of careful archeological and anthropological work to even attempt to identify the ethnicity, let alone the family or personal identify of the remains. Still, he felt certain she was correct. Here lay Hannibal Barca, the mighty Carthaginian general.

"We did it," he said, caught up in the discovery, exalting in the moment. Placing himself in the narrative of history. Planning how to return to the world a lost giant. The thrill was exhilarating. Almost enough to make him forget why they were here. "Rivka," he said, "where's the data?"

She bent over the body, passing her hands over it as if verifying it wasn't a mirage.

"Don't touch it," Ward said, afraid the corpse would crumble to dust.

But she did touch it. She freed the sword from its skeletal grip. Only when she turned, did Ward finally get a good look at the weapon, a sickle-style sword called a khopesh. It was in wonderful condition, nearly flawless, as if it had been forged no more than a few decades ago. It was an odd choice for a Carthaginian soldier, who would have relied on a spear as his primary weapon, but not an anachronistic one. The khopesh was popular from Egypt to Mesopotamia a thousand or more years before Hannibal was born, but attestations had been found as late as the second century BCE, which aligned it with the latter years of Hannibal's life. And a specimen this fine surely would have been prized by a general of his stature.

Rivka shifted the sword into her left hand, and for a moment, Ward thought she was going to hand it to him. But she didn't. She drew her pistol with her free hand, shining the light in Ward's eyes. As she had earlier. Not a mistake at all.

"What are you doing?" he said. Then her words came back to him: *I didn't come here for ashes.* Too late he understood. It had never been about saving Sam. It had been about finding the tomb. For the sword.

"What God commands," Rivka said. She guided him out of the chapel.

"Is Sam even still alive, or was that a lie too?"

"A C-section isn't usually deadly, even at Masada."

"C-section?" Ward said, slowly, finally, seeing the full thread of Rivka's betrayal. "The baby is alive?"

"It was when we took it out."

"Where is it?"

"Someone already claimed that prize."

"Who?" Ward asked, horrified at the dispassionate way the doctor spoke of the baby.

"Not your concern."

"What about Sam's coma?" he asked, his hands in front of his face to keep from being blinded, edging to the wall, seeking anything to save his life. "Was that real?"

"You brought her in that way."

"So she's still alive?"

"Her condition is interesting to Bar-Ilan. I assume he'll take her when they abandon Masada?"

"They're leaving? For where?"

"Not your concern."

"Will Bar-Ilan keep her alive?" Ward's foot hit a pile of rubble.

"Again, not your concern."

"You're a doctor!"

"We are servants of God."

"We?" Ward slumped against the wall, hoping he appeared defeated, his fingers closing on a mug-sized stone.

"You know who *we* are."

Her hand recoiled slightly as if gathering to stab at him with the pistol. A habit Ward had picked up on. A tell.

He ducked.

The first shot sounded like a bomb. Ward imagined the wall exploding where his head had been a half-second earlier. He rolled, scrabbling for the closest chapel. Three more shots detonated, the muzzle flashes moving away, toward the channel entrance. Ward timed her pace, coming up on a knee, and threw the stone as hard as he could and dove flat once more. There was no grunt indicating a hit. He found another stone and pressed to the chapel wall, vaguely aware he was back in Hannibal's chapel.

There was no fourth gunshot. He leaned around the wall as Rivka's light retreated into the channel. Relief flooded him. Then panic and a crushing sense of failure. He was alone in a tomb no one on earth could find, certain he was about to be trapped inside. Worse, he'd failed Sam once more.

No, he corrected. Twice more. He'd failed her and he'd failed her child. If he couldn't catch Rivka and get out of this tomb, they were both lost. If they weren't already.

It was enough to get him moving, even as he wanted to collapse and weep. He started into the channel faster than was prudent. He had to reach Rivka, to stop her, before she climbed out of the tomb and took the rope with her. When he reached the sanctuary, her light was visible through the low tunnel to the entrance. He hit his knees hard, sliding into the tunnel, crawling like a drowning man trying to make it to shore, realizing too late he'd left his spade—his only weapon—back at the channel.

Rivka's light went out. The sound of her climbing the rope up and out of the tomb was unmistakable. And then a hiss, like a curious snake, or a kid's sparkler.

He saw the light first. He didn't need to see the stick. He knew what it was and what it would do. There was no turning around in the tunnel. He could only crawl backward, hoping distance might save him from the dynamite.

CHAPTER 38

Finding a vehicle that ran on gasoline turned out to be fairly easy. At least half the houses in the small town had a car or truck in the garage, or beside it, which violated Republic laws about such things. They chose a sixty-year-old Camaro because it was fast, and its air conditioner worked. It was black and yellow and in cherry condition and, best of all, its tank was almost full of explosive-as-fuck gas. MacKenzie, who almost couldn't believe their luck in finding such a pristine ride, insisted she would drive this time.

It was difficult at first, getting out of town with her injured leg and the car having a manual transmission, but once they were in the desert, cruising in sixth gear, it was sublime. The Camaro drove like a rocket. She imagined how difficult it must have been for the owner to leave it behind when the town was evacuated. Bryce seemed to enjoy the drive as well, far more than he had the helo, and Reina in the back seat was ecstatic to hang her head out the window and lap at the wind whipping by at over eighty miles per hour.

They didn't talk much, allowing MacKenzie to find a zone in the open road for a portion of her mind to drift to the *after.* What would the country look like once the tyranny was thrown down and Faith was restored? She'd never imagined it in more than the vaguest terms, ghosts of ideas, the way she'd thought of her father, Simon, when she was a little girl. He would be tall, bright-eyed, and strong. She never imagined his reality. His strengths and weaknesses. His habits and prejudices. She never imagined him growing old. She never imagined him dying in her arms.

That was how she'd always pictured the *after*. An archetype. A flavor with no texture. An emotion free of consequence. A certainty with no time for doubt. Judgement would come for those who'd hunted Believers. Justice and Faith would reign benevolently for those who accepted it. As the miles rolled by on their way north to Fort Stockton, however, she found details creeping into her ideal of the *after* like wrinkles in a shirt. What of those who didn't accept the new paradigm? Would they be rounded up like the monsters who murdered the Grossmutter? Would even silent dissention be punished Biblically? And what of President Barclay and the rest of the government? By all accounts, the president was a politician far more than an anti-Faith fanatic. He accepted the law as is and expected it to be followed. Those who didn't, he left to law enforcement. To the REC.

Wasn't that as bad as pulling the trigger yourself?

She had no answers. Nor, she found, did she have a desire to be a part of the discussion. She liked the fantasy of retirement she'd been playing with. A small house. A dog. A garden, perhaps. She could restore old cars, she added, enjoying the rumble of the Camaro's engine. It was difficult not to slide so far into the fantasy she became trapped, like falling asleep while driving. There was much to do before she could allow herself the vulnerability of her retirement fantasy. There were too many people who wanted her dead. Too many people to kill.

Maybe soldiers didn't get to retire after all.

Fort Stockton appeared on the horizon like a magic trick. One second, the view was flat and empty. The next, it wasn't. They roared into town as the sun reached its zenith, cruising through empty streets to the courthouse. Here, soldiers scurried about like ants radiating from a nest: a large tent in the grassy plaza before the boxy and pillared courthouse. In the old days, criminals would be hanged on display outside courthouses, MacKenzie knew. She tried to imagine that here. Would they have been hanged from the portico, swinging gently between the pillars? Or from one of the large trees in the plaza?

Would that be Barclay's fate, to swing from the gallows in public? Or would the Seer show mercy? Would he deliver their enemies publicly back to the people?

He'll do what God directs, she thought, but found little comfort in the idea.

They parked at the curb in front of the tent. Reina yawned and began pawing at the back of MacKenzie's seat. She could feel Bryce itching to get out, but he wasn't going to move until she did. He would make a good soldier.

"What would you do if you caught one of them?" she asked.

"One of them," Bryce said. He didn't ask who. The continuation of their discussion about Eagle Pass was expected. "Put them on trial."

"You said, but I'm not talking about after. Right now, right here, one of them comes up the street. You know it's one of them. What do you do?"

Reina yawned. Bryce stared straight ahead. In the rearview, MacKenzie watched a row of soldiers line up in front of the Courthouse like a receiving line for the Seer himself. Lieutenant Porteus stood at attention before them, looking comically uncertain.

When Bryce still didn't answer, MacKenzie drew her sidearm and put it in his lap. "What would you do?" she insisted.

"I would take them if I could."

"And if you couldn't?"

"Then I accept God put me in the position to do His work."

"His vengeance."

"His justice," Bryce said. He handed back her pistol.

"General," Lieutenant Porteus announced.

He was waiting, MacKenzie knew, for permission to approach. A soldier not a thinker. An officer who wouldn't pull down his zipper to take a piss without orders. One who sure as fuck couldn't decide when it was best to ignore orders rather than follow them into a meat grinder.

She got out of the Camaro. Bryce and Reina followed, the dog barking and bounding about before relieving herself on a tree. MacKenzie watched this a moment, enjoying the way it increased her lieutenant's discomfort, before crossing the street. Bryce followed. Reina continued to run and play in the grass.

"Report," MacKenzie said.

Porteus saluted. "Sir, the helo?"

"Loyalists. We're fine, thanks, but we need a replacement."

"Sir?"

"A new helo," MacKenzie said, annoyed to have to spell everything out for him. "To return to Bravo Company."

"I can recall one from Las Cruces, sir. Word came they took the city an hour ago."

"Excellent," MacKenzie said, impressed but not surprised at her troops, especially Major Talbot. "How long?"

"Two hours maybe, plus refuel time on arrival here. Would you like to be seen by a medic?"

"Recall two helos, one for transport, maybe that retrofitted Venom, and prepare orders to transfer Bryce to my command."

Porteus's eyes shifted to the cadet. He appeared both puzzled and conflicted.

"Is your confusion with the helos or the transfer order, Lieutenant?"

"He's a cadet, sir," Porteus said. "A runner. He has other tasks—"

"We're at war, Lieutenant. There are no cadets. I'm promoting Bryce to staff sergeant to serve as my personal adjutant."

Bryce and Porteus made the same choking sound.

"Is there a problem?"

"No, sir," both soldiers said at the same time.

"Good. You have engineers here?"

"Yes, sir," Porteus said.

"I want a squad of engineers and a strike team to fly down to Eagle Pass in the Venom at high altitude. Are you listening, Lieutenant?"

Porteus looked like he'd just gotten off a roller coaster. "Yes, sir."

"They are to fly above two thousand feet. I can confirm loyalists in the region have access to antiaircraft gear ranging more than a thousand feet. There's a field of bodies beside the high school at the north end of Eagle Pass. I want them buried properly."

"Buried, sir?"

"Every one of them. With care. However long it takes."

"Understood, sir," Porteus said. He did not, however, move on to request the helos.

"Is there something else?"

"You have a comm from Horeb," he said, as if he'd been holding this news in the whole time and was finally relieved of its burden. "Eyes only. It's set up in the courthouse."

The Seer. MacKenzie didn't bother wondering how he knew to contact her at Fort Stockton. As far as she knew, he got all his intel from God. Why would this be any different? She ordered Porteus to round up some dog food for Reina and then started toward the courthouse, unable to help imagining bodies swinging between the pillars.

As she reached the pillars, she realized Bryce was still at the curb.

"Sergeant," she said.

Bryce only stared.

"Sergeant Bryce."

He flexed to attention, as if she'd shocked him with a stun baton. "Yes, sir!"

"With me."

Bryce double-timed it across the street, catching up as she neared the entrance. Inside, the courthouse atrium was clad in marble and bright plaster and gold leaf. Two soldiers waited at the far end, flanking a small array topped by two monitors.

"Sir," Bryce said as they approached the soldiers, "may I ask a question?"

"Because you think, Bryce," MacKenzie said. "You understand initiative. How to evaluate orders. And because you've got a moral compass."

"We all do, sir."

"You're also naïve as fuck," MacKenzie said. "We'll work on that. For now, I want to you to pay attention, to follow orders, and to tell me when my orders start tugging at that compass needle. Can you do that?"

"Yes, sir."

"Good. What's your first name?"

"Elijah, sir."

"Elijah? I thought that was on the censor list," MacKenzie

said. The obvious Biblical names had been blacklisted from the start, long before Bryce was born. Unspeakable names like Abraham, Miriam, Esther, and Moses began to be outlawed in some cities even before the Reclamation. The more common names like Michael, Jonathan, and Mary were allowed simply because there were too many people with them to enforce changing them all, but they fell out of favor quickly. How the name Rafael made it through the censors, she had no idea.

And here I am thinking of Rafe again.

MacKenzie's hands closed into fists. They were steady, but she could feel tremors waiting beneath the skin, somewhere between bone and muscle.

"My birth name was Charles, sir," Bryce said. "A lot of us change our names when we join Horeb."

They approached the two soldiers at the array. MacKenzie dismissed them. When they'd exited the building, she said to Bryce, "Stand post at the entrance. No one comes in, and you don't hear a damn word spoken. Understood?"

"Yes, sir."

MacKenzie was struck by how skinny the boy seemed. And unarmed. She drew her sidearm, safety checked it, and handed it to Bryce, who took it with a careful but steady grip.

"You did well in firearms training?"

"Well enough, sir."

"This is yours. From now on, you don't go anywhere without it. When we're done here, I want to you find whatever passes for an armory around here and pick up combat supplies for both of us. Standard strike team gear times two. Got it?"

"Yes, sir."

When Bryce had taken his post, MacKenzie switched on the array. The left monitor flashed to life. It wasn't the Seer.

"General," Thomas Aldrich said. The digital image made him appear younger and less burdened than the last time she'd seen him in person. "I trust your detour to Fort Stockton has achieved its intentions."

"Do you have a problem with the way I run my company?" MacKenzie asked, careful to keep her face impassive and her tone neutral. Her personal relationship with the Seer allowed a measure of freedom and honesty which Aldrich—who struck her as obsessed with rank and structure—opposed.

"Only if it affects Horeb."

"I'd like to speak to the Seer."

"About Eagle Pass?"

MacKenzie lost her words for a moment. "Are you tracking me?"

"I track all of Horeb's resources."

Resources! As if she were a piece of field ordnance to be tagged and tracked. The desire to switch off the array and strip down and throw all her clothes and equipment onto a bonfire flushed MacKenzie. She'd been unplugged, untethered, since she abandoned the Republic army a decade ago. Even a hint of being monitored made her feel betrayed by her own flesh.

"Get me the Seer," she ordered, though she had no right to do so.

Aldrich shrugged and backed away from the screen. A moment later, the Seer moved into view, his face lined with worry and the weight of God's expectations.

"Hannah," the Seer said, his tone fatherly despite the fact he couldn't have been more than five or seven years older than her.

"The Grossmutter is dead," she said, those four words taking the wind from her.

"I know."

They watched each other. MacKenzie wondered how she looked to the Seer.

"Nogales is secure," she said. "Bravo Company is ready for Phase Two. El Paso will fall before dawn."

"The Lord was wise to place His faith in you."

The Seer's words were uplifting, but there was a disappointment to his tone MacKenzie found unfamiliar and disconcerting. She wanted, suddenly and viscerally, to be back in Horeb. She wanted to feel the Seer's hand on her shoulder, assuring her they were still on God's path. She wanted to hear him say the word she'd loved hearing Simon say: *Providence.*

"You have a question," he said. A statement. A fact.

"Question, sir?"

"Hannah, please. You may be an excellent soldier and spy,

but your soul hides no secrets from me."

What God knows, she thought, far more uncomfortable than she should have been at the idea, *the Seers knows.*

"I want to hunt down the ones who carried out the Eagle Pass massacre."

"Do you think this is the time for an exercise in vengeance?"

Yes!

"The executioners of this slaughter deserve to be brought to justice."

"To trial?"

"Yes."

"While we're at war?"

"The war will be over soon enough."

The Seer smiled wearily, the smile of a man who knew a flood was coming but had no materials to build a boat.

"I miss you here, Hannah," he said after a beat. "I fear we lose our balance without each other. I, perhaps, lose some of my humanity as I commune with the Lord, and you lose some of your spirituality out there in the world."

Something inside MacKenzie felt like it was breaking, a sliver of herself cracking off and falling into a chasm so deep the sound of it hitting bottom would never reach her ear.

"Are you telling me not to go after them?" she asked.

"I'm telling you there are more important tasks."

"More important than justice? If we don't do this now, we'll never find them, not all of them. There'll never be trials. The Grossmutter—"

"Not all justice is courts and trials."

"God will deliver their punishment?"

"The Lord delivers all judgement."

"That's not what I mean, and you fucking know it."

The Seer sighed. Disappointment. He never explicitly said as much when she used that kind of language around him, but she knew.

"Do you think Moses was angry at watching the Israelites cross into Canaan?" he asked.

"What?"

"When Moses stood upon the summit of Mount Nebo,

knowing he would never enter the Promised Land, was he angry at the Lord?"

He thinks I'm losing my Faith. The thought was like a chill through MacKenzie's body. She could feel the Seer watching her, the way her mother used to watch her when she was a child and knew she should apologize for whatever her temper had made her do.

"Is God angry with me?" she asked.

"All is as the Lord wills it." His mouth remained open as if about to say more.

For a moment, MacKenzie thought the screen had frozen. "Sir," she started.

The Seer put up his hand. "We need you in Horeb."

She was being called home. Elation filled her, only to be pushed aside by fear. "Have I failed you?"

"We need Bravo Company, Hannah."

"But El Paso..."

"We are betrayed," the Seer said. "The Republic has our location. They're coming."

"How?" MacKenzie said. The only word she could muster. The location of Horeb was the most important secret they had. The base was their Holy Land. If they lost it, would they lose their way like the Israelites in the desert who built the golden calf when their Faith faltered?

"Ba-el has chosen a prophet. He has turned an ally against us."

A panic MacKenzie hadn't felt in years, not since the night she went AWOL from the Republic army, set her trembling. Somehow, she was freezing. That cold hardened to a point. As it had that night. It became a weapon. She honed it. Owned it as part of her. Wielded it.

"Who is it?" she said, intending to return to Horeb and root out this traitor. Expecting this was why she was being recalled. "Who betrayed us?"

"It doesn't matter. The damage is done. We need Bravo Company now, Hannah. Our forces are preparing to engage Republic troops across the width of I-40. You're the only one with the mobility to get here in time. You're the only one I trust."

But she couldn't let it go. "Who is it?" she demanded.

The Seer bowed his head as if disappointed she wouldn't let this go, and then he switched off the comm.

CHAPTER 39

L uck.

Because despite all he'd witnessed, Ward still couldn't believe a god would take an interest in him. He didn't have the type of Faith Simon and MacKenzie had, confident their god would champion them no matter what. Providence, they liked to say.

Ward went with Luck.

Because Providence didn't make one fucking bit of sense considering he'd survived the dynamite only to end up buried alive, to die slowly and in agony from dehydration and starvation. Unless the Providence of it was that he would run out of air first and simply fall asleep and never wake.

Like Sam.

It was that thought which kept him digging for the first few hours. Or maybe minutes. Days. He didn't know. Time had no meaning in absolute darkness. He dug at loose rubble simply to have something to do other than think of Sam and how he'd failed her again.

How he failed her twice at once: her life and her baby's.

Eventually, however, he stopped digging. It was pointless. He knew he was in the inner chamber—he'd made it through the channel and flung himself around the corner of the tomb's L shape before the dynamite exploded—but he had no idea if he was making progress or even if he was digging in the right direction. He could dig all the way through the channel and never know it if the tunnel to the entrance had collapsed, or if Rivka had replaced the slab over the hole above. He wouldn't see a light at the end of the tunnel—he couldn't help chuckling at this—only more darkness. And death. Another body in the ground. His. Hannibal's. Billions and billions of others who'd died over the millennia.

Except his mind found its way to a specific horde of bodies in a subterranean hole like this one. The golgotha beneath Masada. A thousand dead. Mingled in their remains, glints of steel.

Their escape route through Masada replayed for Ward. The way Rivka knew her way through those tunnels. The way she knew those bones would be there. A thousand of them. The same number of defenders of Masada against the Roman legions. The same number who, according to Josephus, committed suicide rather than be taken alive and forced to convert to Roman paganism, though their bodies had never been confirmed by Roman histories or discovered by archaeologists.

He thought of the dagger Rivka had put to Zee's neck, the curved dagger, and the pieces fell into place. She was Sicarii. They, all of them at Masada, were Sicarii, carrying on two thousand years after their ancestors fell.

She was an assassin.

For the moment, questions of Hannibal and the khopesh and Rivka's role as a doctor fled, leaving Ward comfortably cold and focused. He saw Rivka's face. Her eyes. Her cold, lying eyes. He hadn't wanted to harm anyone since he destroyed the Tower, but a desire was pumping through him, fueled by those lying eyes. He let himself feel that impulse. In the absence of light and food and water, he drank that murderous need to kill.

Irrationally, he got up, intending to dig with his fingers until there was nothing left of them but bloody stumps, as if there was any chance of escaping this pit to enact the vengeance he so desired. The chamber ceiling had been brought low by the dynamite and resulting cave in, however. At full height, his head smashed the stone above, knocking him back onto his ass. Dirt and dust and ash filled the air, choking him.

I'm breathing Hannibal. He laughed, maniacally to his own ear, which only made him choke harder, collapsing into a mess of hysterics and gagging.

Eventually, he found his composure. There was no point in

digging. No point in trying. He was only alive so he could die in this darkness. A twisted agnostic Luck. Not Providence.

"But I'll make you a deal," he said, the Hannibal-dust gritty in his mouth. "Yes, you. Whichever one you are. Let's make a deal. A covenant. You get me out of here, and I'll believe."

He waited for answer, aware he was probably running out of air and becoming delusional. That was okay. He'd had conversations with himself before. His sentinel used to watch out for him. He'd settle for a return of that hallucination before he died. It was no less, he suspected, than the comfort Believers held as they died.

"No? Not in a bargaining mood? Or maybe I'm just not worth it? How about vengeance? Get me out of here so I can kill Rivka. Bet you haven't had many human sacrifices recently. How would you like me to do it? Slit her throat? Set her heart on fire? Name it. Give me a sign."

He closed his eyes. Or maybe they'd been closed, and he opened them. He couldn't tell. He'd heard of it being so dark a person couldn't see their hand in front of their face. In this darkness he wasn't even sure he had hands. Or a face.

"I thought so," he spat, wanting his final words to carry the full weight of his accusation. "Frauds, all of you. Prehistoric superstitions. Fantasies sold by snake oil peddlers of the worst kind. I'll take my Luck, shitty as it is. I'll die with it. You can shove your Providence up your holy asses!"

Right then, as his voice continued to echo in the darkness, the earth began to shake.

PART 4: THE OATH BREAKER

By nature, was Hannibal eager for action, an oath-breaker,
a cunning master, yet unbound by justice.
—Punica, by Silius Italicus, c. 90

Ye thralls of meanest vengeance, tyrant gods,
Who mar the sacred nature in her fruit,
Who relish all disorder and unfaith,
Whence your authority that frame such deeds?
—Niobe, by John Warren, 3rd Baron de Tabley, 1864

...should not have to convince any of you. Our loyalty to our
neighbors should be enough to enact our oaths. Our duty to the
Republic should be enough to demand our presence in this fight.
Let it never be said that we stood by, our hats in our hands, with
the enemy at the gates.
—Internal memo, El Paso Police Department,
    17 November 2056

CHAPTER 40

The girl was in a cave again, of sorts. She liked the isolation. She liked the darkness. She could remember liking the sun, the real sun, once upon a time, but isolation and darkness were better, even if it wasn't a real cave.

Her new friend, her dark friend, brought her here. Told the girl there were people looking for her. Told the girl her name had once been Samantha. The girl recognized this was true, but she didn't like the name. It didn't fit, like a shirt two sizes too big.

We don't need a name, Other said.

"You don't like my new friend, do you?" the girl replied.

Other had gone away, deep down where the girl could barely feel anything, when her dark friend arrived. Only when she was alone, her dark friend having left her here in this metal cage to wait, did Other return and insist the single light bulb hanging from the ceiling be put out. Darkness, Other explained, was as close to home as they could get above ground. An impulse to smash the light filled the girl. She'd come to understand the difference between her own impulses and ones originating from Other and chose, instead, to rise up on her toes and unscrewed the bulb.

Not our friend, Other said. *A liar. An abomination.*

The girl didn't know that word, but she felt Other's revulsion, as if her dark friend were something outside Other's ability to comprehend.

Other wanted to kill her dark friend. The impulse was unmistakable. It was Other's primary response to most things. Kill. For Other it was as natural as seeking water when thirsty. At times the girl liked that impulse. She let it fill her the way coffee—*I remember coffee!* she thought—filled a mug to overflowing. At other times, a part of the girl, maybe a part that remembered who she once was, didn't like killing, but that part was small and distant and unable to be heard when Other became parched for death.

"I like my new friend," the girl said, enjoying the way her voice echoed in the metal box, each reverberation bringing part of a memory. She'd been in a metal box before. A much smaller one. A man had put her in the box, and when he'd taken her out, he'd hurt her.

Her hand began to ache. The one that wasn't there. The one that had been replaced with the metallic cuff began to ache. She cradled the cuff to her chest, trying to find the rest of her hand, and the rest of the memory, in that pain.

It is your new friend's fault.

It wasn't often Other referred to the girl as *you*. It was usually *we*. Other's animus toward her dark friend was visceral. It was thirsty.

"My friend did this to me?"

It is your friend's fault.

The girl understood the difference immediately, even as she was aware Other hoped she would not. She knew her dark friend had not been entirely honest with her. Now, Other was offering the same kind of incomplete truth. In that place where Other couldn't hear her thinking, she told herself these half-truths were okay. They indicated weaknesses on the part of those who told them. Fears. She could wait. She had time to decide whose fear would serve her best.

She sat on the cool floor in the middle of the box, letting the darkness comfort her, content to wait for the doors to open.

CHAPTER 41

Ward had been awake for some time before his brain finally made that information available to the rest of his body. He was sprawled on a squishy, musty couch. His head felt like it was stuffed with gauze, thoughts having to fight through to make sense. He sat up and immediately regretted it. His vision became a whirlpool of bright lights and muted colors, and he fell back on the couch.

Slowly—he had no way to judge time—his head began to clear, and memory began to return. A bag of fluid, maybe saline, had been hung on a peg in the wall beside the couch and run into his arm through a thick tube. Before that he'd been dumped on the couch. Before that he'd been brought through... tunnels? To where?

He raised his head enough to look around. Had there been more tables and chairs, he might have thought he was in an old, unused in many years, restaurant. There remained a single round table beneath a single yellow bulb hanging from a line. Four chairs surrounded the table. A swinging door led, presumably, to the kitchen. A narrow hallway led into darkness behind the table. The front wall was boarded up the way people at the Jersey Shore boarded up their windows during hurricane season. The wallpaper and rugs gave the place a Mediterranean feel. No, Middle Eastern.

Am I back in Jerusalem?

That thought led to Rivka. Which led to sex. Then to the bomb. The tomb. The dynamite. The cave in. Then what? The dots wouldn't connect. One moment he'd been buried alive, and the next he was here, plugged into saline, with a smashing headache and no one around to explain the gaps. Was he on this couch as a patient or a prisoner? Did he have someone to thank, or someone to fear?

The only recollection between then and now was himself in the darkness of the tomb bargaining with…who? Himself? A god? *The* God? Or, even crazier, El or Ba'el?

I'm becoming a Believer, he thought, as if it were a disease he'd somehow caught. But he knew better. He'd been scared. Injured and delirious. There were no gods.

Right?

He pulled the tubing from his arm. "Damn, fuck," he said at the pain, his voice cracking. He got to his feet and almost pitched right over. Gripping the arm of the couch, he steadied himself.

But he was no longer alone. The sounds of people approaching, voices and footfalls, from the narrow hallway announced he had only seconds to act. He tried to cross the room, to get to the wall beside the hallway for cover. He made it only as far as the table, where he fell into one of the chairs.

"My friend," said the first man through the opening. "You're awake. You must be thirsty."

Ward went for Zee's throat almost before he registered who had arrived, determined not let himself be held a prisoner as Sam was by Ker. No matter he barely had the strength to stand. No matter two more men appeared from the hallway, tipping the odds horribly out of his favor. He went for Zee, and got as far as knocking over the table.

Next thing, he was on his back, the knee of one of the other men pressed into his chest. He knew the man. One of the three from Turkey. The men who'd come after him and Rivka with dart guns. The other man with Zee had been there as well. Of the third man from Turkey, Ward saw no sign. He did note, however, none of the three were armed.

"Let him up, Nasir," Zee said. "And get him some water. Would you like food? Dates? Falafel?"

The man called Nasir took his knee of Ward's chest slowly and offered his hand. Ward got to his feet on his own, albeit unsteadily. Nasir righted the chairs first, which Ward took advantage of by slumping into the closer one, and then the table. The other man, meanwhile, disappeared into the kitchen.

"I must admit," Zee said, "I didn't think you would be awake yet."

"Sorry to surprise you," Ward said, searching Zee's face for a hint of intention. Interrogation? Torture? Holding for the highest bidder. He found only the face of a smuggler, a man he'd once thought of as a friend.

"You now know Nasir," Zee said. "And this is Farooq." He nodded toward the man returning from the kitchen with bottles of water and a plate of dates.

Ward kept his eyes on Zee. "You're Sicarii, like her, aren't you?"

Zee laughed. "No, we are nothing of the sort, though I am happy you figured out who Masada is on your own. It will save some explaining."

"Masada? All of them?" Ward asked. Thinking still felt like running underwater.

"I'm sure you have many questions. Please drink, and I will try to answer them."

Farooq offered Ward a bottle of water, his outstretched hand revealing a hint of the familiar tattoo Zee, and presumably Nasir, also sported. He'd seen nothing like it at Masada. And Rivka certainly wasn't sporting a similar brand anywhere on her body. Whatever it meant, he could accept that Zee wasn't Sicarii. That didn't mean the smuggler was an ally, however. He took the bottle from Farooq and considered what to do with it. Throw it at Farooq? At Zee? Pour its contents on the floor in act of defiance?

In the end, however, his thirst won out. He drank.

"How about those answers?" Ward said after finishing half the bottle.

"Of course," Zee said. "But first I must ask, has she found the sword?"

"What sword?"

"The only sword that matters. The key to everything."

"What are you…" but Ward remembered as he said it. The khopesh Rivka had taken from the tomb on Malta.

"The Barq," Zee said. "The sword of Hannibal. Does she have it?"

"Is that why you came for me?" Ward said, a strange jealousy rising in him. It was the sword everyone was after. No one gave a shit about him anymore.

"I must apologize for how long it took us to find you," Zee said. He took a seat at the table opposite Ward, placing his hands on the table, palms up, the tip of his tattoo visible. "You didn't wear the shoes I provided, and then we had to make sure you weren't one of them."

"What are you talking about?"

"Drink. Eat. I will explain."

"Can't wait," Ward said. He took another gulp of water which then caught in his throat, going down the wrong pipe. He choked it down, chasing it with two more swallows. The bottle was almost empty.

"I did not trust Rivka," Zee said, "and I have never trusted the Sicarii. They did not all die at Masada two thousand years ago, I'm sure you've surmised. Otherwise, we wouldn't have their story, would we?"

Ward wasn't interested in rhetorical questions. He motioned for Zee to continue while he planned for an escape. The hallway was a poor choice. Farooq hovered at its entrance. Nasir stayed near the kitchen, which might have a back door. But no one blocked the boarded-up front of the restaurant. Boards meant windows. Maybe a door. If they were as old as the dust and smell of the place indicated, he might be able to break through. At the least, he might break off a plank with a nail or two in it as a weapon.

"I had tracking chips placed in the soles of the shoes in the apartment. Rivka chose a pair. You didn't. It made tracking you difficult. Once we realized she was alone, we had to backtrack to Malta. I'd say we got there right in time."

"I'd argue that 'in time' would have been before Rivka buried me alive," Ward said.

"You're not dead," Zee said as if announcing it was Ward's birthday.

"And you expect that to make me happy? You tried to kill me, too."

"My friend, you offend me. I have never done anything of the sort."

Ward wasn't sure what to believe yet, but he couldn't see how a Zee-Rivka alliance made sense. Which meant that even if the Zee wasn't his friend, at least he might not be his enemy.

"Then what do you want?" he asked.

Zee said, "The same thing you want."

"I want to find Rivka, make her tell me where Sam is, and then kill her. Then I want to rescue Sam and never come back to this part of the world again."

"Okay, so not exactly the same," Zee said. "But close enough that we should help each other. The Sicarii have been planning to infiltrate the Republic for some time. When you were brought to them, their plans accelerated. They used you like a bird for two stones. Is that the saying?"

"Two birds with one stone," Ward corrected. He calculated that with a good jump he could make it to the boarded windows, maybe even yank one off to use as a weapon, before Nasir or Farooq overtook him. The odds of success, however, were obviously shit, so aside from shifting his weight in the chair, he stayed put.

"Yes, that," Zee said. "The sword is their primary goal."

"Why? What's an ancient sword to them?"

The answer began forming in Ward's mind before Zee even spoke. The sword was something powerful, like the Vase of Soissons or the River Lethe. Believers would kill for it. They would die for it, accepting that some god or another was smiling on them as they bled out.

And if Ward accepted that? If he were willing to believe others saw power in the sword, wasn't the next logical step accepting that the sword actually had power. From there, would it be much more than a nudge to make him like Rivka and MacKenzie? To make him a Believer?

"The sword is a tool," Zee said. "A gift. Perhaps the first gift a god ever gave. But we must discuss the present times first. The Sicarii want your revolution to succeed. They want your Republic to fall. But they also will not allow the Seer to control the new nation that rises."

"It's not my rev…" Ward bit off his objection. "They're blaming me for the bomb in Jerusalem, aren't they? They're spinning it that I blew up the Consulate on the orders of the Seer so they can rally other governments against him."

"Yes."

"But they're Jews. The people they killed in the bomb were Jews. How does killing their own advance their goal? How is that sacrifice worth making a play on the Republic? What do they care about North America, anyway?"

"The Sicarii are fanatics. All who do not follow their god, El, with the same fervor as they do are their enemies. The Republic. The Seer. Jews who lack the conviction the Sicarii expect. They're all the same to Masada. Anyone who is not them is an enemy. Like Baghel."

Zee's face fell as if he might weep. Ward didn't have to ask to know Baghel's fate. The same as Sam's if he couldn't find Rivka and make her tell him out where they took Sam.

"And Rivka did that, right?" Ward asked. "She set the bomb, not you, right?"

"You want me to convince you?"

"You're damned right I do!"

"We dug you out of the tomb. Is that not enough? Then consider this: if I wanted to blow up my own building, don't you think I could have done so without setting off an alarm? I am not your enemy, Rafael."

It made sense. It fit in with Zee's men in Turkey coming after them with darts rather than live ammunition. Maybe it was the result of being buried alive, but Ward found himself wanting to trust that the smuggler was the same man who'd helped him on Santorini.

"Our objectives are the same," Zee said. "We must find Rivka."

"For the sword?"

"For the heavens and the earth and humanity itself."

"That's a lot for a sword, isn't it?" Ward asked.

Zee only stared, as if daring Ward to disbelieve.

"Look," Ward said, "if you want the sword, or anything else she has, you can have it. All I want is her. She's my only link to finding Sam. You said you're tracking her, right?"

"We've lost her signal. I suspect she changed clothes or found the tracker."

Which meant every minute they spent talking, Rivka was getting farther away. "Fuck this," Ward said. "Tell me the last place you tracked her to, then I'm going."

"You cannot."

"You're going to stop me, *friend*?"

"For your own good, yes. It is not safe to go outside here."

"Why not? Where are we?"

Nasir made a sound. An objection.

"Al-Shatrah," Zee said.

"Southern Iraq?" Ward said, confused by the ridiculousness of the lie. "In the Quarantine Zone? Bullshit."

He got up as quickly as he could, swaying slightly, and went for the boarded windows. He expected to be tackled, but no one stopped him. He grabbed at the boards, but the planks were screwed onto a metal sheeting that covered the front of the restaurant. A hard foam filled the seams where wall, ceiling, and floor met. He grabbed a plank and pulled anyway. It didn't budge. He sought a better handhold. Got his fingers under the edge of a plank. The steel was warm on the other side. He pulled until he thought the muscles in his arms might tear. There was a slight rattle but no more.

"Please stop that. You'll bring unwanted attention."

"From who, the Sicarii?"

"Remember the Nephilim?"

Ward stopped pulling on the board. "Where are we really?"

"I told you. Al-Shatrah, in the Quarantine Zone. It is not safe to go outside."

"Radiation?"

"A concern, yes," Zee said. "You wiped Riyadh off the Earth and drew a boundary on a map and told the world not to cross the line, but you never come here to move the people. The survivors. You never provided assistance or refugee camps. You never negotiated with the nations in the region to absorb the people you displaced."

Ward barely kept his temper. "Not me! Not my fucking war, get it?"

"Please, come away from the windows. They'll hear you."

"The Nephilim?"

"What survived here is different than those we encountered in Bethlehem," Zee said. "More feral."

"So, no tanks?"

"It is not a joke, Rafael. We are in a dangerous place. This is what makes it the perfect place to hide. The Levantine Authority has no presence here, and our enemies would never think to look for us in the Quarantine. Please sit, and I will explain everything."

Less reluctant than he expected, Ward returned to the table and sat.

"We have a source inside Masada," Zee said. "Things have been gearing up there for a move for some months."

"Since Sam and I arrived?"

"More or less, though we think you were only a fortuitous piece of the overall plan."

Ward thought of the comm tap he'd placed about a week after his arrival at Masada. Right about the time he and Rivka were becoming friends. He doubted the coincidence Zee was ready to believe in, but it didn't matter. Not now.

"As soon as you and Rivka left the mountain they began evacuating the fortress," Zee said. "It is all coming to a boil. Jerusalem is on the brink of war thanks to Rivka's bomb. The Seer will win his revolution and demonstrate the folly of disbelief. Which brings me back to my first question: does Rivka have the sword?"

"She took it, yes."

"I feared as much. The Sicarii are not only assassins. They are infiltrators. They aspire to be conquerors. They whisper into the ear of every powerful military on Earth. They plan to assert their god and their doctrines over all humanity."

"I don't see how this is my problem. I was content not existing for two years. I'll happily go back to that life after I find Sam and shove that sword into Rivka's heart."

"Listen to me then, my friend. They evacuated Masada in four waves. My source says they unplugged Samantha from life support and left her behind with a few soldiers, possibly as a trap for you. They lost contact with those soldiers not long after the Consulate was destroyed."

"What are you saying?" Ward asked. "She's still there, at Masada?"

"She was."

"Alive?"

"Yes."

Ward was on his feet again. "You have to take me there."

"I will help with your friend," Zee said, "but first you must help me. The sword—"

"Fuck the sword. You and Rivka can choke on the damned thing. All I care about is Sam."

"I know you don't want to hear this, but we are fighting the same war. The usurpers will destroy us all if we don't stop them."

"Usurpers?

"The Tyrant Gods: El and Ba'el."

"For fuck's—you're a Believer. I must be blind."

"There is a place in the world for all of us, even those who don't have Faith, but only if we overthrow the tyrants."

"Usurp the usurpers?"

"Don't mock me. This is a dangerous time. The Sicarii are El's dagger. Now they possess Ba'el's sword. They possess the ability to kill a god, and more."

"Let them kill a god," Ward said. "What do I care if they murder an imaginary friend?" Except, he found, he did care. The idea of deicide suddenly struck him as repugnant. Abhorrent. Like sending a medieval relic to the Crematorium.

An academic reluctance, he told himself. *That's all. Not Belief. Just a distaste for destroying myth and history.*

"Rafael, you must open your eyes. You must—"

"The only thing I must do is find Sam. You want Ba'el's sword back for your museum or whatever, go get it. I don't..." Ward was going to say more, but those two words—*Ba'el's sword*—stuck in his brain when he spoke them the way the water he'd drunk too fast had stuck in his chest. "Hannibal's sword is Ba'el's sword?"

Zee stood. "Yes."

"You called it the Barq."

"Yes."

"Barq, from Barca, meaning *shining fire,*" Ward said, shocked he hadn't seen it earlier. "And Hannibal, meaning *the grace of Ba'el.*"

It was a simple etymological leap any historian or mythologist should have picked up on from the start. What had his obtuseness cost? Sam's life? Her baby's?

"Do you know the story of Ba'el's battle with the serpent?"

"The serpent resides in Paradise, shedding its skin for a new life whenever it grows old," Ward said. "It's the god of life and death, and Ba'el is jealous of it. He wants to kill the serpent and steal its Paradise, so he asks the god of craftsmanship, Kothar-wa-Khasis, for a special weapon, a god-killing weapon, and is given a flaming sword."

"The Barq."

"And you want me to believe Hannibal Barca was Ba'el's prophet and wielded the god's sword?"

Zee placed his hands on Ward's shoulders. "You must see it. You must feel how close we are to the gods."

"The only thing I must do is find Sam."

As Ward pushed Zee's hands away, he saw again the smuggler's tattoo. From tree roots to vine-wrapped trunk. Only, they weren't vines at all. They were two snakes wrapped helically around the trunk.

It all came together with where they were. Al-Shatrah, in southern Iraq. The heartland of Mesopotamia, only a few kilometers from the city of Lagash, where four thousand years ago a great temple stood to an ancient god. A serpent god of life and death.

"Ningiszida," Ward said, speaking the name of the Mesopotamian god.

Nasir and Farooq bowed their heads. Zee did the same.

"Lord of the Tree of Life," the smuggler said.

CHAPTER 42

"You weren't on Santorini for holiday, were you?" Ward asked, already certain of the answer. "That wasn't a coincidence."

Zee appeared amused. "No, it wasn't a coincidence."

Ward finished his water. "Who hired you?"

"You think I was hired to be your friend?"

"Don't tell me it was a coincidence I happened to bump into the one person with the contacts and skills to help me get back to the Republic."

"I did not say it was a coincidence."

"Who told you to be there? Who put you on that beach?"

"The Lord of the Tree of Life came to me in a dream and showed me the beach outside my flat on Santorini. She told me the secret to breaking El and Ba'el's hold on Paradise would reveal itself to me if I went fishing. I thought She meant I would find enlightenment within the peace of fishing. Imagine my surprise when She brought you."

"The REC and a deranged priest brought me to Santorini, not your...did you say *She*?"

"The Lord of the Tree of Life."

"Ningiszida is a woman? The Lady of the Tree of Life?"

"She is what She wants to be, and She is always the *Lord* of the Tree of Life."

"Forget it. I'm not doing this," Ward said. He didn't want to hear about another god. El and Ba'el. Kerberos and Garm. Now Ningiszida? If one was real, were two? If two, why not four? If four, why not all of them? When would it stop? What role did humanity even have if there were hundreds of gods, maybe thousands, warring for…what? Souls? Power? Bragging rights?

But if none are real, who was I asking to save me in Hannibal's tomb? Who was I praying to?

"You are caught in a wave, my friend," Zee said. "We all are. The only way out is to ride it to shore."

"I'll show you another way out." Ward went for the kitchen, hoping for a back exit. What he found was a tiny kitchen with a rotted butcher block island in the middle and a rusty refrigerator without a door on the right beside a countertop with a hole where the sink should be. There was no exit. No way out.

Zee appeared in the doorway. "Please," he said. "Come drink more water and eat the dates. They will refresh you."

"Ask me politely again, and I'll shove that bottle of water up your ass."

I sound like her, Ward thought. *Like MacKenzie.*

With nowhere else to go, Ward followed Zee back to the table. The smuggler sat. Ward didn't. Farooq and Nasir remained near the hallway.

"I'm going to tell you a story," Zee said. Not polite, but the message was clear: *You're going to listen.* "When humanity began experimenting with civilization, they sought to bring their gods from the fields and the rivers and the islands to their cities. Gods, however, are fickle. Like cats. Some came. Some didn't."

"And then El made a pact with Abraham, and the rest is bullshit anyway," Ward said, feeling like he was trying to convince himself, not Zee. Regardless, he was certain Sam didn't have time to entertain more stories. "I don't need a theology lesson."

"You do! El and Ba'el are latecomers. You know their story. They arrived upon catastrophe, killing thousands. Since then, their bickering has killed millions. They turned humanity against itself, praying on the civilizations our indigenous gods helped us build, and driving many of those older gods to extinction."

"Which is all true of course because you believe it, as compared to what's obviously true for others who believe different."

Zee fixed a glare upon Ward, his eyes forbidding Ward to look away, forcing him to ask questions as if the smuggler were stitching them into Ward's mind.

What did I see rising from the Mediterranean on Santorini?

What about the old man on the cliff, and at the café in Paris, and in the photo of the Grossmutter's husband?

What about Ker and what happened to Sam when she swallowed the water of Lethe?

"You know better," Zee said. "The conflict between experience and belief is plain on your face. Listen to me. For the first time in your life, my friend, *learn*. The people of the Fertile Crescent called Ningiszida to their cities, to this city, to beg for a second chance, for She is the green earth and the withered netherworld and the Tree of Life around which we revolve. She is Paradise and rebirth, and they begged Her to save them."

"This isn't a lesson," Ward said, clinging to denial as if it were a life raft. "It's the same fable in a different language. An older version of Persephone and her six months above and six below. You might as well label Persephone as Ningiszida 2.0, and the Japanese goddess Izanami as the 5.0 version. And the Tree of Life? Come on. Yggdrasil. Shajarat al-Kholoud. It's the same story rebooted for a different time, like Gilgamesh's flood retold as Noah's. Ningiszida's residence in Paradise surrounding the Tree is no different than any other paradisiacal garden."

"The people of the Fertile Crescent prospered with Ningiszida in their hearts and in their cities," Zee continued, as if Ward hadn't objected. "And when they passed from this world, Ningiszida brought them to the eternal garden, called Dilmun, to bless them in preparation for rejoining the Tree of Life."

"More parallel mythology," Ward countered. A reflex. He didn't even know why he was arguing anymore. He didn't know what he believed anymore. "Dilmun was an ancient city between Mesopotamia and the Indus Valley. Its exotic people and beautiful gardens inspired the myths of Paradise and Eden."

"So, we agree."

"On what? No, you know what, I don't care. I don't want to care. All I want is to find Sam."

"That is not *all* you want. You want truth."

"There is no truth! There's your point of view and other people's beliefs and still other's hopes. It's all the same. It's all killing and dying for lies people want to believe so badly that they won't accept there is no god damned truth!"

Then what have I been studying all these years? The thought popped into Ward's head as the others had, as if stitched there by Zee's will. *What have I been searching for in all those old manuscripts and censored books?*

Meaning.

What is meaning without belief? What is truth without faith?

"What did you do to me?" Ward asked. "Did you put something...did you put Lito in the water?"

"Are you finding it difficult to remain skeptical?" Zee said. "Do you think this is how your students feel when they near epiphany from your lectures? Maybe, professor, all these similarities you cite are signs of truth, not imagination or drugs."

"I..." but Ward no longer knew what to say. In the last twenty-four hours his skepticism had begun to abandon him, the same way anger at Rivka had begun to erode his desire to never again spill blood.

"When the Tyrant Gods came to Dilmun," Zee said, "they stole the hearts of the Fertile Crescent and desecrated the eternal garden. They exiled Ningiszida from Paradise and cast Her in a new narrative as the insidious serpent tempting humanity away from Eden. Once Paradise was theirs and humanity lost faith in Ningiszida, Ba'el went forth into the world to hunt down the old gods while El remained in Paradise to safeguard their prize. Ba'el, with his flaming sword called Barq, was unstoppable."

It sounded both ridiculous and right, insane yet logical. Though not ready to give himself over to Belief, Ward found he was able to accept that Zee believed. Maybe that was enough. Maybe it was the belief itself that made it real, the way European Christians in the Middle Ages knew witches were real. They didn't believe it. They *knew* it. The way Ward knew he was trapped in his Holmesian locked-room pattern.

"What are you asking me to do?"

"For now, continue to listen," Zee said. "The earth is decaying. Humanity is decaying. Our weapons, our betrayal of nature, the sufferers we saw in Bethlehem are all mere symptoms. Only the return of Ningiszida to the Tree of Life can rescue us from our own corruption."

"You want me to help sneak a god into Eden?" Ward knew he should be playing along, but this was too much to pretend he could believe. "Why me? Why was I chosen?"

"No one chose you, Rafael. Have you not been listening? Are you so vain to think the gods have been waiting millennia for you? You put yourself in the game. You listened to the voice in your head. You reported your neighbors and submitted relics for cremation. You also saw through the lies and refused to accept the totality of the Republic's atheism. You gave shelter to El's champion, Hannah MacKenzie. It was always your choice to play the game. It was always your choice which side to play for. It's still your choice. You've listened this long. Will you listen a little longer? Will you fight for the only side that matters?"

"Which side is that?"

"Humanity's side," Zee said. "Ba'el slaughtered the old gods. For each one you know, there are five whose names will never be remembered."

"And these other gods want to start a revolution like in the Republic?"

"There are no other gods," Zee thundered. "Not anymore. Ba'el was relentless. When he returned to Paradise, he did so with the blood of thousands on his blade. The only survivors were Ningiszida and some of the base deities. Regional avatars of rivers and mountains. Spirits of eagles and jaguars. Keepers of dreams and escorts of the dead."

"Kerberos," Ward said.

"Do you believe he was what he claimed?"

"It doesn't matter. Sam killed him."

"That is a separate story," Zee said. "We'll come back to it. When Ba'el returned to Eden, El suggested they should take turns guarding the gate, for Ningiszida might return to take back what once was Hers. They drew lots. Ba'el was to stand the first watch. He dutifully took up his position, and when the gate closed behind him, he cast a spell on it so that none could open it without a key: his special sword, the Barq. Only, he didn't see El follow him out of Eden. It was El who struck the first blow in the war between the Tyrant Gods. That story you know. The war was won by El, and Ba'el was imprisoned."

"In the Vase of Soissons," Ward said, "which I sealed and sank into the Mediterranean."

"Yes, Ba'el is banished once more, but not destroyed. Now, listen. Yes, El defeated Ba'el, but not before Ba'el hid his sword. For thousands of years since, he influenced the minds of humanity, floating among us like a fog, occasionally finding someone to be his champion. His prophet. In the ancient world, there were many such prophets. Each was shown to the sword, and each used it to sow chaos in the world. Hannibal was the last in that line of prophets. Until now."

"And you want me to believe that the sword Rivka took from Hannibal's tomb is Ba'el's sword? That she is Ba'el's prophet?"

"The sword is the Barq. It can kill a god or open the gates of Eden whether you believe it or not. But Rivka is not Ba'el's. She is Sicarii. She is El's. But Ba'el's prophet will not be far from the sword, or from where the sword is going."

"Where is it going?"

"Not far at first. Then the Republic."

"And what's in the Republic?" Ward asked. "A god to kill, or a gate to open?"

"Perhaps both."

"Eden is in the Republic?"

"Eden is not a physical place," Zee said. "It exists outside the geography you see on a map."

"Of course it does."

"Damn it, Rafael! If the champion of either El or Ba'el gets the sword, they will kill the other. They will destroy Ningiszida. They will rule in Paradise forever. Humanity will burn."

I don't believe, Ward told himself. *I'm going along because it gets me to Sam. Because it gets me to Rivka. Because if we have to go to the Republic, maybe I can see MacKenzie again.*

"What do we have to do?"

Zee stood. "The sword can serve only one master at a time, and it cannot harm its master or its master's prophet. It cannot open Eden for anyone other than those who serve its master. It has served Ba'el for millennia, but his prophets have never been able to find Eden's gate. Rivka will seek to cleanse the sword and rededicate it to El. As of an hour ago, she is back in Israel preparing to perform the ceremony that will re-consecrate the sword."

"El can't do it himself?"

"For all their power, gods need us for such things."

"And your plan is to get the sword and make it serve Ningiszida, right?" Ward asked. "Because your god is more benevolent than the others, right? Your god has humanity's best interest at heart."

"You can trust that," Zee said, "or you can allow El and Ba'el to continue in their ways."

"Not much of a choice."

"Precisely."

A sudden feeling of familiarity crept over Ward. He knew what was coming next. If he had pen and paper he could script it.

"You know Rivka is in Israel, but you don't know where," he said. There was no need to ask.

"Yes," Zee said as if reading the same script.

"And you think I can find her."

"I do."

Ward sighed. The script demanded he go along. "It has to be somewhere special, right?"

"Somewhere holy to El. The older and purer the site, the stronger the sword will become."

"Somewhere ancient?"

"You have an idea?"

"Why should I help you?" Ward asked, even though he knew he had to help. Even though he found himself wanting to help. But there was something he needed to do first. Something Zee would have planned for if he was as familiar with the script as Ward suspected.

"You want to find Samantha first, yes?" Zee asked.

"Yes."

"My source in Masada says she is different now."

"Different how?"

"In a way that I, though Ningiszida, can cure. And I do so, but only after you help us. Do we have a deal?"

"Cure? What are you talking about? Her coma?"

"Come," Zee said. "I'll let my source show you."

"Where?"

Zee started for the hallway. "Downstairs."

"Your source is here?"

"Yes," Zee said. "She is."

CHAPTER 43

The hallway forced them single file. Farooq and Nasir first. Zee next. Then Ward. No one behind to prod him along. No worry he wouldn't follow. Zee had the carrot tied nicely to the stick.

Ten meters in, the hallway became stairs leading down to a dimly lit second kitchen with deep corners and deeper shadows. Like upstairs, it was in disrepair, but it was larger, with two sinks, a brick oven set in one wall, and two industrial sized metal freezers in the other.

"Where's your source?" Ward asked.

"Tell me," Zee said. "The events in Spain, did they go exactly as they've been reported?"

"Reported? What are you talking about?" There'd been only a handful of people at the River Lethe beneath the Abbey of Sacromonte: Ward, Sam, MacKenzie, Ker, Garm, and, at the end, Compano and her two men. One of Compano's men, plus Ker, and probably Garm, died there. Sam was in a coma. MacKenzie was...

"Wait, who is your source?" Ward asked.

"First, you never answered my question. Do you believe Kerberos was what he claimed?"

"A dog?"

"Don't pull the blindfold back on now. He claimed he was one of the guardians of the underworld. The river, he claimed, was Lethe. Do you believe him?"

Belief. It all kept coming back to that one idea. That one trust that had killed his mother and MacKenzie's father. Even if he wanted to, Ward didn't know if he knew how to do it. How to have it. Belief. Faith.

And yet, after all he'd seen and done in the past few years, how could he not believe? How could he not at least stop denying Believers their Faith?

Maybe that was enough. Maybe accepting was enough to allow him to start making moves in the game instead of simply being a pawn.

"If I say yes, you'll tell me who your source is?" Ward said.

"Very soon," Zee said, sharply. Like an order. "First, do you remember what the texts say of Kerberos? Do you know his story?"

Ward knew two stories. Mythology said Kerberos was the three-headed dog guarding the gates of the underworld. His most detailed escapade was being captured by Hercules as one of the hero's Twelve Labors.

The man himself, the one called Ker who'd been a soldier in MacKenzie's army, a tech specialist of some sort, claimed he was the underworld guardian. More, he insisted Garm, the Norse equivalent of an underworld guard dog, and Cadejo, a similar South American spirit, were his brothers. The three guardian hounds rather than a three-headed beast.

"The offspring of Echidna and Typhon," Ward said, telling the myth, "Kerberos is a chimera with the heads of snakes rising from his spine to go with three heads of his own. He guards the gate of the underworld, Hades, to prevent the dead from escaping."

"And Typhon's story?"

"Is this a test?"

"Yes," a new voice said. A heavy, mechanical voice.

The darkness between the two freezers seemed to thicken. To move. Taking on form. Substance. Bulk. Then she was there, as if she'd come through a portal. Compano standing massive between the freezers.

"You," Ward cried. He was already moving. Already making fists. Already flying into her.

It was like trying to tackle a truck. She closed her arms around him, servo motors whirring with each motion. He fought, pounding on her metal chest. Seeking the human part of her face. Finally getting an arm free for a good blow. She rotated her head, taking the punch on the side of her helmet. Pain flared in Ward's hand. He screamed. She let go, and he dropped, his legs refusing to stand him up. Nasir and Farooq pulled him to his feet. He yanked away from them and stood toe-to-toe with Compano. It was all he could do. Until he found a gun.

"Where's Sam?" he demanded.

"It's good to see you, Rafael," Compano said.

"Fuck you, you...appliance."

Compano made a sound that might have been a laugh.

Ward asked Zee, "What is she doing here?"

"She came to us," Zee said. "What she was offering, we couldn't refuse."

"She's your source?"

"I was," Compano said. "Until they kicked this operation into gear."

"Then you know where Sam is."

"Let me tell you a story."

Ward wasn't interested in another story. He'd had enough stories to last him a few lifetimes. He thought maybe, if he ever found a life of his own again—one not enveloped in the never-ending wars of Believers and their gods—he might take up gardening or woodworking.

"They saved me to use me," Compano said. "They pretended to teach me, to indoctrinate me, but they never really wanted or needed my belief."

"That must have hurt your feelings," Ward said. "If you have any."

"Of course, I understood. They are Sicarii. They are convinced of their own singular righteousness. No different than my Agents. No different than your girlfriend and her rebels. No different than the Seer."

Ward flinched. He couldn't help it. First, the surprise of thinking Compano meant Rivka—how could she have known about the night they'd spent together in Jerusalem? Then, realizing she meant MacKenzie. That old wound. Compano never missed an opportunity to stick her robotic fingers into it and twist.

She didn't miss the flinch, either. Her head tilted. Had she learned something new or merely confirmed a suspicion? Ward was certain she was playing them for something, but with only half a face, she was impossible to read. Like trying to guess a toaster's intention. It had purpose not intent. Unlike a toaster, however, Compano was deadly. He would have to be more careful.

"The whole base went dark after your little escape," Compano said. "My comms were deactivated. I was an experiment. This," she tapped her chest, "was an experiment. They want to conquer death. They believe if they become immortal through technology, they won't need anyone else. They won't need to interact with people of other faiths. They'll be able to kill them all."

"Genocide?" Ward asked.

"Victory," Compano said. "Is there a story of a god anywhere in human history that doesn't involve dominance over others? They believe they can achieve what their god set out for thousands of years ago. In any case, I became obsolete once they had the girl."

"Her name is Sam."

Compano offered an awkward motion Ward equated with a shrug. "I returned to Masada anyway," she said. "I don't like being outmaneuvered. They were gone already."

"When did you get in bed with this thing?" Ward asked Zee.

"I've done work for the REC for years," the smuggler said. "Our lines of communication are mutually beneficial."

"Then why didn't you know what Rivka was planning? To that point, if keeping the sword out of her hands is so important, why didn't you take it yourself?"

"No one knew. We didn't even know the sword was in their plans until I overheard you on our drive from Ein Gedi."

"I never had access either," Compano said.

"How many sides are you playing, exactly?" Ward asked.

"One. Mine."

"To what end? What do you want?"

"To win."

"Like the Sicarii? Genocide?"

"Look at me," Compano said, her one eye blazing and bloodshot and shattered by lightning cracks of gold. "All of you, take a good look. Make no mistake, I am still alive. That is my victory. I would watch the world burn for another five minutes of breath, even in this thing they built around me."

Ward couldn't hold that staring eye. There was something horrifically sad in the way it no longer blinked, in the desperate way Compano voiced her desire to remain alive, as if trying to convince herself she was. It was such a grotesque sadness it made Ward miss his training Agent in the same way he missed MacKenzie and his mother and Sam.

"As I was saying," Compano said, "they were already gone when I arrived, except for about two dozen soldiers, a doctor, a few medics, and a girl in a coma. Their orders were to unplug her, to monitor her, and to report on her condition until she finally died. That was all. But something went wrong. When I arrived, the girl was gone, and the rest were all dead. Some looked like they'd been taken by surprise. Some had barricaded themselves. Some stood to fight. All had their skulls bashed in."

"Your people?" Ward asked Zee.

"No, and we have no intel on any other forces active in the area."

"What about those Nephilim?"

"They don't come to Masada."

"It wasn't a force," Compano said. "It wasn't a breach. It was internal." She paused, maybe for effect. "I found her."

"Found who?"

"Your little girl."

"Sam?"

"She wasn't in the infirmary."

"You have her?"

"She wasn't anywhere in the fortress."

"Where is she?"

"She was deep in the belly of the mountain. I almost couldn't find her."

"Where is she!"

"She was among the dead."

Everything stopped. To Ward, it felt like the earth had stopped spinning. Compano was perfectly still and silent. Zee and Nasir and Farooq were nearby but motionless. Even the mechanical sounds of Compano breathing disappeared. There was only Ward and a tableau. A half-vision, half-memory. A young girl, barely eighteen, her right arm missing its hand, sitting naked in a dark cave. Covered in blood. Her face empty of self, as if who she was had been driven away and what had slipped into the vacuum wasn't enough to fill the mind that remained. Surrounded by the bones of a thousand long-dead martyrs.

"Golgotha," he whispered, giving name to the setting of the tableau.

"You've seen it," Compano said.

"How did you find it?"

"I can't explain it. There was a pull, like a magnet. Like I belonged there with her."

Ward thought it might have been the most honest thing Compano had ever said to him, but he had no idea what it meant.

Zee, however, did. "You were dead once. So was the girl. She has death inside her. You will always be drawn to people and places of death, the way a salamander is drawn to water."

The comparison between Sam and Compano made Ward's skin squirm. He wanted to wipe the idea from his mind, but he kept returning to the tableau. To the blood.

"Death inside her?" Ward asked.

"It's the only explanation for what I saw," Compano said.

"Make sense, damn it."

"Kerberos," was all Zee said.

"No, that's crazy," Ward said.

"I saw it, Rafael," Compano said. "I saw what she did."

"What did she do?" he asked despite himself.

"She killed them. She killed all of them."

"Bullshit," Ward said, but not emphatically. The look on Sam's face when she killed Ker, the man who'd cut off her hand, said more than any testimonial from Compano meant. The look on her face when she pulled that trigger was one of eagerness. Of intense satisfaction as the bullet exited the barrel. Of supreme joy when it exploded Ker's head.

Are we all monsters inside?

"Where is she?" he asked.

"She's here," Compano said, a twisted sort of delight creeping into her mechanical voice. "I brought her to you."

CHAPTER 44

The girl had been dreaming. She didn't know when she fell asleep or when she woke, but she was awake now. She didn't know if she was remembering the dream or an actual memory, but she was losing the thread. It had been there in her fingers and now it was slipping away. A bright room. A distant man. A kind woman. A warm plate topped with a stack of semi-round cakes dripping with syrup.

Pancakes.

I remember pancakes!

The realization was like a victory. She could almost taste the syrup.

They're coming, Other said, startling her.

"My friend?" she asked aloud.

Her voice echoed in the darkness. Were it not for the echo, she could imagine her voice going on forever. But it came back, giving the box she was in size. Dimension. It wasn't a large box, but it wasn't small either. She had the impression she'd been in a small box before and didn't like it. This was different. Though she couldn't touch two walls at the same time, it was only a few steps from one to another. And it was quiet, aside from the echo of her own voice.

She liked her voice. She didn't particularly miss sound or voice when they were absent, but she liked them when they were present. Like a tree. Didn't it need sound before it could understand a forest? Or before it could fall? Before it could be a tree? She didn't understand exactly, but she knew sound was important, especially for other people. Like light. Though, she also knew, neither was necessary.

It occurred to her that Other hadn't answered. Other did that sometimes, retreating to that deep space inside her. It occurred to her also that if she stopped thinking so much and listened, she would be able to hear people outside the box. The ones Other said were coming. Their voices soaked through the walls of the box like rain through a pair of jeans. She'd never seen rain, but she remembered liking it when it fell from the sky. She heard two voices. Maybe three. Sometimes talking. Sometimes yelling. The walls of the box muffled the words too much to understand, but she knew what they were talking about.

Her.

"Must we kill?" she asked.

Other remained in the deep space, which meant there would be no killing. That was okay. She was tired despite the sleep and the dream.

The clang of a lock echoed off the walls. A crack of light broke vertically in the darkness. Then, horizontally above and below, brightening the room quickly and uncomfortably. The girl closed her eyes and rubbed her fist into first her left eye then her right before opening them slowly.

Five of them stood there, watching her, including her dark friend. Three of the others were familiar. She'd seen them when her dark friend brought her here and told her to wait in the box. The fifth, she didn't know.

Except she did. She knew him the way she knew pancakes and rain. Knowing him was intrinsic, elemental, like breathing, as was the knowledge of what was going to happen next. He was going to say her name. He was going to break free of the crowd. Wrap his arms around her. Ask if she was okay. Tell her he was sorry. Promise never to let anyone hurt her again.

As if she required protection from a man who stank of such neediness.

Is he my brother? she asked Other, knowing as she spoke he wasn't.

Other returned from the deep space but did not speak.

Is he my father?

A snort only from Other.

"Sam," the man said, weakly, chokingly, just as the girl knew he would.

She'd expected *Samantha*, the name her dark friend had used, but this shorter name was more comfortable. It fit. Like old shoes. She liked it.

Still following the script, the man broke free of the crowd of five as if waking from a trance. She let him come to her, seeing no reason to break the inevitable. Let him wrap his arms around her. His embrace was comforting, like the name he gave her. Like darkness, but different. He was warm. She hadn't realized she was cold until now.

"Are you okay?" he asked.

She said, "Yes."

He shuddered. "I'm so sorry, Sam."

Can I see the future? she asked.

A shifting of mass inside her mind told her Other was uncomfortable.

"I won't let anyone hurt you again," the man said. "I promise, I won't let anyone near you ever again." As he said this last part, he looked over his shoulder at the crowd of four. At the girl's dark friend.

They will fight, she thought. Not yet, but soon.

The man was looking at her again, holding her at arm's length so he could examine her.

"Sam," he said. "Are you okay? You don't look okay. What did you do to her?"

At first, the girl thought he was asking Other, but he was asking her dark friend.

"I haven't placed a hand on her since Spain," her dark friend said.

Spain. There was a river in Spain. And a bad man who'd hurt her.

The man was looking at her again. "Are you alright, Sam?"

"What is your name?" the girl asked.

The man looked back at the crowd again, as if seeking help. No one spoke. He let go of her arms and marched to the girl's dark friend.

"What did you do?" he said. "What's wrong with her?"

Is something wrong with me?

Still nothing from Other.

"Am I a doctor, Rafael?" her dark friend said.

"You're Rafael," the girl said, the name as familiar as pancakes. "That's your name."

He came back to her. "Yes. Rafael. Rafe, remember? I'm Rafe."

"Rafe. Smaller than Rafael. Like Sam is smaller than Samantha. I like Sam better than Samantha," she said.

The man, Rafe, laughed. It was full of relief and happiness and still some neediness, but not enough to ruin it.

"Are you my friend too?" she asked.

"Yes, I—too?"

The girl—*my name is Sam*—pointed at her dark friend.

Rafe followed her finger. He tensed. Looked at Sam hard. "She's not your friend."

Sam backed away from him. She didn't like the contradiction. Her dark friend was good to her. She brought her out of the mountain. She brought her here.

She took us from home, Other said.

She's my friend, Sam insisted.

She's not our friend.

And Rafe?

No!

Then who is our friend?

The sudden sensation of warmth, soft and furry, nuzzling Sam's hand made her flinch.

"Are you okay?" Rafe asked.

Sam ignored him. She focused on the feeling. It was so real, she thought she might be able to see whatever was tickling through her fingers if she looked, but when she did look the sensation disappeared. There was no creature nuzzling her hand. There was no hand.

She made a phantom fist with her phantom hand, imagining it grabbing the fur of a phantom creature.

"Dog," she whispered. It was a dog she was feeling.

"Yes," Rafe said. "Reina. You have a dog named Reina."

At first, it didn't fit, but then she remembered. Reina. Yapping and mottled and loyal and needy. But not the same disgusting neediness Rafe spewed. A different neediness, like a reflection of herself. Like a partnership. An embrace to immerse herself in. to wrap her arms around. To love unconditionally.

"Where is Reina?" she asked. "Where is my dog?"

Rafe's face darkened. She knew what he was going to say. He'd left Reina the same way he'd left her.

"We can go find her, Sam," he said. "We can go get her together."

"How could you leave her?"

"We left her. You and me together. You agreed to leave her in Texas with the Grossmutter."

Sam's head exploded in agony. Headache. She grasped the word, barely, through the pounding of her skull which became more than pounding. It became a storm. Chaos. She couldn't find Other. She couldn't find herself. Or maybe there simply was no difference between Other and herself anymore. Not in the maelstrom that was expanding inside her mind, growing and growing until her consciousness threatened to pop like an overinflated balloon.

Then it did.

CHAPTER 45

"I'm not leaving her," Ward said.

They'd brought Sam upstairs and laid her out on the couch. Compano stood nearby, insisting she was fine and would wake when she was ready. Ward didn't like it. He didn't like the way Sam had just collapsed, as if someone had pushed a button and sent her back into a coma. He didn't like the way Compano watched over her. He didn't like any damn thing about this place or what Zee was trying to get him to do.

"Recovery of the sword must be our goal," the smuggler said, sitting at the table. "I will do everything I can to help your friend *after* we get the sword."

They'd been going around in circles since they came upstairs. That was the only thing Ward was fine with about this whole thing. He didn't care about Rivka or her sword. Not now, anyway. He would find her in time. That was his strength, his curse: finding things. For now, the longer they remained stalemated, the longer he got to stay with Sam. The better the chance he could negotiate a way to help her.

"Then go find it without me," he said.

"Rafael," Zee started. He didn't finish. He looked tired. Older.

It occurred to Ward he had no idea how old Zee was. He'd always assumed they were about the same age, but the man before him—tired and seemingly nearly defeated—could have been ten years older. Maybe even twenty years older for his slumped posture and the crow's feet around his eyes.

"I'll let the whole world burn for her," Ward said.

"I believe my former Agent has finally found the hill he's

willing to die on," Compano said.

Ward didn't look at her. He couldn't stand to see her hovering over Sam like a nightmare cloud.

"I need your promise," Zee said. "I need to trust you will find Rivka for us."

"You first."

Zee sighed and exchanged looks with Farooq and Nasir. Neither moved or acknowledged his glare, but he must have seen something in their faces because he nodded and pointed to the chair opposite himself. Ward sat.

"Kerberos sought to force you from your own body," Zee said. "That was why he took you to the River Lethe. He wanted to give your body to another. When the dead drink from Lethe, their memories are obliviated. It does not work that way for the living. A ritual is necessary to open the doors for the soul and for consciousness to evacuate."

"I thought you worshipped Ningiszida," Ward said. "What's with the expertise on Greek mythology."

"It's not mythology. It's sleeping right there on the couch!"

Ward looked over at Sam, but his eyes kept rising to Compano. "She drank from the river and lost her memory?"

"No," Zee said at the same time Compano said, "Yes."

Ward wanted a drink. A slug of whiskey. A focusing agent to make sense out nonsense. To allow him to believe things no sane person should believe.

"It's more complicated than that," Zee said. "Consciousness is like any other vessel. When it is emptied, it creates a vacuum. It welcomes whatever is nearby to fill that vacuum."

"You want me to believe she's Kerberos now?"

"She's not Kerberos," Zee said, "but he is in there. The ritual was incomplete. The door opened, and then she shot the guardian of the underworld in the head. Some of her memories made it out. Some of his consciousness made it in. The door slammed shut."

Despite himself, Ward found belief was no longer a problem. All he had to do was close his eyes and remember Sam's eyes before, and Sam's eyes now. They were different. Deeper. More dangerous. They were knowing. Like Ker's.

"You're serious," Ward said, though there was no hint of humor in anyone in the room. "She's carrying Ker like," he almost said a baby, "like a person with multiple personalities?"

"Like that a bit, yes, but we can remove him. We can exorcise Kerberos."

"More rituals."

"The Lord of the Tree of Life has offered Her gifts for this task, and I will happily undertake it once we have recovered the sword. We are almost out of time. Rivka will perform her ceremony when the moon is high. We have a few hours, five or six maybe, before it will be too late."

"Is it dangerous, this exorcism?"

"The ritual is dangerous, yes. Life is dangerous. It will only become more dangerous if we don't recover the sword."

"Okay," Ward said. Zee visibly exhaled. "Do the exorcism and then I'll help you find Rivka."

The smuggler popped out of his chair. "No, my friend, we do not have the time to do it now. We must go. We must not lose Rivka or the sword."

"I'm not leaving Sam."

"You were far from my best trainee," Compano said, "but you were never an idiot or a coward. Don't start either now."

"What are you even doing here?" Ward said, never taking his eyes from Zee. Unable to look at the thing that used to be Compano, not because of what she was but because he blamed her for Sam being in this mess. For Sam losing her baby. For Sam not knowing who she was.

Which was all horseshit. He was the reason, and he knew it.

"Taking care of my new friend," Compano said.

"You're so full of shit it's practically coming out of what's left of your eye."

She did that mechanical thing Ward correlated with a shrug. He wanted to grab her mask and see how difficult it would be to tear it from her skull.

"How many sides are you playing?" he asked.

"There's only one side."

"The winning side," He said, not bothering to hide his contempt.

"You did learn something from me."

"She a kid," he said.

"Not anymore."

Tension hung in the restaurant like thick summer heat. It was apparent on everyone, even Farooq and Nasir. Everyone except Sam, who slept peacefully on the old couch.

"Her baby," Ward said, the thought popping into his head so easily he didn't have time to feel guilty for not bringing it up previously. "You were there. Where's her baby?"

Compano said, "They took it."

"Who?"

"The Sicarii."

"Is it alive?"

It. What kind of a monster am I, calling the baby an it?

"It was, last I can verify."

"Boy or girl?" he asked.

"I don't know."

Ward wondered if she was lying about that one, but he didn't think she would admit as much. "Why did they take the baby?"

"For the same reason they put me in this, and they covered her stump. Experimentation. The mother has a god in her, after all."

"And what about you? What do you want out of all of this?"

"I want to help Samantha," Compano said.

Ward didn't believe it. She was withholding.

"I want her child returned," he said.

"Go get it."

"You're not hearing me," Ward said. "Today is all about making deals. You're here because you've got some play in this with Zee and his buddies, right? Back me on this, and I'll back you afterward."

"Rafael," Zee started.

"You had your chance," Ward said. To Compano, he added, "Whatever you're after. Back me, and I'll back you."

"Anything for you, Rafael," Compano said. The density of her smugness almost cost his control of the situation. "We're not leaving without Sam, Ziyad. Sorry."

"And the baby," Ward said.

"Yes," Compano said. "We don't leave Sam now, and once she's free of Ker, I'll help you find her baby. Now, Rafael, don't you want to know what you'll be helping me with?"

"Not even a little bit," Ward said. It might have been the truest thing he'd ever said.

"You two leave me with no choices," Zee said. "The exorcism ritual takes too long to prepare to do now. We cannot delay finding Rivka. We'll bring Sam with us. Will that satisfy you?"

"Yes," Ward said, but the victory was a hollow pit in his gut.

"I will have the temple at Lagash ready for her upon our return," Zee said. "Now, can you find Rivka?"

"Tell me again what she needs."

"A temple, ancient and powerful and blessed by El."

"You're certain? It can't be a circle of candles or a modern synagogue?"

"To break one god's hold on the sword requires the Word of another. Direct contact with the earth where that god has tread. The very breath of that god itself if possible."

"Ancient and holy. Got it," Ward said. "It's a big list. Bethlehem. Hebron. Megiddo. Jerusalem, of course. Where do you want to start?"

"Maybe she mentioned a place when you were with her," Zee offered. "Did she tell you of a temple or a location she wanted to visit?"

Ward tried to replay their conversations, but each time he thought of her was a blend of sex and blood, naked flesh and ash. "No, nothing. Help me out. Is she north of the Line or south of it?"

"The Line won't stop her. I don't know what else to tell you other than she will need a place of immense power, maybe a place her god, El, spoke his Word upon the Earth."

"Spoke his Word," Ward repeated, remembering something Rivka had said near the start of all this. "The Word of God. The secrets of His garden."

"You know," Zee said.

"I think I do."

CHAPTER 46

Someone was brushing Sam's hair. With a hand. A warm hand. A calming stroke. Her eyes were closed. She opened them. She was in a new room, a long room with small windows, her head in Rafe's lap. The hand brushing her hair was his.

I'm on a plane, she thought. She understood that meant she was flying through the air in a metal tube. She also understood that should have terrified her, but there was something comforting about the droning of the plane's engines, like static. White noise. Almost like another form of darkness.

She sat up. They were on a row of black, not very plush seats facing another similar row of seats on the opposite wall of the tube. The three men with the brown skin sat on that side fifteen or twenty seats up the tube. Her dark friend stood by a door.

"Where are we going?" Sam asked.

"We have to get something that was stolen," Rafe said. "How are you feeling? You fainted. Compano thinks it was a seizure."

"Compano?" Sam asked, unfamiliar with the name.

"The big one who brought you here."

"My dark friend."

"She's not your friend."

Sam considered this a moment. It felt true in his voice, but it felt false in her head.

"Is she not your friend?" she asked.

"Do you remember me?"

"Yes.

"Not just my name. Do you remember what we did together? Do you remember how you feel about me?"

He understands...something, Sam thought.

He is a liar, Other said.

"I remember you helping me," she said. "Not actions. I don't remember things. I remember impressions, like the impression of my name. It seems right, like it fits."

"That's good. That's a start."

The plane dipped suddenly. Rafe tensed and sucked his breath through his teeth. The movement seemed to shake loose more memories.

"Did you protect me?" she asked.

Rafe shifted. "Yes."

It was a lie. Or a half-truth. She sought more in his face. He seemed to understand she wasn't going to accept that answer.

"We met by accident," he said. "You got in trouble because of it, because you saw me. I tried, I truly tried, to protect you. I'd like to think I did, for a while, anyway."

"You did bad things."

"Yes."

"You killed many people."

He lowered his eyes. "I'm not a bad person. I'm not, but you were kidnapped because a man was angry at me for something bad I'd done."

Other began moving around uncomfortably, like an unsettled stomach after eating too much.

"Why did he kidnap me if he was angry at you?"

"Because I care for you. Because he saw a way to hurt me by hurting you."

The hand that wasn't there tingled uncomfortably. She cradled the cuff to her belly. It was cool and heavy.

"I crossed an ocean to get you back, to save you from him, but by the time I found you, he'd already done that." Rafe pointed at the cuff.

"You weren't there when I woke. The first time I woke as this self, I was alone."

His guilt was palpable, as bitter as his neediness.

"You were in a coma. I was told you were dying. I left to try to find a way to save you."

"Why do you keep trying to save me?"

"I don't...I just want to do one good thing. I've done so many bad things. If you hadn't met me you wouldn't be in any of this trouble." Tears rolled down his cheeks.

"I don't need to be saved," Sam said. "And the girl who was in trouble isn't here. I don't remember her. Not really. I'm not who I was."

"That's okay. Maybe you'll remember. Maybe you won't. Either way, I'm not going to leave you again."

"I think I would like to remember you more."

"We were talking while you were asleep. Zee says he can help with your memory. Maybe get it all back."

"Will it take away who I am now?"

"I don't know."

"Will it hurt?"

"I don't know. Possibly."

"Would the person I was, the Sam you remember, miss her memory?" she asked.

"Oh yes. She was a strong girl. A strong woman. She would have missed her memory and Reina and telling me what an ass I am."

"Are you an ass?"

He shrugged. "I keep trying to save you."

Sam laughed. It came on suddenly. She didn't know what it was, and then she couldn't stop doing it. It might have been the first time she'd ever laughed. Soon Rafe was laughing too. It was strange, and it hurt her cheeks and her belly, and she loved it. She never wanted it to stop. But it did. It died away in chuckles and wet eyes and a moment of hiccups, and then it was her and Rafe again. Strangers who weren't quite unfamiliar. And the promise of regaining some of who she once was.

"Who is Zee?" she asked.

Rafe pointed at one of the men opposite them. "He believes part of the reason you can't remember things is what happened in Spain, in the river, with the man who took your hand."

He's lying! Other shouted.

Sam winced.

"Are you okay?" Rafe asked.

"Tell me," she said.

He's trying to take me away from you, Other said.

"It's a kind of ritual," Rafe said. "Zee says it's the only way to remove what's keeping you from remembering."

He wants to kill me.

Who are you? Sam asked.

I am you.

Sam didn't understand. Both Rafe and Other said they wanted what was best for her. Could they both be true? She tried to weigh their words. She tried to taste them, seeking the flavor of truth, but mostly she tasted desperation. The need for her approval. Her alliance. Oddly, both tasted of age. Rafe's as if he'd rolled in history, like a dog rolling in the grass. Other's as if he were history, so old the number didn't exist to count his age.

I am you! Other insisted.

"I think I would like to remember," Sam said, "so I can know the truth."

CHAPTER 47

They landed in a red sand valley in what was once Jordan. To Ward, it looked like the surface of Mars in an old science fiction film. From the plane, they hurried into a military truck. Farooq and Nasir drove. Ward, Sam, Compano, and Zee rode in the canvas covered cargo bed. It was an old, loud, gasoline powered machine that made it difficult to converse at a normal volume.

Zee, who'd inserted a comm into his ear, said, "Ali says they've located her."

"Who's Ali?" Ward asked.

"The one who tried to shoot you in Turkey." There was no humor in Zee's tone.

"Great. Is she where I said?"

"Yes. The temple ruins on the cliff north of the Ein Gedi synagogue. You have not told me how you knew."

"That's right." Ward did his best to match Zee's tone. "Is it just her?"

Zee put up a finger to indicate he was getting more intel.

Compano said, "Sam should come with me."

Ward said, "Never going to happen."

"Pull your head out of your ass a moment, Rafael. I need a set of eyes, and you're going with Zee into the assault, yes?"

"What assault? It's Rivka and a sword. We've got this."

Zee put this finger down. "Ali counted twelve Sicarii before they shot down our Eye-D."

Compano said, "You were saying, professor?"

Ward didn't answer. He'd been outmaneuvered again. Their basic plan had been set while still in the air. Compano, with her extensive modifications, claimed to be as accurate with a scoped rifle as a computer performing advanced calculus. She would set up on the western rise over the temple ruins with the best sniper rifle Zee could acquire on short notice, a slightly outdated Russian model called a Pobeda, which sat on the truck bed between her legs. Meanwhile, Ward, Zee, and the other two would approach from the promontory from the east.

All of that, however, had been before they found out there were at least a dozen Sicarii on site.

"Ali has thirteen fighters with him," Zee said. "Once we cross the Dead Sea, we'll meet with them and proceed."

A few minutes later, Nasir banged on the window separating the cab from the truck. They slowed. Turned. Stopped. Got out. They were on a rise above the Dead Sea, dots of light dancing in its waves below. Stars reflected from above. Ward couldn't help looking up. He'd never seen brighter stars. He pointed, hoping to show Sam something beautiful, but she sulked off near Compano. It occurred to him she hadn't spoken since they got on the truck, and even though she sat beside him the whole ride, she'd remained distant.

"There's a boat below," Zee said, pointing down a slope toward the Dead Sea, which spread out like never-ending glass reflecting the stars.

The boat was an inflatable assault raft that reminded Ward of the crafts Agents trained with for quick cross-river assaults. Zee herded them on board, the boat dipping low on Compano's side, and they headed out into the Dead Sea, the raft's engines purring along almost silently.

"What will Rivka be doing?" Ward asked when they were far enough from shore to feel like they'd glided into the ocean. He pulled his leather jacket tight around him, the only one on the boat, as far as he could tell, who was cold.

"The ceremony is two parts," Zee said. "According to Ali, she is already engaged in the first part: removing Ba'el's blessing from the sword. Then she will cleanse herself and prepare for the second part where she will offer the sword to El and ask his blessing. Once complete, the sword will be bound to El's will. With luck, we will allow her time to finish the unbinding."

"Luck?"

"Do you not believe in luck either?"

"I figured you would ask Ningiszida for help."

"It doesn't work that way, my friend. I thought you knew."

Ward wasn't sure how to respond. Was Zee making fun of him? Chiding him? Nudging him toward a conclusion? Or a mistake?

"El and Ba'el are of the same fabric," Zee said. "The prophet of one can undue to the binding of the other. But the old gods are as different from the Tyrant Gods as you are from a gecko. Noncompatible. We need the sword free. It's the only way into Paradise."

"Yeah, about that."

Zee waved him off. "Not now. We're almost there."

Ward searched the darkness but couldn't find a shore. The only way he knew there were mountains ahead was the stars stopped shining as he scanned closer to the horizon. One by one, Zee handed out comms to everyone but Compano. They looked like little beans designed to fit into the ear.

"They translate," Zee said.

Ward pushed the comm into his ear as Zee pointed around the raft labeling everyone, starting with himself as Z1. Nasir and Farooq were Z2 and Z3. Ward was Z4. Sam, Z5. Compano, Z6.

"Ali is Z7," he continued. "The others you can figure out. When the comm translates there's a half-second delay. Most of our people don't speak English, so it's the best we have."

As Ward fiddled with the comm, hating the way it felt like it was perpetually on the verge of popping out of his ear, the beach appeared. A single figure awaited their approach.

"That is Ali," Zee said.

He ordered Nasir and Farooq into the water to pull the boat ashore. Ward, feeling useless, joined them. Once the boat was on dry sand, everyone else climbed out. Zee and Ali embraced. The smuggler held the soldier's face in his hands a moment before kissing him hard on one check, then the other. They held each other another moment, sharing a look, before separating. There were no other introductions. Just nods between Nasir and Farooq and Ali. Just a scrutinizing glare from Ali over the others.

"You better get going," Zee said to Compano.

She checked her rifle and let her bloodshot eye fall on Ward first, then Sam.

"Rafe," Sam said, a familiar tone to her voice. The can-I-have-extra-credit tone. The I-need-an-extension tone.

"Go with her," Ward said, voicing the surrender he'd already decided on. "She's right. It'll be safer up there."

Sam offered an odd smile. Compano made no comment at all. She simply started north. Sam followed. Ward watched them go until they were lost to the night and then turned his attention to Zee and Ali who had walked off a few meters to talk quietly. Ali was a soldier, no doubt. He was stocky, with a shaved head, and a nose that had been broken enough times it probably wouldn't hurt much if it were broken again. Ward imagined himself looking like that if he'd stayed in the REC and remained a good Citizen. Not the shaved head or the crooked nose, necessarily. But the attitude. The posture and visible mindset of absolute assurance in both cause and his own personal capability. He wondered which version of himself he would despise more: the current Rafael Ward, who'd ruined everyone he'd ever cared about, or the hypothetical Agent Ward, who would serve Compano without complaint or fault until one of both of them were dead.

Or option C, professor: All of the above, with a bullet and shot of whiskey on fire.

He stalked back to the raft where Farooq and Nasir were unpacking their gear. Nasir handed him a bundle containing a short barrel assault rifle, a Jericho pistol, a utility belt, and three extra magazines for each gun. He put on the belt and checked both weapons. He assumed Zee had a map of the area, but even without one he was reasonably sure they had no more than five or six minutes before they had to get moving.

Ward's comm crackled to life. "Z6," a mechanical voice stated, followed by Compano's own, quite mechanical, voice. "Beginning climb. Estimate five minutes until we're in position."

"Z1: Confirmed," came Zee's reply, again preceded by the mechanical voice of the comm.

Zee and Ali returned from their conference. "We should get moving," Zee said.

Nasir commented they were ready, and the group hiked west, single file, with Ward and Zee in the middle.

"Z1: The Eye-D showed them in a cross defense, three soldiers at each of the four directions, one facing Rivka in the middle, and two facing out. Our approach puts four eyes in our general direction, the eastern and southern positions. Z6, you have the west position. The three Sicarii to the north are the wildcard. Whoever gets to them first has the green light. Keep an eye west."

Ward hurried to catch up with Zee, who'd started for the rise. "What's to the west?" he asked, having no idea if his question were being broadcast to the entire team.

"You know," Zee said, without the interference of the comm voice.

"The Nephilim?"

"The Eye-D picked up movement a few kilometers into the desert."

"I thought they didn't come to the sea."

"I thought you didn't believe in gods."

They reached the cliff where nine soldiers waited, seven men and two women, one of whom was the tallest woman Ward had ever seen in uniform. Ward didn't ask where the remaining four were. He assumed they were already in position. It was go or no go time. Zee asked through the comm if everyone was ready. The responses came at dizzying rapid fire. The team of Ningiszida worshippers, along with a machine, a teenage girl, and a college professor, were set. They began the climb, Zee and Ward heading right up the middle, directly at the Sicarii's east position. Not far to their right, Nasir and another soldier made excellent time. To their left Farooq and the tall woman scaled the cliff like the rope ladder in basic training.

Ward lagged behind. His leg brace kept him moving at a brisk pace, but his rifle kept sliding off his shoulder, slapping his back or his thigh, forcing him to readjust. Zee kept in line, refusing to leave him behind, but the smuggler's impatience was palpable. Near the top, the cliff face became almost concave.

Mounting the rim would be difficult. Making it worse, the earth was little more than loose gravel. Each push up was a potential landslide. A possible betrayal of their position to the Sicarii, the most dangerous assassins who'd ever lived.

"Z3: In position."

"Z11: In position."

"Z9: In position."

"Z6: In position."

Sam didn't report in. There was no reason for her to, she was with Compano, but the absence of her voice made Ward anxious. He was here to stop another holy ritual. Like the Vase of Soissons. Like the River Lethe. Each had ended in death. Was he ready to take part in another? Was he ready to pull the trigger?

On Rivka, you bet your ass.

But it felt like bravado, not resolve. Could he really do it, even after all she'd done? Could he go against the dream, the hallucination, of his mother whispering, *No more fires*, *baby*, back in the library in Arizona, the last home he'd had?

Then, the most ridiculous thought: *If gods are real, why can't Mom have come to me in a dream?*

Zee tapped Ward's knee. He signaled with his hands they would be go in ten seconds. The smuggler shifted to the left, putting space between them. Two targets, not one. He got on his knees, ready to call the charge. Ward did the same, raising his rifle to his shoulder, wondering if he could climb the rim with two hands on the weapon and not fall over backward.

"Z1: Five seconds."

Ward counted the beats. At two, his comm clicked on. "Z6: Hold."

Zee flattened onto the cliff, repeating the order. "Z1: Hold, hold."

Ward dropped to his belly, his heart hammering away in his chest.

"Z6," his comm said, announcing Compano's call sign. "They're changing position. Shifting to intercardinal. Same formations."

"Z1: Can we take them on the move."

"Z6: Negative. They're on high alert. Hold and wait."

"Z1: The ritual?"

"Z6: Appears in progress. Hold."

The look on Zee's face said he wanted to scream in frustration. It also said he was terrified Rivka was already on the second part of the ritual. Compano was their eyes, however. No one else was above the promontory. They had to wait.

Ward's comm crackled again, a longer static.

"Rafael," Compano's mechanized voice said. "Welcome to my secure channel."

"Secure?"

Zee rolled in Ward's direction, his eyes asking a question. It took Ward a second to understand. Zee was trying to figure out why Ward's lips were moving but no voice was coming through the comm. It was because Compano had somehow tapped into the feed and was running an out-of-loop link. Ward motioned for Zee to keep his position, and then he turned his head so Zee couldn't see his lips moving.

"What are you doing?" he asked.

"We need to talk," Compano said. "I want to give you a chance."

"A chance? I don't want any chances from you. Where's Sam? Is she okay?"

"Shut up," Compano said. "Pay attention. The revolution is at a crossroad. The Republic's forces are disorganized. The REC is fractured. Its infiltration and strike divisions have been ordered to the Canadian Districts, more than a thousand miles north of the fighting."

"Your divisions, the Reapers, they're all out of the fight?"

"Not all of them, but the REC will not sway this war one way or the other. But it may still be swayed. Your girlfriend and her Seer are in trouble."

"She's not my..." Ward stopped. He wouldn't get trapped like this. Not in one of Compano's games. One of her familiar tests. "What kind of trouble?"

"Their secret base isn't a secret anymore. The next few weeks will determine everything. The Republic will not be the same regardless of who wins. And you can bet it won't be godless anymore."

The implication was obvious. "The Sicarii," he said.

"They're the infiltrators now, and they have no interest in a utopian paradise for Believers."

"Why tell me? Why now?"

"You trust too much."

"You're the case in point."

"Not me, Rafael. You never trusted me. Don't start lying to yourself about that now. Your girlfriend. The Seer. Zee and his snake worshippers. Stop trusting simply because their goals are aligned with yours for a moment."

"Stop trusting them about what?"

"Everything."

"Great warning. Thanks. Can we get back to what we're supposed to be doing?"

"Wait," Compano said. Then: "Z6: Continuing shift. It's not intercardinal. They're rotating. Will advise."

The crackling in Ward's comm indicated he was back on Compano's secure channel. He said, "You're good at this. You should get a job as a spy."

"Shut up and listen. Gods, prophets, governments, men, women, none of them are what we ever intend."

"Not even your god?"

"I have no god. Gods crave humans. I'm…no longer what they want."

"Maybe you are a god," a new voice said.

"Sam?" Ward almost shouted her name.

"Maybe you are a new kind of god," Sam said. "Maybe we both are."

"Sam, don't listen to her. She's crazy."

"That's the brilliance of the Sicarii," Compano said. "They've found the in-between. They think they're bringing themselves closer to their god with their biotech and their modifications, but they're really setting themselves apart. They're making both humanity and gods obsolete."

"I don't give a fuck about humanity or gods. I only want Sam to be safe."

"So you can be her hero?" Compano asked.

"Whatever she needs me to do or be."

"I don't need you to be anything," Sam said.

"Fuck this," Ward said, wishing he were on a telephone call so he could hang up. Or better yet, wishing he were face to face with Compano so he could prove to Sam what a monster the former Agent was. "None of us have time for your games."

"Right you are," Compano said. "Time is almost up. Two last things. First, one thing you seek is on Cyprus. Second, your girlfriend is in danger. She's trusting the wrong people too."

"Who is she—" Ward tried to ask, but his comm crackled, kicking him off Compano's secure channel.

"Z6: Positions resumed," came Compano's full channel report. "Assault ready."

"Z1: About time. We go on three."

Ward pounded his fist into the earth, clutching at focus, needing to set himself in this moment, knowing divided attention would get him, and maybe everyone else, killed. He ground his teeth. He shouted silently. He imagined placing the muzzle of his gun in Compano's bloodshot eye and pulling the trigger. None of it helped. His focus was shattered. MacKenzie and Sam. Compano and Rivka. The impending battle. He was a kid at the state fair being shaken up in that ride that tried to get its patrons to vomit all over each other.

"Z1: Go!"

CHAPTER 48

The crack of her dark friend's rifle filled Sam from her ears to her toes the way sand runs through an hourglass. It was exhilarating. Apotheosizing. Orgasmic.

Home, Other said, creeping up through the filtering sand.

Yes, they were home. This is what they were meant for. The way others might seek a couch and place to put up their feet, she and Other sought these moments when the veil between life and death became thin. When they could squeeze lives through their fingers like clay.

I do not have all my fingers, she thought.

More, Other said.

Sam couldn't deny the impulse. She couldn't deny Other. Gunshots were detonating below like drunken music, her dark friend's cannonade setting the beat. She couldn't sit out this dance.

She charged down the hill, her dark friend rising as she went over the edge but making no attempt to stop her. The plateau below was in chaos. For Sam, though, it was beautiful. Better than a dance. It was sex and violence and ecstasy. The closest soldier was alone, a dead man at his feet. He was facing away from Sam, lining up a shot. She noted his target—Rafe grappling with a much larger man—but never slowed. Never doubted her victory. She was made for this. She and Other were born for this.

Other made a lip-smacking sound as Sam hit the soldier in the back, knocking him face first to the ground. Her live fingers pushed on the top of the man's head while her ghost fingers clenched into a fist. She drove her cuff like a piston into the back of the man's neck, up and into his skull.

She spent no time exalting in the kill. One down, she bound to the next. After that kill, the next, and so on until she reached Rafe, who was on one knee, trying to keep his adversary from burying a knife into his chest. A bullet came for her, oddly slow and visible. She understood innately that Other was protecting her as she twisted away from the projectile, delaying her ability to assist Rafe. She slid on her calf and thigh, bouncing up onto the path she'd temporarily abandoned. Rafe had made a move. He'd used the larger man's mass and momentum against him and was drawing his pistol. Aiming it at the man who was scrambling away like a crab.

Kill, Other said.

Sam slowed. It wasn't her victory. It was Rafe's. He'd earned it.

I don't care, Other said. *I want to feel it. I want home.*

Death is death, Sam told Other, already seeking a new target. Only, there was no gunshot from Rafe. There was no death for him to claim.

She returned to him. The pistol trembled in his hand. His enemy had stopped trying to escape and was seeking a weapon. One of them would be dead in less than two seconds. Even Other didn't seem to know which.

"I told you to stay up top," Rafe said. It wasn't a command. It was concern.

That concern filled her with an appreciation, a need, and a desire to give she didn't understand. The part of her mind that remembered things like pancakes and airplanes gave her a word: love. It was a complex word, not like coffee which she understood the moment it was given a name. It was an incomplete word, indeterminate if it meant the giving or the receiving of all that it encompassed.

It was a word that came with two faces: a fat man asleep on a couch, and a long-faced woman being taken away by men in uniforms.

Mom, she thought. *Dad.*

Kill! Other cried.

Sam saw Rafe's time was up. His pistol had dipped. His

enemy had found a rock. The end smelled sweet within the miasma of gunpowder, sulfur, and blood that covered the plateau. Other wanted her to let it happen. Other didn't care who died so long as death reigned.

Except that wasn't quite true. Other's panting for blood had direction. The scent Other wanted most was Rafe's. There was no time to examine this desire. No time to weigh one death against another. She had to choose. She went for Rafe.

"Sam," he cried as she slew footed his braced leg. The rock missed his skull by the space of a fist.

She never stopped moving. The man on the ground found a knife, but she'd already taken a better angle. Her knee hit him in the chest. His ribs cracked like muffled shots as he landed on his back. He wailed. The cuff on her arm, as if alive, plunged into the man's gaping mouth, shattering teeth and tearing flesh and exploding through his skull so that it punched the earth beneath.

More! Other screamed.

She sought her next target. Two enemies, a man and a woman, were dug in across the plateau, exchanging gunfire with three of Rafe's allies. Between her and them, the woman, the one called Rivka, was kneeling in the center of the ruins, a sword on the earth before her.

Someone approached. She spun, her arm withdrawing from the man's skull with a sickening-yet-appetizing squelch, and aimed for her attacker's throat.

Kill! Other roared.

But she was facing Rafe. He backed away, nearly tripping over his own feet.

Kill!

"Sam," Rafe said.

"The woman in the middle is yours, yes?"

Rafe looked dazed, as if he'd been hit in the head.

"The woman in the middle with the sword. She is yours, yes?"

"I—yes," he said.

"I will find battle with the other two. Be safe."

She bounded across the plateau, passing close enough to

snap Rivka's neck. Other howled for it, but the woman was Rafe's. She'd betrayed him. That death was his, so long as he was willing to claim it. She homed in on the two enemies, Other's disappointment becoming a bloodlust that was intense even for him.

CHAPTER 49

She didn't look like Sam anymore, the thing hurdling across the plateau like a nightmare wolverine. This wasn't the girl who had turned eighteen less than six months ago, who had been looking forward to graduating high school and earning Citizenship, who had worked in a convenient store like every other teenage kid in the Republic. That girl was gone.

What stalked the temple ruins in her skin was fearless and confident and deadly. It was like MacKenzie's worst impulses, unchecked and without balance, combined with Ker's raw lust for death.

All because she met me, Ward thought.

"Z1: The sword."

The sword. Rivka. A two-headed bargain for Sam's chance, maybe her last chance, to regain some measure of the person she used to be.

If Zee had told the truth.

If Ward could bring himself to believe.

"On it," he told Zee.

He couldn't locate his rifle, but his pistol was still in his hand. Unfired. Rivka knelt at the center of the plateau before a crumbled stone altar, her back to him the way it had been when he'd found her reading the spell at the synagogue on the plain below. He locked in on her, forcing himself not to see the soldier Sam had killed, the man whose head was broken open like a melon. Forcing himself not to hear the gunshots and screams. Not to remember the boiling eyeballs that haunted him in the years after he destroyed the Tower.

As he closed on Rivka, he could hear her chanting, the

words thick and unfamiliar. Aramaic or another obsolete Semitic tongue. A precursor to Hebrew, perhaps.

He pointed his pistol at her back and said, "Stop."

She kept on chanting, her arms extended like she was warming them over a fire. He sidestepped to the right revealing the sword—the khopesh that Zee insisted was Ba'el's own sword, the Barq—on the ground before her. If he got too close, she would be able to slice him in half with it.

"Stop the prayer," he said.

"Z1: No!"

Rivka stopped chanting.

"Z1: Is the first part complete?"

"How should I know?" Ward said.

"Z1: Find out."

"Are you finished?" Ward asked her. "Both parts of the ritual?"

"Not yet," she said, never taking her eyes from the sword.

"Z1: Report."

"She says the ritual isn't complete."

"Which part?"

Ward took the comm out of his ear, having to reach across his body awkwardly with his left hand, and let it drop.

"It's not easy having a voice in your head, is it?" Rivka said.

"Get up," he ordered.

"Ba'el's prophet must be killed," Rivka said. "Let me finish the ceremony, and together we can destroy his influence on humanity forever."

"Fuck humanity."

"The man I slept with doesn't believe that."

"The man you slept with was an idiot."

Rivka shrugged. Ward almost squeezed the trigger.

Get a grip, he shouted inside his head. Killing her was acceptable. It was good even, but he had to make sure he fulfilled his end of the bargain. For Sam.

"Is the sword free of Ba'el's blessing?"

"It is."

Ward's hand tightened on the pistol, but doubt kept him

from firing. He couldn't read her, and he had no confidence in her honesty.

"All you have to do is nothing, Rafael," she said.

Somewhere distant, between gunshots, Zee called his name.

"All you have to do is not kill me," she went on. "I'll take care of Ba'el and his prophet."

"Fuck Ba'el and his prophet."

Rivka, still facing west, her back to Ward, raised her head as if scanning the cliffs. Seeking escape, maybe, as the battle faded, gunshots bursting now at intervals like the final kernels of popcorn in the microwave. The others would be coming soon.

"Who did Zee promise to save," Rivka asked, "the girl or the general?"

Ward flinched as if she'd swung at him, completely unprepared for the staggering amount of guilt that cut through him at the thought of MacKenzie. At his culpability in her fall from the Seer's grace. Rivka used that moment to lift the sword in her palms and turn on one knee until she was facing Ward.

"We could do this together," she said. "We could save them both. We could save everyone. Zee can't offer you that."

The temptation to ask how, to demand to know what she knew about MacKenzie, was overwhelming. It was stronger than his desire to kill Rivka and fulfill the pact he'd made in Hannibal's tomb with the delusion he'd almost let himself believe was a god. It was so overwhelming, he couldn't do anything. Not ask, nor pull the trigger.

This is what gods do, he thought. *They give us what we ask, but they prevent us from taking it. Then they punish us for failing our word. That's what they get off on, the punishment.*

"I'm not your enemy," Rivka said.

"You're Sicarii," Ward said.

"I am God's surgeon."

"You're an assassin," Ward said, determination returning. "You killed all those people in Jerusalem and framed me for it. I should kill you for that alone."

"You should let me finish," she said. "If the Republic wins, the war goes on until all Belief is dead. If the Seer wins, Ba'el will raise a new Gehenna on Earth. But there's a third option.

Together, we can root out the corrupted."

Corrupted.

The same word Daniel had used when they spoke over the comm at Masada.

"Who is this corrupted?" Ward asked.

Rivka's eyes darted away. The gunfire behind Ward had stopped. He was still alive, which meant Zee's people must have won. They would be coming. But Rivka wasn't looking at them.

"The Seer's general," She said.

"You're lying," he said, sighting the pistol on her chest, but it trembled in his hand. His finger wouldn't squeeze the trigger.

What if she was telling the truth?

Your girlfriend is in danger, Compano had said. *She's trusting the wrong people too.*

Wrong from whose point of view? What if MacKenzie had become the wrong person? What if she'd become the one who couldn't be trusted? He thought of the way MacKenzie killed, especially in Old Mexico, without mercy, relishing each pull of the trigger. He couldn't forget the way she tortured that poor museum usher. He couldn't unsee her tattoo declaring the Sixth Commandment, *Thou Shalt Not Kill,* did not apply to her.

"Not to you," Rivka said. "Not anymore. I'm out of time. Here's the truth: we tattoo them on the wrist. That's how you'll know. Number thirteen is the one you want."

"The one I want?"

"The baby."

"Baby?" Ward asked, his gut filling with hope and dread. "Sam's baby?"

Again, Rivka's eyes flicked away. To the west. "They're coming," she said. With uncanny speed, she let go the sword and produced a knife, the curved dagger of the Sicarii, and drew it across her own throat.

Ward didn't stop her. He didn't try to shoot her in the arm or shoulder to keep the blade from slicing through her veins and arteries. Her blood spurted and arced. He looked at the pistol in his hand, cold and dark, and wondered if he would have been fast enough anyway.

Someone behind him made a sound. He looked over his

shoulder. Sam was there, next to Compano. Zee, too, and Farooq and Ali. That was all. No Nasir. None of Ali's soldiers or Rivka's Sicarii. These made up the dead lying indiscriminately around the plateau. Sam separated herself from the group. Slowly. One step. Two. Into a jog. A run. Straight for Rivka. No one stopped her. She knelt beside the body and lowered her face over Rivka's as if attempting to inhale the assassin's last breath. Then Compano was beside Sam, speaking in her ear.

Zee, Farooq, and Ali put their heads together in a huddle, making plans. They might have wanted Ward to join them, but he stayed where he was, stuck on Rivka's last words. *They're coming.* Who was coming? Sicarii? Ba'el's prophets? It wasn't an idle threat or a distraction. It was a warning.

Something skittered along the desert to the west, near the cliffs. The direction Rivka had looked before cutting her own throat.

They're coming.

"Zee," Ward said, forgetting he'd removed his comm. No one heard.

It was too late anyway.

The Nephilim swept down from the cliffs like locusts across the desert. They reached Ali first, swallowing him like a pebble in a flash flood. Zee cried out. Gunfire erupted. One second Farooq was standing his ground, the next second parts of him were being passed about like a trophy. Zee stood his ground, firing into the coming swarm. Ward saw no point in fighting. It would have been like trying to shoot individual drops of water in a tidal wave. He turned east to the ridge to flee. Ahead, Sam and Compano were descending toward the Dead Sea, the sword clearly visible in Sam's arms.

Ward stumbled. Maybe he was tripped. He hit the ground hard but never stopped running. Claws grabbed at his jacket, tearing it from him in strips and shreds before the Nephilim overtook him.

PART 5: TO CANAAN

Say, Brothers, will you meet me
On Canaan's happy shore?
—Camp Meeting Hymn, c. 1856

CHAPTER 50

It was all MacKenzie could think. It was all she could do. Kill.

She shot a Republic soldier through the eye at thirty yards. Another in the knee and then the chest. When she got close enough, she drew her utility knife across that soldier's throat. Then a three-round burst from her assault rifle decapitated an Agent trying to reach cover behind a bench. All around her, men and women fell. Her soldiers. Her enemies. It didn't matter. She would continue. She had to reach Horeb.

She'd met Bravo Company at El Paso, prepared to order in all of Horeb's helos if that's what it took to get them to Denver in time. Bryce, however, had argued against an air approach. He'd done so quietly, aside from the rest of the company, insisting Horeb was the morsel in a trap. Coming in hot aboard a significant percentage of Horeb's helos without proper ground support, he'd said, would be foolish at best. More likely, it would be a slaughter.

He'd been right, of course, even if the operation did go wrong almost from the moment they arrived in Denver four days ago. The Republic had been waiting. It took a full day for Bravo Company to fight its way north to the city center. Once they were close to Horeb, MacKenzie ordered the company west. She wasn't going to walk face first into the trap. They swept around, coming through the abandoned amusement park called Elitch Gardens northwest of the base.

The slaughter wasn't waiting for their air approach or direct route from the south. It was waiting at Elitch Gardens.

The Republic used the decommissioned Ferris wheel, roller

coasters, and bumper cars to confuse scans and lay ambushes. They came at Bravo Company five to one, equipped with artillery, flame units, and air support, not to mention two mine fields that decimated MacKenzie's soldiers.

It wasn't her mistake—she had little doubt the same ambushes were waiting at the university to the south and the casino district to the east—but that didn't assuage her guilt as her troops were cut down and burnt alive, nor did it make her decision easier now that it was clear Bravo Company was lost.

"On me," she shouted to the remains of the squad that had been advancing with her, Bryce, and Reina.

She switched her assault rifle to fully automatic and took out a handful of Agents lurking on a carousel—one of the few teams of Agents taking part in the ambush. The significantly low number of Agents concerned her, but getting into Horeb was all that mattered. If they were waiting to ambush her within, so be it. She had to survive long enough to get inside for them to have a chance to kill her.

She changed out her magazine, her last, and switched to single shot. Her squad swept over the carousel, gathering weapons and ammo. Moving in pairs, the team headed for the corpse of a giant steel roller coaster. MacKenzie picked off soldiers with brutal efficiency. Every hint of movement ahead received a bullet. Each body took her hard-toed boot to the skull as she passed, preserving bullets. At the coaster, a solider, a kid no older than the loyalists in Texas, came at her with a knife. She knocked the blade away with her rifle, catching the kid with her elbow on the follow through. He went to a knee. She put the barrel of her rifle to his ear and fired three times before the body hit the ground. A waste of ammo, but she fired once more into the boy's throat, barely aware she was screaming.

"We're here, sir," Bryce said.

The squad had set a perimeter. They saw the landscape. They knew their responsibility, even if they didn't know their destination.

"All set, sir," the squad leader said. Her arm was bandaged, and a bruise was forming under her eye, but there was no quit in her face.

MacKenzie couldn't remember her name. Holly something, MacKenzie thought. She'd never forgotten a Bravo Company soldier's last name before. It was all she could do to keep from touching Holly on the shoulder and apologizing, but the soldier wasn't interested. She was shouting orders to her troops. The Seer would be proud of Bravo Company. MacKenzie sure as fuck was.

With Bryce and Reina, MacKenzie broke off south into the water park. Holly and her soldiers did their job. The last thing MacKenzie heard as she uncovered the piping beneath a ruined waterslide was Holly shouting, "To Canaan!"

MacKenzie's hands were shaking as she worked the latches sealing the pipe, the secret emergency exit from the Temple deep inside Horeb. Until this moment, the pipe had never been opened. Until this moment, only she and the Seer, and presumably Aldrich, even knew about it. That it was still sealed filled MacKenzie with hope. The Seer remained inside. Horeb hadn't yet fallen.

The pipe led into Horeb's ductwork, which should have taken them directly to the Temple, but Horeb had been breached. Signs of battle lay below each duct vent giving louvered sightlines into the base's narrow corridors. Bodies and blast marks and rubble and bullet holes. For every dead soldier of Horeb, MacKenzie counted three or four Republic corpses. Alive, however, she saw only Republic soldiers and an occasional Agent crossing below in pairs, calling out cleared halls and rooms and reliving the dead of their weapons and gear.

"Still no Reapers," MacKenzie said. Was it a sign of impending victory or a warning that the trap was about to get much worse?

"There's been no confirmed Reaper encounters so far, and only a bout thirty Agents counted," Bryce said. "Maybe they're somewhere else."

MacKenzie didn't buy it. If Reapers were on site, they would have seen them by now. Something was wrong with the REC. But what?

Reina whined. It was the first noise she'd made since they entered the base, as if she understood the need for stealth. They continued deeper into Horeb until they reached the mess hall where the ductwork had been sheared off in the middle of the room. The ceiling was scorched, and bodies littered the floor and tables. The ductwork continued at the far wall, but it was crimped and blackened. It would take tools and time they didn't have to gain access.

"They made a stand here," Bryce said, angled for a better view through the open end of the duct. "Bad spot with three entrances."

For all his instincts, he was still an unexperienced soldier. Reality didn't allow for textbook solutions.

"There are no good spots," MacKenzie said, thinking of Holly and her squad giving their lives so MacKenzie could reach the pipe. Dying to protect Horeb and the Seer.

Because I was too weak to stay here and keep my job.

"The hallway outside would be better," Bryce said. "It's narrow. Two abreast could hold the line. It wouldn't matter how deep the enemy lines ran."

"You can teach a fucking class when all this is over," MacKenzie said. "Stay here until I give a clear."

With her rifle slung over her shoulder, she dropped from the open end of the duct, the impact on her still-healing leg painful but not debilitating. She took up position facing the north entrance where the tables had been piled up to barricade the entrance. There was no movement or sound. She circled the mess, checking the south and west doorways as well. Each had been similarly barricaded, but the tables had all been shoved aside, and the doors had all been blown off their hinges. Twenty-one of Horeb's soldiers lay dead in the mess along with thirty-seven Republic soldiers, including three Agents, the enemy forces concentrated near the three doors. A bad spot to make a stand, but Horeb's troops had done so admirably.

"I'm getting a table," she told Bryce.

"I can jump," he said.

"For Reina. Wait up there."

MacKenzie dragged a table beneath the duct. Reina knew her cue and hopped down, landing spryly on the table and then jumping to the floor. She whined and sniffed at the dead. Bryce followed, landing loudly on the table. He scrambled down and took up position facing the west entrance, the Republic's primary breach into the mess according to the carnage. Once more, MacKenzie was impressed with how calm and collected he was.

Like Holly had been.

"I can create a better barricade in the hallway after you go," he said. "Let them bottleneck inside the mess."

"We can't give them the mess. That duct is the only way back into the piping."

He examined the corridor leading from each of the three doors like a critic circling the walls of a gallery. Finally, he came to the south entrance where MacKenzie and Reina waited.

"I'll hold the mess as long as I can, sir," he said.

Tell him he doesn't have to. Tell him to come with. We'll find a way.

"Bryce," she said, her voice cracking.

He's a kid, for fuck's sake, tell him!

"I've got this, sir," Bryce said. Reina yipped and trotted to the kid. "We've got this," he said, rubbing her ears.

The sound of boots approaching the mess from the north ended the conversation. MacKenzie saluted Bryce and Reina, but they'd already turned their backs like good soldiers.

"Good luck, kid," she whispered as she took off toward the Temple.

CHAPTER 51

Agents were usually more diligent. They should have staggered themselves at the corner. At least one should have been watching this corridor for approaching enemies. At least one should have positioned himself to be visible to their comrades around the corner. Instead, clearly thinking the battle was over, they leaned on opposite walls five yards from the corner, talking about returning to their families in the Atlantic District. Neither noticed MacKenzie watching. Neither had a hand on a weapon. Neither knew what hit them.

MacKenzie chose her knife, leaving her rifle behind, to keep from alerting whoever was around the corner. She took down the first Agent with a sliding tackle and an elbow to the throat. The second barely got his pistol from his holster before she buried her knife up through the bottom of his jaw. She left it there to spin back to the first Agent and punch him twice more in his throat while he struggled to find his breath. When he crumpled, she smashed in his skull with her boot. Five seconds. Two down. No shots fired.

She gathered her rifle and peered around the corner. Twenty yards ahead, the hallway terminated at the door to the Temple, the Seer's inner sanctum. The heart of Horeb.

Before that door knelt too more enemies, silhouetted by the light of the plasma torch they were using to try to break in. The use of the torch was a good sign. It meant they wanted the Seer alive; otherwise they would have blown the door, and possibly the Temple itself, with explosives.

Their attention on the door, MacKenzie was able to get within ten yards of them before one stood and turned. Not a soldier or an Agent. A Reaper. There was no mistaking the armor. No mistaking the ghoulish helmet and mask. A calmness came over MacKenzie, a patient anticipation, even as she charged. She wasn't leaving Bryce and Reina alone after all. Horeb would be their tomb, together.

The Reaper didn't alert his companion. He didn't hesitate or overthink. He positioned himself defensively before his companion and raised a pistol. MacKenzie dropped her rifle and dove into a roll. The Reaper's first two shots went high. She came out of the roll into a leap, drawing her own pistol as she did. The Reaper's third shot went low. The next one would hit her center mass. Her only chance was speed and diversion. She shot the Reaper in the shoulder. His armor absorbed the impact as she knew it would. As her own armor had absorbed the impact outside. Absorbed it and displaced it, but not entirely. The impact was still felt. The Reaper's aim went wide. It was enough. MacKenzie hit him at the waist.

It was like tackling a tree. The tree went down, but the impact hurt, and she lost her grip on her pistol. She recovered in time to avoid a haymaker, twisting to drop a solid punch to the Reaper's groin. He didn't even grunt. She tried to roll off, but he grabbed her hair and pulled her face into a solid fist. Her vision flashed white. She gave up a fistful of her hair to pull free, spinning off into the wall. Facing the wrong way. The Temple. The Agent with the plasma torch—a standard Agent—remained focused on his work. She had that going for her, at least.

Until the Reaper got a hold on her again. She turned into the motion when he yanked, coming in under his pistol before he could shoot, and threw an uppercut into his armored jaw. It felt like punching a cinderblock, but it rocked him back. She got a hand on his wrist, the one holding his pistol, and twisted. The gun flew from his grasp, but it cost her positioning. The three punches he landed to her kidney felt like gunshots.

Then he hit her with something else.

The mechanism must have been part of the Reaper's armor. It sent a jolt through her worse than any stun baton. Her muscles clenched and spasmed. It was all she could do to remain conscious as she fell, twitching in agony, her bladder releasing. Then it was over. Her muscles were numb, leaving her defenseless on the floor. The Reaper picked up his pistol.

This is how I die.

Gunfire erupted somewhere else. MacKenzie didn't have to guess where. The mess hall.

The Agent set down his plasma torch and said, "Should I go?"

"No," said the Reaper. "Open the door."

In fits and jerks, control returned to MacKenzie's muscles. She got erratically to her feet only to find the Reaper pointing his pistol at her forehead. Inches away. No chance of missing.

"To Canaan!" a voice cried. Bryce's voice. A soldier's battle cry.

Two more shots, and then silence.

"It's over, General," the Reaper said.

Before MacKenzie could say something snarky, another salvo of gunfire erupted. The Reaper's head twitched in the direction of the mess hall. A reflex. A half-second delay. Enough for MacKenzie to do one thing.

Praying her muscles would comply, she went for his knee. She expected to fall on her face. She expected the Reaper to put a bullet in the back of her head. Instead, she hit him hard. He cried out as his knee bent the wrong way. She grabbed the side of his helmet and used his momentum to slam his face into the wall. Something crunched. The Reaper fell onto his back but kept hold of his pistol. His free hand went to his helmet which had shattered over his nose, exposing the bloody center of his face.

"You bitch," he growled.

MacKenzie dove on top of him, grabbing his wrist, pushing his pistol wide. Like last time, his shot missed. Like last time, he shocked her. This time, however, she knew it was coming. This time, she twisted his arm and bent his wrist before the attack. When it came, when it forced all her muscles to contract, he was pointing his pistol at his own face.

The Agent at the door never looked up. MacKenzie took the Reaper's pistol and put four bullets in the back of the Agent's head. He fell. The plasma torch winked out. MacKenzie listened for more gunfire from the mess hall, hoping for a reason to backtrack, but there was no barking. No shouts of victory from Bryce. They'd done their job. There was no time to mourn. She banged on the Temple door.

"It's me," she shouted. "MacKenzie."

The clang of the locks echoed. Two of them. Three. Four. Not the fifth.

"Password," a voice said.

"Open the door," MacKenzie said, "or I'll pull your liver out through your eyes, Aldrich."

There was a pause, during which MacKenzie thought he might insist on her reciting the emergency password they'd agreed upon, a password she couldn't remember after taking the equivalent of two bolts of lightning through her system. But the fifth lock clanged. The door swung open.

"Hannah," the Seer said, enveloping her in a strong hug and pulling her inside.

"It was an ambush," she said.

"We know," Aldrich said. He appeared uncomfortable with the display of affection between the Seer and MacKenzie.

MacKenzie removed herself from the Seer's hug. "The traitor," she prompted, wanting to know who to blame, who to kill, when everything was over.

"It won't matter if we don't get out of here alive," Aldrich said. "The escape route is a dead end."

"It picks up in the mess hall," MacKenzie said. "I had a man there, but..."

"All will be as the Lord desires," the Seer said.

He seemed sad but not defeated. Calm but not at peace. He seemed older as well, as if the past five months had aged him five years.

The sounds of marching boots came down the hall. MacKenzie had little doubt it would be Reapers. Teams of them.

"The door," she said.

Aldrich, who himself seemed older as well, put his weight into the door, but the Seer stopped him.

"The time to hide is over," the Seer said. "The Lord has asked us to restore Faith to the Republic. We cannot do His will from in here."

He opened a cabinet on the far wall, revealing a full stock of small arms. He handed Aldrich a submachine gun and took a short barrel assault rifle for himself. The pride that swelled in MacKenzie was almost enough to balance the grief of losing Bryce and Reina. The Seer was with her. God was with her.

"Providence," she said.

"Providence," the Seer repeated.

He looked on her the way Simon had in those few moments they'd had together. It was, she was sure, the way God would look on her when she finally found her way to Heaven.

"Follow me," she said.

"Always," the Seer replied.

"To Canaan," Aldrich added.

Together they marched up the halls of Horeb to war.

EPILOGUE

By the full moon, Ward thought he could make out the Mediterranean a kilometer or two ahead. A hundred kilometers from where the Nephilim took them. It had been over a week since Sam and Compano escaped with the sword. Since Farooq and Ali and Rivka and all the others had been killed. It was Ward and Zee now, naked and alone, escorted by dozens of Nephilim across the desert in hungry, thirsty, exhausted silence.

They were allowed to whisper during the day when the Nephilim made camp. Some would turn a circle facing out, some would turn a circle facing in, with the prisoners in the center, and the rest would bury themselves in the sand like lizards and sleep.

At night, however, when they marched across the desert at a methodical pace, any talking was met with angry hissing, as if the sound of human words offended the Nephilim. As if they were afraid something out there would hear them.

"The other tribes," Zee had guessed a few days ago when Ward asked who might hear them in the Waste.

"Like the one with the tank?" Ward had said.

"That could have been this tribe."

"Then why are we walking? Where's the trucks to drive us wherever we're going? Where's the weapons to keep us in line? Where's any technology at all?"

"Maybe they're punishing us by making us walk."

Or purifying us, Ward had thought but not said, irrationally afraid that saying it out loud might make it true.

"Maybe they just don't want to share their prize," Zee had said.

"Their prize," Ward had mused. "Us or the bee?"

Zee had shrugged.

That was the last time they'd spoken out loud. Since then, Ward had tried to distract himself from his healing wounds, his sunburnt and peeling skin, and his cracked and painful lips, and his gnawing hunger by studying the Nephilim academically.

They were tribal, Zee had said. After watching the way they worked together with occasional bug-like hisses and clicks, Ward began to wonder if they weren't more like a colony or a hive. There were clearly different classes of them, each with separate tasks. The ones who hunted for bugs and small lizards, as well as underground water, were clearly different than the ones who stood watch during daylight hours. The hunters were slimmer, less scaly, and skittered about more than walking or running. The ones who took the water and meals from the hunters and gave them to Ward and Zee—the smuggler chewing up the insects eagerly each time, while Ward gagged and choked on his portions—had webbing between their finger-like digits that the others lacked.

Hunters. Guards. Feeders. Like a colony.

Like bees.

It kept coming back to that. Childeric's golden bee. The one Ward had rescued from the Tower, a sort of token or reminder of who he used to be. A historian. A protector of the past and its stories.

Only he no longer had the bee.

The first wave of Nephilim had hit him seconds after Rivka slit her own throat, sending him to his knees. He tried to get up, to run away, but they were too fast. Too many. The last thing he saw before they crushed him into the ground was Sam and Compano disappearing down the ridge. Then it was all claws and kicks and that horrific hissing. They tore his clothes from his body like starving children unwrapping a meal. First his jacket. Then his shirt sleeves. A shoe. All ripped away and passed above the crowd of mutated faces and craterous mouths.

One of the Nephilim held the shredded leather jacket over its head the way the others had held Farooq's torso aloft. Something fell from its pocket. Something bright and glistening in the moonlight. It hit the sand with no more sound than a dropped pebble, but the Nephilim halted their attack immediately. The desert went silent.

A Nephilim came forward. A female, Ward thought, though he couldn't see anything to differentiate it from any other. She picked up the golden bee and examined it by placing it near her mouth. The crowd seemed to collectively hold its breath. And then the female held the bee in the air and trilled and hissed. The other Nephilim responded in kind, like a cheer. When the noise died away, the female sniffed at Ward, her face as mutated as the others. Her breath was like rotted meat. Ward gagged and his eyes watered. She trilled again, and the crowd parted so two Nephilim could bring Zee to Ward. He was bleeding from the forehead and appeared dazed.

"You look terrible," the smuggler said.

The Nephilim hissed and buzzed angrily. Then they tore away what was left of Ward's and Zee's clothes, leaving the men naked. The female sniffed at each of them, spending a moment at Ward's hands and another at Zee's genitals. Then she snaked off into the crowd, leaving the rest of the Nephilim to prod their prisoners into the desert.

That was at least eight days ago. Maybe ten or twelve. The first few days and nights were a feverish blur of confusion and fear and endless marching through the desert and horrific dreams of dragons and burning babies.

Now, as they crested a massive dune above the Mediterranean, the moon was sinking, and the stars were fading. It would be morning soon. Whatever the Nephilim had planned was imminent. The hunters and the guards were gathered in two groups, one to the north and one to the south, behind the prisoners. Another group was burying itself in the sands while the feeders skittered about here and there. One offered the prisoners some beetles and water. Ward declined the beetle but choked down the warm water from a leathery waterskin. Zee took a gulp too, and then popped a beetle into his mouth, savoring it like a hard candy.

"I think this is Ashqelon," the smuggler said, though they were surrounded by nothing but gray sand and the sea. It was the first either of them had spoken aloud in a long time.

Ward surveyed the landscape, seeking traces of ruins or relics from the famous seaport and site of a decisive Crusader victory at the end of the eleventh century, but saw none.

"Why?" he asked, his lips splitting. He grunted from the pain and put his fingers to his mouth.

"Direction," Zee said. "Best guess."

"No, I mean why would they bring us here? There's nothing left if this ever was a city."

"For the sea."

Zee didn't explain. Ward didn't ask. He'd already resigned himself to whatever fate the Nephilim had in mind. He would fight, of course, but likely not with much verve. Beetles and fetid water didn't offer much energy, and his sunburned skin, now turning a deep tan, was still tender.

"What about the bee?" he asked. If the Nephilim were going to kill him, he wanted to know why now. Why not at the temple? Why had the bee stayed their execution? What did it mean to them? Was it the shape that mattered, or the gold, or the ruby? Or was it something else more important? Something about colonies or hives?

"Other than the two tribes trying to kill each other," Zee said, "our knowledge of the Nephilim is limited. Maybe they like shiny things. I don't know. The bee bought us time. What else does it matter?"

"It matters to me."

"Always the puzzle solver."

To my dying fucking day, Ward thought.

Zee licked his lips, not bothering to hide how much it hurt. "We know they believe they are El's chosen people, and this land is theirs, a gift from their god. Perhaps they see the bee as a sign of El's favor on us. Or on them."

Ward didn't understand how fifth century relic from France could signify such a sign. At first. He'd been focused on how the bee could relate to the Nephilim themselves, but now Zee's words took him in a new direction. Not the Nephilim but the land.

"The land flowing with milk and honey," Ward said,

thinking of the promise El made to Moses in the Book of Exodus, to bring the Hebrews from Egypt to the Promised Land. "They believe the bee is a symbol of that honey?"

"Sounds like a good enough theory to me."

A nearby hiss said it was time for their conversation to end.

Zee mouthed, *Is it important to you?*

The bee?

Yes.

Not more than our lives.

A moment later, the female approached, the bee clutched in her claw. She examined the prisoners, sniffing at them similar to how she first examined the bee.

"I think she's getting hungry," Ward whispered.

The female responded by trilling loudly and putting her face in Ward's. Bile rose in his throat at the smell of her breath, but he fought it down. She seemed to know. Her eyes flashed in what Ward could only think of as amusement. She continued trilling and clicking, louder and louder until it stopped sounding like bugs. Until patterns emerged. Until Ward recognized it wasn't hisses and clicks at all. It was words.

"Zee," Ward said.

"I hear," he replied.

"Is it Hebrew?" Ward asked, thinking he'd heard the word *HaShem*, Hebrew for *the Name,* an epithet for God.

"Older," Zee said. "But maybe close enough." He translated: *"Not. Hungry. Important. Task."*

The female's craterous mouth elongated into a mockery of a smile.

"A task for us?" Ward asked, pointing at his own chest.

The female's head jerked awkwardly up and down. A nod. She spoke again, her language like a radio broadcast thick with feedback and static.

Zee's eyebrows came together.

"What did she say?" Ward asked.

"I don't..."

It spoke again. The same words, Ward thought. Two of them, the pair repeated three times. Zee repeated each. The female gave another jerky nod.

"*Larvae*, I think," the smuggler translated. "Then: *children*."

The other Nephilim approached, creating a perimeter around Ward and Zee on three sides with an open path to the sea.

The female pointed out into the Mediterranean and said one more word. This time, Ward didn't need a translator. He said the word himself.

"*Kittim*."

The female nodded enthusiastically.

"What is Kittim?" Zee asked.

Ward didn't answer. He was grasping at something Compano had said. Something he'd not really listened to because the next thing she'd said was about MacKenzie.

"Rafael," Zee prompted.

"Kittim," Ward said, "was the name of the island of Cyprus in ancient Hebrew. Have you noticed there's no little Nephilim?"

"Children?" Zee said.

"The Sicarii are all about experiments. On Compano. On Sam. On Sam's baby."

The female Nephilim howled and repeated the word. "Bay-bee." Then, "*Zachal*," the word she'd used earlier for *larvae*.

"They want us to find their children," Ward said. It was a leap, but the female's reaction made it seem right. He felt certain of it, the way MacKenzie was certain of her Providence. "They think we're part of their god's plan."

The female's attitude changed. She grew louder and more agitated. She spoke again, different words.

"*Not. Our. God. All. God*," Zee translated.

"Of course," Ward said. "Apologies."

The female lowered herself into the sand as if readying for a nap. The others followed suit.

"Does she really understand me?" Ward asked.

"At this point," Zee said, "I'm ready to believe they understand everything."

"What do we do now?"

"We go."

Ward looked down the dune once more. There were no towns. No roads. No cars. No boats.

"Go where?" he said. "Paddle to Cyprus completely naked?"

Zee shrugged.

Ward looked up at the fading stars. Even now, they shone so brightly out here in the wilderness, so sure of themselves and their place in the universe. Of course, each was a lie. Their light was billions of years old. The stars themselves could have burned out eons before humanity first discovered gods. It was a nihilistic thought, and a comforting one. If that light could find its way across so much distance and time, maybe he could find his way back to Sam. And to MacKenzie.

To Daniel.

But what then? What had Ward ever done in his life that hadn't led to pain and loss and death?

"Come," Zee said, starting for the Mediterranean. "We'll think of something."

Behind Ward, the Nephilim began to hiss and trill and buzz. It was time to go. He was no longer welcome here.

ABOUT THE AUTHOR

Michael Pogach is the author of the award-nominated Rafael Ward series: The Spider in the Laurel (2018 Kindle Book Award finalist) and The Long Oblivion (2019 Kindle Book Award semi-finalist), as well as the chapbook Zero to Sixty. His short fiction has been featured in Tales from the Combat Zone, the CAM Horror & Science Fiction Charity Anthology, and Blackest Spells. He is a professor of literature and creative writing in Pennsylvania where he lives with his family.

www.michaelpogach.com
@michaelpogach
facebook.com/groups/MichaelPogach

Curious about other Crossroad Press books?
Stop by our site:
http://store.crossroadpress.com
We offer quality writing
in digital, audio, and print formats.

Enter the code FIRSTBOOK
to get 20% off your first order from our store!
Stop by today!